A REAL KISS

"Try to get some sleep," he growled, draping one arm over her.

She was sharing his body warmth, nothing more. This was the wilderness, she reminded herself. Not London. This was no indiscretion, it was survival. "Don't be getting any ideas that I . . ." she stammered.

Before she could pull away, he stole an impetuous kiss, a quick peck. "I am not a man of ideas, *ma petite,*" he murmured, "but a man of action."

"How dare you!" she exclaimed. "I am engaged to be married, sir. I am helpless to defend myself against your most . . . ungentlemanly advances, so . . ."

"You have nothing to fear from me, mademoiselle."

"Then why did you kiss me?"

"To torment you," Alain said.

"Not only are you my enemy and a heathen," she breathed against his shoulder, "but you are ill-mannered and ignorant as well. I shall speak not one word more on the subject"

"Bon!"

"And my father and my fiancé will hunt you down and make you pay for this!"

Alain's mouth hardened as reddish gold curls bounced defiantly beneath his chin. He tightened his arms around her. "That, I believe," he whispered, "was several words more."

This time he stopped her mouth with a kiss . . . a real kiss.

DANGEROUS GAMES   (0-7860-0270-0, $4.99)
by Amanda Scott

When Nicholas Barrington, eldest son of the Earl of Ul-
combe, first met Melissa Seacort, the desperation he
sensed beneath her well-bred beauty haunted him. He
didn't realize how desperate Melissa really was . . . until
he found her again at a Newmarket gambling club—being auctioned off by her father to the highest bidder. So,
Nick bought himself a wife. With a villain hot on their
heels, and a fortune and their lives at stake, they would
gamble everything on the most dangerous game of all:
love.

A TOUCH OF PARADISE   (0-7860-0271-9, $4.99)
by Alexa Smart

As a confidence man and scam runner in 1880s America,
Malcolm Northrup has amassed a fortune. Now, posing
as the eminent Sir John Abbot—scholar, and possible
discoverer of the lost continent of Atlantis—he's taking
his act on the road with a lecture tour, seeking funds for
a scientific experiment he has no intention of making.
But scholar Halia Davenport is determined to accompany
Malcolm on his "expedition" . . . even if she must kidnap
him!

AUTUMN ROSE

Linda Windsor

Zebra Books
Kensington Publishing Corp.

http://www.zebrabooks.com

ZEBRA BOOKS are published by

Kensington Publishing Corp.
850 Third Avenue
New York, NY 10022

Zebra and the Z logo Reg. U.S. Pat. & TM Off.

First Printing: December, 1996
10 9 8 7 6 5 4 3 2 1

Printed in the United States of America

*To the Montreal Historical Center,
the McCord Museum of Canadian History,
and the Montreal Bureau of Tourism for their
friendly and invaluable research assistance.*

One

The geometrically engineered streets of Albany were lighted only by lanterns on a few public buildings as Alain Beaujeu left the waterfront, where taverns and ale houses were beginning to ring into the night with ribaldry. Three off-duty regulars in English scarlet staggered, arm in arm, down the opposite side of the muddy street, the one in the middle sagging between his comrades. They were too full of West Indian rum to notice him, although keeping in the shadows of the buildings was certainly to Alain's benefit.

It was not chance but precaution that the Canadian voyageur exercised. Even though the practice of illicit trade between his kind and the English was commonly known, the hostilities between England and France made its execution more difficult than before. At least prior to their outbreak, the merchants of Albany merely dealt in black-market goods, avoiding the King's taxes as reward. Now, they traded with an undeclared enemy as well and officials were not as likely to turn their heads.

There were many in Albany, however, who did not consider Alain's fellow countrymen enemies in this English-French conflict. Neither businessman nor farmer wanted his trade interrupted by politics and consequently ignored edicts not to trade with the British-held country to the north.

Alain had divorced himself from politics years ago to adapt to the liberated life of the voyageur—the middleman, who ventured into Indian territory to trade staples and dry goods for furs, which they returned to exchange with Albany merchants for a handsome profit. In fact, he himself was now a stockholder in the New York Company as a result of wise investment of his savings, for that was where the real profits were.

To boot, there was still a tidy sum, enough to live comfortably for a year or so, were he inclined to do so. Price, not politics, dictated where he unloaded his pelts. He enjoyed the rewards of free enterprise.

Tonight, however, he was not pleased. Squire Stewart had reneged on his offer of last fall and lowered the price they had agreed upon for pelts from the Indians of the inland wilderness. The news had not caught Alain by surprise. He had heard it from one of his fellow smugglers, who was on his way out of the city when Alain ventured in. Unlike his friend, however, Alain was not afraid to go over the head of the warehouse manager, with whom he'd dealt for seven years.

It wasn't the money. Alain did not need the ten percent, which the squire attempted to cheat him of. It was the principle! Who was to say the man would not try this same trick next year? There were those of his trade who did need the money—men with wives and children, responsibilities Alain had yet to assume, as his mother so often reminded him.

He knew the squire thought Canadians were half animals and illiterate, and he had not bothered to correct the man's misjudgment. Sometimes it paid to appear the fool. Tonight, however, was another story. Tonight Stewart would learn differently.

Not only was Alain's English good, but, thanks to his mother's socially prominent family in Montreal, his education was well rounded for a man of his twenty-eight years. While the La Tours, too, had barely suppressed their disdain for the son of their poorly-married relative and his simple paternal Acadian heritage, Alain had robbed their condescension of substance with exceptional performance, exceeding that of his higher born cousins.

When he traded his hand-me-down brocades and velvets for buckskins and left Montreal for the Indian country, however, he felt as if he had been set free of the confinements of civilization and all its glitter and trappings. What could his mother, who hoped to see him rise to a prominence equal to that of her family, say?

She had given it all up for a brave Acadian trapper who had rescued her from the Indians and won her love and respect. And his father certainly could not blame his son for pursuing the same freedom he had enjoyed in his youth, before love planted his feet firmly in the soil belonging to his father.

Alain slowed his brisk gait long enough to appreciate the full moon, which bathed the beautiful countryside and the rooftops of the city in an ethereal glow. They were much alike, this Albany and his Montreal. Both were neat, well planned, and full of rules and regulations, enough to choke a man born for the wilds. He rubbed his chin, covered with dark bristle, and laughed. They did not know the meaning of freedom, these city people.

Accustomed to climbing mountains, the young man found the hills leading up to the wealthier homes on the bluff no challenge at all. Sinewy thighs strained against the leather reinforced trousers tucked into the tops of his roe deer leggins. Beneath them, fringed moccasins permitted a silent ascent, although there was no need for stealth, now that he was away from the waterfront and municipal buildings where British guards remained on duty at all times. It appeared that most travelers had arrived at their destination and no doubt supped on the food, the tempting aroma of which wafted in the spring air, along with that of woodsmoke.

And locusts, Alain realized, inhaling the sweet fragrance of the trees lining the drive up to a palatial home. These Yorkers did love their flowering locusts. He picked one of the fragrant white bracts from a low hanging branch and tucked it into his hatband, next to the egret plume presented to him by a particularly friendly mademoiselle upon his leaving Montreal last autumn.

Shaking himself before his thoughts led to more stirring recollections of that last parting, Alain concentrated on the brilliantly lighted mansion ahead. Carriages and wagons of every description lined the long drive to the two-story Georgian structure. Its windows, even those in the attic dormers of the roof, were aglow and all four chimneys stood starkly white against the moonlit sky. Owing to the break in the weather, many guests were ambling about the gardens—gardens which had been only drawings on paper when Alain had last seen Squire Stewart's plans for the estate. The house itself had been framed then and no more.

He spied uniformed servants standing on the columned portico. Wishing to avoid a public announcement, he made his way around to the back of the house, where food was being rushed from the brick kitchen under a vine-canopied colonnade to the main house of matching stone and brick.

Coquettish laughter drifted his way from the seclusion of the garden, serving to remind Alain once again of how long he had been without feminine company. There was no time for such things when he was in the wilderness, although the Indians could lend a new dimension to the word *hospitable* regarding their women.

"Pardon me, sir, but . . . are you lost?"

Alain directed his attention to the manservant standing at the back door of the manor, banishing the memory of the night in the smoky lodge completely. "Non, monsieur, I am not lost if this is Annanbrae."

The manor would be called Annanbrae, so the squire had once told him, after the Scottish town from which the Stewarts had come. The *brae* part of the name meant a hill overlooking a river or lake. Alain had to admit the owner had a gift for applying apt names. The Hudson curled like a silver ribbon below the bluff.

The doorman seemed taken back by the Acadian's backwoods garb, not to mention his accent. Once he was able to drag his eyes from the animal skins clinging to the well-formed and compact physique of the stranger, he glanced about as if expecting savages to spill from the trees and shrubs. For a moment, Alain nearly laughed. Perhaps he should have changed his clothing.

"I would see your employer . . . Squire Stewart, *s'il vous plaît* . . . on business," he added, trying to put the man at ease.

At the mention of business, the doorman regained

his air of superiority. "The squire has a manager for that, sir, at the warehouse down on . . ."

"I have spoken to him and have not found satisfaction," Alain interrupted, his patience and humor waning. "I would speak with Monsieur Stewart personally."

The servant glanced around again, as if still unconvinced that Alain was not the forerunner of one of the savage Indian attacks instigated by the Canadians of New France against innocent British settlements. The English outcry struck Alain as ironic, considering their like courtship of the Iroquois to do the same thing for them. But to an Englishman, everything English was right. Anything else was as if it did not exist, much less matter.

"Unless, you would have me go to the front door," Alain suggested wryly. His threat was exactly the winning argument. Cowering under the intimidating gaze of the insistent guest, the doorman motioned him to follow.

"This is highly irregular, especially during Miss Stewart's homecoming party. I can assure you, the squire will not be receptive to whatever you have to say."

Alain was undaunted by the man's warning. He had no doubt that Squire Stewart would not be receptive, but the merchant would hear him nonetheless.

Elegantly dressed men and women milled in the wide hallway which divided the house down the middle, but Alain was ushered through a paneled passage under a grand curved stairwell and into a magnificent library. Oriental rugs decorated the floors, reminding him belatedly of the mud on his moccasins, so that, when the servant turned to notice his tracks with an air of disgust, Alain was prepared with an apologetic shrug.

A low burning fire, just enough to take the chill off the spring night, glowed on the hearth, which was situated between two ceiling-high bookcases filled with leather bound volumes. Distracted by such a display of wealth and intellectual bent, Alain found it difficult to believe the Squire Stewart he knew had read one of them, much less all. On Alain's twentieth birthday, he and the Scot finished two bottles of good brandy, exchanging lessons in swearing in their native tongues. It had been Alain's first trip into the wilderness.

"Whatever you do, sir, remain here until I fetch the squire. He will not be very happy."

"So you have indicated, monsieur."

Alain flashed a devilish white smile that sent the servant struggling through the sliding paneled door before it was completely open. It was a wonder the man had not torn off his pewter buttons, the Canadian mused, turning about to examine his surroundings further. A home's furnishings and accouterments told much of its owner aside from purse size, yet what Alain saw did not fit in with the character of the earthy man he had met seven years earlier.

The Squire Stewart he remembered would sooner have died than set foot in the Presbyterian church he'd helped build. Yet, there was a scriptural painting on the wall, which the young man recognized as Moses ascending Mt. Sinai. Alain's mother had also seen to his religious education, for all the good it had done him. If the genteel soul knew half of the things he'd done, it would finish her weak heart.

It wasn't that he was what he considered a bad man;

he was honest and fair to Indian and white man alike. Alain preferred to think of himself as a free man, free to follow his own values and mores. Left to his saintly mother, he would live the life of a priest. The wry twist of his lips froze as he instinctively followed the wall around to the back window, where a portrait of a young woman rested, unhung, against the sill.

She was eighteen, if he was half the judge of women he considered himself to be, with free-flowing locks of reddish gold cascading about her neck and shoulders, bare but for a black velvet choker adorned with a jeweled brooch. A dress of autumn orange was draped over the ripe swell of her bodice, as if the nubile globes were all that kept it from dropping to a black-sashed waist a man might span with his hands. And her eyes were those of an enchantress, Alain marveled, captured by their spell.

He removed his hat and placed it on the desk, which was the central piece of furniture in the room, before taking up the portrait to get a closer look. The eyes were a rich brown, but not the same hue as those of the Menominee chief's lovely squaw. No, there was too much emotion, as if they'd taken on that dark cast in fiery defiance of her fair coloring. Never had he seen such a bewitching creature, Indian or white.

"I see you have an appreciation for art, Monsieur Beaujeu."

Alain felt his neck growing warm as he put the portrait back in its place and turned to face Squire Stewart. It wasn't like him to be caught unawares, especially this side of the border. He crossed the room and extended his hand. "Monsieur Stewart! It has been many years.

I see you have been most successful since our first meeting so many years ago."

Instead of taking Alain's hand, James Stewart marched to his desk and took a seat. His once-red hair had thinned considerably since the Canadian had seen him last, and his taste in clothing had improved as much with his income. He was as foppishly attired as Alain's cousins.

"I don't like the idea of ye coming up here, young man. I would have no aspersions cast on my character by your company . . . these breeding hostilities, you understand."

And the man's vocabulary had increased over that of the swearing Scot Alain had known. Casting aside all pretense of the courtesy he had been taught, Alain replied in kind.

"Nor do I like the idea of your cutting your price on my pelts. They are as good or better than the past year's and I will have the same price."

James Stewart leaned back against his chair, his rich velvet coat falling away from his vested abdomen. A gold watch chain draped from its pocket and disappeared beneath the swell of excess flesh around his waist, indicating his purse was not all that had fattened with his success. Eyes that always reminded Alain of a weasel's sharpened, undermining the helpless shrug he effected.

"There is a war on, sir, declared or nay, in case you have not noticed. The cost of goods has increased. My capital is not . . ."

"Indeed so, monsieur, which is why I asked for *twenty* guineas now, instead of the ten you agreed upon."

"That's ten too much!"

"The risks are much more as well," Alain pointed out.

Momentarily stymied, his host turned to the task of lighting his pipe from one of the rushes by the hearth. "How is your family, boy?"

When in doubt, change the subject. Alain knew the ploy well. "They will be even better off with the extra moneys I have made this winter, non?"

With a low chuckle, Squire Stewart turned back to him. "What if I refuse to meet your price, boy? What then?"

Alain shrugged and picked up his hat from the polished surface of the desk. *"C'est la vie.* There are others who will."

It was good to play the negotiation game with an experienced profiteer, rather than the hunchbacked warehouse manager, who was more comfortable with ledgers and figures. Alain's hand was on the latch of the sliding paneled door when his worthy adversary called him back.

"Wait! Fifteen guineas and not a pence more."

As if considering the offer, Alain threw back his head and stared at the dancing shadows on the ceiling, cast by the sconces over the hearth. He would have been content with the agreed upon price, but an extra five guineas was well worth the walk up from the landing. Tonight, he would join his partners a rich man instead of his usual impoverished self.

"Fifteen it is, monsieur," Alain agreed.

"You can collect it from my manager tomorrow."

"But non, monsieur. I would have it tonight. Tomorrow I rise with the sun to return to Acadia." His aging father was too proud to accept his money, so Alain intended to spend the summer helping to work the family farm.

Squire Stewart scowled and pushed himself up from the desk. "Strike me blue, I like ye, boy," he began, hooking his thumbs in his waistband. "But take my advice and stay clear of that place. There's a lot goin' on there and you don't want any part of it."

Alain knew of the English fears that the Acadians threatened New England, not to mention Halifax, a growing English settlement in their midst. While it was true that his people had not signed the oath of allegiance to England, required by the English intendents there, he knew the people of his parents' community, which was not so far from Halifax.

The Acadians were a peaceful people, dedicated to their land, regardless of which mother country claimed it. They hesitated to sign such a contract for fear of retaliation from the Micmacs under the zealous and righteous leadership of Abbé Le Loutre and were content to leave the politics to those who had time for such. Survival was their priority.

"Merci, monsieur, but I will be fine. My family does not resent the English and I surely do not, as my being here proves."

Squire Stewart sighed heavily. "These are unsettled times, boy. People are forced to do things that don't always make sense." He shifted uneasily under Alain's expectant look, but instead of going on to explain himself further, he pointed upward. "I'll get your money. It's upstairs. Ye stay here and wait."

Alain smiled. "But of course, monsieur."

He would not think of joining the gaiety taking place

in the front rooms where a musical ensemble had now begun to play. To end all that laughter with a gasp of horror at the sight of his half Indian, half French attire would not bother him, but it would ruin a certain young lady's homecoming, he thought, recalling the servant's words. Even a backwoodsman was too gallant to do such a thing.

Alain turned to study the painting once again, with renewed interest. Some artist had obviously been infatuated with this woman to have painted such life and beauty on canvas, for surely no female was ever so perfectly breathtaking. The eyes of love did tend to need spectacles, Alain reminded himself, for he'd seen men perceive some of the homeliest creatures as beauties when in that state.

The door from the main hall burst open and once again Alain put down the picture hurriedly and straightened. Instead of Squire Stewart, a gowned woman stepped into the room.

"Father, what's keeping . . . oh!" she gasped, blinking to adjust to the dim light so she might focus on the Acadian.

Her hand flew to her throat, fingers clasping the brooch on her black velvet choker, the same one she wore in the portrait. Her hair, instead of flowing free, was piled upon her head and bedecked with a cluster of ribbons, from which black *aigrettes* had been delicately anchored. Curls and feathers bounced as she took a step backward, her eyes, those enchanting eyes, growing wider with her increasing alarm.

Alain knew instinctively that she was going to scream. Even as the perfect "o" of her lips parted to release her terror, he leapt across the room and clasped his hand over them. In his own confusion upon seeing the girl in the portrait come to life, he implored in a husky whisper, *"Tais-toi, mademoiselle!"*

His blurted French, intended to quiet her, only increased her struggles, leaving Alain no choice but to forcibly pin her against the bookcase with his body to keep from hurting her. Even as he did so, he heard the rip of the front of his shirt and felt her nails rake down his chest.

"Be quiet, mademoiselle!" he repeated, regaining his wits and his English. "I promise, I have no intention of harming you, or anyone. I am but waiting for your father to return to conclude our business."

His soft and sweet-smelling captive froze. What he could see of her face behind his hand was clouded with suspicion. "If I let you go, will you promise to be quiet and wait for your father to return to vindicate me of your . . ." Damnation, ordinarily he had no problem with fluency. "Your . . . *mistrust,*" he finished with a sigh of relief. "What do you say, non?"

He felt her acquiesce, her muscles relaxing slightly as she nodded in understanding. Realizing that she could hardly express her answer otherwise with his hand over her mouth, he eased away cautiously, prepared to seal her lips again should the panic swimming in her gaze find its voice.

"Bon . . . good! I will let you go and step away with my humblest apologies for frightening such a beautiful lady."

She *was* real, Alain told himself again, backing away with a gallant bow. The artist had painted exactly what he had seen . . . a goddess of fire and innocence such as never had walked this earth before. As he snatched up his hat and swung it across his waist, the locust blossom fell to his feet.

What games was fate playing, he wondered, reaching down to retrieve it. First, a beautiful woman steps out of a painting and then he is prepared to present her with a token of his worship.

"A blossom for a . . ."

An explosion in his left temple choked the rest of his compliment off and sent Alain reeling sideways, as if he'd been struck by the blunt end of a rifle butt. The fire smoldering before his eyes became a yellow-orange blur as the weapon came at him again, this time assaulting the back of his head with a nasty crack which brought him to his knees.

Swaying unsteadily, he blinked, trying to focus, to see the assailing behemoth with a fist like an anvil, when a slippered foot flashed in front of his face in what would have been an entertaining display of petticoats and feminine charm had it not caught him under his chin with a terrible clip that not only knocked him backward in an awkward sprawl, but snuffed out the dancing lights on the whirling ceiling overhead.

Through the darkness, Alain could hear a woman's hysterical voice. "Mother of God, I've killed him!" He laughed skeptically within the confines of his netherworld at the very idea that it was she, the fragile beauty in the portrait, who had rendered him unconscious. It was no doubt a brute with a fist of ungodly proportion, sent by that arrogant servant. "Father, look what I've done! I've killed a French spy!"

"Strike me blue, lassie! 'Tis no spy, but one of my voyageurs! Grab his arm and help me get him into the chair."

"*Your* voyageurs?"

Squire Stewart's reply astonished even Alain, who was gradually coming back to life with the heavenly press of silk, lace, and lavender against his cheek. "He works for the English, Tamson. He's one of *ours.*"

"Oh God, he's bleeding. The binding of the book must have broken his skin!"

Book? Alain struggled to open his eyes with the incredulity that washed over him, but the pain was such that emerging too quickly might cause him to sink back into the senseless limbo. She had struck him with a *book?* A swell of manly indignation overrode his queasy dizziness as he grasped the arms of the chair into which he'd been half lifted and half dragged. He, Alain Beaujeu, who had outwitted and outfought the craftiest of renegades, knocked unconscious by a hysterical woman with a *book?*

Whether it was the result of his pain or anger, when he focused on the concerned face hovering in front of his, its perfect features were no longer irresistible. Whatever gallantry he possessed had been ungraciously walloped out of him by the same delicate hand that brushed his coal black hair from his forehead to test the swelling.

"Oui, it *hurts!*" he grumbled irritably, shoving himself upright in the chair. "What manner of woman is it that assaults a man with a book for giving her a flower?"

"Will ye . . ." The girl stopped, as if some unseen tutor stood over her with a stick. "Will *you* listen to the man, Father, saying *I* was the assailant, when it was he that slammed me into the bookcase and held me helpless, gagged by his hand!"

Alain whipped his gaze about in challenge, but the

sharp pain shooting through his temples made him think he was going to slump down into the chair again. Knuckles clenched white, he held himself up and turned his attention to the master of Annanbrae.

"Monsieur, this *woman* bursts into the room and, upon finding me instead of you, started to scream. I thought it best not to draw attention to my presence and tried to quiet her in the only way available to me."

"This *woman,* Monsieur Beaujeu, is my daughter Tamson, freshly arrived from England, where she's been attending school the last eight years since her mother's death."

"Ah, so *that* is where she has become so good with the books!"

"I apologize, Monsieur Beaujeu. What with the impending war, I am a wee bit jumpy. When you spoke French, I thought you were one of those Canadians."

Canadians. The word was spat out, as if it put a bad taste in her mouth. Alain stared at the smooth, jeweled hand before him, a hand which had never seen a day's work. Spoiled and pampered like the rest of her, no doubt.

"And your clothes did resemble those of the savages I've heard about. I vow, I thought I was going to swoon!"

Alain rose to his feet cautiously and straightened, before looking down into the wide, mercurial depths of the gaze turned up at him. It was appropriately anxious, yet certain of forgiveness. After all, what man could not accept an apology from lips so provocatively pursed, as if begging not only for forgiveness, but for a kiss as well. It was just as well her father was present, for at

the moment, Alain was not feeling the least bit forgiving
or gentlemanly.

"But how could you swoon, mademoiselle, with such
an armory as you have behind you?" Lips twisted wry
at his tone, he took up the hat Squire Stewart handed
him and, seeing the bound weapon she had wielded so
well against him lying on the desk, flipped open the
cover and read the title.

"Ah, Shakespeare. *The pen is mightier than the
sword,*" he quoted dourly. "I did not realize, when I
studied his works, that his words were so true."

"*You* studied Shakespeare?"

Alain could not miss the incredulity in the young
woman's voice. "Yes, even I, the bloodthirsty French
Canadian, have read the bard of old England." He
turned to the squire, who watched the exchange between him and his daughter with interest. "Monsieur,
I would have my money and be on my way."

Squire Stewart took a pouch from his coat and
dropped it into Alain's extended hand. "Excellent idea.
I am certain ye wish to return to the riverfront. I'll see
ye next year?"

Alain nodded, weighing the purse cautiously in his
hand. He could almost tell the amount of coin in a purse
by its feel and weight, without counting. That gift had
won him many bets during nights around a campfire,
when boredom set in.

"Perhaps Monsieur Beaujeu would care to bathe upstairs and change into fresh clothing to join us for supper, Father," Tamson Stewart suggested, turning a
whiskey-tinted gaze to Alain.

Her impassive expression further served to confirm

her disdain. Alain had been a source of contempt among the aristocracy enough times to recognize condescension when he saw it. The bluebloods were the same in any society, French or English, and were gifted in the art of veiled insult. He was well aware that a bath and change of clothing was in order, but it was impolite of the woman to say so.

He was almost tempted to accept, just to see her squirm as she walked into the parlor with a French Canadian on her arm. Being a private man, however, he did not wish to be inundated with questions, particularly by the authorities in attendance tonight. Besides, his head was pounding like a blacksmith's hammer on an anvil.

He would go back to the Red Bone Tavern and join his companions instead. If he was to suffer, he might as well earn it by savoring a good bottle of brandy and, perhaps, some feminine company.

"Merci, mademoiselle, but non. While your father and I are business partners of a kind, we do not travel in the same circles. It's better business that way, non, monsieur?"

Squire Stewart nodded, eager to have the Frenchman on his way before someone else came looking for the host of the evening. Half his guests dealt with voyageurs, but it didn't do to flaunt it. Smugness was the first step to a man's downfall.

"Ye're a smart boy, Beaujeu. If ye ever want employment in Stewart & Company, all ye have to do is ask. I could use more men of your caliber."

Alain nodded stiffly, for fear of aggravating the thunder in his temples. "Merci, monsieur, but non." He saluted daughter and father in turn as he slid open the panel door which disappeared into the wall under the stairwell. *"Au revoir, mes amis."*

Two

Autumn was Tamson Stewart's favorite time of year. Perhaps it was because she favored the beautiful, rich colors with which Mother Nature bedecked herself.

This particular autumn was even more special. Not only was she home at last, but a certain Captain Mark Heathcote, whom she'd met while studying French and the arts in Paris, had asked her to marry him. Her friends, those who flocked to Annanbrae to welcome her home after eight years away in England, were positively green with jealousy.

They made a beautiful couple, she thought wistfully, recalling the engagement party the previous week. Mark's impeccably cut uniform of blue and buff with scarlet trim was the perfect match to her scarlet gown. He'd even indulged her by letting her wear his bicorn hat perched mischievously upon her reddish gold curls. They'd danced the night away, trying to make it last as long as possible, for Mark's new orders would carry him the following Monday into the upriver wilderness to join General Johnson with the captain's new command of regulars.

Now, not only was Mark gone, but her father as well. After extracting a promise from her not to leave Annanbrae, which curtailed her plans to ride over the estate, Squire Stewart left for a meeting of New York merchants downriver. The very thought of one of those French-Indian raids this close to the fort was absurd. They were happening further north in New England, along the borders. Everyone said so.

"Miss Tamson, the misses you invited over for tea are in the hall."

Tamson rose from the windowseat overlooking the slope down to the river, where boats and barges of all description went about their way. Since she could not visit or ride over her father's lands, she'd invited neighbors to her. How else was she ever going to get to know them again?

"Thank ye . . . *you,* Prudence," Tamson reiterated, unable to stop Aunt Penelope's well-worn lecture on the inappropriate Scottish burr eight years in London had almost eliminated. She'd promised her aunt not to let her father's *bad* influence affect her carefully groomed lady-like demeanor, but she was already starting to sound like him again.

"Please see to our tea and cakes while I join them in the parlor."

Smoothing her russet skirts over an embroidered quilted inset, Tamson made her way down the steps to the parlor where young feminine voices chattered gaily. Of all the ladies in the county who attended Squire Stewart's gala parties, the three she had invited were her favorites.

They came because they wanted to see Tamson, with whom they had corresponded since she'd left eight years earlier. They also possessed undying curiosity and plagued her with questions about London and the latest fashions.

"Good day, ladies!" Tamson greeted brightly. "I am so delighted that you indulge me with an afternoon of your company."

"Oh no, Tamson, it's our pleasure!" Abigail Whittington insisted. "And sending an invitation on playing cards! What a novel idea!"

"It was a broken set," Tamson admitted wryly. Realizing her guests, although divested of their wraps, were still standing, she motioned around the room. "Please be seated. I can see you've brought your stitchery. The light is excellent in this room in the afternoon. I think Papa planned it that way."

"I hear a seamstress from downriver helped him with the planning," Beatrice De Lancey informed her in a tone that suggested more. "A Mrs. Van Dorn, as I recall."

Tamson had heard the rumors that her father had certain scandalous relations with that woman and attributed it to those male urges men were often consumed with, but didn't realize the flaming color that crept to her cheeks until Abigail Whittington turned to Beatrice in an aggravated tone.

"For heaven's sake, Beatrice, you're embarrassing our hostess! It isn't Tamson's fault. You know how men are."

Beatrice's air of superiority dissolved, followed by genuine apology. "I didn't mean to come all the way over here to insult you, Tamson. Now tell us about Captain Heathcote! Don't you just love that southern drawl?"

"Yes, and his French, why it's impeccable! I truly thought he was Paris born until he confessed his real purpose for being in the city. But, while I could talk about Captain Heathcote all afternoon," Tamson averred, "that is not the reason I asked you ladies over."

"Pray tell then, why?" Amanda's eyes twinkled in anticipation. "Is it to play cards? I brought my invitation in my purse, just in case we needed it."

"You mean, so you could cheat!" Beatrice teased.

"Not so!" the younger woman shot back with a pout that bespoke anything but innocence.

Of the three, Amanda had not changed one bit. It was always Amanda and Tamson who were perpetually in trouble, much to the horror of the older Beatrice and Abigail.

"No, it's to plan my wedding!" Tamson announced. "I've been gone so long and I do need help in making out the invitation list. I feel I hardly know anyone now— Albany is so different from London."

"I can't imagine why you bothered to come back," Beatrice snorted with a roll of her eyes. "If I had relatives in London . . ."

"You'd do just what Tamson did and come home to your father," Abigail finished smugly. "Besides, what would Willie McShane do without you?"

"I couldn't say," the minister's daughter replied sharply, although her blush betrayed her feigned indifference. "Perhaps you could have that captain of yours talk to Master MacShane. He asks me to dance at all the dances, he stops by for supper on Sundays to speak with father, *so he says,* and he's always in town when I go in to shop, but not one advance has he made!"

"Beatrice De Lancey . . . and you a minister's daughter!"

"That doesn't make me any less a female and wanting a man's attentions, Abigail Whittington."

"But Willie's been busy trying to prosecute those merchants on Tide Street for buying stolen goods from the French and Indian raids along the border and upper New England," Amanda spoke up in the young man's defense. "I don't think Governor Shirley can continue to turn his head away from the blood money being exchanged."

Abigail shuddered at her sister's comment. "I couldn't do it. I just couldn't do it!"

"Do what?" Tamson inquired, totally at sea as to what the girls were speaking about.

"Buy a set of dishes with the initials of some slaughtered soul engraved on them!" Amanda put in with repudiation.

"It's giving the good citizens of Albany a bad name. Everyone in New England will hate us for trafficking stolen goods for the enemy."

"I hear they already do," Amanda chimed in with her cousin.

Astonished, Tamson leaned against the back of her father's chair. "Dear God, it's no wonder! I had no idea!"

For some reason, the night of her homecoming party flashed in her mind, along with the strange visitor she had assaulted in her father's library. He had been French, but was evidently an ally. Odd, but for several weeks after, she kept thinking about him and his funny little accent—a ruffian, but somehow gallant in his own way . . . until she'd clobbered him with a book.

Tamson wasn't ordinarily prone to violence, but when he had forced her against the bookcase, not even her crinolines and skirts could fend off the disconcerting effect of such a hard and manly body upon her own. He was so . . . *virile*.

That was the word that came instantly to mind to describe him, followed immediately by *dangerous*. She'd reacted out of instinct, she told herself, for this was surely a man who took what he wanted. It wasn't until she helped her father get him into the chair that she'd seen his face clearly—a handsome face, rakish and unshaven, with thick black lashes a woman would die for.

The conversation about the blood money trade on Tide Street was dropped when Prudence came in with the tea and cakes Tamson ordered. With all the grace her aunt had so carefully taught her, the young woman served the tea. "Will you have one lump or two?" she asked Beatrice politely.

"Just put two on the saucer," her friend answered, causing Tamson's eyes to widen in wonder.

Upon seeing her expression, Amanda laughed. "Actually, Tamson, we sip our tea *with* our sugar. It saves the need of a spoon!" To demonstrate, the girl popped a lump of the sugar Tamson had dropped on her saucer into her mouth and proceeded to sip the tea.

"Amanda!" her cousin gasped. "That is not so! It's . . . it's just the way we drink tea."

Tamson considered the strange habit. So different, she thought again, drifting momentarily back to London. But she didn't find it objectionable. "Then I shall try it. If I'm to be a New Yorker, I must learn their ways."

"And then you'll be moving down south!" Amanda piped up dreamily. "It's so romantic!"

Over fresh lemon cakes and pecan rolls, the making

of plans for the wedding ensued. Each of the girls had her own ideas, while Tamson wondered how they did such things down south. After all, people who sucked sugar lumps with their tea may not be the best advisors.

Much as she was enjoying her company and their antics, she found herself wishing her Aunt Penelope were there, or, better yet, her mother. Her father had turned all the plans over to her, saying she could have whatever she wanted. Money was no object.

"Excuse me, Miss Tamson, but there is a visitor here to see your father," Prudence announced.

Tamson rose. "Did you tell him Squire Stewart will not return until next week?"

"Yes, ma'am, but he said it was urgent and that you might be able to help him."

"If you ladies will excuse me, I shall be back shortly," she promised, certain that, now that the girls were involved in making her plans, she would hardly be missed.

The lighting in the library was just as good as in the parlor because of the position of the house overlooking the river. When Tamson stepped into the room, a gentleman turned from admiring the apple orchard through the window to address her.

His clothing was worn and illfitted across the broad span of his shoulders, but it was a considerable improvement over the skins he had been wearing the last time. She stared at the Canadian voyageur, speechless that he had so recently crossed her mind and was now here in person.

"Bonjour, mademoiselle. I am sorry to interrupt your party, but . . ."

"We were just discussing my wedding plans." Now why on earth had she said that?

The Frenchman bowed shortly. "My congratulations then, as well as my apologies for the interruption. I must know the whereabouts of your father."

"He is in New York City on business, sir."

"Your fiancé is here, then?"

"Captain Heathcote is away on duty. There's no one here except myself . . . and the servants, of course."

An inner alarm went off, warning her too late that she should not have made such an admission. For all his manners, there was something about this man that made her nervous. She had not forgotten his swift overpowering of her the night of her homecoming.

One corner of his mouth curled slightly, as if he'd read her thoughts. Yet he made no attempt to ease them. "Of course." He turned to look out the window again, in no apparent rush to be on his way.

"Is there anything I can do for you, sir?"

"Yes, there is, mademoiselle. Stay calm and no one will be hurt." The man spun about, a pistol brandished from inside his coat.

Tamson stepped backward in surprise. "What are you doing?"

"Tell your friends and the servants to get down into the basement . . . quickly!"

"I . . ." She stiffened and tried to moisten her suddenly dry throat so she could speak. "I will not, sir!"

The Canadian stepped aside, his pale blue eyes glittering like a morning frost. He pointed out the window. "If you do not, I cannot promise what *they* will do with them. I have given orders that those in the house be spared."

To Tamson's horror, what had been a peaceful orchard only a moment ago was now swarming with Indians of the most hideous sort. Skins, paint, and feathers abounded everywhere. "My . . . my father will kill you for this, sir!"

"Will you warn your friends and servants, or shall I take you with me and leave them to my *companions?*"

Tamson inhaled deeply to steady her nerves. Indians! A hundred horror stories flashed through her mind.

"Now, mademoiselle!"

Her feet tangled in her petticoats as she whirled about to enter the parlor. In a flash, a strong hand caught her arm and righted her. "Stay at the door, where I can see you," the man whispered threateningly.

God in heaven, Tamson prayed, her heart pounding against the back of her tightening throat. She had been right all along. This man had fooled her father and now . . . now God only knew what he intended to do. From the unrelenting hold on her arm, and the instinctive alarm riddling her body, it involved her.

"Indians!" she shouted, stepping halfway into the adjoining parlor. "Everyone, into the basement! *Prudence!"* Where *was* the woman?

The three visitors looked at Tamson as if she'd lost her mind, but when the crack of a rifle erupted outside, they bolted to their feet with startled screams.

"Miss Tamson!" Prudence cried, bursting into the parlor from the hall. "Indians!"

"Get everyone in the basement!" Tamson commanded urgently. Her voice broke as she added, *"Please!* If you do, I've been assured there will be no harm done!"

"They'll burn the house down!" Beatrice wailed, hesitating at the door.

The maid was close to hysteria, but remained ever loyal to Annanbrae's mistress. "What about you, miss?"

"I'll be fine and so will you," Tamson reassured her, ". . . but you must do as *the man with the gun at my back* says. Now get to the basement!" Dared she trust his word? For all she knew, she could be sending her friends into an incinerator. God help her, she couldn't think!

"Let her go, you Canadian butcher!"

Tamson gasped as she was suddenly thrust to the floor beneath the body of the Canadian. A gun went off simultaneously, its explosion splintering the wood where she had just stood. Before she could tell where the shot came from, the gun in the Canadian's hand went off. From the hall she heard Prudence's scream and caught a glimpse of their doorman's body falling in the passage under the stairwell.

Seizing the only chance to catch him armed with an empty weapon, Tamson turned on the man who had saved her, reaching for his face with manicured nails. He discarded his pistol and caught her wrists, but not before she had drawn blood. Of the three welts on his cheek, one seeped scarlet.

"Don't make me hurt you!"

Hurt her? If she hadn't been so frightened, she might have laughed at the statement. Instead, Tamson continued to struggle, kicking and scratching until her assailant wrestled her to her back and pinned her to the floor. The sand on the floor bit into the flesh on the back of her hands, while her stomach knotted in icy panic. Her breath was growing ragged with her efforts, as if hammering home the futility of her situation. She knew bet-

ter than to believe him, she thought, terrified. God help
her, she knew better.

When he released her left hand, a thin thread of hope
glimmered briefly before her eyes, only to be replaced
by a drawn fist. She would have at least tried to block
it as it came at her, but for the savage blue eyes that
flash-froze her defenses and bore coldly through her.
He was going to kill her! Her echoing conviction
blended with the husky apology her stronger adversary
whispered, and then blackness came upon her with a
painful clap of deafening thunder that burst into shards
of light, flickering and fading with her consciousness.

Three

Heavenly Father! Tamson would have prayed more, but after days of relentless riding and pushing through woods and over hills, she didn't know what to pray for . . . unless it was her sanity. It was still like a nightmare, she thought, lifting her head to scan the campsite. Two of the savages were still awake. The rest, like the man lying peacefully next to her, were asleep, scattered here and there on blankets.

The homesteads and farms they'd left unscathed since leaving Albany had long since ceased to appear and now nothing but *forests* and lakes, *forest* and rivers, and *forests* and falls surrounded them. Tamson had never seen so many trees, nor heard so many frightening sounds emanating from the dark cover beyond the glow of their campfire at night, making sleep almost impossible.

Nor had she ever been more miserable, so tired and yet too anxious to sleep. The incessant push of the day astride the Canadian's sorrel stallion, or rather, her father's stolen prize thoroughbred, had robbed her not only of her energy, but her spirit as well. She'd just existed, tight-lipped and stiff as her waning stamina would permit, riding, and sometimes sleeping, in front of the buckskin-clad man with the ice blue gaze that could burn and chill at the same time.

The bloody bastard had never once let her out of his sight, even when nature demanded relief. While he turned his back to her, he kept her tethered, like an animal on a leash, affording her the barest privacy. He was one endless source of humiliation, she thought, resisting the temptation to kick him soundly in the stomach while he slept to deal at least a portion of the justice she owed him.

She'd lost track of the number of days that had passed since her abduction. All she knew as she lay on the bed of leaves he'd made for her near the campfire was that she was his hostage, taken in order to force her father to use his considerable influence to find the young man's family among the Acadians exiled from Nova Scotia.

While she was dragged over hill and dale and subjected to all manner of degradation, however, he had assured her he meant her no harm. His statement was so absurd, she'd laughed in his face. She was bruised, scratched, driven to the point of exhaustion, and mentally abused beyond her capability to comprehend.

She wasn't laughing now, however, nor did she fully trust his word concerning the savages. Tamson shivered beneath her blanket, more from fear than from the fall chill. They had to be considerably farther north now, for this was the bitterest night yet, she told herself, trying not to dwell overmuch on her future.

"You are cold?" The blue eyes that had rested beneath shadow black lashes were now fixed upon her, instantly alert.

"Don't be absurd," Tamson grumbled irritably. She

dropped the blanket she was trying to get up over her shoulders, but, instead of admitting her discomfort, stubbornly retrieved it again.

"But of course you are," he answered himself, stirring from his sprawled position. He reached for her shoulders, his tone surprisingly sympathetic. "Come here."

Tamson pulled away, shaking her head violently. "I'd rather freeze. Dying might be preferable to what you have in store for me."

"Which is why I wish to keep you in good health," her companion shot back dourly.

With a grimace of determination, he grabbed her again and tugged her down into the nest he'd made in the leaves.

There was no fighting him, but she did have the option of turning her back. Pulling away with as much indignation as she could summon, she did just that. His breath blew warm about her ear as he reached over and retrieved the worrisome blanket. After a few moments of rearranging the covers, he curled about her and tucked the double layer of wool over her shoulders, securing it with his arm.

"You meant it, didn't you . . . when you said you weren't going to turn me over to them?"

She wished her voice had not grown so small. She would have preferred to keep up her stalwart front. Being this close to her captor, however, made it impossible. It was the same helplessness she'd felt awakening in his arms when they were riding. As totally unacceptable as it was, it was entirely too comfortable to be safe, especially now that they were sharing a bed—if leaves and blankets could be labeled that—and not a horse.

What if she closed her eyes and fell prey to his animal nature? He hadn't revealed it, but it was there. Alain Beaujeu was many things, a virile male paramount among them.

"Of course I did, *ma chérie.* Now try to get some sleep. I can promise you, that is *all* I wish to do," he reassured wryly, as though he'd read her thoughts.

As if to prove it, he relaxed, one arm draped over her shoulder to hold the covers there, sharing his body warmth and nothing more. That it worked so quickly, male to female, unsettled her even more, for she was more aware of him as a man than ever. Worse, she was reacting to that unspoken communication between them, for every nerve in her body was alert, almost expectant. It was . . . too strange to put into words, she decided.

After a while, she heard his breathing, rhythmic and low, confirming further his intention of wishing only to sleep. Convinced her sigh was one of relief, Tamson tried to relax her aching muscles. One of Aunt Penelope's hot toddies would be just the cure right now. Instead, there was one distractingly warm Canadian lying next to her, which would have to suffice. She needed to accept that, no matter how much her proper upbringing was insulted. This was the wilderness, not London. This was no indiscretion. This was survival.

The sleep that eventually ensued was dreamless. Wrapped in a cocoon of blankets, she was no longer a victim of the cold autumn air. The buckskin clad arm and leg thrown over her added a further sense of security in a place where such feelings were practically nonexistent.

She was awakened just before the break of dawn to the low whisper so close to her ear it startled her.

"Wake up, *ma petite*. We must be going."

Tamson went stiff within the circle of his arms for the three blinks it took to focus and then shoved at his chest with her bound hands as if he were Satan himself.

Eyes rolling skyward, she stammered in utter mortification, "Good heavens, I'm sorry! I . . . I didn't mean, I mean, I had no idea . . ."

"It was my pleasure, mademoiselle."

The nutmeg irises of her gaze were flecked with gold anger as she lifted a stubborn chin. "I was cold! It means absolutely nothing, so don't be getting any ideas that I . . ."

The cocky grin on her abductor's face slackened, but before Tamson could heed the warning, he stole an impetuous kiss, a quick peck. Then the grin was back, smug as ever.

"I am not a man of ideas, *ma petite,* but a man of action."

Even as he climbed to his feet, Alain Beaujeu regretted his capricious response. He was her kidnaper, not her seducer, he reminded himself sternly. Unlike many men, he could certainly overlook the fact that she was beautiful and desirable. He was not without discipline. Yes, he was attracted to her, but not as much as he was repelled by the actions of her kind.

Never would he forgive the abduction of his family from their small cottage where, upon his return to Acadia, he'd found the dried and rotting remnants of the supper which had been interrupted. To be rounded up ruthlessly like cattle and shipped off to God only knew what destination was such an unthinkable crime that Alain had to be told the horrible story of the exile again and again by the few remaining villagers before he actually believed it.

"How . . . how dare you!" his captive sputtered. "I am engaged to be married, sir! Worse, you have trussed me like a chicken, so that I am helpless to defend myself against your most ungentlemanly advances!"

Her chin quivered in a devastating manner, which, despite his inner rage against the English, nearly brought Alain back to her with an apology. *Dieu,* but this was a dangerous woman!

"I told you, you've nothing to fear from me, mademoiselle!" he said. She was naught but a means to find his family—the proverbial *eye for an eye.* Squire Stewart would pull the right strings to find the Beaujeus in order to get his precious daughter back, of that Alain was certain. If he did not, he would never see the girl again.

"Then why did you kiss me?"

"To torment you," Alain replied, "so that you would make a goose of yourself by asking such silly questions!"

"How dare you speak to me like that after you so rudely stole a kiss!" Scrambling to her feet, Tamson drew to her full height in front of him, her wounded pride evident in the depths of her gaze. "Not only are you my enemy and a heathen, but you are ill-mannered and ignorant as well! I shall consider the source and speak not one word more on the subject!"

"Bon!"

"My father and fiancé will hunt you down and make you pay for this!"

Alain's mouth hardened as reddish gold curls

bounced defiantly beneath his chin. "That, I believe, was several words more, but who could expect the English to keep his or *her* word."

Four

After passing streams riddled with muskrat holes and a large stretch of forest, Alain and Tamson arrived at the limestone walled fort called St. Frederic. Despondent that her hope of rescue was all but nil now that they were so far within French-held territory, Tamson nearly jumped out of her skin when the savages burst forth, breaking the self-imposed silence they maintained during their travel.

Alain rode straight through the melee and into the garrison, where he was surprised by the appearance of his trading partners. They were a gay lot, less given to brooding than their comrade, and instantly and utterly devoted to Tamson's comfort. While Alain saw to business concerning a letter waiting with the commander of the fort from Montreal, they showed her to her quarters for the night—a small room in the thick wall of the fort with actual walls, windows, furniture and, to her delight, a bathtub.

It was actually a hog scalding trough, but the wood had been scrubbed clean and Tamson had no compunction whatsoever in taking advantage of the unexpected and thoughtful luxury her newly appointed benefactors had provided. When she finished, a bundle of fresh, clean clothing awaited her, shoved in the door by Jacques Dupré, the stocky leader of the group, who claimed the feminine articles were compliments of his friend, the Marquis de la Galisonne.

Never did Tamson dream that, when Alain came for her later with an invitation to dine with the fort commander, she would discover that the generous marquis was none other than her rough-hewn captor. Even more incredulous was his reaction to the title and estate that went with it, for he grew adamant that the inheritance was a mistake—that his father was Jean Beaujeu, a poor Acadian trapper turned farmer, not some member of the noblesse of southern France. The fort commander's persistence in addressing the voyageur as Monsieur Le Marquis irritated her traveling companion no end.

Not even the fine Madeira the superior officer served with the succulent roast of venison topped with pepper sauce tempered the voyageur's aversion to his patronizing manner. Tamson, however, enjoyed everything from the gentlemanly company of the fort's officers to the food and drink, particularly after her ordeal with the Indians still howling and celebrating outside St. Frederic's walls. And naturally, she favored anything that made Alain Beaujeu uncomfortable.

When conversation turned to the political controversy between the New France's Governor General and Crown to have the Canadian's brother appointed as the new governor of Montreal, not to mention the French's estimation of the prospects of her father's friend and colonial Indian agent William Johnson in winning Indian neutrality among the Six Nations, she was almost relaxed for the first time since being dragged from Annanbrae against her will. The bath, the clean clothes, and the food and wine had made her feel almost human again as she walked with Alain from the blockhouse which housed the commander's second-story quarters.

They were almost to the gate before she realized they were not heading in the direction of the quarters she'd been assigned. Although she thought the mistake an oversight, she fingered the clasp of her cloak nervously and came to a stop, halting her companion as well.

"My quarters are *that* way, sir."

"I know, madmoiselle, but there is something we must take care of first."

To her horror, he took her arm and started for the gate again. The revelry of the Indians on the outside made Tamson dig in even more, instantly sobered. She had no idea what he was about, but she wanted no part of it. "No, please! Can't *you* take care of it?"

"Non, I must bring you to the chief and trade my horse for you."

"I thought you said it was understood that I . . ."

"It is," her companion assured her. "But there is the matter of the transaction." Suddenly his voice softened. "All you have to do is stand still and keep silent. I give you my word, no harm will come to you." Cupping her chin with his finger, he lifted her face to the moonlight. "I will not let them keep you, *ma chérie*. Have I yet lied to you?"

Battling the dread which welled up at the idea of rejoining their heathen traveling companions, Tamson stepped into the circle of Alain's arm. Instinctively, she reached from under her cloak and snaked her own about his waist, as if to make sure they wouldn't be separated. Upon glancing up in uncertainty, she spied the kindling of a smile in his gaze.

"Wh . . . what about the horse?"

"It's with the others."

"I don't see why *I* have to be there if the bloody horse doesn't! It doesn't . . ."

Tamson broke off as two of the frolicking painted pagans rushed at them, shrieking and waving war clubs over their heads. Tightening her hold on the buckskin of Alain's jacket, she stepped closer, barely missing his foot.

"Chin up, *ma chérie*. They admire bravery," he cautioned. "Now I am going to step away and they will escort you to the chief."

"What?" Tamson's objection caught in her throat, but she did not cling to Alain as she was inclined to do. Instead, she stood stiffly, trying not to tremble visibly as she concentrated on his advice. *They admire bravery.*

How she ever walked the distance to the painted chief of the raiding party without her fear-weakened legs causing her to stumble, she had no idea. With the roar of the celebration now dead as the night, all she could hear was her heart drumming in her ears as she was abandoned in front of the stern-mannered leader, who addressed Alain in a jumble of unintelligible syllables.

"Take off your cloak."

Tamson refused to take her gaze from the man who'd sworn to protect her as her bumbling fingers finally released the clasp of the blue woolen hooded cape he'd procured for her from the wardrobe of the second-in-command's late wife. Had the woman been killed by Indians, she wondered, praying there was no stigma attached to the garment as she let it fall to her feet. At that moment, she wondered that her frantic heart did not stop from sheer fright.

The chief stepped back, taking in her appearance

from head to toe, as though he was seeing her for the first time. His expression might well have been one of the totems carved on the pole outside his hide-covered lodging for all that it revealed of his thoughts. His hand smelled of oil, liquor, and smoke as he reached for her bottom lip and pulled it out, staring at her teeth as if she were a horse!

When he inserted his finger to inventory her back teeth, however, Tamson snapped at him with involuntary indignation. The reaction startled her as much as the furred and feathered Indian. Her fear rising bitter in her throat, she froze in anticipation of some bloodthirsty reprimand.

To her astonishment, however, the stern countenance of the chief faltered, softening briefly with something akin to respect. Again he said something to Alain, who shook his head in denial and pointed to the remuda of horses tethered nearby. At this, the Indian held up four fingers, shaking them in the Canadian's face.

Again Alain shook his head and replied in a battery of syllables totally foreign to Tamson's ears. Suddenly, he whipped out his hunting knife, its blade gleaming in the light of the fire as he took a step toward her.

"I am going to make a small cut on your hand like so, see?" he whispered urgently.

Tamson flinched as he made a quick slash across his palm and inadvertently buried her hands in the folds of her skirt. "You said I'd not be hurt," she averred, staring at the red blood seeping slowly from the wound.

"Mademoiselle, s'il vous plaît . . . please, do not cause a scene!"

A scene? Tamson almost laughed hysterically. She'd been living a *scene,* moving from one nightmare to another, and now this! She tried to shake her head in denial, but was too frozen to do more than implore with her wild, terrified gaze.

"It is to show you are mine, so that none of their warriors will be tempted to steal you from me. You would not wish that, non?" he asked, lining his voice with a velvet-like quality that was oddly reassuring.

Although she knew that she was going to be physically ill at any moment, Tamson reluctantly put her hand in his extended one. She had to trust him. As he'd pointed out earlier, he hadn't lied to her yet, and he certainly was the lesser of the evils she faced. As the blade stung her palm, she winced, her lip clenched painfully between her teeth. Then the sting was numbed by the warmth of Alain's hand pressing against hers, his fingers entwining with her own as blood mingled with blood.

Around them grunts of approval and acknowledgment rose from the witnesses to the bizarre proceeding, but she was only aware of the strange exchange that seemed to be taking place between her and the man standing beside her, watching her every reaction. Uncertainly she sought solace in the glowing depths of his pale blue gaze, highlighted by the firelight. Gooseflesh rose on her skin as an unfamiliar warmth riddled her body, more disconcerting than her initial fear.

"We can go now, mademoiselle," Alain told her, letting go of her hand to pick up her cape.

She stood like a child, permitting him to wrap it about her shoulders and fasten it, and waited for him to acknowledge his heathen companions once again before departing. She was cold, and now that she was on her way to safety, her defenses threatened to crumble.

Yet, somehow she summoned enough strength to get to the stone cell near the end of the officer's row. After building up the fire in the hearth, Alain tore a strip of his handkerchief off and wrapped it around her still trembling hand. "You were very brave back there, ma chérie. Much more than I thought you would be."

Not even the soothing quality of her companion's compliment managed to penetrate the aftershock of the strange ceremony. "Does this make us blood brothers?" Tamson asked wearily as he tied the bandage securely. She thought she'd heard some grim account of the blood exchange before from Mark.

"Not exactly," Alain answered, a grin spreading cautiously on his lips. "It actually makes us man and wife."

"What?"

"It is the Indian way, madmoiselle . . . but you have nothing to be alarmed about. I intend to sleep on the bunk over there. You can sleep there," he said, indicating the second cot on the opposite wall. Suddenly he lifted her hand and brushed his lips over her bandage. "So, I will leave you for a short time to prepare for bed and then I will join you . . . *so to speak,*" he added at the sharp arch of Tamson's brow. *"Bon soir, ma chérie.* I wish you the sweetest of dreams."

Dreams? Tamson stared at the door her companion closed behind him. The devil he says! Glancing down, she picked at the knot Alain had tied, the most absurd thought coming to her mind. Most women at least get a wedding ring. Suddenly she laughed—not her usual lilting merriment, but a high-pitched version akin to hysteria. The truth of it was, nightmares were more likely to haunt her sleep . . . horrible, hideous nightmares.

Five

If she never saw another Indian, it would be too soon, Tamson thought with a shiver of repugnance, her appetite for the tasty joint of the wild turkey the voyageur cook Gaspar had served her fading. Weary from the three-day journey by canoe and foot to Prairie de Magdelene, she supposed she should be grateful for the separate encampment set up by Alain and his partners. Unlike that of this new tribe of Indians, who overran the small farming community, it was complete with a tent to protect her from the early snow threatened by gray skies overhead.

Although the obliging and attentive voyageurs were her captors, she still felt guilty, seeing the group of them huddled under the protection of their overturned canoe. They'd done their best to make their trek bearable despite the cold silence of Alain Beaujeu, who was now in the village seeking lodging. Considering the number of additional camps on the outside of the palisade besides their own, however, he had already expressed his doubts as to his potential success.

Each day had gotten progressively colder as they moved further north. Now, in addition to her *two* dresses and petticoats, she wore a pair of borrowed woolen trousers, two sets of stockings and some sort of moccasin boots over her kid slippers. Were it not for the thong lacings, she'd have walked out of them a number of times on the journey afoot from the shore to Prairie. Although she did not complain, what she wouldn't have given for a toasty foot warmer and a carriage!

She supposed she should be relieved that her legs, abused by the constant hours on horseback during their earlier journey, no longer ached or made her walk as if the blasted horse were still there. Using the heat of the mug from which she drank her bark tea to keep her fingers warm, Tamson lifted it to her lips, but stopped upon seeing Alain Beaujeu returning in the company of the trader from the Ottawa camp. They were deeply involved in conversation and did not look up until Jacques Dupré hailed them heartily.

"Any luck, *mon ami?*"

At this, an increasingly rare smile spread on Alain Beaujeu's lips, giving Tamson heart. She might be able to forgive him her previous trials if he had found her lodgings in a warm inn for the night.

"We have luck, *mes amis,*" he announced as he joined them. "Monsieur Du Bois knows a good hearted widow who will permit us to sleep in her kitchen, since we have a lady with us . . . even if she is English," Alain added with a mischievous wink at Tamson.

Tamson nearly dropped her cup. As it was, the weak tea sloshed over its rim. Something had certainly improved his humor of the last few days. The thought had no sooner registered when the trader Du Bois produced a flask from inside his fur vest and passed it over to Alain. So it was alcohol that had thawed his icy withdrawal. And not unbecomingly, she mused, certain that his rakish smirk had turned the widow's head quicker than the sad story of a poor English girl forced to camp out in the worsening weather.

"Come, mademoiselle! Monsieur Du Bois and Jacques will take you there while I make arrangements for my journey to Montreal tomorrow."

"*Your* journey, monsieur?" It was one thing to swear silently at her captor and hold him responsible for all her discomfort, but the idea of his leaving her alone in the wilderness to which he'd brought her was even less agreeable.

"Oui, I have business to attend to there, but Jacques and the others will see you are taken care of. Unless," he added upon seeing her frown, "you wish to take a *bateau* across the river."

He pointed to the white-capped water beyond the fields. Across its stretch, the mist-shrouded island that Gaspar identified as Montreal rose like a shadow on its western horizon.

The idea of crossing the wave-tossed surface in a small *bateau* was less appealing than taking on the lake in the birch bark canoe. Hardly a sailor, she'd suffered two weeks of deathly nausea before acclimating herself to ocean travel during her return to the colonies. Besides, Dupré and his companions were still with her.

"If I have a roof over my head and firm ground under my feet, I shall be content."

"Oh, and one other thing," Alain cautioned, lowering his voice for her ears only. "I have told Madame Lusignan that you are my wife." He silenced Tamson's spontaneous protest with his finger against her lips. "She is a devout woman, mademoiselle. It is the only way she would permit us to stay with her."

"I wonder what she'd say if she knew you had kidnaped me from my home," Tamson accused, brushing his hand away.

Alain shrugged. "Then she would throw us both out. Because you are married to a Frenchman, she does not consider you the enemy, but a guest."

Marriage to Alain Beaujeu may have gained Tamson entry to the cozy little cottage not far from the village church, the steeple of which she had seen over the tops of the palisade from their campsite, but it did not completely erase the suspicion in the widow's hawkish eyes. Widow Lusignan was a petite woman with graying hair.

Not unattractive, she had retained her youthful figure, which was bedecked in a short jacket and colorful skirt, hemmed scandalously short. Tamson could see not only her buckled shoes, but a good length of stockings as well. From what she'd seen of the other women that day, it was the fashion.

Later that evening after a hot meal of rabbit stew, which Tamson, full from Gaspar's turkey, hardly tasted, she glimpsed even more of the woman's shamelessly revealed legs. The voyageurs joined them, bringing Gaspar's fiddle, and the widow danced to her heart's desire with each of them, leaving Tamson to wonder how long she had been without a husband.

Truly warm for the first time since they'd left Fort St. Frederic, Tamson sat on a three-legged stool by the fire and watched the gaiety taking place beneath the heavy beams, hanging with all manners of dried herbs. Her companions had been exceptionally kind to her, but they were still the enemy and she was too tired from the long day's walk to dance. She did, however, enjoy a warm toddy, which lulled her into a state of sleepy contentment and made her wish the revelry would come to an end so that the dance floor of packed dry earth could be made into a bed.

The bench next to her creaked with the weight of the trader to whom she partly owed her gratitude for her lodgings. "This is very different for you, non, *Madame* Beaujeu?"

Tamson's expression was blank at first, her charade long forgotten under the lure of the inviting fire and blood warming toddy. "Yes . . . yes, it is, Monsieur Du Bois."

"I would be honored if you called me Anton."

"But I do not know you that well, monsieur."

Anton Du Bois afforded her a half smile and lowered his voice. "You must come from a very wealthy family to have such arrogance. I would wager they would pay dearly to have you safely delivered back to them, non?"

Tamson's attention sharpened on the man thoughtfully stroking the point of his close-cropped beard. "My father would make it worth one's while, if that is what you are asking." She'd given up hope of escaping, much less of anyone helping her!

"It would be very dangerous and very hard travel. My Indian companions will be drunk tomorrow night after their trading is done. Do you think you could slip out of the house unnoticed?"

Tamson leaned forward, unaware of the tantalizing view the low square of her bodice afforded her unexpected ally. After her recent traveling experience, she could ride through hell to get home to Annanbrae. For the first time in days, her hope rekindled.

"I can try . . . at least Beaujeu will not be here." She'd heard Alain telling the others he would be in Montreal overnight. If she figured correctly from her recent experience, that could give them nearly a fifty mile lead, if they wasted no time.

"Tomorrow night I will wait in the alley until the bell of the church rings the midnight hour. If you are not there, I go without you."

"Without me?" Tamson was perplexed.

Du Bois' smile was crescent-like, framed by his beard and mustache. Between his ample teeth he held a chip of wood that he'd been chewing. "I have some documents that may be of value to certain parties at Ft. William Henry. If I have to deliver one plum already, why not two?"

"Oh!"

Tamson's lips formed a perfect circle, no better at concealing her shock than her round eyes. Who would have thought the man an English spy! Perhaps her luck had changed after all. At the sudden burst of cold air from the outside, which brought in with it a fur-wrapped Alain Beaujeu, however, she banished all trace of her wonder and finished the last of her brandy laced toddy to conceal her excitement.

"So will you dance with me, madame?" Du Bois queried, raising his voice to a less suspicious level and keeping up the charade he and Alain had concocted to ensure Tamson's lodgings.

"Thank you, Monsieur Du Bois, but no," she answered, summoning a collected and lofty demeanor. "I could not favor you any more than my companions . . . and as I told them, I am very tired."

At least she was tired until the idea of escape became a possibility. Like her captor and his companions, Du Bois looked like a man who could handle himself in the wilderness. She wondered if he were a French traitor or an Englishman in disguise.

"What took you so long, mon ami?" a cheerful Jacques Dupré called out to Alain from across the room. "Your bride will not dance and we need another woman! Even she agrees you have the fairest face of us all."

A general laughter broke out at Alain's expense, but he did not join in. "The courier from La Présentation was found dead a mile from the walls of the fort. His horse came in without him and his satchel."

"Indians?" Tamson blushed as the attention shifted from Alain to her. It was the first thing that came to her mind. After all, the savages were everywhere.

"Non, he still had his hair." Alain straddled the bench next to Du Bois and helped himself to a drink from the open bottle of brandy. "Whoever did it was no fool. Not even the Indians could pick up a trail."

"One of us, mon ami?" Dupré asked, suddenly sober.

"Possibly." Alain shrugged. "However, the *bateau* the unfortunate soul had secured for himself will carry me to Montreal *early* in the morning."

Picking up on his less than subtle hint, Madame Lusignan threw up her hands. "But of course, Monsieur Beaujeu! I am so thoughtless. We must end this frolic, though I have not danced since my Perot died, rest his soul." She crossed herself in solemn respect. "I have prepared my bed for you and your wife and I will take the cot here in the kitchen."

"Oh, we couldn't put you out of your own bed!" Tamson blurted out. Her skin started to burn from her bodice to the top of her head, where the little red cap Gaspar had given her crowned her burnished gold tresses in an impish fashion. "Monsieur Beaujeu doesn't mind sleeping on the floor." Upon realizing that the woman had no idea what she'd said, she tried again in French, only to be interrupted.

"But *non*, I insist!"

Tamson looked to Alain for some sort of support, but all she saw was a hint of a smile lingering on his lips. His words were no help either. "In that case, my wife and I accept most gratefully, madame." He put down his empty noggin and took Tamson's hand. "Come, *ma chérie*. It has been a long day."

"Ah, to be that age and in love again," Tamson heard Madame Lusignan sigh wistfully as she allowed Alain to usher her through the low wooden door to the back room, covered by a catslide from the main roof.

Aside from the bed and a trunk, which served as a table and held the candlestick Alain had taken from the mantel over the main fireplace, the small bed chamber was scantily furnished. There was just enough room to walk around the bed, which Tamson did immediately, putting it between her and her companion. Arms crossed, she waited expectantly for her captor to explain himself, but instead of saying a word, he began to shrug off his outer garments.

"You are ruining me, you know," she said at last, her voice full of accusation. "Everyone thinks I am your . . . your whore."

Alain dropped down on the feather mattress to remove his footwear and leggins, making it swell on Tamson's side in invitation. "They think you are my wife."

"The widow does. Every *man* out there knows different. I could sense what they were thinking and it was not very honorable."

"I cannot be responsible for everything, mademoiselle."

The voyageur stripped off his layered shirts in one sweep, exposing rippling sinew from broad shoulder to narrow waist, where his trousers hung low and loose on his hips. Not the least involved in her quandary, he tossed back the thick layer of quilts and climbed into the bed.

So, that was that! Tamson thought grudgingly. So much for asking him to sleep on the floor, much less his offering to do so. She rubbed her arms briskly, for the back room was much chillier than the one they'd just left. Survival, she told herself, taking up her pillow and shoving it beneath the covers against the wide back turned to her. That's all it was.

Fully clothed, she slipped between the sheets and stared miserably at the ceiling, where shadows moved about from the single candle on her companion's side of the bed. A whole host of condemning faces swam before her glazed eyes—those of her father, her aunt, and Mark . . . Captain Heathcote would never have her after tonight!

She wasn't aware that she voiced her thoughts aloud until her companion rolled over and glanced over his shoulder at her. "This Captain Heathcote . . . he is your fiancé?"

Humiliated, Tamson turned her face to the wall and nodded. "I'm ruined, because you are not gentleman enough to allow me the bed to myself. My only alternative is to sleep on the floor and catch my death!"

"And what is it, mademoiselle; that you anticipate tonight, that has not happened any other night we have been together?"

Alain faced her, propped on one elbow. She wouldn't look, but Tamson could picture that tolerant, mildly amused tilt of his lips she found so annoying. His tone confirmed its presence. He knew bloody well what she meant and was toying with her. She clamped her mouth shut in a thin line, ignoring his comment.

The low chuckle echoing close to her ear, however, was not so easily disregarded. She turned back with a gasp. "You are on my pillow!"

"You are a silly goose, Tamson Stewart." It was odd, the way his pronunciation of her name seemed to stroke the nape of her neck without the least physical contact. "If your concerns were of any consequence, this pillow would not stop me . . . and if the fact that you choose a warm bed over a cold floor will keep this fiancé of yours from wanting you, then he is even a bigger goose, non?"

Despite the distance she put between them, Tamson could feel Alain's presence, warm and disarming to the defenses she maintained between them. It was his pagan spirit searching out her own through layers of ingrained propriety. If he would just touch her, she'd at least have a reason to slap the face hovering no more than a breath away.

A short breath at that, one she could feel on the lips she unwittingly moistened. He was going to kiss her . . . *alone, in a bed!* Panic welled and her heart quickened, yet the fists she intended for him lay indifferent at her sides. She closed her eyes, as if that might make him disappear, when suddenly, the knitted hat she'd neglected to remove was pulled down mischievously to her chin, covering her eyes, nose, and mouth!

"Stop running on about this nonsense and get some sleep . . . or at least allow *me* to rest!"

Tamson tore off the cap as her maddening companion turned back over, abandoning her pillow and the conversation, and blew out the candle. With a growl of irritation, she slapped his back with it and, when that got no response, lifted her knee to thump him soundly on his buckskin-covered buttocks.

"That was not ladylike, mademoiselle," Alain warned, settling down under the covers. "Unless you wish me to respond in kind, I would not do that again."

Left with little alternative, Tamson tugged the hat back on and threw herself against the mattress in grudging resignation, although her anger was as much directed at herself as it was at her companion. How easily he manipulated her! Why, he probably thought she *wanted* him to kiss her!

"If you had kissed me, I would have scratched your eyes out!"

The bed shook with Alain's quiet amusement. "I will keep that in mind should I be overcome by your fair beauty and *sweet* disposition."

Inhaling sharply, Tamson drew back her knee, but checked her retaliation upon recalling Beaujeu's warning. The arrogant . . . *reprobate!* she fumed. After tomorrow night, that condescending smile would be wiped off his unshaven face and it would serve him right. There was justice in this world after all!

Six

"So you did come."

Tamson shivered in the dark cover of the alley and stepped forward. "I'm ready. What do we do?"

Her whisper barely escaped her dry throat. The passing of the day had been interminable and her guilt from leaving poor Jacques, the guard Alain left at the cottage, lying unconscious from a blow on the head with the fireplace poker still riddled her. To think she'd once longed for a taste of the adventure her fiancé had told her about!

"There is a loose section in the palisade along the western wall. We'll leave the fort that way. I have horses and supplies waiting for us in the woods beyond. You *can* ride?"

"Good as most." She fell in behind Du Bois as he took the lead. She'd made the right choice. Here was a man who knew what he was about. There would be no more second guessing Alain Beaujeu and his moods, no more playing the cornered mouse to his preying cat.

The sentries of the fort were few and far apart. Those that were out, kept close to the buildings and walls to be spared from the bite of the river wind. Although her exertion was minimal, scampering from cover to cover and building to building behind Du Bois, Tamson's heart was beating so frantically by the time they reached the loose section of wall that her chest hurt. Her eyes ached, as if they had widened past their capacity as she glanced behind her in fear of discovery.

Although Du Bois had to squeeze through the opening made by the log he lifted from its bed in the upright wall, Tamson had no problem at all getting through it. While he replaced it, her attention was drawn to the Indian encampment a short distance away, where many of the braves were still gathered around a large central bonfire. Most of the other fires in the camp had died down.

"Do not worry. Those still awake are drunk and too involved with their gambling to pay us any heed."

Cupping her elbow with his hand, her companion herded her toward the small cluster of trees he'd spoken of. After moving a long way in slow motion, they reached it and the horses hidden there. Hers was hardly comparable to one of her father's prize steeds. It wasn't even on a par with a tackie or military issue. She could feel its ribs and the spreading blades of its haunches as she tried to calm it. Could the poor thing keep up the pace required?

"I had to borrow what I could from the locals, mademoiselle," Du Bois explained, anticipating the questions running through her mind. "It was the best to be had, but it is strong and wiry." He boosted her up onto—Praise God! she thought—a saddle! What she'd once taken for granted was now a luxury after riding bareback for days with Alain Beaujeu. "I . . ."

Du Bois stiffened suddenly, with a low warning, "Hush!"

Tamson froze, her hands on the reins. She neither

heard nor saw a thing. Suddenly, her companion slapped the farm horse on the hindquarters.

"Ride!" he shouted.

She had no option. With a whinny of protest, the horse took off on its own, nearly unseating her and costing her her hold on the reins in the process. At the same time, the trees erupted with a fiendish yelling. Glancing over her shoulder, she saw Anton Du Bois vault onto his horse, taking off even before his feet were in the stirrups through a living thicket of screaming Indians, war clubs raised. Fear running through her, she kicked the sides of her steed, oblivious to the branches swatting at her face, when, seemingly out of the sky, a large Indian dropped onto the back of the animal and seized the reins from her.

Her scream blended with his loud war cry. Panic-stricken, she bit the arms that took the reins and elbowed his ribs. She fought blindly, as if her life depended upon it, for there was no time to think about what she instinctively knew. Twisting in his iron grasp, she clawed at his face, grease and paint caking under her nails. His chest, hard and barren as the winter land, was impervious to her blows, filling her with overwhelming despair.

Yet Tamson would not give up. She was her father's daughter. If she was to die, she would not make it easy on her murderer. The arm around her jerked fiercely, crushing her frantic breath from her chest and constricting her ribs painfully. Through a glaze of pain, she focused on the bulging muscle exposed by his mantle of animal skin and sank her teeth into it in desperation. The Indian howled, a bloodcurdling sound. The arm about her ribcage loosened. Her own hold slackening, Tamson swung one leg over the galloping horse's neck, preparing to throw herself from it, when the thunder of its gallop and the fiendish yells surrounding her faded with a blinding white flash of pain exploding in the back of her head. It obliterated all other discomfort, except the well of nausea choking her at the back of her throat. Then, even that was gone.

The blackness which followed seemed to lift Tamson in and out of the din around her. She remembered falling, but not hitting the ground. Her hands and feet were bound tightly, cutting off her blood flow, but she could not focus on her grunting, tattooed captors. She heard Anton Du Bois cursing in French and English, but could not place him. Woodsmoke filled her nostrils, along with that musky scent of animal skins and unwashed bodies, and her arms ached, drained of blood.

Consciousness was swimming and intermittent, allowing occasional glimpses of the bright, leaping fire just beyond her. It was close enough that the heat dried her lips and singed her cheeks. There were voices, heathen sounds mixed with periodic bursts of French. Her wrists felt as if they were being cut by dull blades, but when she finally was lucid enough to make out the source of the abrasion, she discovered it was leather thongs, tied wet and drawing tight into her tender flesh with the hellish heat of the fire. She was hanging by them, suspended from long poles crossed and braced above her.

Her head fell forward, its weight still too much for her neck to bear. As she focused on the tattered remnants of her clothing, she realized her cloak was gone, as were her two dresses. All that kept her decent were two petticoats and they were ragged and filthy, as if she'd been dragged a good distance. Her arms were scraped and bruised.

She licked her lips, tasting dried blood. It was too hot to breathe. God in heaven, they were roasting her alive, she thought, as the closeness of the blaze registered. She tried to back away, but her bonds would not permit it.

"My apologies, mademoiselle. We tried."

Tamson blinked, trying to focus on the figure of Anton Du Bois a few yards away. Stripped naked, he, too, was suspended by his wrists from a similar structure. His body was streaked with dirt and blood. One eye was swollen shut.

"I should have killed you when I had the chance."

Bewilderment settled on Tamson's face. What was he rambling on about? She forced her gaze wider, trying to make sense of it all, when the sight of Du Bois was replaced by a hideous, living mask. Head shaved on either side and tattooed, the Ottawa warrior stared down at her with eyes like glittering coals, dark, yet full of fire.

She shook her head, as if to remove him from her sight, but he seized her, forcing her to face him. Mockingly, he cocked his head from side to side, his scalplock, a red crest attached to the single tuft of black hair growing over the center of his scalp, flipping from side to side.

Suddenly he leaned forward, so close that his liquored breath was more smothering than the heat of the blazing campfire, and snapped his teeth together at her, over and over. Tamson's scream lodged in her throat upon recognition of the heathen who jumped upon her horse's back during the escape. The moment the savage

saw she knew him, he seized her by the arms and bit
her shoulder. This time she found her voice and shrieked
with the agony.

"Non!"

With a barrage of unintelligible syllables, Jacques
Dupré forced himself between Tamson and the savage.
The Indian glared down at the Frenchman, unmoved,
until one of the others said something to him in a warning tone. Only then did he back away, looking past Dupré at Tamson and clicking his teeth threateningly.

"You are not hurt badly, mademoiselle." Tamson followed Jacques' fingers to the place on her shoulder.
Teeth marks were embedded in her flesh, but it was not
broken. "You, on the other hand," the man went on,
"took a chunk out of his arm." Jacques gave her a sympathetic look. "You are a very foolish girl."

"She only wanted to go home. She knows nothing
of my mission. You must do what you can to save her!"
Anton Du Bois called out to the voyageur hoarsely.

With a horrid yelp, one of the Indians milling about
the fire brandished a knife from his belt and slashed
out at Du Bois, laying open yet another cut across the
man's abdomen with its tip. The captive made a stran-
gling noise to keep from crying out at what Tamson
could well imagine was an unbearable pain.

"Your . . . Beaujeu will not like it if the girl is
harmed!" he managed, defying his captor's attempt to
silence him.

"You should have thought of her safety before you
involved her in such a dangerous escape plan. Did you
really think you would get away with her?" Jacques
turned back to Tamson. "My friends and I . . . we will

do the best we can for you, mademoiselle, though it will cost Alain dearly. He will be very angry."

Tamson rested her head against her arm weakly. "I don't care what he thinks." However, as Jacques started to walk away in silence, she added, "But I am sorry that I hit you. You . . ." Her voice broke with emotion. "I only wanted to go home."

"You have my sympathies, chérie, but alas, your fate is up to the commander and the chief."

For the first time, Tamson looked beyond the fire, where most of the Indians had gathered. There, a French officer, a scarlet plume flaring from his hat, was in deep conversation with the chief. From time to time, they looked over at her or Du Bois, sometimes pointing as well. Jacques Dupré joined them and, after a lengthy discussion, Anton Du Bois was cut down and dragged before the Ottawa chief.

He had to be freezing, Tamson thought, too distraught to be embarrassed at his nakedness. Everyone else, save the half-naked savages, was cloaked or wrapped in blankets. She tried to rest her tiptoes on the ground, to take some of the strain off her wrists. Her fingers were not frozen, not as close to the flames as she was, but they were numb and would not obey her mental command to move. Surely the officer would intervene and take them back to the fort as prisoners.

While the men continued to talk, much of the time with raised voices that indicated their differences in opinion, Gaspar and Alain's partners arrived carrying two wooden crates. Tamson could not make out the writing stamped on the side of them, but when they were opened, their contents stirred great interest among the savages. Like children after candy, the Indians rushed in and helped themselves to the rifles, aiming them at imaginary targets and making firing sounds.

The chief watched the juvenile display with approval until the brave who had captured Tamson and suffered the consequences stepped forward, arguing fiercely. A few of the other Indians took up the discussion on the chief's part, until the sachem raised his hand, demanding silence. With another dissertation Tamson could not understand, he pointed to her and then to Jacques Dupré and his men. The injured warrior, however, did not go along with whatever he said. Eyeing Dupré with hatred, he spat at the man's feet and stomped off into the distance in an angry tantrum. It was dawn, Tamson realized dully.

"Your life will be spared, mademoiselle, thanks to your friends and the two cases of rifles they paid the Ottawa for you. You will leave with them."

She'd been so engrossed in the dealings among the chief, the warrior, and Jacques Dupré that she hadn't seen the French captain turn Anton Du Bois back over to the savages. Instead of tying him upright, as he had been before, they were staking him out on the cold ground.

"And you?" she asked timidly.

"I, alas, will die . . . *while you watch.*"

Seven

The Montreal docks were crowded, the powder blue French uniform colors predominant among the crowd. Ships eager to be on their way south before the winter freeze were busy loading their hulls for the return voyage to France. Alain, however, left the busier area for the seashore, where smaller vessels were beached or harbored nearby.

Dieu, but things were changing, he observed, and not for the best. It was evident that his cousins were in financial distress, despite the grand show of the harvest ball. Both rich and poor were scrambling to maintain their lifestyle against unbeatable odds. What manner of government would force farmers into the military while their fields lay untended, the grain rotting on the stalk? Now that same government, like his previously indifferent cousins, had suddenly taken an interest in his business.

Alain had thought La Friponne, or *the Cheat,* as the warehouse business run by Quebec's seedy intendant's cohorts was called behind their back, was too busy defrauding the French government and its peoples to worry about the activities of a small voyageur.

Except that now he was no longer an insignificant voyageur. Incredulous as it seemed, he'd seen his

mother's diary, which had been found in the attic by
Isabelle La Tour, wife to his cousin Joseph. Marie La
Tour had been pregnant with Alain when she gave up
her family position to marry voyageur Jean Beaujeu,
her rescuer from the Indians who had killed her husband.

The intendant's men, like his cousins, smelled money
and influence, even if Alain disdained the title and inheritance of his mother's first husband. As far as he was
concerned, he was still the son of Jean Beaujeu and
perfectly content with his own hard-earned fortune.
That, however, did not stop the La Tours' change of
heart from disdain to reluctant adoration or the strong-
arming of Monsieur Chapais, the intendant's repre-
sentative.

Somehow Bigot's people had found out about Tamson Stewart and were using her safety as a means of
forcing Alain into their ranks. As for his cousin, it had
taken Alain all morning to assure the anxious man that
he wanted no part of the La Tour-Galisonne inheritance,
all of which was needed in these times for Joseph, Isabelle, and little Marielle to survive. All he asked in
return was that a house be secured for his new bride.
There was no other way to explain Tamson's presence
in Montreal.

Day by day, he regretted more and more his impulsive
decision to kidnap the girl! He'd lost count of the number of times his mother's caution about one lie begetting
another and another had haunted his thoughts and filled
him with remorse. Now, he was about to drown in the
torrent of fabrication he'd created.

The only news that had been welcome had come unexpectedly in the form of a crudely scrawled letter from

Jean Beaujeu. His father was alive, although not well, and living in an Acadian refugee camp outside Quebec. It seemed he'd not been at home when Marie Beaujeu and her daughters had been seized by the British and forced onto waiting ships for exile. So, Quebec would be his next destination.

"Alain! Alain Beaujeu!"

Alain halted abruptly and turned with a curse upon realizing he'd been so wrapped up in his quandary that he'd walked past the *bateau* he'd secured to cross the river to Prairie that afternoon. To his astonishment, Alain recognized Jacques Dupré waving from the deck of the fishing vessel. In an instant, shock became alarm, for his companion would never have left Tamson's side unless something was wrong.

"What is it, mon ami?"

"The trader Du Bois escaped with the girl and the papers belonging to the courier. The Indians caught them."

"Didn't you stay at the cottage?" Alain demanded.

"She . . . she hit me over the head with a poker and left. When the Widow Lusignan found me, I was unconscious."

A gnawing fury curled in Alain's stomach, threatening to pull the strength from his knees as well. "What happened to them?"

Jacques met Alain's gaze evenly. "Du Bois was turned over to the Indians. We bought the girl back for two cases of rifles."

Alain swore, the warmth of his breath clouding in front of him. "She is not hurt?"

"Not so one can see."

"What do you mean, *not so one can see?*" Alain

queried suspiciously. It rose again, that strength-draining anxiety. If the savages had ravished Tamson, he would never forgive himself.

Jacques took his seat in the *bateau* and motioned for Alain to do the same. "She is scratched and bruised—that is all in the physical sense."

"But . . . ?"

"She does not talk now. It is as if her mind has left her." Jacques' face was imploring. "I am so sorry, *mon ami*. We did everything we could to protect her."

Eight

Smoke drifted skyward from Widow Lusignan's chimney as Alain and Jacques Dupré entered the gates of Prairie. As anxious as he had been to see Tamson and comfort her during the river crossing, he found his pace slowing during the last stretch down the row of wood-roofed cottages. Despite Jacques' sordid account of what had happened, he didn't know what to expect. It wasn't that he didn't trust his friend's accuracy. It was all the conflicting emotions, the guilt and frustration, fear and longing, that contributed to his reluctance to step into the small house.

The widow, out of the kindness of her heart, had insisted that Jacques bring the poor English girl back to the house. No stranger to the tales of Indian torture, Madame Lusignan felt compassion for *any* woman, regardless of whether she was English or French, who had been captured by the savages.

"Oh, I am so glad to see you, Monsieur Beaujeu! It is terrible, this thing. I did not know my late husband's friend was a traitor, much less a kidnaper, to take your wife so. If only I had not been so tired, I might have heard the commotion, but . . ." She shrugged expressively and then smiled. "But I have good news!"

Alain did not correct the woman. Jacques explained

how he'd told her it was Du Bois who had knocked him
senseless, having followed him inside when he brought
in wood for the night. Alain had not been the only one
to notice Du Bois' interest in Tamson, for the widow
had found the story completely believable.

"She spoke your name this morning!"

Most likely as a curse, Alain thought laconically. He
nodded toward the bedroom door, left ajar to absorb
some of the cozy heat that was building back up in the
room after their entrance had allowed some to escape.

"She is in there?"

"Oui, monsieur." Madame Lusignan followed Alain
to the low opening. "I tried to get her to bathe and
change into some clean clothes, but all she will do is
wrap in that blanket and sleep! She has not eaten a bite
since she has returned!"

The moment Alain entered the small back bedroom,
he was struck by the smallness of the figure on the bed.
The red-gold hair that tempted his fingers too often was
strewn in a tangled mass over the pillows. As he walked
around to where she lay, he could barely see her soot-
smudged features, for she'd rolled up in her blanket in
a cocoon-like manner, her face tucked down in it.

His heart constricting in the strangest manner, he
lifted the wild stray strands of silk which further served
to hide the sleeping girl's face and touched the back of
her tear-streaked cheek with his hand. She shuddered
and pulled further into the folds of the blanket, causing
him to curse his thoughtlessness. His hands, he was
sure, were like ice. Self-consciously, he rubbed them
against the side of his mitasses and sank down on the
edge of the mattress.

At the movement of the bed, whiskey-brown eyes

flashed open to stare at him, filled with fear. A small whimper caught in the girl's throat as she recoiled. Before she could roll away in her confinement, however, Alain caught her and dragged her to his chest, cooing gently to allay her fright.

"Easy, *ma petitesse*. No one means to hurt you."

He stroked her hair, sorting out the tangles as best he could, until the stiff body within his grasp gradually began to relax. The heavy scent of woodsmoke assaulted his nostrils as he brushed the top of her head with his lips, unwittingly tightening his embrace. From the corner of the room, Madame Lusignan quietly exited, closing the door behind her to afford the couple privacy.

"I am so sorry that this happened to you."

Like a mother rocking her child, Alain continued to speak softly, moving back and forth. His only encouragement was that the girl had totally ceased to struggle in his arms. When he ran out of things to say, he told her about Montreal and how his father had been found in Quebec.

"He is very ill. I will be going for him."

To Alain's astonishment, Tamson worked her bare arms out of the blanket and clung to him. Bewildered, he lifted her chin so that he could see her face—a tormented, pleading face with new tears slipping silently down her cheeks.

He cleared his throat gruffly. He should never have taken her. He felt as if he himself had inflicted the scratches and bruises marring her smooth white skin. The large blue, black, and red one on her shoulder where the Indian had bitten her was enough to make him ill with remorse.

"I will not leave you again," he promised fervently.

Tamson cocked her head suspiciously, but nonetheless, some of the terror in her gaze subsided. She leaned against him again and shivered, prompting Alain to draw the discarded blanket up around her.

He knew an unfathomable relief that, as surprising as it was, troubled him. She should hate him. If she were in her right mind, she would. He'd heard about people who had witnessed savagery losing their minds, withdrawing into another world where their recollections could not follow them.

"Tamson?"

The girl stiffened at the sound of her name and looked up.

She knew who she was, he thought thankfully. She had not forgotten that, even if she had forgotten that he was her kidnaper and not her protector.

"You must eat. I will get you something." The moment Alain began to get up, Tamson threw herself at him, refusing to let go. Her expression was wild and panicked. "I am only going into the kitchen . . . just in there."

He pointed at the closed door, but the girl would not release her death grip on his waist. Even her eyes were clenched, as if she feared the prospect of witnessing his leaving. Resolve melting with contrite compassion, Alain drew her to her feet with him and secured the blanket on her shoulders.

"Come with me, then," he coaxed gently.

Although she loosened her arms, Tamson's fist was clenched about his belt, bloodless and pale.

"Alons, look who has come to join us!" Jacques ex-

claimed, rushing from his spot by the hearth to hug Tamson.

She did not pull away when the burly voyageur embraced her, nor did she let go of Alain.

Gaspar stepped up next. *"Bonjour, madame!"*

Tamson gave no sign of pleasure or dismay. She simply endured the attentions, staring apathetically at each of the men in turn.

Alain led her over to the kitchen table and offered her the one chair at the end, but it was not until he took a seat on the bench beside it that she joined him. He was too absorbed in ordering food for Tamson to be aware of the despair on his face. It was not missed by his companions, however.

"It is not your fault, mon ami. She will be all right in time."

Time? Alain wondered, glancing at the lovely but blank face of his companion, now attentive to the dancing flames of the hearthfire. How much time? What if she didn't recover? He'd heard of such things. Her father would have him hunted down and skinned alive . . . and rightfully so. The way he felt at the moment, that fate would be a relief.

Tamson did not let go of him until supper was put on the table by a cheery Madame Lusignan. It was another stew, fit and filling. Although the girl nibbled idly on a hot chunk of bread, torn off the loaf and buttered lavishly by Gaspar, she didn't touch her main dish.

When words would not cajole her into eating, Alain resorted to the time-tested technique he'd used with his younger sisters. He took up the spoon and dipped a small portion of the now cool concoction. Tamson watched him disinterestedly until he pressed it to her lips.

"Come, Tamson, eat . . . for me, please."

For a long moment, it appeared as though her lips would not part for him or anyone else. She merely stared over the spoon at him, lost on some tangent of thought far removed from the present. Then, just as he was about to give up, she opened her mouth and took the stew daintily.

"That is my girl!" Smiling, Alain dipped another spoonful, only to have her do the same with the spoon he'd put down, except out of his porringer. "Ah, so that is your game!"

He ate the offering and waited expectantly for her to respond in kind. Childlike, she did and so they went on until half or better of her dish was emptied. When she began to balk at taking more, Alain gave it up reluctantly.

"Half is better than nothing at all, which is what she would do for me," Madame Lusignan consoled him sympathetically. "Now there, Tamson," she went on, touching Tamson's arm to draw her attention from the fire.

Tamson started with a gasp, giving the poor widow a fright as well.

"There now, dear, why don't we clear these men out of here so you can have a proper bath. I'll comb that pretty hair of yours and . . ."

"The Indians, they took her clothes," Jacques reminded her.

Undaunted, the woman went on. "I'm sure I have something she can wear besides those filthy petticoats.

We'll wash them out and they'll be dry by morning, *non, ma petite?"*

Thinking the widow had everything under control, Alain rose from the table. *"Alors, mes amis,* let us go to the trading post and see what we can find for the lady." Impulsively, he took up the small hand resting on the table and lifted it to his lips. "I will come back soon, I promise."

It wasn't until Alain reached for the fur vest he'd discarded before supper that Tamson seemed to grasp his intentions. She overturned her chair as she bolted to the door where he gathered with his friends. Gone was that empty look and in its place, renewed panic.

"We will see what we can find, mon ami," Jacques offered. "Is there anything we can bring you, madame?"

Madame Lusignan shook her head. "Non, just take care of this poor child." The break in her voice drew attention to the mist over her eyes. "My husband and I, we lost a little daughter to the Indians years ago, never to see her again."

"They usually adopt children as their own, madame," Jacques reassured the widow empathetically. "To be raised and loved as such."

"I only pray as much." She stared at the wadded apron she twisted in her hand and then shook herself with a forced brightness. "But that was that! I must get some fresh towels and the washbowl."

"We will return in a while!"

Jacques and the others departed while Madame Lusignan disappeared into the back bedroom. Through the open door, Alain could hear her rummaging about for the articles she mentioned. With the girl firmly attached to his belt, he surveyed the table.

"Well, let us help the madame!" He began to stack the well-sopped porringers, devoid of leftovers. "You get the spoons. Here . . ." He put a few spoons in Tamson's hand and went back to his own task. As he picked up each bowl, she gathered up the spoons accompanying them, never more than an arm's length away, until all the dishes were neatly stacked at one end of the table.

"Stop that this instant!" Madame Lusignan ordered, appearing in the doorway with fresh linens and an old faded dress. "You are paying guests! It is *I* who will do the work. You can take down that basin on the wall there and fill it with the hot water from the hearth. We need to get her bathed before the others come back."

Alain hesitated. *"We?"*

"Well, you do not expect her to let *me* touch her, do you? And if she will not let you go, then we all three cannot gather around the basin."

The heat from the fire seemed to leap to Alain's neck, despite his placid acceptance of her logic. To Madame Lusignan, they were man and wife. He prepared the bath water hurriedly, Tamson on his heels with each step he took. Upon spreading her blanket on the bench he'd pulled close to the fire for warmth, he sat her down in front of him and knelt on the floor.

He was gentle, taking care not to open any of the cuts that had clotted over as he removed the dried streaked blood from her skin with the cloth. So soft, so vulnerable, he thought, stricken by the feel of it beneath his fingers. When her arms and face were done, he deftly tugged the shifts off her shoulders, so that they too were bared.

"You've done this before, monsieur," Madame Lusignan observed from the table where she busied herself with the dishes. "You had many brothers and sisters, non?"

"No brothers, only younger sisters."

Although his movements were impersonal and methodical when he slipped the cloth inside Tamson's damp garments to wash as far as he dared reach, the feel of the firm flesh of her youthful breasts managed to imbed itself in his memory. Later that evening as he lay next to her in bed his wandering thoughts were anything but impassive. Indeed, her softness, the curve of her breasts, the taper of her legs had established a clearer image in his mind of Tamson Stewart's physical charms than his wayward imagination had been able to conjure, despite his conscious effort to remain detached.

He had kept expecting to be slapped unceremoniously at any moment, and then, because of the base and inadvertent reaction of that part of him which had no conscience, he came to wish for such punishment. The girl had submitted to his ministrations in complete, even shy, trust.

When he'd stood her up to strip down her petticoats, wet and clinging with the washing he'd done beneath them, and turned her toward the fire in a feeble attempt to maintain some semblance of decency, his mouth had gone dry at the sight of the perfect sillouette of feminity outlined by the glowing light. His hands were nearly shaking as he hurriedly tugged the old dress Madame Lusignan had given him over her head and wrapped Tamson back up in her blanket.

Combing her hair was as much a trial, although her

frequent gasps and winces managed to distract him from its silken feel between his fingers. It took him better than an hour to work out the tangles and briars matted in it with a comb and brush. But now there was no distraction, only Tamson lying next to him, watching his every move curiously.

He'd left his trousers on, even his boots! Her earlier resistance to him, her quick and cutting barbs, bolstered his own. Now that they were gone, he felt at a loss to deal with this overwhelming urge to make love to her, to kiss her back to reality and show her his remorse in the only way he knew how.

He closed his eyes. It was just as well, he supposed, that she was not in her right mind. Her vulnerability had undermined his, too. It was not a comforting thought. Oh, he was vulnerable to his sisters' pleas and cajoling, and willingly so. But the way he felt about Tamson, it was somehow dangerous . . . threatening.

The touch of cold fingers splayed upon the warm skin of his bare chest beneath the blanket brought Alain's eyes open instantly. He turned to see Tamson raised on one elbow, the wide neckline of her oversized dress hanging impishly off one shoulder. Her face was devoid of emotion as she moved the covers back to consider the hair she toyed with experimentally. When it was fluffed up to her satisfaction, she snuggled closer to Alain, and rubbed her cheek against it.

Aware of the tautness drawing his chest and forcing a rush of blood to already unmercifully antagonized loins, Alain tensed. Ignorant of his reticence completely, she gently smoothed down his furred chest and laid her head upon it with a sigh. Her fingers had found another trail to trace, one which narrowed down the

center of his abdomen to the low slung waist of his
trousers, but before they were even close to the material,
he stopped her hand with his own shortly.

"Go to sleep, *ma petitesse.*"

He would take her home. Alain licked his lips and
turned his face away from the tumble of hair that had
escaped his awkward attempt at braiding. After he
brought his father back to Montreal, he would take Tamson to the nearest English settlement and turn her over
to the authorities there with a note as to whom they
should contact.

"Do you wish to go home, Tamson?" From his vantage, Alain could not see if the girl had drifted off to
sleep or if his attempt to stir her unresponsive behavior
had failed. "I will do that for you, *ma petitesse.* I will
take you back to your father . . . after I take care of
mine. I promise."

Nine

The sound of the bells in the village church nearby reached toward the walls of the fortress housing the Acadian refugees, but starvation and cold made it hard to feel any spiritual serenity. If God were on their side, how could He have let the English exile their loved ones and burn their fields and farms? Yet, the more devout among them did their best to attend the Mass to pray for deliverance from the English scourge. Mostly men, they now trekked back through the barren, snow-crusted plain toward the old fort, a few women who had managed to escape the British here and there among them.

At least Mother Nature left them better off than those in the cities. Once Alain made certain that Tamson was secure in the small stone cell they occupied with his sick father, he had taken a party of men into the wilderness to hunt. While the bread made of peas and flour was not plentiful, the land had provided enough fresh meat to fill the bellies of the homeless, replacing the watery stock made from boiled leather. Whether the supply of game would last throughout the winter without necessitating going further north was questionable, but for today, the cookfires were blazing in the compound and people would go to bed with a full stomach.

To the tune of fiddle music provided by a visiting trapper, some of the ragged occupants danced around the fires. Others watched from behind hide curtains nailed up around the front overhang of the general store to break the wind sweeping down over the walls. With loved ones lost to unknown fates, each and every soul pursued the spirit of the music with a fanaticism, trying just for one day to put aside the fears and troubles that haunted their lives and robbed them of peace.

As Alain made his way through the gaunt-faced people toward his father's cell, he thought he glimpsed Tamson peering out at the dancers. But the moment he spied her, she dropped the curtain over the small window and disappeared. A moment later, she came running through the door, her ragged clothing flying about her.

Alarm filled the young man at first, for the girl rarely ventured out of the cell without him. "What is it? Is it Papa?"

Eyes sparkling, the girl shook her head and pointed to the dancers. She grabbed his hands and skipped toward them, but Alain checked her.

"I will see to Papa first. Then I will dance with you. But first, I have something for you."

He handed her a stick of hard candy he had purchased from the sutler, who had moved out to the settlement from Quebec to capitalize on the new occupation of the fortress. The man's supplies, such as they were, were replenished by Paul René, a young fisherman from his parents' village whose wife had been beaten to death because she would not reveal where he and the few men who had escaped the British occupation by sea were hiding.

Driven like avenging demons, they now left regularly

on expeditions into English-held territory to take what they needed. They justified their plundering as taking back what had been taken from them . . . the eye-for-an-eye concept the ailing Jean Beaujeu swore against with his feeble breath. Alain could not bring himself to confess that he too had taken the Biblical proverb to heart, although his growing guilt over his deed had certainly been fanned by his father's vehement disapproval.

Much improved since the debilitating voyage from Prairie to Quebec during which she was deathly seasick, Tamson took the candy with a delighted grin and rushed ahead of Alain into the single room where they had spent the last few weeks. By the time Alain caught up with her, she was sharing it with the older man on the cot near the fire.

"Now where did you get that, *ma petite?*" Jean Beaujeu queried, taking the small piece she'd broken off for him and tasting it. "It's good, *non?*"

Alain's heart warmed at the sight. The moment the two invalids had laid eyes on each other, it had been love at first sight. His father's attraction to Tamson was no mystery. Like Alain, he loved women—big, little, and in-between. Yet, it was more than Tamson's pretty face. Jean's affection was born of a loving heart and compassion for the mute girl his son's partners had saved from the savages.

"Just like my Marie," he would sigh, watching her as she busied herself with tidying up the room. "A woman's touch makes all the difference in the world, my son."

Alain had to admit his father was right. When they'd arrived, the little room had been dark, dirty, and dreary. It smelled of sickness. After a few days, when Tamson evidently realized they were going to stay there, she began to gather snow in a basin and melt it over the tiny hearth with its stick-and-mud chimney. Where she learned to clean was beyond Alain, for he knew she'd always had servants, but clean she did.

Or, at least she made a difference. The walls were still dark, but diligently brushed with turkey feathers, so that bumping into them didn't automatically blacken clothing with soot. The table she had Alain move against his father's bed for meals and the bench she shared with him were scrubbed free of the built-up grime and bird droppings from years of abandonment. Even the dirt floor, which she brushed every day with a stub of a broom, had little designs drawn on it and the hide curtains had little bows tied on them made of strips from the petticoat Widow Lusignan had given her, which had dry rotted beyond use as a garment. Everything that would stand had a bow on it, from table legs to the door latch.

"Tamson, she has been entertaining me today," Jean Beaujeu told Alain as he approached the cot. "Are you certain she is not Acadian, for the music outside will not leave her feet alone!"

"The Scots like to dance as well, Papa," Alain reminded his father.

Although the man's eyes were bright with affection for the girl seated on the edge of his cot, his pallor was worrisome. The last attack of his weakened heart left him completely bedridden—it would have killed a lesser man. The moment Alain had told him that he had English friends searching for Marie and her daughters, the dying man had managed to gain a little more strength each day. He had been given hope, something that, with each terrible rumor and tale that came in from the outside world, had been hacked into oblivion.

With his new-found hope and Alain's devoted care, he seemed to be improving for a while. Like the cabin, he had been bathed and his bed made with fresh linens. Although his neighbors tried to help him as best they could, they had their own to care for. Unless he was coaxed, he had all but ceased to eat.

"Why do you stand here talking to this old man when you have a beautiful wife who wishes to dance?" Jean tapped the end of Tamson's upturned nose with his finger. "Go, *ma petite*. Take this ill-mannered son of mine outside and remind him it is Christmas!"

Alain took Tamson's hand, but his attention was still fixed on his father. True, his spirit seemed strong enough, but something was definitely wrong. "You are certain you feel well?"

"Well enough to eat that whole shank of venison I smell cooking on the fire out there. If my legs would hold me, you would not even have the chance to dance with this sweet girl. I will lie here and listen to the music."

Tamson leaned over, bussing the man on the cheek in parting, and pulled the covers up around his shoulders. She mouthed the word, "Papa," and looked up at Alain expectantly.

"Not without your cloak! I will not have both of you to care for!"

Like the dress hanging loosely on her, none of Tamson's clothes fit properly. They were hand-me-downs from whomever could contribute, usually garments outgrown or belonging to a deceased family member. That she was unaware of the origins of her wardrobe was a relief to Alain. In some cases, this shock-induced madness had been a blessing, but it would still afford him little peace.

"God will bring her back when she is healed," his father had consoled him when Alain told him about Tamson's ordeal.

He hadn't been completely honest. As vehement as his father was over the bloody retaliation of some of the Acadian men against the new English settlements in Acadia, he knew the man would not approve of his means of finding Marie Beaujeu and her daughters. Although Alain consciously justified his deception in terms of not upsetting the older man, it only compounded his guilt.

He withheld the truth about Tamson for the same reason. And Alain had not been able to bring himself to speak to his father about knowing the circumstances of his birth. The older man was doing so well, Alain hoped that he would regain enough strength to travel down to Montreal in the spring, where he'd left word that news of Squire Stewart's success was to be sent.

Tamson tugged at Alain's arm as they emerged from what had once been an officer's quarters and moved toward the large central bonfire. Men were dancing with men as well as women, due to the shortage of the latter, laughing as if the cares of the world had been lifted from their shoulders. Fiddle music had that magic ability to lift the spirit. Some clapped to the rhythm, while others beat on metal objects and sang, when words could be put to the melody.

Trying to shake off the cloud of concern generated by his father's grayish coloring, Alain waited until there was a break in the circle and pulled Tamson in. It was a simple country dance that anyone could learn quickly. Circling, swinging, and leaping about from foot to foot were the general steps, often taken at the individual's preference rather than the fiddler's call.

A few of the men threw their limbs about wildly, as if bent on dislocating each joint, while others, like Alain, possessed more grace of step and were more merciful to their partners. Not that Tamson was capable of sprawling unceremoniously into the circle of onlookers, as one of the women had done. Light on her feet, she danced with sprightly grace, her eyes twinkling with a magical quality that soon made Alain forget his troubles and throw himself into the celebration.

It had been months . . . a year, since he'd let himself laugh and dance. It was at a wedding of two people he barely knew, but when a social was given for any occasion, the entire parish participated. Laurette had been his main partner, for the young men had the good sense to keep Annette and Lisette on their toes throughout the entire night. Not only had his youngest sister been thrilled with his attention, but her companionship spared Alain from all the matchmaking mothers and their sloe-eyed daughters who knew he was one of the most eligible and well-off bachelors in attendance.

Then all those preying women had been a nuisance. Now, he missed them, not for himself, but for his fellow men. Except for the few dances where partners changed with each round of music, Alain had the loveliest girl he had ever seen on his arm. Not even her tattered clothing and patched cloak could diminish her charms. Scratches and bruises no longer marred her porcelain complexion, healthily rouged by the weather. No rose could touch the color of her lips, invitingly open as she looked up at him in the midst of a fast-paced swing.

The deteriorating battlements of the fort paraded around behind her in a blur, but Alain could not take his gaze from her face. A warm feeling suffused his body, for she looked truly happy. Her broken fingernails and work-roughened hands bothered her no more than her demeaning attire. A laugh hovered precariously about her lips, as if reluctant to break her long silence, as she reached out for him across the arm's length between them.

Alain's heart stopped. For a moment, there was no one there but Tamson. She felt it, too, this magnetism between them, pulling them closer. He battled a strong urge to kiss the girl, who was looking at him curiously, struggling with her own response. Alain felt that if he did not taste her lips now, he would never again have the chance.

"Alors, you have had the girl long enough, Beaujeu. Did your maman not teach you to share your blessings?"

Alain started as one of his newly acquired friends grabbed Tamson by the waist and pulled her into a foursome for the new dance the musicians struck up. Terror flashed in the eyes that had simmered whiskey-warm in the firelight only seconds before, but the laughter of the others in the group, particularly that of the other woman, seemed to diminish it. Tamson marched in the circle, her gaze flitting uncertainly to the faces of each of her merry companions. Still anxious, her eyes sought Alain for reassurance—he gave her a reluctant but encouraging nod.

Once separated from him, Tamson was surrounded

by others wanting to be her partner. Although she had seen all of these men in the fort, with each new partner she found Alain with her gaze, awaiting his approval before allowing herself to relax and enjoy the dance. Eventually, as the men began to repeat their turns, her looks became less and less frequent.

Alain wrestled with his conflicting irritation and relief that she was enjoying herself so immensely. He wanted her to. She deserved some pleasure after all she'd been through. He had no right to monopolize her. It was good that she was coming out of that withdrawal that had so worried him. At least here, she was safe. Well acquainted with the tale of her Indian captivity, everyone in the fort seemed to care for her, always asking Alain about her welfare.

When someone called him over to one of the smaller cookfires, Alain took the piece of roasted venison one of his new hunting partners offered him. It needed salt, but so did everything. To render enough from sea water with the scant pots they'd escaped with was a next to impossible task. The determined people, however, continued to try. In the meanwhile, they used as little as possible to stretch the supply.

"It is good!" he complimented the farmer-turned-cook.

Occasionally used to going without salt on his long sojourns into the wilderness, Alain did not find the meat so distasteful. He had not eaten that day, but gone out to help the men who were trying to make all the dwellings in the settlement habitable. New roofs and doors, wooden hinges and latches were apparent everywhere, bright and raw against the aged wood that had survived years of abandonment.

"I will get a plate for my father."

Alain turned to head toward the cabin when Tamson flew into him with such force that he nearly lost his balance. Face buried against his chest, she held him so tightly her arms trembled with the effort. When he managed to disengage himself and lifted her chin, the flush from her dancing had paled and anxiety filled her eyes.

"I think she did not see you and panicked," one of the women informed him, reaching out sympathetically to pat the girl on her shoulder. "It is all right, little Tamson. Your husband would not leave a pretty thing like you."

Instead of replying, Tamson tugged at Alain plaintively and glanced at the cabin door, indicating that she was ready to go inside. Her hands were like ice when he covered them with his own. "We will go," he assured her. He shook his head in warning as one of the revelers approached her with the obvious intent of asking her to dance, stopping the man with his pale blue gaze. "Are you hungry, *ma petite?*"

Tamson stopped in front of the door, lost in thought. A sinking feeling invaded Alain's chest. Did she know what he'd asked her? Sometimes he felt she was completely alert but other times, far from it. Without warning, she stood up on tiptoe and softly pecked at his lips. When she drew back, she watched him closely, her fingers entwining with his nervously.

Alain could not move. If he did, he knew he'd return the kiss, and not nearly so innocently. But when Tamson dropped her gaze to the ground and turned slowly to lift the latch to the door, he could not help himself. He caught her chin with his hand and lowered his lips upon her own. Shivering, she went into his embrace, clinging as tightly to him as he did to her.

While she did not return the affection, she did not withdraw from it. Indeed, she seemed to savor it, sighing and melting in complete submission and trust. The flavor of the peppermint candy mixed with the sweetness of her flooded Alain with long-denied desire. There were too many layers of clothing to feel the supple curves of her body against his, yet he knew them, just the same.

"Can you not wait until you get inside, mon ami?"

Alain had no idea who shouted the teasing question, but he was grateful, for he felt the hungry beast within about to lose control. Instead, he drew away from Tamson, gave her a chaste peck on the nose, and herded her inside the cabin.

"I will bring in some wood for the fire," he told her, closing the door between them.

He opened his coat and walked over to the stack of wood he'd been building upon as time afforded, yet not even the cold draft could douse the fire that burned in his loins. He shivered, but not from the cold. From frustration and self-reproach.

She didn't know what she was doing. She simply didn't! She was engaged to be married, Alain reminded himself sternly. If he took advantage of her innocence, he was no better than a savage.

He had filled his arms with as many pieces of firewood as he could carry when the door burst open and Tamson stood there waving at him frantically. Dropping the wood, he ran past her inside to find his father lying on the floor beside the cot.

"Papa!"

He slipped his arms under Jean Beaujeu's legs and shoulders to lift him back onto the bed from which he'd evidently tried to get up. His father opened his eyes, blinking in bewilderment. "Wha . . . what happened?"

"You tried to get up?"

"Non, I do not . . . yes," the older man admitted, as if suddenly remembering. "My head . . . it was aching with a terrible pain and . . ."

Tamson put her finger over the man's lips to silence him.

"Tamson is right—you must conserve your strength. Let me fetch you some brandy."

Jean Beaujeu shook his head as Tamson gently brushed his thick salt and pepper locks from his face. Upon feeling the dampness of perspiration on his forehead, she took her skirt and mopped it. When she looked at Alain again, her eyes were glazed and frightened.

"I will go get a doctor from Quebec," he said.

"Non!" the older man protested. "I need no doctor to bleed me to death to restore my humors. Save your money for your pretty wife and . . . and my grandchildren."

Alain's throat constricted as his father's words sank in. "What is this talk about dying? Look, you are frightening Tamson."

"She knows. She and I, we have talked much these last few days?" At the arch of Alain's brow, his father laughed. "Well, I have talked and she has listened. A woman who is a good listener is a blessing."

"I will go to Quebec to get the doctor and I promise, I will let him bleed you no more."

"Get Madame Thibideau. She will tell you I need no doctor." The man waved his hand at Alain weakly.

"Now don't make me weaker by arguing, son. Do as I say!"

Alain glanced across the cot at Tamson. "I will be right back." At her understanding nod, he turned and left.

Madame Thibideau, like Tamson, had no lack of partners. She was dancing gaily when Alain found her. A heavy-set woman who was midwife of the village, she sobered immediately when Alain explained the situation.

"His color is terrible. He looks almost gray and his eyes . . . they are rolled up so that you can see the white under them." Alain had seen the pallor of death before, yet he was hoping the friendly woman would deny what his instincts were telling him.

"He has never gotten over the shock of Marie and the girls being taken from him. It was all he talked about before you came, but your wife, she seems to have lifted his spirits."

Tamson was still at Jean Beaujeu's side when they returned, although a small basin of water and the cloth on his head betrayed the fact that she had not been idle.

"With such a pretty nurse, why do you send for me, old man?"

Jean chuckled tiredly. "I did not wish to interrupt your holiday, but my son, he is insisting on a doctor. Tell him I am dying and to let me do so without that black-suited buzzard and his leeches."

The madame turned to Alain. "Well, you heard the man. Listen to him . . . or at least humor him. If he thinks he is dying, it will do no harm to let him go on with his madness."

"Then he is not?" Alain asked, bewildered by this casual acceptance of the situation by both parties.

"He needs a good supper, but only what he will eat," Madame Thibideau warned. "Do not force him. Let him drink what he will and celebrate the day as best he can."

"Now *that* is sound advice!" Jean agreed breathlessly. "Go back to your party, madame, and enjoy what days you can."

"I'll see you out," Alain said.

Alain was convinced that all was not well, but was reluctant to make an issue of it in front of Tamson. She was clearly distraught, the way she held his father's hand and kept patting it, as if that would help. He stepped outside after the woman, who turned immediately, once out of earshot.

"I do not know how Jean has managed to hold on this far. He is a strong man to live with a broken heart."

"So you are saying you agree with me . . . that this is serious."

The woman nodded. "Oui, it is serious, Alain, but I would send for the priest, not the doctor. I say send, not go yourself. He needs his son with him. I will take care of it," she added with a sympathetic squeeze of Alain's arm.

"Merci, madame."

Alain was surprised at the sound of his own voice. It was as if it belonged to someone else. A year ago he was in control of his life. Now, his family was scattered, his father dying, and even his captive had been taken away from him, at least mentally. Every aspect of his world was out of hand, beyond his ability to do anything except watch and wait. He ran his fingers through his coal black hair and fetched the wood he'd dropped earlier.

"Alain, come fill your plate! *You* led us to the game. It is only right!"

"I'll be right there."

Tamson had not left his father's side. Still holding his hand, she watched Alain as he added wood to the fire and stacked the rest on the floor. His father said she knew, but the placid expression that had settled on her face gave no sign that she did. Apparently, she believed Madame Thibideau. Perhaps it was just as well, for Alain wondered if he could console himself, much less her.

She had mouthed the word *Papa* earlier. Was that the reason she had taken such a liking to the man? Jean Beaujeu was not unattractive in appearance, and he was utterly charming by nature. Marie La Tour had seen past all the furs and the beard and fallen in love with him. Had he worked a similar charm on Tamson or was it that the girl really thought of him as *her* father?

Alain reeled with a dawning idea. Of course! He had told her he was going to take her home to her father! In her unstable state of mind, she thought Jean Beaujeu was the man. She didn't even remember Squire Stewart. His emotions dulled with the shock of this realization, Alain told Tamson where he was going and took a large wooden platter out to get their supper.

Thanks to Paul René and his companions, there had been enough dried peas and flour to make up some bread, which Alain piled on top of the sliced venison. To complete the meal, he added a couple of slices of roasted pumpkin, lightly sprinkled with maple sugar. There was no butter to add to it, as his mother did, but it would serve well enough. His appetite had gone anyway. It was Tamson and his father who dominated his thoughts.

"I was hunting," Alain heard his father telling Tamson when he returned with the scant feast. "If only I had been there, I might have taken the women and hidden them in the hills." He winced and rubbed his left arm.

"You are hurting, Papa?"

"My arm . . . it has some pain," he acknowledged. "You must find your maman, *mon fils,* and your sisters."

"Even as we speak, our people are tracking them. They will find them. Tamson, will you eat? There is sugared pumpkin."

Tamson started to shake her head, but Jean insisted. "Go on, *ma fille* . . . and I will take some of that brandy you found," he told Alain. "Perhaps it will ease this pain."

At her urging, Alain moved the table next to the cot, but Jean did not wish to be propped up on his pillows as was the usual practice. The younger man went through all the motions of eating, for the sake of something to do, but swallowing was difficult. Next to him, his silent companion enjoyed the roast pumpkin, licking the sticky sugar syrup off her fingers from time to time, but once it was gone, she moved back to her post at Jean's side.

At her coaxing, he took a small piece she had cut off for him and tried to eat it, but it remained in his slackened mouth until Alain finally got him to spit it out before he choked. The brandy, straight from the glass and undiluted, was all he could swallow. After a while, his breathing became less labored, but his pulse continued, fast and erratic.

"There are many things I wish to say to you, Alain," he spoke up after a long period of silence, broken only by the strains of music outside and the sound of happy voices. "I am proud of you, *mon fils*. You place honor above your purse and love above your own desires." Jean smiled wistfully. "When you do that, you know you are in love. Do not think my first winter at home, that my heart did not wander into the wilderness with my friends. But I would not trade that or any of the winters I have since spent with your mother for all the furs in the world."

"I learned that working the land had its own rewards," he went on, blinking away the sentimental mist from his eyes. "Just as love rewarded me with children. I do not regret giving up trading and trapping for her. I would give my life, my last breath this very moment, if she were here, safe, with my girls."

"Papa," Alain began hesitantly, "I received a letter from France . . . from the solicitor of the estate of the late Marquis de la Galisonne."

He had to ask. He might never find his mother and he did not trust his cousin and the suddenly convenient journal which had declared Alain the Marquis de la Galisonne. After all, his wealth was certainly a boon to the La Tours in terms of social prominence, something of too much importance in Isabelle's eyes. Then there was the downturn of the La Tour business.

"So?"

"He had died without heirs," Alain explained. "Mother's first husband was his brother."

Awareness flickered in the distant look Jean Beaujeu

had fixed on the low-beamed ceiling. "So now they want you, do they?"

So it was true, Alain thought numbly. Why hadn't his parents told him?

"But *I* am your father, Alain . . . not by blood, but by love. I raised you as my own son. I delivered you. I held you, still wet from your mother's womb. Few real fathers have as much claim." Although he was smiling, tears streamed down the older man's cheeks. "I gave you to your mother and she gave you to me."

Unable to speak for the blade in his throat, Alain knelt beside the cot and took his father's work-roughened hand in his own, fervently pressing it to his lips.

"And now you are a marquis." It was a statement, flat and lacking the least bit of doubt. "Perhaps it is best. You must take your wife and go to Montreal to the house you told me of. This is no place for her."

"Why didn't you tell me?"

Jean closed his eyes as if to recharge his waning strength, and then looked at his son. "What did I, a poor trader who could not even read, have to offer you? I . . . I was afraid you would be seduced by the glamour and money of your rank and station."

"Have I not been my mother's son, too?" Alain asked. Marie La Tour had given up her plush life in Montreal for the hard life on the little Acadian farm.

"Yes, you are Marie's son," his father agreed, his voice softening with affection. "Love means more to you than position. But you do not know how I worried that, when you went to school in Montreal, you might not wish to come home again."

"I am not comfortable there and I know I would not

be comfortable in France. I have no desire to inherit this title. I do not need it."

Jean squeezed his hand weakly in approval. "Non, you do not. You have everything you need in this country. All you need to do is find your mother and sisters." His voice broke. "You must find them and take care of them for me! You must tell your mother that I will wait for her and see your sisters well married." Pain contorted his features. "And you, *ma petite fille,* you will name my first grandson after his gran-pére Jean, non?"

A loud sniff drew Alain's blurred gaze to Tamson, who nodded solemnly. Dieu! Did she believe the lie he'd concocted to keep her safe or was she so upset because she thought her father was passing away? Alain found himself torn between comforting his father and the girl silently crying on the other side of the bed. A knock on the door saved him from having to choose.

He pushed himself to his feet and answered it. A robed priest stood grimly in the light cast from the cook-fires beyond. With him was Paul René, who had evidently driven the sledge into the village to fetch him.

"I am Père Gabriel de Baptiste, my son. This young man has brought me to administer last rites for your father."

Alain stepped back to invite them in.

"They took my baby girls, you know," the man on the cot repeated to Tamson, his mind beginning to wander. "They did not even let maman take her grandmother's chest! I know her heart is broken!" Whether from physical or mental pain, Jean sobbed. "They only had time to take the clothes on their backs. I can't think where to look for them! Help my boy find them for me. You must!"

"*I . . . I will, Papa Jean!*"

"Wait, monsieur!" Alain put his arm in front of his guests, holding them back upon hearing Tamson's trembling promise. Perhaps he hadn't heard right. Hallucination was certainly not beyond him at this point.

"My fa . . . father will find them. I know he will! He's nae a bad man. Nae all of us English are bad. We love each other and suffer as much as ye'selves from this war."

Alain felt his beating heart stumble at the open admission. It did not register with the dying Jean Beaujeu, but he and Alain were not the only ones to hear her.

"*English!*" Paul René swore vehemently at Alain's elbow. "You said she was a *Canadian* Scot!"

Ten

With the onslaught of grief over his father's death, Tamson was once again silent. She didn't leave Jean Beaujeu's side until the women came to prepare him for burial. Then she'd curled in a ball beneath her blanket, shoulders shaking forlornly and tears chafing her reddened cheeks, but not a sound did she make. Alain wondered if he had imagined her speaking, yet there could be no doubt. René and the priest had spread the word like wildfire through the camp, changing the sympathies toward Tamson to guarded suspicion in some and outright hostility in others.

Alain understood their reason. Their families were gone, like his own. That very same bitterness led him to kidnap Tamson. It had been a mistake. He knew that now and he intended to rectify it, whether she completely recovered from her capture by the Indians or not. Perhaps in her own home, she would. As for his mother and sisters, he might use his title to his advantage to search them out through diplomatic channels.

As they walked through the gates of the fort from the gravesite, Tamson clung to his belt as if it were a lifeline. Alain knew she sensed the change in attitude toward her. It was hard to ignore people looking pointedly at her and whispering behind their hands.

Paul René was even less subtle. "So when will you be leaving?"

"Tomorrow morning."

"And *her,* what will you do with her?"

"She is my wife. I will take her with me." Alain didn't like the questions being fired at him. "By sledge," he added cautiously. "I am certain there will be travelers heading for Montreal from Quebec this time of year. You know how they love the parties."

Most of René's men were fishermen. If he left on horseback, he could ride to Trois Riviers. Alain did not like the threat of the revenge he instinctively sensed seething behind René's shadowy dark eyes. To indicate that they would travel in a group, as was frequently done, might discourage any notions from coming to fruition.

"Don't do anything foolish, Paul," Alain warned flatly.

"It is you who married an Anglaise."

The entire world was mad, Alain thought as he stopped before the cabin door long enough to gather wood for the fire. Even the priests preached about the glory of France and of God's being on their side in driving the English out of the fur territory. The Holy Virgin had appeared to an Ursuline convent to further assure them, so rumor had it.

Yet, the English had had their own sign. It was alleged that Oliver Cromwell's ghost had appeared at White Hall to advise Parliament to declare the war they were already fighting. When would they all realize that people filled with hatred on either side would prolong, not end, a war? If England heeded this apparition's calling and war was officially declared, all the misery Alain had witnessed to date was only a prelude to even worse times.

Tamson sat on the bench by the fire as Alain laid on more wood. How could they consider a homeless angel a threat? he thought, noting the way her hair caught and reflected the glow of the embers. No daughter could have been more tender or caring of his father. Her ordeal with the Indians may have staggered her mind, but it had not tarnished the purity of her heart.

That lost look which could tear at Alain's chest settled on her finely sculpted features as she contemplated the flames licking and leaping about the fresh kindling.

"They hate me."

The girl's statement caught him by surprise. He brushed his hands on his mitasses and pushed up to his feet. "They hate the English, who are our enemy, *ma petitesse,* not you."

"I liked it here . . . with your papa." Tears clouded her eyes with her candid admission. "It . . . it was horrible, what the English did to your mother and sisters." She pointed toward the door, a little sob catching in her throat as she added, "And to them out there!" A saline crystal spilled over her cheek, leaving a fresh wet track. "It makes me ashamed to be English."

Alain pulled Tamson to him, bewildered by her words and touched by her body-shaking despair. "How do you know you are English, *ma petite?*"

She shrugged within his embrace. "How do you know you are French?"

"You liked Papa Jean very much, didn't you?" Alain stroked the static strands of hair away from her face, smoothing it into the golden red cloak over her shoulders. She'd combed it out that morning until he had had

to force himself outside to split more wood . . . anything
to get his mind off of her and her silken softness.

"He was special. He made me laugh and cry . . . like
you." Tamson looked up at him timidly. "You won't
leave me here, will you?"

Alain could not help himself. He sealed her trembling
lips with a tender kiss. "I will not leave you, Tamson.
I promised you that when . . . when we left Prairie. Do
you remember?" Part of him prayed she would not. He
unfastened her cloak and let it fall from her shoulders.

"I'm so tired." Tamson stifled a yawn with the back
of her hand. "Can we go to bed?"

Alain ignored the rush of heat her innocent suggestion evoked and nodded. "You have not rested well. You
take the cot. I . . . I have some more wood to split."

"I can't!" Tamson glanced at the small bed Jean
Beaujeu had occupied and shuddered. She rose from
the bench. "I'll make our bed up on the floor, in case
you change your mind."

The blankets and the straw-stuffed mattress they'd
used for bedding were rolled up neatly under the cot.
Alain helped Tamson get them out and make up a place
in front of the fire. Without thought of propriety, she
peeled off the green and white checked kerchief that
she'd wrapped about her shoulders. After folding it
neatly and laying it on the cot, she turned back to Alain
bemused.

"Why are you cutting more wood when we are leaving in the morning? There's already a big stack split."

Alain glanced away from the gentle swell of her
bosom, modestly exposed without the kerchief by the
square neckline of her oversized hand-me-down dress.

"I need to be alone for a while."

As he turned to reach for the axe kept inside the door, Tamson put her hand on his arm. Although her touch was light as a feather, no chain could be more restraining, especially when Alain did not really want to leave her. Her eyes were amber warm, reflecting myriad emotions, compassion overshadowing the rest.

"I understand. I know you loved him . . . and he loved you, too."

Alain stiffened as she embraced him affectionately and planted a kiss on his cheek. He forced himself to relax. "You rest, *ma petitesse*. Tomorrow we have a long journey ahead."

The hard work of splitting the wood for the fire held a two-fold purpose for Alain. It not only helped him release the inner frustration of his animal nature, but gave him time to think, to deal with his grief without Tamson's innocent distraction. As he swung the axe, he took out his hostilities on the wood, splintering it with loud cracks in a rhythmic pattern that eventually became soothing.

A commotion near the gates distracted Alain from his ponderings. A small band of Ottawa Indians, a hunting party by the look of them, wandered into the compound. Women and children immediately took to their huts or watched from behind cover as Paul René and the Abbé Gabriel left the sutler's store to meet them.

Alain knew the savages to be the same Indians who threatened to raid their small farms if their men did not help fight the English. Such allies were tenuous at best and, while Alain more and more disapproved of using heathens to fight a war, he decided it was best to find out what was amiss. He dropped the axe and walked over to the store, knowing full well he would discover nothing but bad news if the tattooed Ottawa were involved.

Even as he listened to the announcement of the arrival of British supplies, the last for the winter, and the ensuing plans to raid the English settlers now occupying Acadian land, the hair bristled on the nape of his neck. Not so long ago, he'd have joined them. Now the prospect was not so enticing. Whatever their plans, Alain knew he would have to get Tamson back to Montreal, the sooner the better.

The Beaujeu cabin was cozy, warmed and illuminated by the soft light of the fire. Tamson stirred briefly from her slumber when Alain added more wood, but settled back down upon seeing it was he who had invaded her dreams. It wasn't until after he'd packed their belongings that he allowed himself the luxury of rest. He stripped off his wet mitasses and moccasins as well as his buckskin jacket and laid them out to dry near the fire before considering the empty cot shoved against the wall.

A sharp pang in his breast would not permit him to consider lying down on it. As long as he had remained busy, he was able to put aside his grief. While he watched his father slip away, he'd thrown himself into helping his friends make the fort habitable. Once Jean Beaujeu was gone, there were arrangements to be made for the burial and for their journey back to Montreal. Now, however, in the loud silence of the room, there was no one but the sleeping girl to soothe away the anguish twisting inside. He dared not dwell overlong on her presence.

Not one given to showing his innermost feelings, Alain tried to swallow the lump in his throat and slipped

under the blankets on the straw mattress. His father . . .
the man who had raised him and been all that a father
should be, was gone, not lost, like his mother and sisters. What would he tell them when he found them?
Would he then see his mother waste away?

The heavy beams of the ceiling overhead blurred, but
Alain forced the distortion from his eyes and stared up
resolutely. Frustration and bitterness welled in the back
of his mouth. At that moment, he felt as lost as he knew
his family must, wherever they were. Perhaps more so,
he considered tiredly. At least they had each other. What
good was a title and money to a man without loved
ones?

He shut his eyes and clenched his teeth to fight the
uncharacteristic and overwhelming emotional tide, dar-
ing himself to give in to the urge to cry. That was for
women, who could do no better, or children. Even as
he scolded himself, the image of his father as he spoke
nostalgically of his wife and family surfaced.

*I would not trade that or any of the winters I spent
with your mother for all the furs in the world.*

Alain did not know his cheek was so cold until he
felt a warm hand pressed against it. Startled, he turned
to see Tamson, propped up on one elbow, watching him
intently. Gone was the earlier sleepy gaze that had made
her eyelids heavy and in its place was a solemn, sympathetic look. Gently, she closed the distance he'd been
careful to place between them and eagerly pressed the
length of her body against his.

Her face was close now, her lips no more than a single
breath away, yet she didn't speak. Silken tresses hung
tangled over one shoulder, bared smooth and white. Yet,
the girl was unaware of the tempting picture she pre-

sented. She continued to stare into his eyes, as if searching for something to soothe the silent despair in her own. Alain could feel the gnawing anguish meld with his, and, yet, the fact that it was being shared, both emotionally and physically, made it suddenly bearable.

He wanted to hold her, to kiss her, to banish those uncertainties. The distraction from his own pain would be welcome. Yet, to do so would demolish the brittle defense he'd maintained. As it was, Tamson's firm but yielding breasts burned into his chest, robbing his mouth of moisture, and the careless leg she'd thrown over him played havoc with every cell in his body.

Like a coiled spring ready to explode, he struggled with his urges, verbal and physical. Time froze to the thunder of his pulse. When restraint finally snapped, a wildfire flashed hot, engulfing them both.

Alain was not certain who kissed whom first. All he knew was the sweet, compassionate demand that would release neither of them. The contact was their sustenance, more compelling than the breath it denied them. Apologies, caution, and all sentiments of reason were scattered beyond his ability to call them back, much less voice them. He was tired of fighting and hungry for surrender and the comfort and release it promised.

They were both captives now, enslaved by the raw need of both body and soul. Breathless from their deep, soul-searching kiss, she began to explore the sinew of his body with tentative fingers—he was paralyzed by her touch.

As she moved from his chest and down the narrow furred trail that dipped below the waist of his trousers, he held his breath in hot anticipation. She could not have missed the throbbing steel of his passion in the explosive frenzy of that first kiss any more than he could help the hands that went of their own accord to clasp and knead her rounded buttocks, preventing any retreat.

His effort was wasted in that respect, for she gave no sign of withdrawing. He forced the breath from his lungs as she tugged at the lacings of his trousers, her lips set in provocative determination.

Dieu, if she but touched him . . . Alain stood up so quickly, Tamson started. Wide eyes filled with bewilderment and alarm as she met his gaze.

"Don't leave me!"

Alain's laugh was not his own. It was a poor attempt to release that which was threatening to explode within him. "I have no intention of leaving, Tamson," he assured her, ignoring the persistent voice of guilt that tried to dash a fire already too far out of control.

Upon seeing him strip off his trousers, alarm left the girl's expression. In its place was wonder and outright interest. Alain steadied his breath and reached for her, avoiding the outstretched fingers seeking to touch him, lest all semblance of control be banished. He kicked his remaining clothing off and dropped to his knees, drawing her up before him. As if reading his mind, Tamson reached behind her in an attempt to unfasten her dress.

"I will help," he offered huskily.

Alain was no stranger to feminine apparel. He'd helped dress his younger sisters until it was no longer considered proper, yet now his fingers refused to work effectively. All the concoctions his mother had created to adorn her daughters could not begin to match the level of exasperation the simple design of Tamson's illfitted garment did; she remained perfectly still, content to let him see to the task.

As if possessed, she stared at him, devouring his body. When her dress finally came over her head, Alain could not refrain from leaning away, the limp garment still in one hand, to drink in her splendor. The ancients' Venus knelt before him, her youthful breasts upthrust and hard with anticipation of that which she was made for. A tangle of copper-gold tresses cascaded about her shoulders, permitting patches of silken flesh and passion-dark nipples to peek through.

"Hold me."

The two words broke the barrier of silence—the only barrier left between them. He pulled her to him, flesh to flesh, to fall together in the tangle of blankets that was their bed. Cautions of a different nature from guilt reeled among the bombardment of sensation assaulting his ready and eager body, for he had enough knowledge of women to recognize her inexperience and know that she was not prepared for the inevitable union ahead.

With the pleasure of giving in mind, Alain rolled the clinging girl over. He found her lips, drinking deeply of her heady submission until she began to react with timid responses, begging for more. When he circled the tip of her breast with his tongue, her gasp of pleasure made him ache to satisfy his own deep torment.

His fingers were frantic as he worked his way over the flat stretch of Tamson's abdomen to the burnished down of her femininity, stroking, caressing, until she was literally trembling beneath him. Her hands clasped about his head, as if debating whether to push him away or encourage him to go on.

"Alain!" Her breathy plea halted him but only momentarily, for he had tested the moist eagerness awaiting him between her thighs and knew their desire was mutual.

"Of course, *ma petitesse*," he whispered, gently making room for himself with velvet caresses that drove her to welcome him with a desperate embrace of her legs.

There was no time to think about any other need; without hesitation, he united with Tamson in a way he had not dared dwell upon before.

She dug her nails into his back and rode the maelstrom of desire, her cry that she could stand no more falling upon ears deafened with the violent passion that consumed his body. He roared with the release that had eluded him for too long and collapsed on the soft body beneath his.

Vaguely aware of the still figure still united with his own, Alain forced himself to his side and reached for the blankets to cover them both. Tamson wriggled closer, fitting into the curve of his body, her limbs entwined with his, as if they had been made to fit together that way.

A druglike lethargy dulled Alain's senses, making everything seem warm and inviting, including sleep. Neither conscience nor Tamson's gentle nuzzling of his chest managed to invade it. Not even her quietly sighed, "Do you think we made Papa Jean's grandson?" could prod him. It did, however, register somewhere in his semiconscious state, to wait along with all the other reservations he'd had about making love to his beguiling captive until another time, when he was able to feel the full sting of repercussion.

Eleven

An icy wind from the north sped Governor General Vaudreuil's ship toward the island city of Montreal through the renewed break in the channel ice. It would, no doubt, seal in their wake until spring with the renewed January blast. Always one to take advantage of good fortune, something which had become scarce of late, Alain Beaujeu walked along the companionway to the officers' dining room in the stern.

Perhaps it was an omen, he mused wryly. He not only managed to slip out of the refugee camp unnoticed, but had used his newly acquired title to gain passage on the last ship bound for Montreal that winter.

His biggest problem came in convincing Tamson to board the ship. She'd balked upon realizing that a sea voyage awaited her and, considering how ill she'd become, he well understood.

She had managed to keep down the broth he'd given her and was contentedly, if not comfortably, keeping to the cabin afforded the new Marquis de la Galisonne. He knew she didn't understand his reluctance to remain in the cabin with her and was hurt when he showed indifference to her small attempts at affection. He dared not let what had happened the night of his father's funeral happen again, not if he intended to return her to her home.

Hence, he spent more than his share of time on the deck, exposed to the elements. To his astonishment, it was there that he had his first audience with Pierre de Rigaud Vaudreuil de Cavagnal, the Marquis de Vaudreuil and Governor General of New France. Without formal introduction, the governor clapped Alain on the back and welcomed him warmly to the noblesse. He had known Alain's uncle, the former Marquis de la Galisonne, and spoke as if he and the new marquis were going to be good friends.

Despite his reservations, Alain found himself gaining respect for the governor, who, unlike his colleagues, stood at the rail with Alain and braved the harsh weather. As the journey progressed, he discovered he had more in common with the man than he would have thought possible. Vaudreuil, for all his formal education and training in France, was still a Canadian, sympathetic to the people and knowledgeable of their hard way of life in a savage land.

At first the canny gentleman played cat and mouse with Alain, much like Monsieur Chapais. Vaudreuil knew who Tamson really was, although it was never discussed outright. He merely made certain that Alain was aware that he knew in order to press his advantage.

The governor was also aware of the fraudulent shenanigans carried on by his rival, the intendant Bigot, and the offer Alain had had to join the circle of traitorous thieves.

"So, *mon ami,* you will accept the office in procurement," the man informed Alain when all his cards were down, "and catch the mice at their vicious play. I want documentation to send to the King of France to show the real nature of Madame Pompadour's pet intendant, enough to leave no doubt about his swindling of the monarchy and the people of New France."

"And my wife, what of her?" Alain questioned, already feeling the constraints of the city life awaiting him.

The fact was, Tamson's safety had to be secured. The stakes were much higher, now that war had officially been declared. What he'd once counted on as his high card was now his Achilles' heel. Neither Bigot nor the governor were above using Tamson to manipulate him to their own purpose. They knew she was no threat to the security of New France, but they did not have to treat her as such.

That had been made perfectly clear by both factions, Alain mused as he returned to the cabin after dining with the governor and his entourage. He dreaded being alone with Tamson, who, unaware of the torturous discipline required, constantly wanted him to hold her. Each time he left, he had to convince her that he would return, that he wouldn't abandon her.

With the heavy scent of the oil burning in the gently swinging caged lanterns combined with the musty, mildewed closeness of the bulkheads, it was little wonder the girl remained ill. Furthermore, he could not convince her to go topside where she might find relief.

He lifted the latch to enter the narrow enclosure. Relief eased the tightening muscles in Alain's jaw as he saw that Tamson had gone to sleep. At least she wouldn't be expecting some slight, intimate favor that tested his restraint. The fact that the basin beside her was still empty encouraged him further, although her illness had made it easier to keep a distance, he thought with a pang of guilt.

Drawn to the small figure buried beneath the buffalo hide from which she had refused to part since leaving Quebec, he studied her face in repose. Her features were flawless, from her neatly arched brows to the tempting lips that could play so much havoc with his heart. Her lashes, darker than the copper gold fringe curling around her face, were fanned against cheeks inflamed by the whipping winter winds.

Against his better judgment, he leaned over and brushed, first one, and then the other with his lips. The heat that met them brought a scowl to his face, for, red as her cheeks had been, they were usually *cool* evidence of the winter's sting. Alain tested her forehead with his hand. Hot! Too hot to be normal. With a muffled oath, he yanked the buffalo robe off Tamson to find the blankets from his own bunk beneath.

"Wh . . . what are you doing?" the girl stammered, stirring drowsily. "I'm cold!"

"You have a fever, *ma petite*. Your skin is like fire. We must not have too many blankets."

Tamson rose in protest, but the quick movement made her sway unsteadily on the narrow berth. Alain quickly pressed against it to keep her from falling off. With a groan, she grasped her temples with trembling fingers and fell back against the flat, hard pillow.

"My head . . ." she murmured, bewildered by the sudden pain. "Alain . . ."

"I am here, Tamson."

"Don't leave me again!" Panic edged its way into her voice.

"I am only going to fetch the ship's physician. I

would have him see you and tell me how to make you more comfortable."

It was probably nothing serious, he told himself, trying to ignore the rising panic that threatened nerves so recently jolted by his father's death. His sisters had had more touches of this and that than he could count. Yet, the fact that he had taken a coddled young woman and dragged her through the wilderness, exposing her to the elements and desperate living conditions of his exiled Acadian friends did little to soothe his conscience.

"I will be back, *ma petite,*" he promised, planting a reassuring kiss on the tip of Tamson's nose.

"And will you hold me and k . . . keep me warm?"

How many times she'd asked that since coming aboard—and just as many times, he'd managed to find an excuse. He knew now that it wasn't solely because he'd misled her into thinking they were legitimate lovers as man and wife, nor was it one of those feminine bids for attention, but because she was genuinely cold. He'd once cockily thought himself an authority on the opposite sex; now he wondered if he knew anything at all about the confounding creatures.

"For as long as you wish, Tamson," Alain said, backing away and yet feeling torn, as if part of him remained. "For as long as you wish."

The ship's physician was still up and playing cards in the officers' mess. An older man with thinning white hair, he was still trim and impeccable in his uniform. Upon hearing of Tamson's illness, he kept Alain waiting only long enough to fetch his leather bag before accompanying the concerned Marquis de la Galisonne back to his cabin.

During the examination, Alain paced outside the

cabin door, battling a torrent of recrimination once again for having abducted Tamson Stewart. She would know nothing but luxury between now and the time when it was safe to return her to her father, he vowed silently. He would make up for it all . . . at least, all that he could make up for. There were some things that could not be undone, no matter how much he regretted them.

The opening of the cabin door spared Alain another bout of grief. The physician's face was impassive, as if he were lost in thought, even as he spoke.

"Monsieur Le Marquis, I must ask you a few questions. Your wife, it seems, is a trifle shy in speaking to me. This sickness she has been having, has it been at a certain time of the day?"

Had it not been for the wall behind him, Alain would have surely sunk to his knees from the impact of the question. He cleared his throat awkwardly and met the surgeon's inquisitive gaze. *Dieu,* he had not even allowed himself to think of such a possibility. After all, it was only one night!

"It has been only since she is aboard the ship and seems to come and go like the tide," he answered. "Besides, a fever has nothing to do with what you might be suggesting. *Mon Dieu!*"

The doctor smiled and patted him on the shoulder. "Do not look so panicked, Monsieur Le Marquis. It is just that she kept referring to *Papa Jean's baby,* as if she thought she might be with child."

Merci à Dieu! Alain swore again silently, this time in relief. He once again renewed his private vow to keep his distance from his engaging captive. Things were complicated enough as it was. "This fever she has. Is it serious?"

"They are always serious, but I have reason to think that this is the result of no more than a contagion which seems to have infected some of the crew as well. If so, it will last no more than a day. She will be weak, perhaps, because of the additional complication of her *mal de mer,* but if you keep her comfortable and continue to give her as much broth and tea as she will take, I have no reason to believe she will not walk down the gangplank of her own accord when we arrive in Montreal."

"And then, monsieur," the physician proceeded in a patronizing tone, "you and she may do what you will about making an heir for Château de la Galisonne. I can promise you, however, that the climate there will be better suited for her than this, if you sent her there during her confinement . . . when the time comes, that is."

"You know the place?" Alain inquired, trying to redirect the line of questioning.

"I have visited southern France many times and enjoyed your uncle's hospitality. *Such a big place and so empty of children's laughter,* he'd complain to me," the doctor said with a crooked grin.

"Then I would say, 'But you cannot have the children without a wife,' and he would shrug the matter off." The doctor tucked his spectacles in the inner pocket of his jacket and looked directly at Alain. "He loved your mother, you know. He pleaded with her not to go to her family in New France. When he heard his brother had been killed and that she had survived, he sent for her, but she had married once more . . ."

"To my father," Alain finished quietly. Had his

mother kept the secret of his heritage out of respect and love for Jean Beaujeu? That had to be the reason.

"To your *stepfather.*" Upon seeing the lift of Alain's brow, the doctor chuckled smugly. "I tended your mother on her first voyage to New France. She was deathly ill and not from the sea. When she disembarked in Montreal, she showed no sign of carrying a child, but she was. I was new in my practice, but *that* I did know."

The older man stretched and yawned, betraying his fatigue and the late hour. "Bon, I must get my rest and you, monsieur, must see to your wife."

See to my wife, Alain echoed silently, watching until the doctor disappeared down the long dim-lit corridor. He put his hand on the latch. But she wasn't his wife. If this charade continued, Tamson would be so firmly established at his side that it would be hard to disentangle himself. Or perhaps he should say, if his deceit were carried out that long, he reprimanded himself sternly.

She was certainly innocent enough, he thought, stepping inside the compartment. It was two berths wide, plus a body's width and no more. Even from his own bed, she was close enough to touch, to watch, to torment him when sleep wouldn't come.

"You came back," he heard made from the cocoon of blankets on the bunk.

"I promised, did I not?"

"And will you sleep with me and hold me? I can make room."

Her voice was so small, so vulnerable. Alain's heart thudded in his chest and the animal within roused immediately.

"Yes, I will hold you while you sleep, but first," he

stipulated, pouring some water into the deep basin, "I will make myself presentable."

Aside from shaving, he hadn't bothered with much of a toilette. He still wore the same clothes he'd left Montreal in weeks before. It was too cold aboard to undress for anything and, until now, he'd seen little need of bathing. Yet, it was not cleanliness which spurred him to strip off his buckskin jacket and shirts, but the genuine wish to be chilled through so that no thought of anything aside from comfort for the girl might enter his mind.

"How . . . how can you do that!" Tamson exclaimed, tucking the woolen blanket under her chin, her eyes wide in disbelief as Alain splashed the icy water on his upper torso and proceeded to soap it up with a home-made bar from his sack that smelled faintly of spice. "You'll catch a fever, too."

Her teeth were chattering and his would be soon, he thought. Alain rinsed the lather hastily and dabbed his chest with a towel. *Dieu,* but the water was surely just short of freezing! Not even the ample servings of burgundy and brandy served to brace him. He shivered as he rummaged through his bag for his spare shirt. Finding it, he slipped it over his head and rubbed his arms briskly.

"I want you to drink this tea. It's cold now, but it is better than the water," he pointed out wryly.

Slipping an arm beneath Tamson, he lifted her upright and raised the cup to her lips. She was warm. Even through her double layer of clothing, he could feel the heat of the fever.

"Take it all," he coaxed patiently. Perhaps they both might be served well by their impending contact, for he was certain by now that he was something akin to a block of ice.

As she sipped the last of it, leaving the tea leaves clinging to the side, she laid her head against his shoulder. "The doctor says my headache will go away if I sleep. He gave me a tonic." She yawned, covering her mouth with her hand as she wriggled against the bulkhead to make room for Alain. "And I know I will sleep if you hold me. I feel so . . ." She stopped, searching for a word. "Special," she decided, affording him a sheepish smile. "Maybe in the morning we can try to make a baby."

Alain felt her suggestion slice through the chill as if it were of no consequence at all. *Dieu,* but how was he going to be able to keep avoiding her? Again, he'd misjudged her. English women were reputed to be cold-natured. Perhaps it was her Scottish blood that made her favor the intimacy they'd shared but once. He settled on the edge of the bunk and drew her into his arms, more ill at ease than ever.

"I love children," she sighed in a voice muffled by blankets. "And I love you, husband. Papa Jean was a good father and I know you will be, too."

She was babbling, of course, Alain reasoned. The fever no doubt had loosened her tongue.

"Will we live in Montreal or in New York? Father would love it if we settled at Annanbrae."

Alain could not stop the caustic chuckle that shook them both at the absurdity of her suggestion. He would be lucky if the influential merchant did not put a bounty on his head, if he hadn't already. Once Tamson was delivered safely home, however, Alain could simply use the cover of the war to disappear, perhaps move on to the north country until the proper channels could locate his family. A marquis' money could work wonders if distributed to the right people.

He felt Tamson slip her arms around him and snuggle closer, molding her soft body to his. Her forehead found its way into the cradle of his open collar, scorching the stubble-rough skin of his neck. The two of them shivered simultaneously.

"Are you cold, too?"

Alain stiffened as Tamson tried to tuck the blankets in about them, confining them even more. "That is much better," he lied, forcing himself to relax as she yawned against his chest. "Now let us get some sleep."

"We didn't get much sleep that last night in Quebec, did we?"

"Non, we did not."

She spread her hands against him, pushing up so that she could see his face. "It was wonderful, wasn't it?"

"Yes, it was." He was going to have to tell her the truth. *Dieu,* he could not continue to bear such sweet torment.

Although he would have taken any bet that he would not be able to sleep with Tamson wrapped soft and warm about him, Alain was startled into a dazed wakefulness sometime in the wee hours of the morning by the snatching, jerking movement of the girl in his arms.

Shaking the fog from his mind, he raised up on one elbow and tried to make out Tamson's face in the dim lantern light. His initial fear that she was sick again was dashed as he realized she was still asleep. She was obviously dreaming, and not pleasantly, judging from the pained contortions of her delicate facial features.

"Tamson! Wake up, *ma petitesse!*"

As he shook her, Alain noticed that not only was her clothing soaked with perspiration, but his own was, too. He rolled off the bunk and turned to address the shaken girl as she struggled to emerge from her terror.

"Don't go!" Her shrill plea cut through the creaking, rolling silence of the sleeping ship.

Alain put a finger to her lips. "Hush, *ma petite,* I am not going anywhere, but you are wet with perspiration. You need to take off your clothes."

"They took my clothes!" she whimpered brokenly. "They took my pretty dresses and he . . . he was naked!"

"Who was naked?"

"That man! That poor man!" Tamson sobbed, backing against the bulkhead as Alain reached for her.

"Unfasten your bodice, Tamson. I will find you something else to put on."

"It was so cold and yet hot at the same time. I thought they were going to cook me and . . . and he was lying there on the frozen ground with no clothes." She looked at Alain through swimming eyes. "It was horrible!"

Alain caught her as she threw herself into his arms, shuddering and sobbing incoherently. "Hush, hush, my Tamson. It was a bad dream. You are here with me . . . Alain. I am not going to leave you, but I must get you out of those wet things. Your fever, it has broken."

There was little doubt in his mind as to the nature of Tamson's dream. She was remembering the details of her capture by the Ottawa. He eased her back against the mattress and began to unfasten the laces of her buckskin shift. Like the oversized dress beneath it, it had already hiked up to her hips, facilitating its removal over her head. Instead of crying, Tamson caught her breath in little snatches. She was awake and retreating back into that silent world of hers.

The moment she was completely stripped, Alain covered her with blankets and turned to rummage through his sack for something for her to wear. He'd known it was futile, for he wore his only spare shirt and it was as wet as her own clothing. With an impatient oath, he peeled it off and slung it on the empty bunk.

"I don't want to go back to sleep," Tamson said in an imploring voice. "They'll come for me again."

Alain slid beneath the blankets and held his breath as she snuggled against him, her chilled breasts spreading flesh to flesh against his chest, as if seeking the same reassurance as the arms that snaked around his waist.

"There, is this not better?" he asked, mustering an unaffected tone when, in fact, he was very much affected. Yet, even stronger than the primitive reaction buffered by his trousers from her entwining legs, was his will to banish her fears. "I won't let anything happen to you."

"But *you* weren't there." It was not meant as a blow, but that did not lessen the impact upon an already guilty conscience.

"I am here now, *ma petitesse,*" Alain whispered tenderly against the top of Tamson's head.

"How long will the war last?"

He shrugged. "I cannot say."

Several moments of silence passed, with only the sound of the winter wind. Alain was just beginning to think that Tamson was drifting off again when she nuzzled his chest with a sigh. "Tell me about your family.

I can't remember them and I know they were very special. I never had any brothers or sisters, you know."

"That is because when your mama and papa had you, they thought that you were the best that they could ever wish for . . . that they could do no better. With me, my parents kept trying and trying to do better . . ."

A giggle erupted, vibrating against him. "I'm serious, Alain. I want to know all about you and your family . . . *our* family," she added softly.

Alain groaned inwardly. It was bad enough that she taunted him with pretty pictures of what could never be, but now she wanted him to dream. It was something that ordinarily came easily to him. He had picked up on Jean Beaujeu's ability to spin a tall tale. A future with this captivating woman was no more outrageous than some of the stories he'd woven in the past, yet, as he began to speak, it was the past he chose to elaborate upon. That was sure . . . the *only* thing Alain was sure of anymore.

Although he willed himself into the past, he was distracted by Tamson's very *present* naked warmth. His voice was taut as he talked about the little farm of which his father was so proud and the smells and sounds that meant home to him. Eventually, he began to relax. Describing his sisters came easy and filled his voice with pride and love. They were all pretty, with dark hair and pale blue eyes.

Annette, the eldest, was a somber, responsible soul who always acted as if she'd been born old. He was grateful that she was with his mother, for she would be a strong shoulder to lean on. Then there was Lisette, a tomboy who was forever getting into mischief and protesting continuously that she was as able as her brother to go into the wilderness. Had she been a boy, no doubt Alain would have taken her this coming summer.

As for Laurette, well, Laurette was the baby. She wasn't spoiled like many youngest children. Time and lack of money prevented that. Like her sisters, she was expected to carry her share, which she did quietly without much ado. She followed Alain about like a shadow when he was home, eager for his slightest attention yet too shy to demand it like Lisette.

It was as he was telling Tamson of his last homecoming that he finally returned to sleep, unaware that he'd lost his audience somewhere during his recollections.

When the morning light found its way through the salt-caked glass of the single portal, Alain was as oblivious to it as he was to the stirrings of the crew and passengers topside and out in the companionway. His sleep was dreamless, for when one held a woman such as Tamson in his arms, naked as Eve, what more was there to dream for? He felt her stir and shift within his embrace and forced his eyes open. The sun dancing off the curls framing her features seemed to form a red-gold halo. A smile pulled at the corners of Alain's lips.

"Are you still warm, *ma petite?*"

"*You bastard!*"

Before Alain could catch himself, he was falling, propelled by the furious kick of his bedmate. Unable to disentangle his arms from the blankets to break the impact, he struck his head on the floor. Pain slashed through the confusion and alarm that numbed his ability to think.

He looked up at the head that appeared over the edge

of the mattress. "How . . . how could you do such a thing!" He caught a glimpse of the tin basin glistening in the sunlight and rolled instinctively as it came crashing down at him, hurled by the fiery-haired fury on the bunk.

"Do *what?*" he shouted, pulling himself to his feet and shedding his confining covers. "Are you mad?"

Ignoring his demand, the girl on the bed snatched up his discarded shirt and pulled it over her head awkwardly, trying to keep the buffalo robe in front of her at the same time.

"I'm not mad . . . I . . . I'm furious!" She slid off the bunk, wielding the fur as a shield. "You've made a terrible mistake, Monsieur Beaujeu. Now get out!"

Alain straightened, the pieces of circumstance gradually falling into place in his sleep-dazed mind. He'd been expecting this, dreading it. "No, mademoiselle, it is you who do not understand . . ."

"Oh, I understand!" Undaunted by the superior height and frame of her opponent, Tamson lifted her chin haughtily and tapped him on the chest with an accusing finger. "I wake up mother naked in your bed and you tell me I don't know what you've been about?" She reached behind him and pulled open the door. "Now get out!"

Alain braced for the hearty shove that struck him across the chest, but the blankets at his feet refused to cooperate. Scraping his shoulder against the edge of the plank door, he reeled out into the companionway, catching himself on the jamb before he sprawled onto the floor beyond. As he uprighted himself and cleared his feet of further obstacle, an amused voice from the corridor beyond called out.

"I take it your wife is feeling better, Monsieur Le Marquis?"

"She is delirious, I think," Alain growled to the governor general, blocking the door as Tamson attempted to close it.

"Wife!" She shrieked. "Is that what you told your companions?"

"For both your sakes, I suggest you settle your differences behind closed doors."

Without acknowledging the governor's advice, Alain forced his way back into the room, pinning the stubborn girl behind the door in the process. "Yes, *wife!*" he shouted, intending that anyone else who overheard the sudden quarrel hear his answer. "You are feverish and do not remember, but we are wed."

The moment he was free of the door, he permitted Tamson to slam it. "Li . . ."

Before she could finish her accusation, he closed his hand over her mouth and seized her, pinning her once again to the bulkhead. "Enough!" he whispered fiercely. "Lower your voice or get yourself hanged as an enemy, that is your choice. Will you cooperate?"

Confusion and fury swam in the whiskey-colored eyes staring at him and Tamson ceased to struggle. She was no longer feverish, the color in her cheeks proclaiming anger instead. Gradually Alain released her and stepped back, ready to silence her again if necessary.

"You . . ." Tamson hesitated, as if trying to put together a few facts of her own. "You seduced me! You abandoned me to the savages and then took advantage of my . . . my unstable state."

"All right, I did make love to you, but not last night. You were sick last night . . ."

"No, you took advantage of me!"

"As I recall it, you were most eager for my husbandly services. Do you remember that as well, Tamson?"

The fact that she did not answer, but leaned weakly against the bulkhead, confirmed that she did.

"I am only human, Tamson."

"You're an animal!" she whimpered, turning away to hide the shame overtaking her. "And you've made *me* one!" She pointed meaningfully to the buckskin shift laid out across the foot of the bed. "But I suppose I should expect no better from an oaf like you."

The sting of her accusation prodded Alain beyond his guilt into annoyance. "I will have my shirt now, madame."

Tamson squared her jaw in defiance. "Don't call me *madame!* I don't recall our getting married. *You* wouldn't be that decent."

"That is precisely the point, Tamson. You don't remember. How can you be so certain that the memory of our wedding is not still waiting in the recesses of your mind, ready to surface like your most recent recollections?"

Tamson shrunk behind the buffalo robe, her face paling. "I would *never* consent to marry you!"

The fact that she would not meet his steady gaze belied the certainty in her declaration. Alain felt a slight relief. "You have slept with me as your husband. Surely, lady that you claim to be, you would not have done so if you had not married me first, non?"

"Non!" she averred, inadvertently mimicking his accent. "But . . ."

Alain did not let his relief show. He had the upper
hand and intended to keep it. "I think it is time you
dress yourself and allow me to do the same, Tamson.
As to whether or not you believe us to be wed, it does
not matter to me." He glanced toward the cabin door
meaningfully. "But to some, it will make the difference
between seeing you as the wife of the Marquis de la
Galisonne or an English spy. I do not think your wit has
left you so much that you cannot see the wisdom of at
least pretending to be my beloved."

Nonetheless, it was hard for him. Were it not to his
advantage, he would have given in to the urge to take
the disconcerted girl in his arms and disavow all the
doubts haunting her gaze—at least all those that he hon-
estly could. He teased women and led them in the direction they chose to pursue, but he'd never deliberately
lied to one.

Nor had he ever kidnaped one, he reminded himself
dourly, until now. Tamson Stewart represented an entire
array of firsts for him and, although one could not tell
from the stern mask of authority he assumed, he was
as disturbed as she by the resulting quandary.

Twelve

Snow nibbled at the water's edge, spreading ice from the frozen bank where bark and log canoes lined the shore of Montreal around the Port du Marche. It was the one market day of the week on the island and Indians and Canadians alike filled the streets, trading as they had done for more than a century. Further along the fringe of the riverbank the Governor General's ship was moored, its gangplank spanning the distance between it and the beach near the Water Gate. A military ensemble stood mustered to receive the official just inside on the Parade, the rat-a-tat of their drums announcing His Honor's debarkation.

Tamson shriveled inside her buffalo robe, as much from humiliation as from the cold. Thus far, since disembarking from their ship, she'd been paraded before fashionably dressed women, the very epitome of femininity in an otherwise masculine atmosphere. And there was she—wrapped like a savage in an animal skin blanket, stinking to high heaven of old grease, and in desperate need of a bath. Even a brush would do wonders, she thought, glancing disdainfully at her tangled hair.

"Are you warm enough?"

Instead of answering, Tamson glared in silence at the

man inquiring about her comfort. Instead, she settled in the seat of the sleigh he'd hired and looked away.

He deserved the sullen silence she afforded him since coming to her senses and he had no right to get angry over it, much less avow how much he regretted their intimacy. *A regrettable mistake!* he'd said. How could he expect her to dismiss such a thing as simply *a regrettable mistake*. And then to act as if it was her fault! One might have thought that *she* was the only one pleasured by it, the way he ranted on.

"But I will not make the same mistake twice, *ma petite!*" he'd growled grudgingly before stomping out of the cabin and leaving her to the four walls. Where he'd spent last night was beyond her, but his absence was just as disturbing as his presence.

Such a long, miserable night it had been, made more so by the all-too-vivid memory of what had transpired between them. God forbid, she *had* enjoyed it—indeed, to her shame, had asked for more. How their relationship had ever arrived at that degree of debauchery still eluded her. She supposed she should be grateful that they had married, even if she could not remember it.

The jingle of harness bells drew her from her introspection as their carriole lurched forward. *"Rue Notre Dame, mon ami,"* said Alain.

"Oui, monsieur."

The wide brim of their cloaked driver's beaver hat flopped with a gust of wind as the horse pulled them easily through the ice-glazed streets. After passing a nunnery and rows of shops built of stone and wood, the vehicle made a turn onto a fashionable street where rows of townhouses separated by firebreaks were interspersed with free-standing dwellings.

Eventually they came to a stop before a rather large townhouse with a rounded portico, evidently added to the older structure for classical effect. The stoop was complete with columns and marble steps, the improvement not unattractive at all. To either side of the large door were two pairs of windows, each with a matching second story set as well as dormers. As it dawned on her that this fine home was their destination, Tamson paled.

"Why are we stopping?" The man was clearly daft if he thought for a moment she'd step inside such a mansion dressed in animal skins! "I can't go in there!"

"Of course you can. You are my wife. My family will be glad to meet you."

Tamson glanced uneasily at the driver, who looked away, as if deaf to their conversation. "Your family was exiled!"

"My *Acadian* family was sent away," Alain acknowledged, "but this is the home of my mother's family . . . the La Tours."

Tamson remained frozen, even after Alain paid the driver. God in heaven, she'd expected to be taken to another cottage like the one at that fort, not an aristocratic townhouse!

"Come, madame."

"Take me to an inn! I won't meet anyone until I have suitable clothes!" Tamson stared at his outstretched hand as she backed into the corner of the seat.

Alain's forced smile faded as a sardonic glint lighted in the frosty gaze riveting her to the spot. Suddenly, he stepped back into the vehicle with a terse *"Pardonez-moi, monsieur,"* to the side. For a moment, Tamson thought he'd changed his mind until, instead of resuming the seat next to her, he gathered her up, buffalo robe and all, in his arms. Her flailing feet found solid footing as he lifted her up on the seat, but it was only momentary, just long enough for him to heave his shoulder into her abdomen and haul her over it.

Her tangled copper locks spilling over her face, Tamson pummeled his back with her fists. All the while she kicked furiously, but when Alain started up the steps and nearly lost his balance, she ceased struggling in an instant, lest they both suffer a fall on the hard frozen ground.

She wanted to curse him, to throw every oath she'd ever heard or read at him, but dared not speak English. As for French oaths, they had not been in the textbooks her schoolmistresses provided. Besides, she was beginning to learn that reasoning with this hothead was an impossibility, so she braced herself by hooking her hands in his belt and collapsed in brief surrender. So help her, he would pay dearly for this!

"Monsieur le Marquis!" the servant exclaimed upon answering Alain's knock. The rest of his words faded upon seeing Tamson, or at least her hinter half, crumpled stockings about snow white ankles and all.

Alain stepped inside and turned as the doorman closed the door behind him when a child's disbelieving voice filled the grand hall, echoing in the ceiling above them.

"Oncle Alain! *What* have you brought home this time?"

Tamson shook with Alain's chuckle. "A wife! Now go tell your maman that I need the key to the house next door. *Vite!*"

"Can she not walk?"

All semblance of cold was banished by the blood that rushed to Tamson's face, the result, not only of her embarrassment, but of her precarious position.

"Marielle, *s'il vous plaît!*" Alain insisted, his annoyance with his little niece infecting his polite request.

At the answering patter of small feet on what sounded like steps, Tamson continued to stare at the bottom of the closed front door, refusing to lift her head to see the face of the liveried servant standing there, no doubt staring at her. The floor was highly polished with a wide imported carpet of a floral design covering the bulk of its width.

Marielle's ear-shattering, "Maman!" was enough to arouse the attention of every mother in the city, much less the lady who was already on her way out of one of the rear rooms of the mansion. "Look! Oncle Alain has brought home a wife! He must have found her in a trap! She has as much fur as the Indians!"

"Marielle!" Isabelle La Tour snapped in reprimand as she broke her step and came to a stop in front of their unexpected arrivals.

"I would introduce you, Isabelle, but as you can see, my wife is indisposed at the moment. If you will but hand me the key to the house next door, I will take her there and restore her to a more sociable humor."

"Oh, I . . . oh, Alain. I do not know what to say!"

"Say nothing then, but give me the key."

"But soldiers are living there," the little girl spoke up.

Tamson saw a small pair of slippers come into the periphery of her view and suddenly a wary pair of blue eyes peered through her hair. As if to confirm her foul humor, she made a face, causing the child to hop back with a small gasp. Indian indeed!

"What is this about soldiers living there?"

"Alain, something terrible has happened." Isabelle broke off, sensing the resulting tension Tamson could feel tightening in the shoulder supporting her. "Armand . . . well, Armand is back and . . ." Her voice faltered with a small gasp of dismay. "It is best that you speak to Joseph when he comes home."

"I gave you money to purchase it . . ."

"Please, Alain. Take your wife to our guest room. Joseph will explain."

The expansion of his chest against her legs told Tamson of the restraint it took to accept their hostess's invitation. "Our old room?" he asked, referring to the room he'd shared with his younger cousin when attending school in Montreal.

"The very one."

"Does she bite, Oncle Alain?"

Tamson shrunk within the confines of her robe. Ignorant little twit!

"Only nosy little girls," he answered, a hint of levity entering his voice as he started toward the back of the hall. Tamson bounced with each step he took as he bounded up them seemingly without effort. Her tangled curls flayed her face, fanning her ill humor even more, yet she held her tongue until they were inside the room. The moment the door closed behind them, however, she let fly the name that had echoed with each head-jarring bounce he'd inflicted upon her.

"You bastard!"

"Ah, ah!" Alain cautioned, raising a silencing finger

in front of her and nodding toward the door. "Little ears with a big mouth."

Tamson slapped it away and glared at him.

"It is you who were not ready to meet my family, so I have saved you the trouble, non?"

"Pig!" she hissed through her teeth.

"Act the lady and I will treat you as such. Act the child and *voila!*" He shrugged. "So be it."

At the telltale tremble of her chin, Tamson turned away, but she could not hide the waver in her voice. "Look at me! I look like I *could* bite! It's bad enough that you've robbed me of my honor, but you've taken my pride as well!"

A heavy breath was the only answer she received, a long, slow one that eventually brought a reply. "I will see that you are properly attired as soon as I take care of more important business."

Tamson's dejected gaze drifted to the single poster bed dominating the room with its high, arched canopy and she stiffened once again. "Where are *you* going to sleep?"

Again Alain raised a warning finger. His gaze was brittle with irritation, yet his voice hinted of a frustration he refused to show otherwise. "Please, Tamson. One battle at a time!" Abruptly, he turned on his heel and left the room, ending the confrontation with the slam of the door and leaving her to wonder what business could possibly be more important than the issues left unsettled between them.

Nightfall in the city was a sight to be appreciated if one was in good humor. The lanterns hung on the houses and burning cressets along the street created a warm social atmosphere, despite the chilling cold. Each candlelit window promised a haven of hospitality. Traffic was sparse, consisting of a few sledges and carrioles carrying people to a party down the street at one of the other gracious homes lining Notre Dame.

Alain, however, barely acknowledged the friendly wave tossed to him by the driver of a passing vehicle. Even if his hands had not been full of packages he had finally fetched from Jeanette Villier de Montigny, he would not have returned the gesture. His thoughts were too plagued by this mystery Isabelle would not even hint at, except to say that the house that had been secured with his money had been sold to the King's officers.

Such a fruitless afternoon, he grumbled silently. Jeanette had been out visiting and, of course, his cousin Joseph was at his store. If Alain was to accomplish anything, he had to wait, something he did not do well. At least, he was able to catch a nap at Jeanette's townhouse to pass the time until she returned from her soirée, he thought as he walked up the steps to the La Tour house. But then, once Jeanette heard that he had brought his "wife" with him, he had narrowly gotten away without her accompanying him back to meet Tamson. *Indisposed* was the excuse he'd made and, considering the girl's recent brooding behavior, it was rather apt.

"Alain! We thought you were still in Quebec!"

Alain drew his fist short of knocking on the front door when he heard his eldest cousin call from the street. He turned to see Joseph approaching, his breath fogging the air in front of him as he labored along. In a few months, that would be he, Alain mused, once again feeling the choking collar of a desk job closing in on him. He would surely grow as soft in such time. But first things first.

"Cousin, what is it that Armand has done that is so terrible Isabelle cannot speak to me about it?"

Joseph stiffened, his smile freezing upon his face. Instead of answering, he opened the door. "Inside, mon ami. The dirty linen is public enough as it is without airing it further."

His curiosity piqued, Alain put down the packages and covered them with his coat before following Joseph into the back parlor where the table had been set near the fire for the family dinner. Never had he seen his Montreal family engage in such a practice. Life in Château La Tour was always formal.

"What is this?" he asked, pointing to the table. "Is something wrong with the dining room?"

"I have lost two ships to the English so far. *Some* of us must practice frugality, if the rest will not," Joseph answered tersely. "We try to limit most of our activities to one room when we are not entertaining . . ."

"But the Harvest Ball . . ."

"Was Isabelle's idea. If we entertained first, we would not likely have people calling on us unexpectedly and she would not have to keep food prepared for such an event. You cannot know how that nightmare hovers over her, Alain, that guests may drop in unannounced and find our home as you have just found it. The cost of everything is at a premium thanks to our intendant."

"Bigot?" Alain asked, taking up two snifters while his cousin opened a crystal decanter of golden brandy.

"The same. He fills the King's warehouses and then sells for the highest price. They will be rationing horsemeat before this winter is over, mark my words, *mon ami.*"

"I hear that the habitants are not the only ones being taken in by this black sheep."

Alain handed his cousin the second glass, once it had been filled. Obviously Joseph was not aware that that was already the case, at least for the Acadian refugees. Actually, horsemeat was a luxury, considering the boiled leather and harness he had seen in some of their cookpots upon arrival at the abandoned fortress where his father had spent his last days.

"But then, I suppose I shall soon be seeing Monsieur Bigot's work first hand." At the surprised quirk of Joseph's brow, he went on to explain. "I have decided to accept the position of administrating the supply of our forces."

Surprise gave way to relief. "Then you have come to your senses and decided to accept the fact that you are the Marquis de la Galisonne!"

"I have decided to take the only alternative left me at the moment, now that I have a wife to consider." Alain tugged a chair out from the table and straddled it lazily. "Now, *mon ami,* tell me, why is it that there are King's soldiers living in my townhouse?"

Joseph La Tour walked over to the hearth and leaned against the mantel, shoulders dropped as if the weight of the world rested upon them. "Ah, Alain, at times like this, I think I understand why you love life in the wilderness so much. There you are your own man, responsible for none but yourself."

"I still have my ties . . . or *did,*" Alain added flatly. "My money . . . I take it you had to use it?"

"I purchased the townhouse as you requested, but

when you left, I was under the impression that you might not come back and . . ." Joseph broke off with an oath and turned to face Alain. "Even if I knew you would come back, I would have had no choice."

"What sort of choice?"

"It was Armand. You know how he loves to gamble. He bet his half of Château La Tour and lost. I had no choice . . ."

"But to sell my house to pay the debt or force the sale of yours."

Joseph's pained silence confirmed Alain's conclusion. Somehow, that his cousin now suffered the embarrassment and humiliation which he'd doled out at every opportunity to his less fortunate relative did not sweeten fate's ironic turnabout. Joseph, for all his airs, worked every day to maintain and increase the La Tour family fortune. Instead of losing respect for him or seeing his misfortune as deserved, Alain found himself responding in quite the opposite fashion. After all, a merchant who did not fare well in the city was one who was not in league with the intendant and his cohorts.

"I shall reimburse you in the spring, when the ships from France begin to arrive, if this godforsaken war does not take me under first."

Alain ran his fingers over the smoothly painted woodwork, a whimsical smile darting about his lips. "I always wondered what it would be like to own this house. Now, it seems, I shall find out . . . at least what owning half is like, that is," he amended upon seeing his cousin's disconcerted reaction.

"Then you are not angry?"

It was a moment before Alain answered, for that fact surprised even himself. When Isabelle had hinted Armand was behind his losing his winter quarters, he'd been ready to throttle someone. Perhaps the wait had mellowed his mood.

"You are many things, *mon ami,* honest among them. Perhaps too much so for your own good."

"I will have the papers drawn so . . ."

Alain waved his hand in dismissal and put it out to his companion. "A handshake is all that I need."

"Oh, *merci à Dieu!"* a female voice echoed from the door, betraying Isabelle's discreet presence. Upon realizing her error, she rushed into the room and planted a chaste kiss on Alain's cheek. "You will not be sorry, Alain. You and your wife, you will be our family, and I promise not to spend a bit more than is absolutely necessary."

"You cannot spend more than we have, *ma chérie,"* Joseph pointed out, stepping up to slip his arm about Isabelle's waist.

"And I have been thinking that if I do not visit so many others, that I will not be expected to reciprocate. That will save wear and tear on my dresses for just special occasions and . . ."

"She's out! Maman, she is out!"

Marielle's frantic alarm resounding in the hall stunned them all for a moment, before Alain grasped the meat of what the little girl was shouting about. As he started out of the room, he collided with her and caught her up before she fell.

"Your wife, Oncle Alain, she is out and wearing nothing but a blanket!"

Swallowing an oath unfit for small ears, Alain handed Marielle to Joseph and rushed out into the hall in time to see Tamson Stewart descending the elegantly carved

steps exactly as the child had described. Never in his
experience had he ever seen bed linens put to such becoming use. A sheet was wrapped about her body like
a long, straight, and strapless shift, knotted in the front
where it compressed her bosom. The woolen blanket
itself, scarlet in color, had been draped over her bare
shoulders and tied in the fashion of a cape, which
dragged royally behind her.

She stopped a step from the bottom to meet his
astonished gaze. Instead of speaking to him, however,
she turned to her dumbfounded host and hostess and
extended her hand. Her French was not perfect, but her
manner more than made up for its shortcomings.

"Bonjour, monsieur, madame. I beg your pardon for
having to introduce myself in such a manner, but to
date, my husband has provided poorly for me in the way
of clothing. With nightfall the room was becoming
colder and I was loath to put on those filthy rags in
which he brought me here after you had so kindly provided water for a bath."

So masterfully put on the defensive, Alain broke
away and gathered up the packages he had dropped on
one of the chairs in the hall. It had been a natural oversight, but this was hardly the time or place to address
it.

"My sincerest apologies, madame. Jeanette has assured me that you will find all you will require in
these."

At the mention of another woman's name, one finely
etched copper gold brow arched imperiously. "The
dressmaker?"

"A friend who was good enough to loan you these
until something can be made for you," Alain explained,

his voice strained as he took Tamson's arm. He really wasn't certain if he should be contrite, amused, or annoyed. Uncomfortable with the first two, he slipped into the latter humor, more irritated at his own confusion than with the girl.

"Now if you are through making this exhibition, we shall see you *properly* dressed." He turned to excuse himself from Joseph, who seemed lost between obvious admiration of the beauty of his guest and amazement, when Isabelle recovered sufficiently from her own shock to intervene.

"Nonsense, Alain. You must let me help your wife. You will join us for supper, non, madame?"

Tamson wavered uncertainly. She had every intention of embarrassing Alain Beaujeu, but she was no martyr. The fact was, the aroma of roasting meat that drifted up to her room had started her stomach growling hours before. "Well . . . it is a bit cold up there, now that night has fallen."

Isabelle made an exclamation of dismay. "What monsters you must think us! When Alain said that you were not to be disturbed, I did not think about lighting the fire in your room. Henri!"

"Right away, madame," the servant, who had come into the hall in the midst of the confrontation, acknowledged stiffly.

Isabelle took Tamson in tow and started up the stairs. "You have my humblest apologies, madame, my very humblest. I do not know how you were able to bathe under such thoughtless conditions. Poor little cabbage! You must call me Isabelle. After all, we are family now."

Alain followed the women, packages in hand, but upon reaching the door, Isabelle took them from him.

"I will take care of her. You . . . you go talk to Joseph," she said, as though he'd become a sudden nuisance. "We shan't be long, I promise."

"Can I help, maman?"

Tamson turned, sweeping her blanket train aside, a hint of a smile toying on her lips. "Aren't you afraid I'll bite?"

"But non! You do not look so ferocious without your furs."

"Marielle!"

This time Tamson laughed, directing an amused glance at Alain. "I don't mind if she comes in."

The little girl was through the door before her mother could give or withhold permission and then it was closed, dismissing Alain with a decisive click. For a moment, he stared at the curved panels, a scowl darkening his countenance. That was too easy, he thought warily, retreating with reluctance to the staircase. Nothing else since he'd kidnaped Tamson Stewart had gone so smoothly. Worse, the girl was enjoying herself, as if she was aware of something he was not. He glanced over his shoulder once again at the closed door from the top of the steps.

"I see we are finding more and more in common all the time, cousin!" said Joseph. "Come, let us have another brandy while we await the women. Sometimes that is the only cure for this constant state of vexation they manage to stir within us, non?"

With a hapless shrug, Alain started down the steps. That was the first suggestion of the day which wholly appealed to him.

Thirteen

"She is a little Scottish lamb!" Isabelle whispered to Alain later after an evening of listening to Tamson and Marielle playing duets on the harpsichord. "Did you know she spent a year in Paris studying art and music? How on earth did *you* ever find her?"

Tact was not one of Isabelle's strong points. Despite her implication that her husband's lowly cousin had found a wife educated in the social graces so important to her kind, Alain was once again forgiving. Perhaps it was the brandy that lulled him into such a contented state—that and the fact that Tamson was adapting perfectly to the role he intended for her.

"Fate has its curious ways, madame."

"Do you not love to hear her speak our language? Her accent is charming. But then, *she* is charming, non?"

When she wanted to be, Alain thought to himself, although he had to admit, in Jeanette's dress, Tamson was utterly bewitching. Joseph had not been able to take his eyes from her while they supped. Alain had begun to think that Isabelle would regret having insisted he and his wife live with them, but when Tamson marveled over Marielle's beauty and accomplishment, the jealous sparks in her mother's gaze dissipated altogether.

"Where did you say you two met?" Isabelle asked casually.

Alain drew his gaze from the stairwell where Marielle and Tamson had disappeared. "I didn't."

Isabelle waited expectantly until it became apparent that she would receive no answer. "Well, I shall be happy to help her find suitable clothing. I am ashamed of you, Alain, dressing your wife in your . . . in that woman's clothes."

There had never been any love lost between Isabelle and Jeanette, the first firmly convinced that the latter coveted her husband—or anyone's, for that matter. Alain's cheeks were pinched to contain the roguish grin which threatened his lips. Jeanette had that effect on her society sisters and reveled in it. The fact of the matter was, his friend enjoyed the men's company over that of their wives.

"Babies, running the house, that is for boring women to discuss," she laughed during one occasion after he'd suggested she join the matrons who were casting dagger-sharp glances at her over their fans. "And I, *mon chér*, am not one of them!"

"Jeanette is the only woman I know who is close to Tamson's size. Certainly I could not expect one with your petite figure to have anything to fit her."

The flattery did its work. A pleased look settled on Isabelle's face. "Well, I shall do my best to see that she is *decently* attired," she reiterated emphatically, leaving no doubt as to what she thought of the dress Tamson had worn to dinner. It was cut scandalously low, so much so that when the girl leaned over her plate to eat, Alain found himself sawing away on the plate with his knife as though to score the linen beneath.

"Isabelle is very good at spending money."

"And what is that to mean?" the woman queried of her husband.

"Only that you are wise with your money and get the most for it, madame. What else?" Joseph recovered smoothly, a mischievous twinkle dancing in his eye as he lit his pipe. "Now why don't you see that our daughter is put to bed so that Alain might retire to his room with his wife."

Isabelle chuckled. "Marielle is quite taken with Tamson. I suppose I should go rescue your wife, Alain."

In no particular hurry to join Tamson in their boudoir, Alain managed an acknowledging nod. Too smooth, he thought again, following Joseph to the back parlor while Isabelle climbed the steps winding overhead. Frankly, he appreciated Marielle's distraction. The night would be long enough as it was.

That he had agreed to work on behalf of the Governor General in his Montreal office at the palace pleased Joseph La Tour no end. Usually as conservative with his speech as he was with his manner, his cousin launched into a dissertation on the problems within the administration of the city, lamenting the passing of Governor Longueuil, who had yet to be replaced. Because of that, Bigot's man, Francois Victor Varin, ruled over commerce and politics with as much authority as the King of France himself, although, from all reports, France was being run by Madame de Pompadour, the King's favorite mistress.

Not even Louis XV was above being manipulated by the female of the species, Alain mused later after several glasses of Joseph's good brandy. That was where man made his mistake—allowing the darling creatures close enough to matter to them. If they were kept in the position for which they were created, to satisfy a man's carnal appetite, the world would not be such a confounding place. But non, instead they turn their wide, helpless gazes up at a man and purse their lips just so and there it is! The man feels sorry for them.

Such an art even comes naturally to the little ones! Heaven knew his sisters all had him wrapped about their little fingers. And that, Alain Beaujeu, he cautioned himself, crossing the legs he'd propped up on the folded drop leaf table, is the beginning of a man's end. *Voila!*

Neither the ticking of the clock on the mantel nor the gentle crumble of the logs Henri had piled upon the hearthfire managed to invade the sleep that overtook the young man. He had been completely content to postpone the inevitable confrontation with his "wife" as long as possible and inadvertently drifted off in the back parlor in the midst of his solitary philosophical debate.

Hence, when a woman's scream pierced the quiet of the house and shook him from his repose, Alain was somewhat disoriented. The fire had gone out, leaving the room in total darkness. Instinctively, he knew it was Tamson, but where was she? A faint light cast from a lamp left burning in the great hall was his only salvation as he emerged from the parlor with a banged knee and started for the steps.

The sound of a crash accompanied by yet another blood-curdling scream sped Alain in the direction of their bedchamber as Joseph emerged from his own, pulling on his robe in confusion. A yelp—masculine, if such a noise could be categorized by gender—preceded a frantic fumbling with the latch as Alain reached for it. Suddenly, the door was flung open and a man catapulted out of the room, colliding with Alain and taking him to the floor in the process.

"Ye drunken sot! I'll flay ye within a breath o' life if ye touch me like that again!"

The man Alain was struggling with cursed and stiffened with the impact of the cudgel the female fury laid across his back. *"Mon Dieu,* but help me, brother!"

"Armand!" Joseph exclaimed, holding up the finger-lamp he'd managed to light.

"Alain!" the liquor-soaked soldier slurred as Alain rolled away from him in distaste.

"What?" Tamson looked from the man crawling on the floor to the one climbing to his feet in astonishment. Slowly, she lowered from its offensive position over her head the rod used to pull the shades and clutched it to her bosom. "I . . . who . . ."

"Madame," Alain announced, grabbing Armand La Tour by the coat and pulling him to his feet. "Permit me to introduce my youngest cousin, Armand. And this, you worthless cur, is my *wife,* whom you have frightened witless."

"Wife?" Armand swayed unsteadily, his gaze sweeping over Tamson longer than Alain thought necessary. *"Mon Dieu,* but you are the lucky one! I thought she was an angel sent from heaven to warm my bed and then . . ." He put his hand to his cheek and came away with blood on his fingers.

"You are supposed to be sleeping next door with your comrades," Joseph spoke up sternly.

Armand drew up before his brother, teetering on his feet. "Well then, *why* am I not there?"

"Oh, Joseph, just take him next door!" Isabelle snapped impatiently from the doorway of her room.

Unaffected by the disapproval of his brother and sister-in-law, Armand swung his gaze back to Tamson again. *"Mon Dieu!"* he swore expressively.

With a hot rush of blood to his face, Alain stepped between his drunken cousin and the girl whose thin nightdress enhanced all that nature had blessed her with. "You will need the help of God, if you do not leave with Joseph this very moment," he warned.

Armand lowered his head, staring up through his dark bushy brow at Alain as if he had to concentrate to focus his eyes. "Do not threaten me, cousin. I claim no fault in this! If you had been in bed with your wife like a real man, this would not have happened."

"You worthless . . ."

The impact of Alain's fist as he struck Armand, snapping the latter's head back, muffled the rest of his oath. Armand's dilated pupils rolled upward as he crumbled to the floor like a tin soldier melting in a fire.

"Oh!"

Distracted by Tamson's gasp, Alain pivoted away from his fallen adversary in time to have the door slam in his face. Fists clenched at his sides, Alain began to count slowly, silently, painstakingly. It was only natural that she was upset, he told himself sternly. What woman would not be if a drunken soldier had come into her boudoir in the middle of the night? He put his hand on the latch, only to hear the bolt on the other side click into place.

"Tamson, *ma chérie.*" He tried to soften the anger in his voice. After all, it was not aimed at her . . . *yet.* "It is I, Alain. Open the door." Armand's taunt, which still raked at him, was more than his patience could withstand. The last thread snapped with the answering silence and he threw his shoulder against it, jarring it sharply. "Tamson, *ma petite chère,* if you do not open this door, I shall have to take it down."

"You wouldn't!" Isabelle gasped, looking down the hall where Joseph and a bedraggled Henri had disappeared with their unexpected intruder.

Alain rested his forehead against the cool wood, as if trying to collect himself. "Indeed, madame, I would, and my wife, I think, knows that."

"Well I don't blame her for locking you out then!" the mistress of the house denounced, slamming her own door in emphatic protest.

Alain's flaring nostrils signaled his growing frustration. "I will count to three, Tamson. Then I would stand aside if I were you. One . . . two . . ."

The bolt on the other side of the door clicked before the third count. As Alain straightened, it swung open to reveal the girl, eyes wide and staring. "I . . . I have a rod!" she threatened uneasily, backing away as he stepped inside.

Alain groaned inwardly. The eyes, the lips . . . "So I can see."

Still unaware of the fetching way the silk of Jeanette's nightdress clung and shimmered in the moonlight on curves begging for a manly caress, she stepped to the foot of the bed where a long upholstered bench stood. It had been made into a makeshift cot with a pillow and blankets. Placing her hand upon its high rolled arm, she cleared her throat, yet her voice was still timid.

"I made this up for you."

"That was considerate." Alain pointed to the cudgel she'd wielded so well against poor Armand. "And that, did you sleep with that in hand in case I chose not to avail myself of your *thoughtfulness?*"

Tamson glanced away self-consciously. Were there more light in the room, Alain wad certain her cheeks would rival the color of a rose. Despite the blood pounding through his veins at the mere thought of sharing the plump bed with this fierce yet shy enchantress, he forced a reassuring smile.

"You have nothing to fear from me, Tamson. I gave you my word, did I not?"

"The word of a kidnaper," she reminded him skeptically.

"My word as a *gentilhomme, ma petitesse.*" Taking the curtain pull from her firmly but gently he raised her hand to his lips and brushed her knuckles. They were cold, just as she surely was, he thought, trying not to notice the hard rosette peaks of her chilled breasts straining against the silk of her bodice. *"Bon soir,* Tamson."

His mouth was dry as he turned away to climb into the makeshift bed she'd prepared for him. It had not been his intention to use it, but considering the rampant reaction coursing through his body at the moment just from the sight of her, caution was the best road to take. Tamson—soft, warm, and inviting—curled next to him was more than any man could resist, he thought, twisting on his stomach as if to crush the sudden desire aching in his loins.

To his dismay, his feet struck the rolled arm, verifying what he already suspected. The bench was not quite long enough to accommodate his height. Alain closed his eyes and sighed into the pillow. It was not only going to be a long night, it was going to be a long winter.

When Alain had not come to the room that first evening at Château La Tour, Tamson was relieved. As night
after night came and went without the slightest show of
interest, however, she grew increasingly perplexed.
Nothing she did seemed to annoy him, which in turn
irritated her beyond understanding.

She was actually beginning to believe that he had
married her, Tamson Stewart, darling of London and
Albany society, for the reason he stated—to protect her.
As for his making such tender and passionate love to
her that one night which haunted her thoughts and body,
it too must have been what he'd said—a mistake which
he regretted. He'd shown no sign of attraction toward
her since, only tolerance.

Which was intolerable, she thought peevishly, as they
emerged from a dress shop laden with the latest addi-
tions to her wardrobe. Blast him, she was starting to
feel guilty for making him pay so dearly for *his* injustice
with the charges she placed on his open accounts!

Poor Isabelle and Joseph were reduced by losses in-
curred by the war to practically depending on Alain to
maintain their status in Montreal society until spring,
when their remaining ship returned with goods to fill
Joseph's mercantile. Even Tamson spent most of her
time in the house helping her hostess mend and refur-
bish her wardrobe and surviving with the cut in domes-
tic staff they'd been forced to make. It was the least she
could do for Isabelle, who had made her feel such a
part of the family.

The fact was, she and Isabelle had become friends
and confidants, at least to a degree. Tamson dared not
disclose the details around her marriage. When their
conversation moved onto those grounds, she simply

pleaded that she could not recall. Having heard the horrid stories of Indian capture, Isabelle did not press her further.

As for the rest of the family, Tamson adored Marielle and found Alain's cousins charming. At least when Armand was sober he was charming. He possessed that same boyish appeal that Alain did when he teased his worshipful niece, except that Armand did not have the common sense to know when to quit. His lack of discipline belied his status as a soldier and constantly landed him in some sort of trouble from which his brother or cousin had to extract him, often at a cost they, or at least the conservative Joseph, could not afford.

Alain's source of wealth was still beyond Tamson's ability to fathom. After all, he was nothing but a voyageur before inheriting his title and fortune. She'd heard her father speak with disdain many times that those types lived lavishly while they had it and then were penniless until their next season's earnings.

Since her abductor had become the marquis just before the winter freeze when most contact with France, where his inheritance lay, was abandoned until spring, it was improbable that he had the means to continually indulge her, yet he did. True, he was sometimes rather tight-lipped and brooding about it, but he never uttered a word of protest.

"Quick, get in the coach!" Isabelle prodded, startling Tamson.

"What is it?"

"That woman is coming."

Tamson needed no further encouragement, but climbed in the vehicle and was barely seated when Isabelle instructed the driver to be on his way. As they passed their neighbor, Jeanette Villier de Montigny stared at Tamson until the girl felt obliged to at least acknowledge her with a smile of recognition, rather than the cold turn of the cheek her companion afforded the La Tour family's former ward. After all, Madame de Montigny had not only planned an afternoon soirée in her honor the first week of her arrival in Montreal, but dressed her for the occasion as well.

"She is family, Isabelle," Tamson reminded her companion.

"That is a matter of opinion. Both Armand and Alain nearly came to dueling over her and she still fancies Alain, especially now that he is a marquis."

"They're friends."

"If you believe that, then you will believe *that* creature is really King Louis in disguise!"

Tamson followed Isabelle's pointed gaze to an old man with weathered brown skin as drawn as his frame. His clothes were in tatters, their frayed remnants whipping in the river breeze as he approached their slowing coach, a battered tin cup in his hand.

"Get away from here!" the driver warned, lifting a threatening whip as they made the turn onto St. Paul.

"No, wait!"

She had no coin left, but there was the small bag of hard candy she'd purchased for Marielle. The ribbon would be enough for the child, she thought, tossing the candy to the man. He caught it with astounding agility and, without looking at the content, tucked it into the layers of his clothing.

"Merci, ma bonne marquee!" he called out, flashing a gum-revealing grin.

"*Alors*, Tamson, you are too kind for your own good!"

"At least the candy won't break his teeth, poor soul," Tamson observed, ignoring Isabelle's well intended comment.

"Oh!" Isabelle laughed, suddenly catching on to her companion's wry effort to distract her from another lecture. "Well, on that we can agree!"

Tamson settled back in their cariole, an open sleigh of sorts on runners that was far better suited for getting about in the winter than the customary wheeled coach. She pulled the lap robe up over her skirts and the packages they'd been accumulating all day. On the corner of the street on which the La Tour mansion was located, a pair of soldiers were adding fuel to a burning cresset in preparation for the long night watch ahead as the cariole glided past.

Upon their arrival at Château La Tour, Henri helped the driver unload the vehicle and cart the goods inside the front hall. From there they were dispersed to their proper destinations. The foyer was chilly—the front entrance had remained open for a while and the interior doors to the adjoining rooms were closed, so Tamson lost little time in carrying her bundles up to the room she shared with Alain, a task which required two trips. She was halfway up the stairs the second time when Alain arrived home for the evening.

As he handed his cloak over to Henri, he took in the cumbersome bundles in Tamson's arms in thin-lipped silence.

"Madame Bouchard finally finished the last of my wardrobe!" Tamson spoke up, somehow compelled to explain by his lack of comment. "I can hardly wait to wear them!"

"I am . . . glad that it pleases you, madame."

The renegade spark flickering in his gaze belied his words. Tamson smiled to herself. At long last, she had managed to strike a dissonant chord in her impassive husband, whose nature was becoming as cold and brittle as the Canadian winter. If she didn't know better, she'd swear his passions did lie elsewhere, perhaps but a few doors down the street.

"And you should see the gown I ordered for the reception! I should think a suit of royal with gold thread for you the perfect match. Maybe I should summon your tailor?" she called from the landing at the top of the steps.

"Hello? Alain?" Ignorant oaf, Tamson mused, turning at the answering quiet to go to her room.

The small fire kindled in the bedchamber in anticipation of her arrival had not yet taken away the bite of the late afternoon air. Like food and everything else in the city, it seemed, wood was scarce and rationed accordingly, at least in the La Tour home. Even the gentry complained at the social affairs, fearing the rationing of horsemeat dealt out to the rest of the population might eventually find its way to their tables.

So far, that had not happened. At least in the Governor General's circles, in which the Marquis de la Galisonne was heartily accepted. While little expense was spared in public, Tamson had grown accustomed to her hosts' frugal way of life and simply wore extra petticoats to ward off the chill. When that did not work, she gathered with the rest of the family in the parlor below or went into the kitchen, where the cook kept a fire round the clock.

She dumped the last of her packages on the bed and surveyed her bounty with satisfaction. Having ordered the gown for Isabelle La Tour had quelled her rise of guilt over her extravagance. Making a game of guessing which accessories were in which plainly wrapped bundle, Tamson attacked the task of putting away her new things, for there was no upstairs servant to attend her, another deprivation she'd adapted to. The war was certainly not favoring the French from what she'd seen, although they were, for the most part, safe from the brutal attacks the colonials on the frontier suffered.

After shaking out a new chemise with fitted arms and a ruffled bodice, Tamson held it up in front of her to admire the handiwork in the narrow gilt mirror when the door to the room opened and Alain barged in. His features were grim as he surveyed the package-littered bed, giving Tamson time to recover from the start his unannounced arrival had given her.

"There will be no reception."

"What?" Tamson asked, her mind momentarily blank.

"You will not call my tailor because there will be no reception."

So he *had* heard her. She laid her chemise out on the bed, taking pains to smooth out the wrinkles. "I thought it was already decided."

When Isabelle came up with the idea of having a reception to welcome Tamson into the family, Alain had been against it, but he was overridden by his cousin and his wife, not to mention Tamson, who threw in with them. When she'd asked if he were ashamed of her, he'd finally backed down, but reluctantly.

"Joseph has lost another ship. He cannot afford it and I will not fund it, so there it is," Alain offered simply.

"Another ship?" Tamson echoed in dismay. Her heart sank, not because of the cancellation but in sympathy for Isabelle. Her new friend was trying so hard to make the best of a situation she was clearly not prepared for. If Tamson recalled correctly, this was the last of Joseph La Tour's investments. They were completely ruined now.

"Oh, Alain!" she whispered in genuine concern. "What will they do?"

"Whatever they must. At any rate, you will not need that ball gown now. I suggest you cancel the order."

"Why? *You* are not destitute."

Again Alain's gaze swept over the bed. "Not *yet,* madame, but nonetheless, I have two families to support now. What you can do without will mean more for my cousin's family. This winter will get worse before it gets better."

Part of her wanted to argue, to throw in his face that he'd promised her anything she wanted as his wife. Yet, she could not, not at the expense of her newfound friends and family. And there was something about the heavy weight that appeared to be on Alain's shoulders, the concern brooding in earnest behind his frost blue gaze.

Despite the mistakes he'd made concerning her, he wasn't a bad man. He truly worried about the soldiers on rations of horsemeat and bread and swore repeatedly at the folly of taking so many men away from the fields and relying on a king an ocean away to supply them with food. Then there were his Acadian friends whom he'd left at Quebec, outcasts among their own people. Now he had three families to fret over—his mother and sisters, her, and now his cousin's.

"Damnation!" she swore, swiping up her chemise and plopping down abruptly in its place on the bed. It was becoming harder and harder to hate her enemy. When the French were merely the French, it was one thing. When they were Alain, Joseph, Isabelle, and Marielle, it was quite another.

Mistaking her exasperated oath for protest, Alain circled the bed to stand in front of her. "Tamson, *ma petitesse,* I am trying to help you to understand this. If you must have the dress . . ."

"It's not the bloody dress! It's just that . . ." Tamson met his confused gaze. "You're making it very hard for me."

"I promise, I'll take you home this spring and, for now, try to make your life here as bearable as possible."

"That's not what I meant!"

Alain rolled his eyes toward the ceiling. "Then what do you mean?"

"I mean I can't even make you angry anymore!"

"I would not go so far as to say that!"

Tamson cut him a sideways glance.

"But why do you wish to make me angry, Tamson?"

"Because you are my enemy and I . . . it's my duty to aggravate you," she said, disconcerted by the difficulty she was having explaining herself.

Cupping her chin with the crook of his finger, Alain lifted her face to his. His voice dropped to a lower timbre, radiating warmth in the chill of the room. "You are not my enemy, Tamson."

Tamson knew the folly of her remark even as Alain slipped his hand behind her, resting it warm against her back. The slight curl of his lips expressed mild amusement while his eyes danced with curious reflection and something else so deep and real that she felt it spreading around her, drawing her closer with unseen arms.

"Were it mine to give, you would have the world to make up for all the mistakes between us. The entire world, *ma petitesse,*" he whispered, leaning forward and brushing her lips.

She should pull away, she thought, her heart suddenly slamming against her chest. An angry Alain was more predictable and didn't see nearly as much of the soul she felt bared by his searching gaze. Yet, when he brushed her lips again, lingering there, she remained frozen, neither yielding nor withdrawing from the tumble of conflicting emotions that suddenly erupted.

"Alain!" A piercing scream shattered the stillness and suddenly Alain was racing toward the door with Tamson following, fear chilling the brief and heady warmth that lingered in the wake of her husband's unexpected attention.

Fourteen

"Alain, it's Joseph and Armand! You must stop them!" Isabelle pleaded from the bottom of the steps, a frightened Marielle clutching her skirts.

Before Alain could answer, a crash echoed from the back of the house, followed by the piercing shatter of glass. He vaulted over the rail and charged into the back hall toward the parlor. By the time Tamson and Isabelle caught up with him, he was solidly planted between Joseph and Armand La Tour, a fistful of Joseph's shirt in one hand and Armand's in his other. Seeing that the fight had stopped, Isabelle nervously herded her daughter toward the kitchen to avoid their angry words.

"Have you lost your minds?" Alain challenged the two men, the seams of his tailored jacket and trousers straining with the rugged sinew beneath as he braced them apart. Of the three, it was he who looked like the untamed savage about to burst from the bonds of civility. "What is this worthless behavior about?"

"My brother, it seems, has lost not only his fortune but his honor and wits as well," Joseph breathed heavily, unaccustomed to the exertion which had overturned the drop leaf dining table and reduced the china to shards.

"I merely pointed out an alternative to ruin," Armand answered defensively, "and this is how my noble brother thanks me." He pointed to the cut over his eye, which was beginning to swell and turn an ugly blue.

"I will not join the ranks of Varin's puppets and dance to the song of betrayal!"

"What does it matter to you where your goods come from as long as you have goods to sell? La Friponne is commonly known and accepted."

"Not to all!" Joseph retorted heatedly. "Better to starve."

"We could pay off my debts and reclaim our house from our cousin, Joseph! Why should we alone suffer, when everyone has their thumbs in the pie, non? That is foolishness, not nobility."

"Out! Out of this house, before I throw you out!"

"It is *Alain's* house now, brother, and I happen to know that our cousin is not so particular as to whom he trades with, so long as the profit is worth his while. Perhaps *you* can talk sense into this idiot, cousin."

Alain glanced at Joseph warily, as if still unconvinced that he'd reined in his explosive temper. He'd only seen Joseph lose his temper once and was glad that he was not the one who had set it off. That time, it had been Armand who had had the nerve to flirt with the then-betrothed Isabelle. "Perhaps if you left, I might be able to . . . discuss the matter, that is. It is difficult to deal with one whose motives are so self-serving."

"Self-serving?" Armand repeated, incredulous. "It is not I who have a wife and child to support. The army takes care of me adequately."

"The King of France could not afford to take care of you, Armand. It is just as well that you are well situated in the intendant's camp as you are, considering your addiction to the gambling tables."

"Oh, so your title has suddenly polished your ethics to an untarnished shine as well? You are not the same cousin with whom I have lifted more than one glass. There are certain mademoiselles who wear a permanent pout, now that they have heard you are married." Armand looked purposely at Tamson. "And this one has the look of wifely neglect."

"Your penchant for drink, cousin, has made fertile that imagination of yours." Alain clapped Armand on the back in an effort to diffuse his cousin's liquor-enhanced indignation, rather than land a well-placed punch in the mouth and start yet another brawl. "I have not changed, Armand," he lied, for there was a time in the not-so-distant past he would have risked Isabelle's ire to satisfy his lacerated ego at Armand's expense—a time before he'd kidnaped a girl. "I simply prefer to remain practical and above politics. Since Joseph can no longer afford to subsidize your frivolous habits and I will not, I would suggest that you try the same tactic."

Armand drew himself up, rearing his head back to stare down his nose at Alain in utter amazement. "Are you saying that if I were to find myself indebted, that you would not come to my aid? After all my family has done for you in the past?"

"Let me see, now. You put a roof over my head during the time in which I received my education and, when you had little choice, introduced me to your associates." Alain handed Armand his cloak. "Well, I know most of the guards at the prison and I certainly owe it to you to see you adequately situated, should you find yourself in their care."

"But . . . but you are family, Alain!"

"I'm aware of that, Armand. If I were not, you would not even receive that much consideration."

Tamson and Isabelle, who had joined her in the hall, stepped aside as Alain escorted Armand to the front door. The latter was clearly taken back by his cousin's frankness.

"But . . ."

"I am a practical man. While such a person might do business with another of dubious background, he does not throw good money after bad. Now think well on that, cousin. The next time you incur a debt, it will be yours alone to honor."

Armand brushed off his shoulders, as if to remove the taint of Alain's hand from it, and stepped back on the stoop, the brass buttons of his jacket gleaming through the opening of his woolen cloak. Tamson was reminded of a spoiled child made speechless by unexpected discipline. He wanted to object—she could tell that by the mottled red of his face and the brittle gaze that assessed his imperturbable cousin—but his foolishness did not go through to the bone. He had enough sense to recognize a man who would not be pushed.

"I should have expected this from a low-born Acadian. What a waste of wealth to have it fall into your hands!"

"Au revoir, monsieur."

Tamson clutched her arms over her bosom and shivered, partially from the cold air and partly from the wintry calm of Alain's voice. Armand read the threat in it just as clearly. Outraged, he abandoned the steps.

Fists clenched at his sides and fire smoldering in his gaze when he turned from closing the door were the only signs of Alain's suppressed hostility. His smile of acknowledgment to the ladies as he passed them and re-entered the back parlor would have fooled anyone who had not just witnessed what had passed between him and his cousins. Without a word, he knelt down and helped Joseph, who was collecting the bits and pieces of the broken china off the floor.

"It is your grandmother's china," Joseph apologized to Isabelle, handing her two surviving plates. He shook his head. "I do not know what came over me."

Isabelle went to her husband's side. "I am proud of you. I was but worried that Armand, full of brandy and with his soldier's training, might get out of hand. He knows Alain will not tolerate his recklessness."

"I have spoiled him, I suppose." The older man effected a laugh. "There! There is a bright side to all of this. Now I can no longer do so. Although he will hate me for this."

"Nonsense," Isabelle objected. "You have spoiled Marielle and me as well, but we still love you. In fact, I love you more. Money cannot buy honor. I will not be surprised if even Armand forgives you, once he is sober and realizes how he behaved."

"And you did not spoil him. He was that way when you inherited him from your parents," Alain reminded Joseph. "They never taught their baby to accept responsibility."

With all hands helping, the table was soon reset and the *sipaille* the cook had prepared was steaming at its center. Isabelle chatted about their day at the market, keeping the conversation moving, for the men had fallen silent aside from polite acknowledgment. Evidently, she had heard about the cancellation of the reception, for she failed to mention the gown Tamson had ordered.

Even Marielle, who now ate with the family since her nurse had been discharged, was quiet. The little girl picked at the economical seafood dish with its herb flavored contents separated by layers of pastry, sensing the unacknowledged tension hovering over them. After the meal was finished, Tamson was almost glad to get out of the room and leave the men to the subject weighing heavy on their minds. When Isabelle planted an affectionate kiss on the top of Alain's head, Tamson followed suit without thinking and was just as startled as Alain by her action.

"You scared him, Tante Tamson!" Marielle giggled. "He didn't see you coming!"

Her face singed with color, Tamson ushered the girl toward the door. She *was* proud of him, the way he stood up to Armand. She had no doubt Alain could have broken every piece of furniture in the room with his cousin, if the latter were inclined to press him. And when Armand made that derogatory comment about Alain's Acadian heritage, why, she could have done so herself! It was about time someone in the family acquainted the frivolous young man with reality.

"It's an old frontier trick I learned," she quipped, glad she was on her way out of the room—and out of reach of that soul-baring gaze of his.

Alain watch the feminine sway of Tamson's retreat until she closed the door behind her, his mind totally devoid of what he had been about to say. Wrapped in thought, he hadn't paid attention to her when she came up behind him. Then one tiny peck on the top of his head and he'd forgotten all but the warmth of her lips he'd sampled earlier.

"She is lovely," Joseph reflected, guessing at Alain's

thoughts. "You were lucky to find her, just as I was lucky to find my Isabelle. I can only hope that you will not fail her as I have my wife."

Until recently Alain would have disagreed with Joseph on his luck in finding Isabelle. He had always thought the woman a spoiled, featherbrained aristocrat and Joseph dry and dour. It was an odd match, but one that was obviously working. The woman's resourcefulness and understanding where her husband's misfortune was concerned had certainly proven her mettle.

That Joseph had turned down Armand's offer of guaranteed profit for ethical reasons had furthered Alain's estimation of his elder cousin as well. For most of the past, Joseph, being five years their senior, rarely associated with either Alain or Armand. Alain was always left with the feeling that he was being tolerated, nothing more, and Isabelle afforded him barely that. It was a novel experience, being eagerly recognized as a family member of the La Tour household, but Alain was certain his newfound title and inheritance had not hurt their change of heart. In fact, he would be just in turning them out, but all that revenge had gotten him so far was the burden of protecting the lovely Tamson Stewart.

"You have not failed Isabelle, Joseph. That is worthless talk like your brother's and I know you have better sense. You are a victim of the war, nothing more."

"Better the victim than the vulture. It is beyond me how our intendant can so boldly skim the King's properties for his own profit. Do they have idiots who cannot count?"

Alain shook his head. *"Non, mon cousin.* They have men who are paid handsomely not to do so."

"The whole kettle of fish is rotten then!" Joseph exclaimed in exasperation. "The enemy within is as bad as the one without!"

"Not quite the *whole* kettle."

Upon remembering Alain's position in procurement for the troops and Indians, Joseph quickly apologized. "I was not speaking of you, cousin. Do not think that I have not seen your frustration when you come home, or heard your despair over the lack of supplies from the King's warehouse. But why do you not say something? You are a marquis now and surely can be lent an ear."

"Because I am waiting to join them, *mon ami.*"

The expression on Joseph La Tour's face was nothing less than dumbfounded. It was clear he had no idea how to respond to the bold admission.

Although he did not like having to take anyone into his confidence, Alain realized he needed to take Joseph into his. The invitation from Armand to join the intendant's crooked ranks was just the thing Alain had been waiting for. Taking a deep breath, he finally broke the strained silence.

"I have a plan, cousin, one I think our Governor General will appreciate very much."

The blossoming of early flowers and the appearance of certain birds usually proclaimed spring in the greatest of glory at Annanbrae. In the city of Montreal, however, Tamson discovered it was heralded by the great increase in the number of Indians and *couriers de bois* who infested the marketplace day in and day out. Arms and liquor abounded in exchange for the furs brought in from the hunting season in the north and west, priming the savages for their fair-weather marauding.

Meanwhile *troops de la terre* from France arrived daily by the shiploads to be disbursed to the frontier outposts. Montreal, like her sister city Quebec, turned out to welcome the heroes from France with parties taking place almost every night of the week. The harbors of both cities were thick with ships laden with trade goods and supplies, requiring those in procurement to work endless hours in storage and disbursement.

Alain and Joseph were both absent from the supper table more times than not, leaving the women of the house free to work on the invitations Tamson had made so popular. When she'd first offered to hand paint and write invitations to Marielle's birthday party, she'd intended to save the cost of having them professionally printed. Never had she dreamed how well they would catch on. Now she had a backlog of orders, especially with so many upcoming activities.

To her astonishment, the endeavor had proven not only a good way to pass the time, but a profitable one as well. She managed to pay Madame Bouchard for Isabelle's ballgown with her own money, having canceled the champagne brocade she'd ordered for herself, and had spending change as well, so that she did not feel accountable to her husband. It did not go very far, what with the exorbitant prices, but her needs were small. If anything, she spent it on her engaging and lively niece.

She and Marielle were inseparable when the child was not busy with her studies, which Isabelle overtook personally. The fact that neither Tamson nor Isabelle was caught up in the social whirl, having dropped out for financial reasons, had been a blessing for Marielle. The little girl had never had such attention before, al-

ways under the care of a hired nurse. She sewed with
the women of the house, entertained with Tamson on
the harpsichord, and matured far beyond her years as a
result. After her birthday party, she confided to her
Tante Tamson that she found children her age annoying
with their childish ways.

The war had changed them all, Tamson supposed,
blowing on the finishing touches of watercolor she'd
applied to her most recent order. When people suffer
together, they naturally pull together. Not only had she
and Isabelle grown close as sisters, but Alain and
Joseph's relationship had progressed as well.

Even Armand tried, but his weakness for cards and
liquor were his constant undoing. Alain had even told
him he could sleep on the sofa in the back parlor as
long as he remained sober, since he'd no longer been
able to pay his share of expenses with the officers
housed next door. But two weeks was the longest the
poor soul was able to abstain from his vices. During
that time, Tamson found herself pitying him, for the
craving of drink was his devil, not greed. It was the
drink which led him to the tables and ruination. The
family's only hope for Armand was a sobering tour in
the wilderness with the *troupes de la marine,* whose
rigorous pace, according to Alain, would either kill or
cure him.

"Oh, Tante Tamson, how beautiful! These are the
prettiest yet!"

"I hope Madame de la Morandière will think so,"
Tamson sighed, coming out of her reverie to hug
Marielle. She stepped back from the table and planted
a kiss on the part down the center of the little girl's dark

hair, which was braided on either side and bedecked with the scarlet ribbon her aunt had given her.

"I like red flowers."

Red tulips were symbolic of the time of year, at least on the banks of the Hudson. Tamson had yet to see one since she'd left. "You like anything red! I am surprised you are not supporting the English because of their uniforms."

"Tante Tamson, how could you say such a thing!" Marielle chided gently. "I think they more likely stole the color from France long ago."

"Marielle!" Isabelle's voice rang out from the upstairs.

Reminded of her mission, the child rose on tiptoe and planted a kiss on Tamson's cheek. *"Bon soir, Tante Tamson."*

"Good night, *ma petitesse.*"

As Marielle bounded out of the parlor, Tamson surveyed her work once more with a degree of satisfaction. She'd let the watercolors dry overnight and finish them in the morning. The light would be much better. With a sigh, she walked over to the hearth and sank into the large chair usually reserved for Joseph. He had gone to bed early that evening with a bit of a cough, rather than staying out with Alain as he often did. Even Isabelle complained about the number of evenings spent alone, but only to Tamson. She was glad that Joseph was enthused about his work again.

As for Alain, there were many nights he didn't come into their room at all. Although she was gradually losing the conviction that they should occupy separate beds, Tamson made his faithfully at the foot of hers each night and removed all evidence of it each morning, even though there were no upstairs servants to notice, much less talk. The fact of the matter was, even if they married for all the wrong reasons and he had betrayed her, she now understood why.

Instead of hating the man as she'd vowed, she found herself respecting and admiring him more and more. Which was why once again she wrestled with the temptation not to make up the second bed. After all, they were man and wife. Their marriage had been consummated. Most assuredly, she thought, the memory of that hungry night of passion still as vivid as though it had been yesterday.

She'd thought that perhaps he too was warming to the idea of renewing that intimacy when he'd put a stop to her spending and she'd admitted that she no longer considered him her enemy. That night she'd lain awake until the wee hours of the morning, waiting for him to return to their room and, instead of falling into the bed on the bench, to take his place beside her and finish the sweet kiss he'd but started when they were interrupted earlier. She learned later from Isabelle that he and his cousin had spent the entire night in the parlor absorbed in conversation—and the last of the imported brandy.

"Ah, the look of a lonely woman is more than my heart can stand!"

Tamson jumped, her hand flying to her chest as Armand La Tour stepped into the room. He glanced at the table where her cards were drying and smiled.

"Beautiful work from a beautiful lady. I am beginning to think that my cousin is blind."

"Alain is working," Tamson countered defensively. She eyed her uninvited companion speculatively, wondering if she should call for Henri, who had retired to his basement quarters with his wife. "And Joseph is not well, so he has retired early. Isabelle should be down momentarily. She is putting Marielle to bed."

"Love is blind, so I am told. I am beginning to believe it."

Tamson followed Armand with her gaze as he went to the burled walnut liquor cabinet and took out a bottle, examining the label. From the face he made, he did not approve of the quality, but it didn't stop him from pouring himself a generous glass.

"I had thought Joseph would have replenished the good stock by now. Will you have some?"

"No, thank you, Armand . . . and I don't think Alain would approve of your doing so. You know how he feels."

"Madame, I am taking this one drink to fend off the night chill. At which point, I shall make up my bed on yon sofa and retire for the evening."

Tamson rose from the chair. "Then I shall leave you to do so. I shouldn't want to be here if Alain came in and caught you helping yourself to the liquor."

"But he will not, at least for several hours, if my guess is correct."

Something in Armand's voice pricked at her curiosity. "You've spoken to him?"

"Non, but I saw him enter Jeanette's coach at the Mont Royal House. Knowing my cousins as I do, I do not expect their liaison will be a short one."

"Their *liaison,* as you call it, most likely consisted of Alain escorting Madame de Montigny home. The streets are hardly safe, what with all the Indians about. My husband is most protective," Tamson averred with more certainty than she actually felt.

"To have such a beautiful woman as yourself love me so blindly would be the stuff my dreams are made of, *ma chère*. I would know what it is that my cousin has that makes women so crazy for him."

Tamson wanted to blurt out that she was not in love with Alain Beaujeu, but the months of acting the part of his wife had tempered her tongue, if not her thoughts. "Integrity, monsieur. He is a man of honor, not some spoiled spendthrift with a weakness for liquor and games, who allows his jealousy to drive him to defaming the very hand that feeds him!"

"Voila!" Armand threw up his hand, as if he had made the point, rather than she. At her puzzled look, he chuckled. "As I said, *ma chère,* love must be utterly blind."

Instead of answering, Tamson spun on her heel and left the room. There was no point in arguing with Armand La Tour, whether he was drunk or sober. He was a stubborn, opinionated bore, she thought, storming up the steps. What a miserable man!

Love must be utterly blind, indeed! As if she loved Alain Beaujeu! She admired and respected him, but she would not go so far as to say she loved him! The sight of the bench at the foot of her bed brought Tamson to an abrupt halt. She leaned back against the door to her chamber, suddenly disarmed by the stark reality of her thoughts. If she didn't love him, why was she thinking of inviting him back into her bed?

Lust! she decided haplessly. That had to be what she was feeling. Love was something to be cherished and nourished, something Alain had certainly not done. All he'd done was turn her into a simple-minded fool—a blind one at that! As she turned, she caught sight of her new cloak, made of soft tawny wool and lined with flannel.

But love or lust, Alain Beaujeu was *her* husband! Tamson snatched the garment off the peg and threw it over her shoulders. Her fingers froze on the fastens as she realized that Armand had not said where Jeanette de Montigny and Alain were going.

If her husband had escorted the woman home, as she preferred to think, that was where Tamson would find her. If not, the two would have to return sooner or later. She put her hand to the latch. That being the case, she intended to be present when they said their goodbyes.

Fifteen

"When can I come along again?"

Alain wiped a smudge of dirt from the impish face his friend turned up to him. This was more the Jeanette he preferred, untethered by the restraints of the station she coveted.

"Tonight was the beginning and end of your career as the governor's agent," he informed her as they walked up the steps to her townhouse.

"But Alain! At last, I feel like I am doing something!"

"The contacts you've provided were enough without your taking Joseph's place with me tonight," Alain assured her. While he'd been reluctant to take her along, he had to admit it was Jeanette who found the secret door leading to the contraband.

"But he was sick!" Jeanette pulled a playful face at him. "And it was exciting!"

"Joseph and I, we have reason to be about the warehouses along the docks," Alain insisted. "The guards know us. As it is, there will no doubt be a rumor about the city by the morning that you and I are having an affair, since you had to sneeze and draw the corporal's attention."

"Everything was so dusty! I could not help it!"

Jeanette exclaimed in her defense as she shoved the key into the lock of the door to her townhouse. Before she turned it, however, the door swung open and her steward stood back in full dress.

"Good evening, madame, monsieur."

"Why Jacques, what takes you up and about at this hour of the morning? I do not expect you to wait up for me."

"You have a visitor, madame." The servant afforded Alain a disconcerted look. "The Marquee de la Galisonne."

"My wife?"

"So you *do* acknowledge that much, you philandering jackrabbit!"

To Alain's further astonishment, Tamson blazed into the room, for *entered* hardly applied to the angry swish of her skirts as they brushed through the elegantly framed doorway of the de Montigny parlor. Her dress, usually impeccable, was somewhat disheveled, as if she'd been sleeping in her clothes. There was, however, no sign of drowsiness in her eyes. The flickering candle in the lamp on the newel post at the foot of the steps was not nearly as bright as the fire that flashed from her eyes as she stood, hands braced on her hips and chin tilted in imperious indignation.

"What . . . you think Jeanette and I . . ."

"It's after three in the mornin'! What do ye think I think?" the girl demanded with a short step backward, as if she'd been pushed.

"Have you been drinking?"

Stiffly, Tamson inclined her head toward the manservant. "The good man gave me some sherry to keep the chill off and I've been waitin' *six* hours!" she reminded him emphatically before foundering, "but 'tis me that's askin' the questions here!'"

"Should I put on some hot water, madame?"

"Thank you, but non, Jacques. You may retire. I will lock up." Jeanette looked from Tamson to Alain and back. "Perhaps, madame, we might step into the parlor where I see Jacques has kept a fire going. Alain and I have walked a long way and the winter chill has not yet left us."

"Of course." Alain agreed eagerly, stepping back to allow the women to precede him.

When neither moved, Jeanette led the way.

"There is an explanation," he told the fuming Tamson, reaching for her arm and ushering her in after his hostess.

Upon entering, he saw her cloak crumpled at the foot of the divan and a pile of pillows at the other end. In front of it on a small butler tray table was a decanter with a single glass still half full of the golden sherry. Tamson took a seat next to her cloak, as if expecting to leave at any moment, and self-consciously brushed a strand of hair off her face.

"I fell asleep for a while," she offered at the quizzical lift of Alain's brow. "It was *six* hours!"

"So you said."

"Alain, since Jacques has retired, would you mind fetching one of my brandies from the basement? I feel the need for something more fortifying."

Upon deciding that his hot-blooded and impetuous wife had spent most of her ire and had fallen into a sulk, Alain obliged Jeanette and started for the hall again, where a door beneath the staircase led to the basement below. He stopped long enough to pick up a

chamberstick and light it from the lamp on the newel.
Then, with one last bemused glance at Tamson, disappeared through the paneled entrance.

"You have flattered me, madame."

Tamson blinked at Jeanette de Montigny, her blank
expression bringing a smile to the latter's face.

"That you think I have lured Alain Beaujeu away
from you."

"Ye've been with him since supper this . . ." Tamson
frowned thoughtfully before going on. "Last evening,
have ye not?"

"What a quaint accent you have! Sherry becomes
it."

For the first time, Tamson realized she'd been speaking in English, the accent her teachers did their best to
erase, burring her syllables without censure. She only
had three glasses of sherry, one on each hour after she'd
awakened from her inadvertent catnap when the clock
struck twelve. Or was it on the half hour? She gave an
accusing glance to the glass in front of her.

"My father was Scottish," she admitted grudgingly,
careful to recall the exact answers to give and remain
within the charade Alain had concocted to keep her safe.

"And your mother English. Oh, I know who you really are, madame," Jeanette told her, upon seeing her
eyes widen in surprise. "I am Alain's friend and confi-
dante," she went on, "but that is all . . . at least, that is
all since he became involved with a certain mademoiselle from Albany."

Tamson might have been elated at this revelation, but
from all Isabelle had told her, Jeanette De Montigny
was not to be trusted, especially where men were con-

cerned. She wiped the inadvertent delight from her face with an effort.

"Well, he must have had a lot to confide to take up six hours."

Tamson watched the woman lay her cloak over the back of the chair next to the hearth and then toss another log on the fire. In the flare of sparks that ensued, it became obvious that the pale blue of Jeanette de Montigny's dress was smudged with a soot-like substance, as if she'd been working, rather than entertaining a gentleman friend. Where the devil had Alain taken her?

As if she'd heard Tamson's thoughts, her companion answered. "Actually, I was helping him take inventory of the latest shipment from the islands. Joseph's shelves will be overflowing by the end of the week . . . many of the supplies of English origin."

"English!"

Tamson hardly knew which was the most unbelievable part of her hostess's story, that she'd helped Alain work or that she'd been inventorying English goods. Unless they'd been pirated, she reflected, concentrating to finish her train of thought before she lost it. Of all the times to feel tipsy! Yet, her nerves had been undone when she'd awakened, cold and in a strange house, only to discover it was past midnight and the suspicious couple had still not returned.

"The black market always flourishes in wartime. It seems some of your officials are not above trade with the enemy if the price is right."

"But that's treasonous!"

Jeanette took a seat on the chair and leaned back. "You are not a stupid girl, Tamson Stewart, but you are

incredibly naive. Perhaps that is what endears you to
Alain . . . aside from your obvious charms, that is."

Tamson wished she hadn't partaken of the sherry.
She'd come here to accuse Jeanette de Montigny of an
affair with her husband and the woman had deftly
turned the pointed finger at her, as if she were the one
who had wrongfully charmed Alain. Here was a smart
one, more the fox than even Isabelle gave her credit for.
Would that Alain truly thought her as dear as her hostess
implied!

Tamson mastered the insecurity Jeanette's compliment evoked and rose to her feet, ignoring the momentary waver of the room about her. She chose her words
as carefully as her footing.

"I have nothing more to say to you, madame, except
to warn you that I will not tolerate your nocturnal liai-
sons with my husband. There are plenty of men in
Montreal with whom you might pursue companionship." Trying to balance, she picked up her cloak and
threw it over her shoulders. "And if you pursue in per-
sisting . . . pursuing my husband . . ."

Tamson stared down her nose, blinking to merge the
two figures seated before her into one. The devil take
it! she thought recklessly, more concerned with the
point to be made than the manner in which it was delivered. "I shall pluck you bald as a stewing hen!"

With an emphatic sniff Tamson pivoted toward the
doorway, only to collide with the silent, broad-shouldered
man filling it. She bounced backward with a start, but
was caught about the waist by a steadying hand.

"As for you, you gallivantin' jackrabbit," she recovered spunkily, "I'll scratch your bloody blue eyes out!"

"You never told me Tamson was so belligerent,

Alain!" Jeanette teased as he swept the unstable girl off her feet before she fell over the table that caught her behind the knees as she tried to back away.

Instead of fighting him as he expected, Tamson fell against his chest. Oblivious to the smug look the girl afforded her adversary, Alain shifted to get a better hold on her and leveled an accusing look at his friend.

"There was no brandy in the cellar." He couldn't believe he'd allowed himself to be manipulated so easily, but Tamson's unexpected presence had left him somewhat rattled.

The perfect coquette, Jeanette put her hands to her cheeks in mock dismay. "Then the last of it must be in the pantry! How foolish of me to forget!"

"I think it best that my wife and I be leaving anyway."

"I can walk!" The girl in his arms protested, rousing from the pillow of his shoulder.

"That is not necessary, *ma petitesse.* Jeanette, *s'il vous plaît,* the door . . ."

"And I am not your little *anything,*" Tamson protested. "I am your wife and I want to be treated like a wife, not like some dressed-up doll!"

"Hush, Tamson, lest you call the guards on the streets down on us!" Alain whispered sharply, effectively silencing the fuming female as he carried her out onto the steps.

"Bonne chance, mon ami," Jeanette called after him gently. "You will need it, I think."

Instead of answering, Alain strode purposefully toward the rounded steps of the portico in front of Château La Tour at the opposite end of the block. Her cloak having fallen away, Tamson shivered within his grasp and sought a secure hold about his neck, her hair tickling his chin. When he reached for the latch to the front door, to his relief, it was open, most likely having been left that way by the girl in his arms when she'd decided to come after him.

Isabelle would have a fit if she knew of the security breach, for his cousin's wife was paranoid about the Indians that roamed the streets with more and more frequency. Although it was rare to see one on rue Notre Dame. They stayed mostly around the marketplace and dockside where the trading took place.

"Alain . . ." Tamson's voice cut through the silence as he maneuvered her through the door and into the hall.

"Shush! We do not wish to awaken the entire house."

"But I need to use the commode!" The girl squirmed in Alain's arms, as if to confirm the urgency of her request.

"Upstairs."

She kicked her feet until he lost his grip and dropped them. "I can't wait!"

With yet one more situation out of hand, Alain released the girl and followed her hurried step into the dining room adjoining the hall. As she opened the sideboard to take out the porcelain necessary stored there, usually for the convenience of the men after a formal meal, he caught it by the handle and put it down for her.

"Well?"

"Well what?" he hissed, impatience tingeing his growing frustration.

"Ye can't stand there, ye gapin' fool! I'll have my privacy!"

Instead of giving voice to the argument that sprang

to his lips, Alain swallowed it and walked into the hall. If the stubborn little idiot fell over, it served her right. A hint of a smile pulled at the corner of his mouth as he considered the possibility. Women were peculiar creatures with their ability to be beguiling and annoying at the same time.

Who would have believed Tamson would have gone to Jeanette's house, much less threatened to pluck her bald and scratch his eyes out? What the devil had prompted her to go out looking for him in the first place? After all, it wasn't the first night he'd spent away. The fact was, aside from his work demanding it, he found it a good way to avoid the sweet temptation she presented sleeping so close that he could hear her breathe softly in the stillness of the night.

Even with his eyes closed, he could see her lying there, hair spread like a copper gold halo around her face when she forgot to braid it. There were a thousand pictures of Tamson embedded in his memory—an imp laughing and playing with Marielle, a madonna carefully working over her stitchery, an artist studying her little cards with a moué of concentration that was enough to drive a sane man wild with the urge to kiss it.

The sound of a chair scraping heralded Tamson's less than graceful approach. Eager to steady her before she knocked something over and alerted the household, Alain found her easily in the darkness and ushered her toward the steps. There she stopped without warning, causing him to collide with her.

"Aren't you going to carry me?"

"I thought you said you could walk."

She stiffened, as if he'd issued a challenge, and turned away. "And walk I will!"

With a hand on the rail, she progressed up the staircase without incident, although Alain was right behind her should she slip. The cold night air had evidently cleared her senses to some extent, for her step was somewhat steadier. With a hand pressed gently to her back, he guided her toward their bedroom, holding his breath until they were both inside and the door closed behind them.

Using the bedpost to steady herself, Tamson perched on the edge of the mattress and addressed him with an air of authority. "What kind of work were you and Madame de Montigny about tonight, sir?"

"Taking inventory at the King's warehouse."

The fire had been banked in the shallow hearth and a turn of wood and kindling lay stacked neatly by it. Using the poker, Alain stirred the embers until they glowed a bright orange before adding a few of the smaller pieces.

"What are the clerks for then?"

"I have a suspicion that not all of them are honest. That is why Joseph and I have been away so much in the evening. Tonight, however, my cousin was sick . . ."

"And Madame de Montigny went with you to the warehouse to count the stores?" Tamson finished with a skeptical note.

"I could not have checked both cargo lists without her help." The silence that followed was encouraging, but shortlived.

"Why didn't you ask me to help?"

"I did not ask Jeanette. She insisted." Alain carefully laid another larger log on the fire and straightened. "But it is my turn to ask you a question, madame. How is it that you knew Jeanette was with me?"

Tamson rose from the corner of the bed and let her cloak slide to the floor. "It doesn't matter," she replied, turning away to work at the fastens of her dress.

Alain hesitated for a moment, his gaze transfixed by the fingers struggling with the laces entangled in the disheveled braid hanging down the girl's back. She was always in bed when he came to their room, Isabelle or Marielle, he supposed, having helped her undress. The dress had been designed for a woman with a servant to attend her. Or a husband, he thought, recalling her earlier declaration of how she wanted to be treated.

"But it does matter," he said, resuming a more detached attitude. "I would know who is watching me so closely."

"Why, are you doing something illegal rather than immoral . . . or is it both?" Tamson dropped her arms and shook them to get rid of the numbness from the fruitless effort of holding them up so long.

"Non, but someone is."

"It would not be untoward, sir, if you were to assist me with this knot . . . unless you'd have me ruin my dress by sleeping in it."

Alain resisted the temptation to remind her she'd already done that. "Nor would it be *untoward* if you were to tell me who is watching me. I could be in some danger."

Tamson reached behind her and drew away her braid, tugging the ribbon which barely held it together off in the process. While Alain concentrated on the knot, she ran her fingers absently through her hair, combing it out.

"It was Armand. He was at the Mont Royal and saw you and Madame De Montigny leave together." She stared up at the ceiling, as if intrigued by the dancing shadows cast there by the fire. "And since there have been many nights when you have not even come to our room, what else was I to think?"

Alain exhaled in relief. Armand was a nuisance, not a danger, although his cousin was envious and spiteful when it came to Jeanette. Since Tamson had arrived, he'd done his best to annoy Alain with his flirtations and, when the girl failed to respond accordingly, he'd apparently resorted to adding fuel to a fire Isabelle had already kindled, Isabelle and Jeanette never having cared for each other from their first meeting.

"With so many ships coming in with the clearing weather, there has been much to do and much to check. I need documentation to bring these brigands to justice. Besides, that bench is not much to come home to, Tamson."

Tamson spun away from him abruptly, the lace which he still held tugging her loosened bodice off one shoulder. "Do ye see the bench made up, Alain Beaujeu?"

A fiery weakness flashed in Alain's stomach at the sudden challenge, robbing him of breath as surely as if he'd been kicked. The secondary bed had not been made and the implication was rapidly overwhelming all the resistance he'd so carefully constructed where Tamson was concerned.

"I understand now, Alain, why you took me away." Tamson went on, her impatience softening. "Since we have been here in Montreal, I have seen much about you that I admire. Your love and devotion to family, your honor and integrity, they make me realize that I could have done much worse in marriage."

The word *honor* cut through the desire rising in his loins like a winter wind, staggering it with the reality of this dream unfolding. Tamson coming to him of her own accord was one thing. Tamson coming to him under the assumption that she was his wife was another. What seemed the best way to control the girl was suddenly his undoing.

"Ah, Tamson," Alain groaned as she stepped up to him and wrapped her arms about his waist.

His mouth went dry at the light brush of her lips against his neck and, despite his misgivings, his hand sought the velvet softness of the shoulder bared to his touch. It was cool, exposed to the night air, yet it fired a heady warmth that spread through Alain at a startling pace. He shuddered with the impact and forced himself away.

Were this any other woman, he'd let the passion raging in his veins run its course. But this was Tamson—not Squire Stewart's daughter, not his kidnap victim, just sweet, fiery, unpredictable Tamson. He had misled her enough as it was without further compounding his mistakes.

His well intentioned restraint, however, pushed her away as surely as if he'd physically shoved her. "You *do* love Madame de Montigny!" There was no sign of anger in the wounded eyes turned up at him, only hurt and confusion.

"Non, Tamson!" Alain averred fervently. "I do not love Jeanette. We are but friends. It is just that . . ."

Dieu, but help him! He stumbled through the desire-ridden fog in his mind, groping for a reason aside from the truth. To tell her they were not married after he'd finally convinced her that they were, would surely set off that unpredictable Scottish fire. Not that he was concerned about his own welfare. He could easily slip away into the wilderness, should suspicion be aroused about his loyalties to the French, but not with her in tow.

Tamson turned abruptly and, upon seizing a pillow from those piled on the bed, tossed it on the bench at the foot. "Don't be explainin', for the love of God! I've been humiliated enough as it is!" The pitiful waver in her voice cut Alain like a knife, compounding his own misery.

"Tamson!"

He grabbed her and forced her around to face him, but one look at the tears spilling down her cheeks and his denial died on his lips, smothered by the consuming kiss that had urged him beyond reason or control. The lingering, sensual assault was for all the times he had coveted her honeyed lips, which parted in wary reception at first and then became infected with the same carnal hunger. The pouts, the smiles, the thoughtful purses, the sleepy, turned-up corners—they were all there and Alain devoured each and every one until there was breath for no more.

Blood hammering through him, he pulled away, but caught Tamson's face between his hands, lest she try to escape. She made no move, but returned his fevered gaze with her whiskey-warm eyes, where emotions kindled as raw and wild as lightning flashing stark against a summer sky.

"Never," he managed hoarsely, *"never* think that I do not want to take you to my bed, *ma petitesse. Mon Dieu,* but   am burning for you." He fumbled to find her hand and guided it to the front of his trousers where the evidence of his declaration swelled. "You make me the wild man, you are so desirable to me, but . . ." Alain struggled with his fledging control.

"You have a disease?"

Alain laughed. Not that he felt the least amused by the situation or her absurd supposition, but he had to find some means of release. Upon seeing irritation kindle in her expression, however, he put a staying finger to her lips.

"Non, non, non! It is nothing of the kind! It is . . . *Dieu,* but you make me crazy, Tamson!"

Leaving her standing by the bed, Alain retreated to the fireplace to a safer blaze and tossed another piece of wood on the hearth. How lies will multiply, he lamented silently, staring into the flames reflecting those tormenting him within.

"It is our marriage, *ma chère.* It is not as it should be and I do not wish to further compound my mistake by renewing it . . . our relationship, that is, because . . ." Alain exhaled heavily. "Because I am taking you home to your father as soon as I can arrange a way and the marriage can be annulled."

"What's wrong with us?"

Alain turned to face the disconcerted girl leaning against the bedpost, and swore at himself even as he expanded on his lie. "The Church, it will not recognize it because you are Protestant, non?"

"Yes, but didn't a priest marry us?"

"We did not tell him. He assumed we both were of the faith," Alain told her smoothly, wincing inwardly at the stricken look on Tamson's face as she sat back down.

"I see." She remained on the corner of the bed for a

moment, as if absorbing what he'd told her, and then
slowly slid off. With a tug, she yanked the blankets
folded at the foot of the bed and laid them over the arm
of the bench. "So what happened at the fort in Quebec
was lust and nothing more?"

"I would not say that," Alain answered awkwardly.
Something akin to panic skimmed along his spine.

"Then you do love me?"

"How could anyone not love a girl such as you, Tamson?" *Love* was not a term Alain used loosely. In fact,
he'd never used it in the romantic sense with a woman.
There was too much commitment that went with such
an admission, and who could commit to anything in
these uncertain times?

Whether Tamson accepted his evasive answer or not
was difficult to tell. She merely stared at him, all the
emotions he'd seen reflected in her gaze, dying to an
impassive glaze.

"I can finish undressing myself now," she said at last,
her tone revealing no more of her feelings.

Taking the dismissal at face value, Alain nodded and
walked to the door. "I'll sleep downstairs in the parlor,
if you would like."

"No, I'll make up your bed. Armand is down
there."

Armand! Alain's lips thinned. It was a terrible temptation to take out some of his pent-up rage on his cousin,
but that would only awaken the household and accomplish nothing. It appeared that was to be the way of
things for him—accomplishing nothing. *Dieu,* but he
was about to explode with such unaccustomed lack of
action!

"Then I will wait outside."

Exercising more will than he would have given himself credit for, Alain stepped into the hall and leaned against the door. Besides, this particular quandary with Tamson Stewart was not Armand's fault. It was his own.

Sixteen

"Listen to the hens cluck!" Oncle Souris grunted, taking great care to keep his mouth closed, lest one crumb of the bread might escape.

When she'd risen that morning to sit by the window and try to assuage her aching head, Tamson had seen the beggar who allegedly lived in the tunnels beneath the city. The "tunnel mouse," as he was frequently called, was in the back alley holding off two dogs with his walking club while he rummaged through garbage to get first choice. He was like a derelict spirit, able to disappear and reappear in different parts of the city, so Isabelle had told Tamson one day with a slight shiver.

Unable to eat the generous portion of toast on her plate that morning, Tamson had slipped the remainder in her pocket to put outside where he'd find it and then finished dressing for her outing. To her surprise, when she'd stepped out of the house, leaving Isabelle involved in Marielle's studies, the old man was waiting for her.

She hadn't seen him at first, merely sensed that she was being watched. The idea had frightened her until she caught a glimpse of the ragged blanket over his bent shoulders as he ducked into an alley. Emboldened by the presence of two guards in powder blue chatting with a tavern wench who had carried them out a complimentary refreshment from the proprietor, she'd gone back and confronted him.

"Just making sure *la bonne marquee* is safe," he'd replied, shrinking back against the moss-coated masonry wall of the alley. "These streets are not safe for a lady alone."

While Isabelle had indicated that the old man wasn't stable, much less the sort one would wish to have about, Tamson insisted he join her, if walking a few steps behind could be called that. It was as close as she could convince him to come without breaching his inbred sense of propriety. After all, if anyone knew the city, this man should. Besides, the bag of her belongings he carried for her was heavier than she'd first thought.

"They will chew the governor's ears, but the man cannot give what he does not have," the beggar observed bluntly. "Men can't fight and harvest at the same time. Them hens'll find horsemeat's a fine fare compared to what I've had to make do with." Souris snorted in amusement. "That's why I like my drink as I do. Then I don't care so much."

Tamson glanced down the adjacent street which ran alongside the Château de Vaudreuil, where the women protested—habitants, most of them. The intendant's henchman Cadet had forced them to sell the wheat that had been harvested at a fixed price, allegedly for the army, and then sold it back to them through La Friponne's various merchants at more than twice as much. Now they had to contend with rations of horsemeat, for the barrels of fresh pork and beef brought in by the ships from France were being sent straight to the French outposts. Alain predicted it would be even worse the following winter if the same men remained in charge.

Now that the merchant vessels had arrived, first choice was being snatched up by the *troupes de terre* and *de la marine,* and rightfully so. The city would fare worse, should their armies starve or die of neglect. The citizens would have to sacrifice and make do a bit longer, although Tamson knew the noblesse had suffered little, even if Alain had insisted on the Marquis and Marquee de la Galisonne keeping a low profile socially. After all, his job demanded his attendance at many functions, most of which he visited alone.

Isabelle fretted over the gossip that one could expect no more from a voyageur-turned-marquis, but Alain let the slander roll off his broad shoulders. Tamson herself suspected the fact that he didn't care to take his English wife into the public any more than necessary. No doubt he would hardly miss her, now that she had left Château La Tour.

"Does the Marquis de la Galisonne know you are doing this, madame?" Although the street beggar valiantly tried to hide his disapproval of her mission, it was obvious.

"Non," Tamson answered truthfully, "but he will understand."

"You should not be on the streets alone."

"But I have you, monsieur."

Her companion fell into silence once again, shuffling on his rag-wrapped feet behind her, and Tamson was grateful. It had been hard enough to convince Isabelle that she had to go to the convent. Her new friend had been beside herself, but Tamson had remained stalwart in her decision. If her marriage was not recognized by the Church, then she would do whatever was necessary to make it right. She would study and live at the nunnery until such time as the sisters thought her a suitable wife for Alain.

Leaving would solve many problems, for surely the shameful longings she felt for her husband would not follow her there. They would not give her peace as long as he remained in the same house, much less the same bedroom. When she looked at his face her gaze gravitated toward his lips, which reminded her of their overwhelming masculine possession. His searching gaze could kindle a flame deep within her with its fire-blue caress. His laughter when he teased Marielle lifted her heart and his consternation over his work made her ache to comfort him in the only way she knew, a way he had shown her.

She loved him. It came to her after the long sleepless night like the dawning light filtering through the shutters as she'd feigned sleep while watching him through veiled eyes as he'd hurriedly dressed in the cold morning air. She loved the man who had abducted her and taken her away from all she knew because of the very reasons he'd done so—his devotion to his family and his fierce capacity to love. He had made her his wife to protect her and was still doing so, even from himself and the desire he'd made known to her the night before. Now, she would do what she had to to be worthy as his wife because somewhere, somehow her grudging admiration had turned into love.

The stone half-wall surrounding the nunnery did not serve as well to insure privacy as the great hedge that grew on the inside and spread over it. Oncle Souris handed over Tamson's bag at the iron arched gate with a toothless grin and bade his goodby there, leaving her alone to enter. Gathering her courage, Tamson walked toward the main building through the well kept grounds, which were beginning to show the promise of spring with little bursts of color here and there amidst the winter brown and evergreen ground cover.

What exactly was she going to tell them, she wondered, not for the first time. Would they think her a fallen woman?

"Bonjour, madmoiselle. May I help you?"

Tamson's thoughts fled as she came face-to-face with one of the grey-robed women, whose benevolent smile failed to assuage her nerves. "I . . . I wish to work and study here."

"I see." The sister gave her a speculative look which did not miss the fine cut and material of her clothing. "Then you must see Mère Marie."

With that, Tamson was promptly shown inside the east wing of a long stone building with a cluster of rooms on either side of the clean-scrubbed hall. If the positioning of doors was a sign of importance, Mère Marie ranked highly, for hers was central in the wing and quite large. Scantily furnished, a single bed stood neat and curtained in the corner, with a trunk along the wall and an altar with candles and religious ornamentation at the opposite end. They found the older woman at the desk in the center of the room, studying what appeared to be ledgers, although Tamson did not presume to try to make out their nature for fear of appearing impertinent.

"Mère Marie, this young woman has come in the hopes of joining us."

"To study and work," Tamson corrected. "I am married . . . that is, I wish to learn the faith of my husband.

He says our marriage is not recognized by his church and . . ."

"Madame la Marquee? Is that you?"

Tamson turned toward the door in time to see Jeanette de Montigny sweeping in unannounced, her light *pelisse* flowing over her dress in the back.

"It is you! But what brings *you* to the nunnery?"

The sight of Alain's avowed *friend* made it easy for Tamson to recoup with a cool, "I would ask the same of you, madame."

Jeanette tossed her dark auburn curls over her shoulder, where they fell into the silken folds of the liner of her hood. "Why, I volunteer to help the sisters at the Hotel Dieu three days of the week. With all the soldiers coming in suffering from their weeks at sea, I am learning so that I might be ready when the fighting begins again. Monseigneur Pichon sent me with a message for Mère Marie." She looked at Tamson's bag in surprise and quickly put things together. "Does Alain Beaujeu know of this?"

"This is the Marquee de la Galisonne?" the sister behind the desk exclaimed, taking another look at Tamson.

"The same," Jeanette affirmed.

Tamson pivoted away from her adversary to Mère Marie. "I wish to live here and learn your faith until I'm considered a suitable wife in the eyes of the Church. I was captured by the Indians and suffered amnesia. I don't even recall the wedding, but it was the result of desperate circumstance and I want to make it right. I will work to earn my board and lodgings."

"It is not that simple, child, especially if you are married to the marquis as you have said. Were you wed by a priest of the Church?"

Tamson grimaced. "I cannot remember. But I am willing to work very hard. Can't you see, I want to make it right."

"Pardonez-moi, Madame Mère, but I think that perhaps la marquee needs a friend more than she needs your services. There is much she has to learn of our culture, coming from the far west as she does with her Scottish heritage."

Tamson stepped away as Jeanette reached for her arm. "I know my own mind . . ."

"But you do not know that of your husband, *ma chèrie."* Upon handing the missive from the monseigneur to the mother superior, Jeanette motioned to her. "Come, there is nothing here for you. If you are intent on learning our faith, you must be instructed by one of the priests. Let us walk back to the hospital. There is where your help is needed and you might find what you are looking for."

Left with little alternative, Tamson picked up her heavy tapestry case and followed Madame de Montigny out of the building. Of all people to witness her being turned down at the nunnery, much less to offer to come to her aid! And, as always, Jeanette looked exquisite, as if she had not spent the better part of the night before cavorting with Alain Beaujeu. But then, Tamson reasoned, no doubt Jeanette had slept once her guests left, instead of lying awake, listening to Alain breathe softly at the foot of her bed as Tamson herself had done. It was small consolation that he had not slept well either, the way he'd tossed and turned on the creaking bench.

The ghost of the headache which had plagued her

upon rising began to make itself known, aggravated by this new distress. Tamson groaned silently. Never had she felt so tired, so broken, so defeated. She was married to a man she could not have, at least in the eyes of his church; she was a stranger in the enemy's camp, although she bore no threat to them either physically or politically; and now, she was in the hands of her husband's mistress. After all, who was she going to believe—Alain, who had lied to her more than once, or Isabelle, who had taken her to her bosom like a sister?

"Come, Madame la Marquee," Jeanette announced, slowing at the street corner. "You look as if you might need some refreshment before meeting Père Martin. If you would like, I have a powder from the apothecary which will do marvels for that headache."

Tamson halted in abrupt astonishment at Jeanette's accurate assessment of her current state. If she were only half as sharp, she lamented silently. Too tired to spite herself over pride, she nodded in acquiescence and crossed the street to a small tavern nestled in a row of buildings, mostly shops with apartments overhead, which served as homes for the proprietors.

The establishment was alive with customers, most of them soldiers newly arrived from France. The conversation slackened as Jeanette commanded a private table in a corner and more than one pair of eyes sought them out. As if totally unaware of the commotion they had caused, Jeanette summoned one of the tavern maids with an imperious snap of her fingers and ordered coffee for two while Tamson wearily wedged her bag beneath the small table.

One taste of the chicory brew, however, brought her

impassive gaze to life with shock. Not even a third lump of sugar managed to take away its edge.

"This is my own special blend," Jeanette laughed, the silver tones of her merriment once again drawing attention. "There is that . . . how do you say, hair of the mongrel . . ."

"The dog."

"*Oui*, the dog that bites you!"

Tamson looked at the dark liquid again. "There's liquor in this and you're about to take me to meet a priest?"

"Ah, Alain is right. There is something charming about you which makes one wish to watch out for you." The woman leaned forward in a conspiratorial manner. "And I do not often feel that way toward those of my own gender, particularly those who falsely accuse me of indiscretions with their husbands."

Tamson flushed. "Perhaps I owe you an apology. Alain would have me think so. After all, Isabelle . . ."

"Isabelle thinks that I want her dull, dreary Joseph! Until she came along, Joseph was like a big brother to me . . . almost a father figure after my own passed away. She is simple, that woman! What would I want with a ruined merchant, if I were as desperate to find a man as she thinks?"

"I am certain a marquis would be more to your liking."

Jeanette smiled, catlike. "A title would be nice, I suppose, but I am content to have all the money I can spend and my freedom as a widow."

Tamson fell silent and sipped on the drink. It was hot and steamed through her, spreading slowly with a warm, invigorating effect.

"And I am not foolish enough to sct my heart on

Alain Beaujeu. I left it with him once and he put it aside, like his tailored clothes, and went out into the wilderness. I am not the sort of woman to wait." Her companion shrugged as if that was the end of it. "And you are not foolish either, madame. So it is best that you stop acting it and realize just what you have so that you do not lose it."

"Lose what?"

"The heart of Alain Beaujeu. It is something he has never given before. No doubt he has been clumsy at it."

Clumsy was hardly the word that came to Tamson's mind. Reluctant, obstinate . . . they were more accurate descriptions.

"What makes you think he has given away his heart?" Tamson bit off the addition that he'd acknowledged her as his wife only in name since their arrival at Montreal. She couldn't admit that, at least not to Jeanette de Montigny.

"Because, my silly cabbage, he no longer shares my bed."

The frank admission brought a scarlet hue to Tamson's pale cheeks.

"He has not since . . ."

"I don't need to know that."

"Since he abducted you," Jeanette finished stubbornly. "The night you tried to escape his men, he spent with me . . . *talking about you!* You see, we have always been friends first, then lovers. It was then that I realized Alain Beaujeu had lost his heart. It is just that his head, perhaps, has not yet discovered it missing."

Tamson looked over the table warily. There was a time she knew her enemy. Now she did not trust her instincts.

"And I can see that Alain is not the only one who is in love and is not yet reconciled to it." Jeanette scanned the room, taking note of those who appeared interested in her with a practiced eye before returning her attention to Tamson. "So tell me, if you are in love with him, why is it you are leaving?"

"It's because I love him that I'm leaving. I can't bear living as man and wife, yet not really being . . . acting as such," Tamson stammered awkwardly. "I . . . Alain told me our marriage is not recognized by the Church because I am not of his faith. Sooner than risk further disgrace, I intend to remedy that."

"You mean to say that Alain and you do not share . . ."

"That's why I thought that you and he were having an affair. I recognize he is man of considerable appetite, so to speak . . ."

Jeanette's laughter interrupted Tamson's explanation, leaving the girl disconcerted. What on earth was she doing, speaking of her intimate affairs to a complete stranger? Suddenly, she wished the beverage she'd consumed was more than lightly laced with liquor. A straight shot was more appropriate for the occasion.

"This *is* serious!" Jeanette managed, assembling her composure with a degree of difficulty, as if the very idea of Alain Beaujeu exercising such restraint was incredulous. "Alain will not take you to his bed because you are not of his faith?" she reiterated. "Your marriage is not consummated?"

"Of course it is . . . was," Tamson corrected, indignation adding to the deep rose of the complexion so admired by a group of young French officers a few tables away. She glanced away from Jeanette to where they smiled expectantly, as if awaiting some subtle invitation to approach. Her topic of conversation alone was unthinkable. That she was having it in a public tavern was even worse. Bringing her hand to the side of her face as if to shut them out completely, she returned to the immediate conversation, her voice lowered further.

"And Alain has apologized and promised that he will not make the same mistake again, as if *that* will restore my honor."

"And you intend to remove that excuse so that he will have no reason not to see to his husbandly duties in the boudoir, non?" Jeanette chuckled, more to herself than at Tamson. "So the fox has finally met his match."

"I intend to make honorable what has already transpired," Tamson insisted, "what he led me to believe was honorable at the time. Had we not . . . well, if we had not acted that one night as man and wife, none of this would be necessary."

"You love him, Tamson Stewart. That is why you are willing to do this."

"I admire and respect him. I think I could have done worse for a husband, since I had no choice in the matter."

Somehow she couldn't bring herself to admit that to Jeanette de Montigny. That was something for her to know only, until Alain admitted his feelings for her. He wanted her, he'd made that known most convincingly. He'd yet to say that he loved her, not without coercion.

"And what will you do if he does not wish to continue with this marriage of yours, even after you have completed your studies and been approved by the monseignor?"

"Go home."

As the biggest fool in the entire world, Tamson thought, refusing even to acknowledge that possibility. They'd been through too much together for this bond, this attraction between them, to be meaningless. It simply could not be. The honor she loved in him would not allow such a thing.

Whether it was the stimulant in Jeanette's special coffee, the fact that Père Martin readily agreed to teach Tamson in exchange for her volunteer services and influence with Alain Beaujeu in obtaining supplies, or the astonishing idea that Jeanette de Montigny had in one morning changed from rival to ally, Tamson was in high spirits as she made her way down Notre Dame toward Château La Tour.

She was to start her classes first thing in the morning, before going to work with the Sisters of the Congregation who staffed the hospital. The priest was grateful enough for the word she promised to put in with Alain, but she'd insisted on working in the wards as well, especially after seeing the need for extra hands.

With a spring in her step, Tamson bounded up to the front door and raised her hand to knock, only to have the door jerked open. In the entrance, Alain Beaujeu stood like a pillar of silent thunder, lightning snapping in the gaze that slipped over her and came to rest on the bag in her hand. He started to speak and then appeared to think better of it. Instead, he sighed and stepped back.

"Welcome home, madame. I would see you upstairs," he added tersely, revealing that his black humor had not dissipated.

"Guess what I have done!" Tamson declared proudly,

undaunted as she handed him her bag. Helping Isabelle was hardly a full time job and they'd repaired just about every linen and item of clothing in the house. Besides, her work at the hospital was something far more worthwhile than the silly invitations she made. It was a gratifying task, a small way that she could make up for the treatment of Alain's family by her own people.

"I heard, madame, and I still cannot believe it!"

"But I thought you would be pleased."

"Pleased?" Alain reined in his voice and pointed upstairs. "I would discuss this in private, Tamson, not that the entire city does not know," he grumbled beneath his breath. *"Dieu,* but you are an exasperation!"

Rather than argue on the staircase, Tamson hurried up the steps with Alain stomping behind her. It was beyond her what he had heard, but she was in too high a spirit to let his irritation dampen it. She not only would make him proud of her as a volunteer, rather than one of the dimwitted hostesses whom he frequently derided as worthless, but she would surprise him upon her confirmation into the faith.

"Alain, I was wrong about Jeanette and I apologize for last night," Tamson admitted, stepping inside the room. "We've spent the day together at the Hotel Dieu and . . ."

"Thank God! So it was she who kept you from making me the total fool!" her husband interrupted hotly. He approached her, wildly waving his arms about like a madman. "What is it that you hoped to gain by all this? A rope about your neck, possibly mine as well?"

"No, I . . ."

"The whole city is buzzing like the bees! The Marquis de la Galisonne's wife wishes to enter the nunnery.

The poor dear has been locked up in Château La Tour and he has obviously neglected his husbandly duties. I can assure you Armand is gloating over the tables, collecting his bets . . ."

"Oh, pooh on Armand! Who cares what he thinks?"

The moment the words were out, it became very obvious to Tamson who did. Alain consciously lowered his voice. "His associates are influential, Tamson! Whatever possessed you to . . ."

Unable to think of any other way to stop him long enough to defend herself, Tamson resorted to the only course she knew to be effective. After all, he'd silenced her more than once in the same distracting way. Stepping up on tiptoe, she threw her arms about Alain's neck and covered his mouth clumsily with her own. Her impulse was not quite as masterful, but it was effective nonetheless.

Startled by her unorthodox assault, Alain backed away, but she followed him until the closed door at his back stopped him short. Then, and only then, did he submit, warily at first, as if her initial assault had only softened his outrage. As his shoulders relaxed beneath her arms, she let go the death grip she'd held on his ears to prevent his escape and spread her fingers through his hair. Bourbon, she thought, tasting the lips that had begun to kiss her back, correcting gently, nipping and coaxing her own to increased boldness. She'd never cared for bourbon's strong sapor until now.

"You crazy little goose, I have been mad with worry!" her victim stammered, clearly thrown by her aggressive behavior.

"Is that the kiss of a prospective nun, Alain Beaujeu?" she murmured against the corner of his mouth, praying her voice didn't sound too hopeful. It was hard to play the practiced seductress when one had not had the experience.

"Isabelle told me you had left, that you were going to the convent because we were not legitimately married."

Alain's terse explanation faded to a guttural sigh as Tamson dropped her attention to his Adam's apple, bobbing beneath a rippling stretch of bristled skin. It was such an unprecedented surrender that Tamson nearly giggled with the heady power of her success.

"I did not believe her until I saw that your clothes were gone. I was on my way out when you arrived."

"To do what, Alain?" she whispered huskily behind his ear.

"To fetch you back home where you belong!" Upon realizing the fervent extent of his spontaneous confession, Alain straightened to recoup his scattered defenses, so that Tamson had to tilt her head upward to read his unsettled expression.

She nearly melted in her resolve to keep her studies a secret. It was instinct which held her back. If he was not ready to admit all that had become of their relationship, then neither was she. Instead, she planted another short kiss on his mouth and spun away. She would allow him his stubborn pride for now. Besides, his inadvertent admission was enough to send her heart soaring. *Mad with worry.* He'd been mad about her, mad enough to be angry and unreasonable and absolutely adorable.

"Well, Isabelle misunderstood. I said that I was going to the nunnery to volunteer to study and do hospital work."

"Study what?"

"Why, nursing the ill, what else?"

"For that you needed your clothes?"

Tamson shrugged. "I thought, in view of our situation, it might be easier on us both if I lived there, but they didn't want anything to do with me either, my not being of the faith, so to speak."

With a mumbled oath, Alain closed the distance between them in a step and engulfed her in his arms. He was still trembling inwardly from the shock of finding Tamson gone. When Isabelle had told him that Tamson was so shaken upon realizing that their marriage was not recognized by the church that she'd decided to become a nun, he'd thought his cousin's wife was playing a game with him. Then he'd seen the empty drawers and closet and had been on his way to find her and tell her the truth this time, when she appeared on the front step, bag in hand.

"Tamson, that is not what I said last night."

"It's all right, Alain. I realize now that the very honor that has kept you a gentleman, when you might not have been, is part of the reason I love you so much. Honor is such a scarce quality in these times and I'm so proud of you I could burst."

"But you see . . ."

She kissed him again. She liked this. For once, it was he who was off balance. He looked like a boy who had been caught with his hand in the candy jar.

"No other man would have denied his passion as you have for my sake. It only proves how very much you do love me." Catching his face between her hands as he started to speak, she added emphatically, "And I am going to prove myself worthy, Alain Beaujeu. I'm going to show you we didn't make a mistake and, when we say our vows again, monsieur, even *your* church bells will ring."

With an emphatic hug, she drew away, leaving him in discomfited silence. There was an appealing desperation in his pale blue gaze, as if he were groping for the right words. How often she'd felt that same way.

"I think I like Montreal, Monsieur le Marquis," she quipped saucily, taking a quick step which placed her between the door she opened and its frame. "And I *know* I love you!" She kissed her finger and planted the affection on the tip of his nose, his inadvertent start lifting her even higher as she spun away in retreat.

Alain stared speechlessly at the abandoned doorway, listening to Tamson's light steps echo down the stairwell. He hadn't been sure exactly what he had in mind when he confronted his unpredictable *wife*, he'd been so distressed to find her gone. All he knew was that *this* would never have been a consideration. This bolder side of her was something that had taken him by surprise.

A clashing assortment of emotions struggled for dominance, resulting in extensive confusion as he grasped the latch and pulled the door behind him. Part of him wanted to dance and shout with glee. Tamson loved him. Yet there was another, more practical side that dealt with a reality she had long been out of touch with—a side which recognized the impossibility of her sweet promise.

Even if the war were to end tomorrow, he knew there would be no reconciliation with Squire Stewart, Tamson's father. That man would no more forgive him than Alain would forgive those who had taken away his mother and sisters. There were some wounds, he feared, not even love could heal.

Seventeen

Chouaguen. Speculation about the fort and trading center referred to by the English as Oswego and when the enemy stronghold would fall was on everyone's tongue throughout the spring and into the summer. Governor Vaudreuil had wasted no time in dispensing his troops into the English colonial frontier from Forts Niagara, Duquesne, and Frontenac. The French successes only added fuel to the fervor stirred by the arrival of Louis Joseph, Marquis de Montcalm-Gozon, the new French captain general, and an array of bright officers and seasoned *troupes de la terre.*

Siege had already been laid that spring at Chouaguen and then abandoned, but the result was the loss of British stores, horses, and men, and above all, the gain of time. Vaudreuil's quick assault set the English back before they could launch an offensive and once again, the French held the advantage of the aggressors. The enemy was losing valuable time resupplying and rebuilding while the *troupes de la marine, de terre,* and their Indian allies harassed English fortifications and settlements at strategic points to keep them disorganized.

The effort to supply the forces was monumental. Keeping track of the pilfering and illicit trade was next to impossible. There was no end to the demand on

Alain's time, both from requisitioning officers and belligerent Indians. Thankfully, there were others in the commissioner's office to handle the ransom of those English captives fortunate enough to make it back to the trading center alive in exchange for liquor, as well as dole out the blood money for scalps.

In the midst of it all, there was Tamson, gently slipping into his office from time to time to remind him of the needs of the Hotel Dieu, which was now inundated with patients beyond those homeless and unfortunate citizens for which it was built. It was one of the few times he saw her, for this new nursing vocation she had insisted upon kept her away from the La Tour house as much as his work did him.

Although he had been assured by several officers that he need not fret over the safety of the lovely Marquee de la Galisonne, Alain was far from comforted. It seemed that Tamson was conquering the French and Canadian army from within the ranks with her charm and compassion in tending the wounded and ill. Each night she had an escort of at least two officers of the *troupes de la terre,* those of the marine being outranked by the distinction of French, rather than Canadian, birth.

Like her other conquests, Alain managed to find whatever it was that she asked for. How could he not, when it was requested so endearingly. Still, he did not like the idea of her volunteering at the Hotel Dieu any more than he had originally. Jeanette was the rebellious sort, always willing to take on the unthinkable, but Tamson . . .

There was all manner of disease and vermin a lady of her station should not be exposed to. The exertion was telling on her face and the strain of exposure to

sickness and death showed in those autumn-fired eyes
that often haunted his mind, making it difficult to concentrate on the task at hand.

He'd planned to return her to Annanbrae in the spring,
but the hostilities renewed with such intensity that to
undertake the journey by land was too risky. Now it was
midsummer and there was no sign of any change for
the better. Prisoners of war had already revealed an omi-
nous and prospective change in the British command—
the appointment of the Scottish Lord Loudon, a fighting
man of considerable reputation; the war at sea seemed
to roll more and more to the enemy's favor, as evidenced
by the increasing list of French ships reported taken or
missing.

Yet, Alain knew that a sea route was the best chance
he had of insuring Tamson's safety. As his cousin Joseph
had pointed out, living in Montreal was becoming like
living on a lighted powder keg. Between drunken,
bloodthirsty Indians stomping about the Place Royale
market, frightening the inhabitants of the city with their
increasing aggression, and the clashes between the
troupes de la terre and *troupes de la marine,* it sometimes seemed that there was as much hostility within
the city as without.

That added to the poorly concealed division between
Governor General Vaudreuil and Montcalm's camp—a
gap which seemed to grow with each planned military
engagement—and Bigot's pirates bleeding both sides,
spelled inevitable doom for New France. The question
was not *if,* as far as Alain was concerned, but *when.*
This year, next? It was no wonder Joseph had so readily
accepted Alain's offer to take Isabelle and their daughter

back to France before the winter freeze and assume the role of overseer for the Marquis de la Galisonne.

Now all that remained was to convince Tamson to accompany them. It was, perhaps, the longest way to get her home, traveling to France and then to England, but it was by far the safest. Alain had already made the contacts. Having been drawn into Bigot's inner circle along with Joseph as he had anticipated, he now knew the names of the privateers and smugglers who had stocked La Friponne with choice English goods, one of whom owed Alain his life. As a voyageur, he had saved the drunken sailor from losing his scalp as the result of an unsatisfactory trade with a disgruntled Iroquois.

All he had to do was broach the subject with Tamson, who appeared perfectly content to go about her charitable work like another Jean Mance, who had founded the hospital years before. *Dieu,* but she was so different from the way he had originally considered her. Instead of spoiled and haughty, she was as open and giving of herself as his own mother had been, without regard for her station. In the face of hardship, she had done without like the rest of the family, despite his promise that she could have whatever she wished. That pride and stubbornness he had once disdained were her strength and durability as a woman in every sense of the word.

Odd as it was, Alain wondered just how he would manage without her. Not that he'd spent much time with her as he perhaps should have, he mused guiltily. He closed the ledger in front of him and abandoned his work. The others who worked at the commissary, including the new aide assigned to him from Montcalm's command, were across the street at a tavern or had gone home to pass the noon hour. The numbers he'd been studying were hardly competition for his attention when his *wife* entered his thoughts.

It was just that she was there, where he could find her, if he were so inclined. She might be reading to some weakened soldier or folding bandages, but she was just a block or so away, in case he needed to see her smile or hear her gentle voice with that funny burred French she spoke with considerably improved fluency. Sometimes he watched her without her even knowing he'd been to the hospital. Something about her serenity in the chaotic surroundings calmed him like a strong tonic and assured him that there was still hope for this world.

Tamson was worth the boring parties, the endless nights of keeping a second set of books for the governor to send back to France to expose Bigot and his followers, and the torturous denial he'd imposed upon himself in dealing with the reality that sooner or later he would have to give her up. He had to, for her sake. He didn't want her here among the savages or facing another winter that would make the last look bountiful. Unlike most of his contemporaries, he held little hope that the crown would send sufficient food supplies for the troops, much less the habitants. The coming year would be one hell he could deliver her from.

"Monsieur Le Marquis! You must hurry. *Vite! Vite!*"

Alain bolted upright, snatched from his deep ponderings by the high pitched screech of the little man they called the tunnel mouse. Despite the hot weather, the derelict still wore his tattered blanket over his shoulders. It flapped comically as he hopped up and down in the open doorway.

"What is the urgency, Oncle Souris?"

His manner of begging ordinarily consisted of an extended gnarled hand, so it was unusual for the man to speak, much less appear so excited. Old Souris usually blended into the shadows of the buildings, or kept to his tunnels, although he had been spending more and more time in the alley behind Château La Tour. Isabelle complained he was like a stray cat and that Tamson was to blame for having fed him. But then, that would be Tamson's way.

"It is the *bonne marquee,* she is in danger! The Onondagas at the market . . ."

The squeaking declaration drove through Alain's chest like a stake of ice, seizing him in alarm. Waiting to hear no more, he ran out of the office after the old man.

The street leading to the Market Place was thick with traffic. Carts and wagons had slowed to a halt by the mixture of people there to shop and trade and visit crude stalls set up in haphazard fashion so as not to provide a thoroughfare. The sight of the chaos hindered Alain as he strained to see beyond a large produce cart for a quick way through.

"This way, monsieur. Souris, he knows a quick way to the Market Gate."

Frantic, Alain followed the old man into an alley, barely wide enough for him to pass through without turning. Once behind the warehouse belonging to one of the fur companies, Souris shuffled to what appeared at first to be a pile of broken crates. After moving them, however, Alain discovered a narrow hole about four feet deep. Ignoring his instinctive reluctance to try the tunnels, most of which were either flooded or caved in, he dropped in immediately after the old man. There was no time to be squeamish.

"Which way?" he asked, glancing dubiously at the dark stretches which branched away from them in three directions.

"Follow old mouse," his companion answered, his cackle far from reassuring.

Alain dropped to his knees, feeling the damp earth soak them, but obeyed. A hundred stories told about Oncle Souris and his subterranean habitation beneath the city failed to override Alain's initial panic at the old man's inference. Tamson was in danger in the market from Indians. That the savages were causing trouble was nothing new. There was no end to the complaints issued against them at the Château de Vaudreuil, most of which went unheeded. Allying oneself with the Indians required more tact than any of the diplomatic exchanges with the English.

But what was Tamson doing there, he wondered, having extracted her solemn vow never to go there, now that the warm weather raids had resumed. The very idea had left her decidedly pale and fear haunted her gaze as she'd given her word. Alain had been certain she would not break it.

So consumed were his thoughts as he stumbled to his feet after the old man in a slightly higher section of the blackness, that he lost track of his approximate whereabouts. The passage had run parallel to the walls of the city beneath the warehouses, but now had taken a turn. In the distance, a dim light filtered into the stone-lined space, silhouetting his companion's frail form. Suddenly, Oncle Souris fell back breathless against the wall and dropped to his knees.

"Go there, monsieur. You are beneath the trading post."

Alain reached the opening and moved the old boards covering it aside with a sweep of his arm. In a moment he was out of the dank, musty darkness. The ground was cool and drier beneath the wooden building raised by squat stone pillars above the floodline. Without bothering to brush off the dirt and sand that clung to his clothing, he pushed his way through the crowd to where four uniformed *troupes de la terre* had squared off before a small party of Indians, who had been trading stolen blankets and household goods for powder and the cheap brew the merchants often passed off to the redskins.

Behind them, a French officer held a dazed Tamson in his arms and shouted at the offenders brokenly in their tongue. While Alain had to give the young man credit for trying, he was not making much of an impression with the plunder-rich and brandy-satiated savages.

"What is the meaning of this?" Alain demanded in perfect Onondaga, disregarding his urge to claim his wife in order to disarm the brewing confrontation. "Who dares to assault the wife of one of the French chiefs?"

"Red Beaver wishes to buy her! He offers two horses, two blankets, and . . ."

"She is not for sale. Did you not look at her hand?" Alain lifted the cold, delicate hand of the woman in the officer's arms and turned it palm upward, along with the matching one of his own. "I claimed her on a raid with your Abernaki brothers. She is my woman."

"He is the chief of the blue jackets' powder and musket lodge. Black Otter will not be pleased if he is angered."

"Black Otter will not be pleased that his warriors have insulted his brother Beaujeu," Alain spoke up, producing a pouch of soft deerskin, decorated with beads and shells, from inside his shirt. From it, he took out a length of string, unimpressive in itself, but the pattern of knots and beads confirmed what Alain had declared.

Clearly startled, the Indians examined it and handed it back, studying Alain more closely. "It is him," one observed, his dark gaze sweeping over Alain once more. "We do not know our brother in these clothes."

Alain smiled. "I gave up my skins and mitasses to help the big chief supply his troops and allies. Tell Black Otter Beaujeu wishes him good hunting and many fine sons."

The Indian who had apparently started the confrontation nodded solemnly. "Beaujeu has the apology of Red Beaver." The brave reached down and took up a red blanket. "Take the blanket the fire squaw admired. It is my gift."

"Alain?" a small voice ventured behind him, distracting him as the Indian placed the present in his hand.

With frightened eyes only for him, Tamson squirmed out of the officer's grasp and stumbled toward Alain and into his arms.

"Take me home!"

"Shush, it is all right, *ma petite*. Look! See, they are leaving," he assured her, holding her as tightly as she held onto him.

She wouldn't look. Instead she buried her face against his chest, shivering uncontrollably, as the Indians picked up their goods and moved to another location.

"I thought we were going to have a fight on our hands for a moment, monsieur. The lady, she is really your wife?" The officer who had come to Tamson's defense appeared to anticipate the answer with a degree of disappointment his good breeding could not hide.

"She is, corporal, and I thank you for coming to her rescue."

"Alain, please . . ."

Instead of asking the officer what had happened, Alain gathered Tamson protectively under his arm. "But of course, *ma chérie.* Perhaps, corporal, you will find a carriage for the marquee and I and accompany us so that I might hear what transpired."

"A marquee?" the officer mumbled in surprise, taking in Alain's disheveled appearance once again. "But then that must make you . . ."

"The Marquis de la Galisonne, monsieur. Now if you would . . ."

"But of course, Monsieur le Marquis! Right away!"

The open carriage was reserved for the officers dining at the inn on St. Paul, but upon hearing that it was the lovely Marquee de la Galisonne who was in need of it, they gladly offered its use. When they arrived at the La Tour home on Notre Dame, Tamson was still deathly pale and shaking, despite Alain's attempts to reassure her. Her rose-patterned dress was stained from the swoon that left her lying in the dirt where the young officer had come to her aid and taken her into his arms.

"I would not have presumed so much, monsieur, but she was in such distress . . ."

"I understand perfectly, corporal. Again, you have

my thanks," Alain told the young man as he helped
Tamson into the house.

Isabelle met them in the hall and shrieked at the sight
of Tamson and Alain. *"Mon Dieu,* but what has happened?" she asked, looking past them at the timid officer who followed them inside.

"Tamson was frightened by the Indians at the market."

"But what took you to the market?" Isabelle exclaimed, taking Tamson into her arms like a mother hen.
"Has working at the hospital made you lose your
senses, Tamson?"

"I . . ." Tamson broke off and glanced uneasily at
Alain. Suddenly she shuddered, as if the sheer terror
that had robbed her of her consciousness had raised its
ugly face in her mind. "I'd like to change and lie down,"
she said at last, directing her request to Isabelle.

"But of course, *ma chérie.* Let Alain entertain his
guest and leave us women to ourselves. Henri!" her
hostess shouted. "Please bring up some blackberry cor-
dial and my tonic."

"I don't think I need . . ."

"You're white as a corpse," Isabelle countered
authoritatively as she urged Tamson on ahead of her up
the steps.

Alain stood at the steps until Tamson reached the top
and then turned away, but not before he caught the
searching look she cast over her shoulder at him. She
was in good hands with Isabelle, he told himself, ending
an inner debate with an inclination to dismiss the corporal and hear the story from Tamson. Besides, he
needed something to calm his own nerves, which had

sustained him sufficiently to see her to safety, but now, in the aftermath, were rapidly dwindling.

According to the corporal, he and his colleagues saw Tamson approach the marketplace and, struck by her beauty, continued to observe her at a discreet distance. She seemed distracted at first, as if she were looking for someone, and hardly saw the Indians until one shook the red blanket in front of her, giving her a start. When he dropped it and showed his tattooed face, she froze to the spot, unable to move until he matched one of the scalps on his belt with her hair, whooping in triumph. Suddenly the stricken marquee gave a bloodcurdling scream and swooned. Naturally, the corporal and his colleagues were instantly at her side and Alain arrived shortly thereafter to end the standoff.

"I believe he was trying to impress her with his wealth, but instead, frightened her witless," the corporal offered sympathetically before taking his leave.

He had to get her away from this place, Alain thought as he climbed the stairs later. Isabelle had said Tamson was resting, but was troubled that Alain might leave the house, so he could think of no better time to propose that she leave with Joseph and his family, although his cousin's wife had already warned him of the unlikelihood of his success.

"She is a woman in love, Alain. Like me, she believes her place to be with her husband, no matter how bad things might be."

But Isabelle did not know the full extent of what he had done, unlike Joseph. Alain had finally taken him into his confidence.

Alain quietly lifted the latch and stepped inside the room. The afternoon light was dimmed by the partially pulled shades and the trees growing in the back that sheltered the house from the western sun. A breeze toyed with the curtains, cooling the room despite the summer heat outside.

Tamson lay on the bed, her dark lashes fanned in repose against her cheeks, while her copper gold hair spilled in silken disarray over the pillow. She wore only a chemise of thin white cotton, baring her arms and dipping low over her breasts. From beneath its lace-adorned hem, her stockingless feet and a fair portion of leg peeked out. The linens had been neatly folded at the foot of the bed in the unlikely event that she feel chilled and need to pull them up.

Frozen at the sight of the serene sleeping beauty, Alain found his gaze gravitating back to the gentle rise and fall of the breasts he knew to be the perfect size for his hand. An inner voice warned him that retreat was the best tactic, for he could not be very persuasive with Tamson like this. How could he convince her to leave when he ached to take her to him and never let her go?

Instead, he turned his back to her and pulled his soiled shirt over his head. He would change his clothes and wait downstairs for her to awaken, he decided, working at the fastens of the trousers, black and still wet at the knees from crawling through a section of old Souris' tunnel. A hint of a smile curled at one corner of his mouth. Even the old derelict was enamored with the girl.

"Alain?"

Instead of shoving his trousers down over his hips as he'd been prepared to do, Alain approached the bed cautiously. "So you are awake. I tried to be quiet."

"I was waiting for you. I told Isabelle that I didn't need that blasted tonic, but I finally drank it to silence her fretting. She is such a dear. I think it's sad that she and Jeanette cannot be friends." Reaching over to the nightstand as she sat upright, Tamson deposited a handful of beads with a small crucifix on it. "I suppose Isabelle is too bound by her strict upbringing to allow for the freedom Jeanette enjoys here."

"What is this? A rosary?" Alain asked, arching one dark brow in surprise. "Don't tell me the nuns are making you one of them after all."

"Would you care, so long as it didn't reflect on your manly ego?"

From any other woman, the question might have been delivered with malice, rather than the earnest hope that lighted in her otherwise impassive gaze. Realizing he was treading on dangerous ground and yet reluctant to hurt Tamson any more than he already had, Alain sat down on the edge of the mattress. With a crooked finger he lifted the dimpled chin which could, when provoked, assume the most obstinate pose.

"It would be a sin in itself to allow such a gift to man to go unappreciated, neglected for the purpose for which God created it."

Even as he declared the words, he knew the trap he set with them. Tamson recognized it too, yet she did not make an issue of it. Instead she lay back against the pillow again, the telltale quiver of her chin the only sign of the hurt dealt by his well intentioned rejection. No matter what he did, he was damned, not only by this vulnerable creature in his bed, but by himself. The days when right was white and wrong was black had somehow slipped away, enveloped in grey clouds of war.

"Why did you go to the Place Royale today, Tamson?" It was a cowardly turn in the conversation.

Her gaze shifted from the open window to his own, suddenly widening with alarm as well as despair. "Something terrible is going to happen, Alain. You're going to leave me again. I feel it."

"Nonsense!" Alain replied, gathering her up in his arms. He stared at the ceiling as she clung to him, her fingers digging into the flesh of his back.

"Then why do you look so guilty? I've seen the way you watch me, as if you have something to tell me, but are holding it back." She raised her face to his, a small tear having escaped the corner of one eye. "I've tried so hard to be a good wife. I don't know what else to do, Alain."

"Tamson, how could you doubt . . ." Alain broke off at the edge of the same gaping hole he had just climbed out of. "If one of us leaves, *ma chérie,* it must be you. This is no place for you and it is only going to get worse. We are too busy arguing and cheating among ourselves to last as the victors of this conflict."

"Wh . . . what are you saying?"

"That I think it best if you go with Joseph and his family this fall." There, it was out.

"No!" She shook her head emphatically. "I won't leave you. I am your wife . . . and I hate ships," she added, as if that were the end of it.

"Tamson, look what is happening. The corn is once again rotting in the fields. Yes, there is meat now, but this winter, even horses will be scarce. And that hospital is no place for you. If you were to become ill, I could never forgive myself."

"Do you love me, Alain? And don't answer with another question this time. I need to know."

With an oath, Alain pulled away from her and paced to the other side of the room. *"Mon Dieu, madame!* Why do you think I am trying to keep you safe?"

"No bloody questions!" Tamson reminded him, slipping off the bed to her bare feet and closing the distance between them.

"I have wanted you so much that just to look at you makes me weak and aching. I tremble at your touch like a young pup with his first woman. I burn at the thought of your kiss . . ."

"So you avoid me . . ."

"Because you are my undoing, Tamson Stewart. You are my weakness, my . . . my addiction . . ."

"And reject me . . ."

Alain swung around to face her, his gaze as tormented as his voice. "Because you can never be mine, *ma petitesse!* Can you not see this?"

Tamson reached up, catching his face between her hands to stop him from shaking his head. The rich amber hue of her gaze smoldered, alive and full of emotion. "It is you who are blind, Alain Beaujeu. I *am* yours before the eyes of God and man . . . and if your Church does not recognize our love, then the devil with it! The only one I care about is you."

Alain turned away from the kiss meant to seal the argument once and for all. "And what about your father, Tamson? Do you think Squire Stewart will accept it?"

"By all that's truly sacred, Alain Beaujeu," the girl before him swore fervently, lapsing into her native tongue. "He has no choice. 'Tis only you that can decide, here and now, for I'll wait no longer. Do ye love me?"

"I do, Tamson Stewart, more than life itself."

Alain was stunned by the ease with which the words had come out. They shouldn't have. This was not what he planned. It had all gone wrong, as wrong as Tamson's inferring that he had a choice. There were times in a man's life when he had no choice and this was one of them. The choice had been made that night in the run-down fortress north of Quebec. He had made her his and, in doing so, he had become hers, body and soul. Dunce that he was in such matters of the heart, it had taken this long to realize and accept it.

Made brittle by the months of denial, the dam of emotions gave way. Astonishingly enough, the timid girl he had first made love to was just as anxious to divest him of his trousers and boots as he was to do away with the embroidered chemise. He could not move quickly enough, either for himself or for her, for the waiting had been too long and untethered desire coursed too strong through his veins.

They fell together onto the bed, their bodies entwining intimately even as they settled on the mattress. There was no time to move the seductress beneath him onto the pillows. He needed her there, now, stretched across the bed with her toes tripping up the back of his legs with such dire effect that he nearly forgot to be certain she was ready for him. Withdrawing from the sweet lips that were as hungry as his own, he reached for the burnished down of her womanhood with a shaking hand and discovered the moist invitation awaiting him.

Once again, he nearly lost his control and ground his

hard body against her soft yielding one as he struggled to recoup it. *"Dieu,* but I have never met a woman such as you, Tamson. You . . ."

The sight of her passion taut breasts heaving beneath him in anticipation demanded he wait just a moment more. They had tempted him too many times to ignore, warm and firm yet pliable to his touch. As if to punish them with the fiery lash of his tongue, he assaulted first one and then the other. In response, the girl beneath him raised her hips against him in a gyrating, imploring manner and then locked her limbs over his buttocks as if to remind him of his ultimate goal.

She met him as he claimed it, taking all he had to offer as eagerly as he gave it. As he bore her deep into the mattress, he ventured to lift his eyes enough to see her, this angel who, even as she gasped through parted lips, was taking him higher and higher into the heights of paradise. Her eyes, those beautiful bewitching eyes, were shaded, as if enjoying a tempestuous display of her own, boiling up from the perspiration-dewed body now writhing beneath him, while her hands kneaded his taut buttocks as if to force the building thunder in his loins into release.

Quick and torrid as lightning creasing a stormy sky, it obeyed the frantic loveplay, wracking Alain's body with convulsion after convulsion, while the straining globes beneath him quivered and shook with each one, as though they too rejoiced at the sudden ecstatic free-dom. It was only after he was completely spent that he noted his mate was trembling, too, and clinging to him as if she might fall from the clouds of heady fulfillment without him.

Rolling over to spare her his now dead weight, he

dragged her with him, careful not to break the intimate union. Tamson . . . *his* Tamson, he thought, returning the sheepish smile she gave him as she lifted her head. Her gaze met his and Alain felt a swell of emotion surge through him and within her, as if azure and whiskey had bonded as intimately as their bodies. Here was something he had never known with any other woman and he knew what it had to be. For better or worse, it was love.

Eighteen

Tamson left the hospital at noon the following day. She complained of a headache, but the fact was, she was exhausted. Her husband had not only remained with her the better part of the afternoon, but, after a short visit to his office, returned home for the evening. *Her husband.* She caught herself smiling again at the thought, as she had been ever since Alain had truly become so, in body and soul. *I do, Tamson Stewart, more than life itself.* That's what he'd said.

It had been impossible to hide from Isabelle and Joseph the fact that things had finally been resolved between them. Even Marielle noticed, long enough to tease her precious Oncle Alain for staring so at Tante Tamson, but she was so delighted with the red blanket Alain had brought back from the market that she was content to spend the remainder of her waking hours reading on it on the parlor floor. They had all but forgotten it until the little girl discovered it in one of the chairs in the hall and begged them for it.

With an uneasy glance down St. Paul toward Place Royale, Tamson pivoted toward the intersection with Notre Dame, a course which would carry her away from the nightmare of yesterday. Alain had allowed little time for her to consider it, for there was much time to make up for. Thankfully, the mutually longed for turn in their relationship had made her ardent lover forget his question as to the reason for her venturing into the marketplace.

It was of course a foolish thing to do, but Tamson could have sworn she recognized one of the gentlemen standing in front of the tavern on the corner of the market. As she started toward the group, he looked up, accidentally meeting her gaze, and then glanced away almost as quickly as she. His sudden departure from the group, however, left a lingering suspicion that she might possibly have been right; that the gentleman she saw was none other than Mark Heathcote, her fiancé from Carolina.

If there was anything at all to it, she reasoned, perhaps it was that the man was a cousin or relative of Mark's. After all, his grandmother's family was of Parisian origin. During his diplomatic assignment to Paris as an interpreter, where he had met Tamson, he had visited with them. It was not so far beyond logic, that one of them might be here in Montreal. Besides, Mark was assigned to Colonel Johnson's militia, no doubt holding out against the very troops Alain was responsible for supplying.

Preoccupied with her thoughts, Tamson did not see the man waiting by the break in the thick hedge lining the street until he stepped in front of her. Before she could so much as gasp, he had pulled her into the cover of the tall, neatly-pruned bushes, a gloved hand over her mouth. Slightly taller than Alain but of a slighter build, he whispered urgently in her ear in English, "Shush, Tamson. It's all right. It's me, Mark."

Although he immediately released her, it was some

moments before she could speak. After all, she had just rationalized that the man she had seen yesterday could not be the one standing before her now. Garbed in a wine-colored broadcloth jacket, his brown hair modestly powdered and tied back in a queue beneath a feathered tricorn hat, he looked like any other of the city merchants.

"You *do* know me, don't you?" he asked, concerned when she still had not spoken.

"It's just . . ." Tamson broke off, too staggered to think. Mark here in Montreal? But why? "It's just that I can't believe it!"

She glanced over her shoulder and was comforted that Mark had thought more of their privacy than she. The cover of the mulberry trees and boxwood hedges was ample to segregate them from the business on the street. As she turned back, Mark drew her to him and hugged her emphatically.

"God, I had almost given up hope of finding you! The thought of you captured by savages nearly drove me mad when I heard. Were you ransomed by the French?" he asked, releasing her just to arm's length.

"No, I was . . . Is that why you are here?" Tamson asked suddenly. "Are you a spy?"

She had no idea of the stirring effect her steady gaze had upon the man smiling down at her, almost as much as the rose flush that tinted her cheeks beneath her straw bonnet. It matched the ribbons which held it in place with a bow, setting off the dimpled chin he had once professed to be a sore temptation to kiss. All she saw was the kindling light that sparked in his dark brown gaze.

"I would prefer to think of myself as your ally, not

to mention your fiancé. I couldn't think of another, Tamson, and then to see you again yesterday, more lovely than ever . . ."

Emotion made his voice husky. He was going to kiss her. This Tamson did know. She stepped away, crossing her arms in front of her. "No, not here!" she managed.

Whatever was she going to do? Avoid being seen with Mark Heathcote, that's what, she decided quickly. To have lived among the enemy nearly a year and then get herself, and possibly Alain as well, hung for associating with an Englishman in their midst would be the worst irony.

"There is a fallen-down warehouse near the Champ de Mars. It was built from an old fortification. We will go there at once."

Although she did want desperately to speak with Captain Heathcote about home and her father, Tamson held back. "We can't go together."

"Aye, we can, my love . . . through the alley there."

Perhaps her trepidation showed more than she intended, for Mark kept a firm grip on her arm as he escorted her along the hedges lining the back properties of the establishments along Notre Dame until the Parish Church came into view. Before they emerged on the street, however, Mark led her through another smaller passageway between two buildings and into a side door.

This time, there was no avoiding the kiss he planted on her lips. It was chaste, compared to those she had shared with Alain, but then, Alain was her husband, not her betrothed. Tamson withdrew hastily. The first thing she had to do was be honest with Mark. She owed him that much.

"You mustn't do that!"

"There was a time you seemed to rather enjoy my attentions, Tamson."

Tamson swallowed dryly and tried to ignore the creepy atmosphere of the abandoned building. The light filtering in from the hole in the roof, instead of offering brightness in the dusty dark, only served to make it appear more ghostly, casting eerie shadows on the walls and giving the giant cobwebs an ethereal glow. There were probably rats. She refused to let her imagination go any further and concentrated on the matter at hand.

"Things have changed, Mark. I'm not the same woman I was."

"Whatever the savages did to you won't change my feelings toward you, my love. This bloody war has changed us all."

"I married my kidnaper."

"A savage?"

"No, one of my father's Acadian voyageurs, except that he was not Acadian, but a Marquis."

"He forced you?" Mark's voice had grown taut and dry as her own.

Tamson shook her head. "Not exactly. I . . . I don't recall." Upon seeing the incredulity threaten to unleash the building outrage in her companion's gaze, she added quickly. "I was captured by the Indians when I tried to escape from him and suffered amnesia. I witnessed the most horrible torture on this God's earth. The savages killed the man who helped me while I watched, but I was returned to Alain." She shuddered involuntarily. "When I came to my senses again, I was already married. He'd married me to protect me, my being English. He didn't even want to accept his inheritance as the

Marquis de la Galisonne, but he did, because he wanted to take care of me in a proper style."

"That's rather grand of him, considering he abducted you from your father's home and carried you into enemy territory."

Tamson winced inwardly at the bitterness in the young man's voice. "Alain had a reason. His stepfather was Acadian and his mother and sisters were exiled by the British in charge at Halifax. He knew of Father's influence with the Belchers and Lawrences and promised to return me as soon as Father could locate them. Alain was desperate!"

"Gad, Tamson, you sound as if you approve of the rogue!"

"He was wrong, he admitted that!" she blurted out in Alain's defense. "What was done was done. He couldn't undo it. Can you imagine his heartbreak, Mark? His father died from the shock of losing his farm and family and his mother and sisters have been shipped off to God knows where! I still cannot believe how inhumanely those poor people were treated!"

Mark grabbed her shoulders and shook her, as if to rid her of the nonsense she babbled. *"Inhumane* is what the Indians under the French leadership are doing to our own people! You just admitted you saw it for yourself! Strike me, what has he done to you, Tamson? Are you still affected from your capture by the Indians?"

"He frightened me at first. Then he taught me to trust him and now . . ."

"Now what?"

"Now he loves me."

"And?"

"And I love him."

Flinching at the muttered oath that escaped her companion's lips, Tamson backed away as Mark stormed over to a boarded window, staring as if he could see out of it. But for his tapping finger on the ledge, there was no other sign of the inner rage eager to be loosed. She feared that what she had to say would not lessen it.

"So if you came to rescue me, I fear it's too late. I cannot leave my husband's side." She held her breath, braced for another oath at the least, but her companion's ability to control his temper was admirable.

"I didn't come to rescue you, Tamson," Mark said after a while. "I thought you were dead, beyond rescue." He chuckled humorlessly. "Perhaps you are."

Tamson leaned against a support post, suddenly tired once again. She could not blame Mark for his reaction.

"After all, you are *consorting* with the enemy. I can well imagine Squire Stewart's reaction to that. It certainly won't help his current quandary."

"Quandary?" Tamson queried. "Is Father all right?"

"He is being investigated for trading with the enemy . . . buying goods plundered from English forts and settlements and selling them at a blood profit."

"Father would never do such a thing!"

Mark smiled crookedly. "His daughter married the enemy—why not?" Upon seeing her distress, however, the young man softened his tone. "I'm sorry. I'm not taking this in a gentlemanly fashion, I fear. The fact is, I'm certain your father's generous donations to the militia of supplies and monies will weigh heavily in his favor. I think Mr. MacShane has gotten too carried away with his vendetta against the black market, although he has netted some rotten fish."

Tamson twisted her pursestrings about her hand nervously. "Since you didn't know I had been abducted for a ransom, I suppose you don't know what, if anything, Father has found out about Alain's family, do you?"

"I should have known the day you brought that stray puppy to your hotel room that you had too kind a heart, the sort that would allow for a kidnaper's shortcomings and find a place in it for him. He treats you well, does he?"

"Oh, yes. He gives me everything I desire. He's a good man . . . *really,*" she emphasized.

The rakish twinkle that had once caught her eye and sent her heart aflutter lit in Mark's eyes as he shrugged. "What can I say? You have excellent taste in choosing your romantic interests." It was only his fixed smile that gave away the shallowness of his front.

Tamson straightened and glanced at the sagging plank door of the building, no more square than its frame. "Well, I had best be going before I'm missed. I had promised my niece that I would take a nap with her and share her new red blanket."

"From the Indians?"

Startled by Mark's curious interest in Marielle's blanket, Tamson nodded. "Why, yes. Alain got it yesterday in the market when that horrible Indian accosted me. I'd gone there looking for you. I thought I recognized you, but couldn't believe . . ."

"For the love of God, get rid of it!" As if catching himself, Mark forced indifference into his tone. "It's hard to tell what vermin infest it."

"Oh, I'm certain Isabelle washed it right away."

Then it was lost again, indecision and alarm taking its place. "Tamson, for your sake and the sake of the child, get rid of it. I'll find you another, if she must have one."

Tamson looked at her companion quizzically. "I'm not certain that the war has not affected *you*. Tell me why, for heaven's sake."

Instead of doing so, he turned away. "I can't. You will have to trust me, just as I have to trust you by letting you go." He glanced over his shoulder in gentle challenge. "I *can* trust that you will not let on that you know me, can't I, Tamson?"

"I would never endanger your life, Mark. It's just that I don't understand why . . ."

"Just trust me. Leave now and get rid of it . . . burn it."

"Why are you here, Mark?" she asked, her hand resting on the wooden bar latch on the alley door.

"It's as well that you don't know, Tamson. On that you must trust me, too."

"So I'll see you again?" The hinges creaked as she pushed against the rough planking.

"It's very possible."

Instead of answering, she nodded and stepped out into the damp muddy alley. Her slippers already wet and stained from the walk there, she paid them no heed and trudged out to the cobbled street in front of the Parish Church. Mark was right. It was just as well that she did not know his mission here. As for who he was, well that was something that belonged in the past, before she'd lost her heart to Alain Beaujeu.

Squinting in the afternoon sunlight, she started down the street toward Château La Tour. An open carriage carrying acquaintances of Isabelle and Joseph's passed, its passengers calling out to Tamson and distracting her momentarily. She returned the wave of the mother and daughter, both shaded by twirling parasols to protect their china-like complexions, and maintained her smile until they were behind her. What was she to do, if anything? And how was she going to explain to her family why she wanted to burn the Indian blanket?

The blanket issue was solved before she had even reached home. Marielle met her at the door in tears. "Oh, Tante Tamson, it is so horrible. Oncle Alain has hauled my blanket away to burn it! Those worthless *Anglais*, they have sent us diseased blankets!"

"Diseased!" Tamson echoed, a sickening feeling constricting in her abdomen and weakening her. "What do you mean *diseased?*"

"An English courier who was captured by Villier's *troupes de la marine* had documents telling of supplies of blankets infected with *petite vériole* abandoned purposefully, so that the Indians would take them back to their villages . . . *and ours,*" Isabelle La Tour answered from the parlor door.

Smallpox! God in heaven, Tamson prayed silently, holding the distressed Marielle even closer. *Dear God, don't let this little child come down with it. This isn't her war.*

Nineteen

Château *Ailleboust* blazed with light against a starlit summer sky. Located on the outskirts of the city, beyond which stretched fields of green tasseled corn, the home of one of Montreal's wealthiest merchants rang with the music of the ensemble hired for the occasion while wedding guests danced in its large hall and nibbled at the bounty piled on the tables in the dining room. The powder blue of the soldiers' uniforms was prevalent, for the groom himself was a captain in the *troupes de la terre* and the bride, one of Montreal's own lively beauties.

Clad in new ballgowns, Tamson and Isabelle held their own court of admiration. Isabelle fairly beamed with the attention paid the dress Tamson had had made for her that winter, while Tamson found herself aglow for entirely different reasons. She supposed that was a common consequence of love.

How long Alain had had the champagne ballgown, the order for which she had canceled with the seamstress at his request, was a mystery. All she knew was that when she returned to her room, there it was, laid out in all its splendor across the bed. For the first time, her husband actually helped her *into* her clothes, although he did delay long enough to accept her gratitude properly—or most improperly, depending on one's point of view.

With no time left to work on her hair, Tamson had simply swept it up off her neck, unfashionably without powder, and secured it with combs, leaving her dark honeyed curls bouncing to one side. Nor did she have time to dab more than a dot of rouge on her cheeks before Alain was standing at the door, handsome in a dark blue jacket and braided waistcoat over fetchingly fitted puce trousers tucked into polished knee-length boots.

Like her, he had done away with the hair powder, not out of the impatience with which he tapped his foot at the door of their boudoir, but arrogant disregard of any fashion practice he considered a bother.

"You do not need that! Why paint a masterpiece, *ma chérie?* Now come, we are going to be late."

"But I recall you saying we had plenty of time earlier," Tamson quoted mischievously as she scurried by him, her ample skirts gathered in her hands.

"Ah, but if we arrive early, we can leave early. I will need the extra time to get you out of all that nonsense you've bound yourself in!"

Now that they were truly husband and wife, there had been such a change in him. Not only was he at home at night more frequently, but he was always saying little things like that, teasing her until her heart warmed and her cheeks grew hot. Just as they were now, she mused, perusing the elegant room for a glimpse of her irascible escort and found him involved in conversation with Monsieur Chapais and Joseph La Tour.

As if he sensed he was being observed, Alain looked up, catching her eye. His genteel demeanor vanished with a roguish wink, which drew the attention of his colleagues to her as well. Tamson felt the initial warmth in her cheeks flare to full-fledged heat at the unsolicited male interest and would have turned away but for her husband, who motioned for her to join them.

"Monsieurs, permit me to introduce my lovely wife," he announced brightly.

His voice was a bit over-loud, giving her cause to wonder just how much of the imported wine he had ingested. She had never seen him overindulge in liquor and the idea, especially in his humor of late, was not altogether intolerable. In fact, it held promise, she thought, blushing even deeper at her own wicked musings. Love did have a way of corrupting one's thoughts, despite a lifetime of proper upbringing.

He met her halfway and escorted her the balance, placing her in the midst of the circle, as if to show off a cherished possession. "This, monsieurs, is my wife, La Marquee de la Galisonne. *Bonne madame,* these are Monsieurs Chapais and Ailleboust, whom you have met, I believe, and these are their business associates from our mother country, Monsieurs Bourdon and Ferrier, and the assistant who has allowed me more time to spend at home, Monsieur Marc Lepage."

Had the previous introductions not allowed Tamson enough time to compose herself, she might have indeed given away the fact that, regardless of his warning that this might happen, she knew the last gentleman. With the same smile she had assumed for the previous four, she presented her hand to her former fiancé.

"Now I see why the marquis is so anxious to get away from the office. I cannot say that I blame him,"

Mark Heathcote told her, fixing an admiring gaze upon her face as he lifted her hand to his lips.

She had hoped to forget he existed, even to the extent that she asked for an escort home each night, lest he be tempted to try to intercept her again. No one thought it odd, considering the episode that had happened in the marketplace. Yet, here he was, being introduced to her by her husband!

Alain had mentioned that someone recommended by the Marquis de Montcalm's camp had been assigned to his office, but never in her wildest imaginings did it occur to her that Mark Heathcote was that person.

"Since I have managed to afford him so much personal time, I hope that he will not object if I claim you for a dance later on," Mark went on, affording her husband a solicitous glance.

"I suppose I owe you that much," Alain conceded good-naturedly. "But for now, I will claim her myself. If you gentlemen will excuse me?"

Alain, in his exuberance, did not wait for their reply. Instead he hooked Tamson about the waist with his arm and swept her toward the hall, where the furniture had been cleared away for dancing. A group was forming two lines of equal length, due to the long, narrow floor space afforded. Like a child slipping into the door, just under the ring of the schoolmaster's bell, Alain snapped up the last place in a minor set and stepped away from Tamson to assume a starting position with a totally unceremonious grin.

The ensemble playing on the landing above the hall struck up a chord for the honors and he bowed gallantly to her curtsy. "I am the envy of every man here."

"I thought that I was the one with the intolerance for spirits, monsieur," Tamson teased.

"It is your presence, madame, that makes my spirits soar to the point that I feel the giddy goose." As if to demonstrate, he purposely stumbled and hurriedly fell back into a chassé, or sideward step. "So what do you expect from a simple Acadian voyageur?" he challenged in a louder voice to the couple next to them, whose shock was poorly disguised. "My saving grace is my exquisitely proper wife and your kind understanding."

"Think nothing of it, Monsieur Le Marquis." Madame Ailleboust's acknowledgment was as stiff as her posture. "My Panis has outdone herself polishing the floor, I must admit. She has improved greatly since Louis purchased her from the Iroquois."

Tamson didn't know whether to giggle outright or act horrified. As it was, one urge canceled the other, leaving a demure smile on her lips as she turned in time to the music to face the man on her other side.

"So, what do you think of Monsieur Lepage?"

The sobering question which awaited her return to Alain wiped the smile momentarily from Tamson's face. "What is there to think, monsieur? He has a charming way with words and I am equally indebted to him for sparing you time to spend with me."

She placed her left hand in his at her back, while assuming the same position with right hands at the small of his. The tickle of his fingers against her palm brought her gaze to his suggestive one, where she found no hint that suspicion about Mark Heathcote lurked there at all. They were supposed to be staring straight ahead, yet Tamson could not interrupt the heady message she was receiving until the time came when she had to link hands with the remainder of their set for a six-handed circle.

When they separated into couples again for a turn, Alain smiled at her smugly. "I told you you needed none of that rouge. No flower in all of Montreal can compare to the bloom in your cheeks, madame. I am tempted to ask you to marry me again, I am so stricken with admiration. You deserve a proper wedding, I think, with a grand reception like this one. We shall plan it before Isabelle and Joseph leave."

Such was her shock that this time it was Tamson who stumbled. She had had a second wedding in mind, a small ceremony performed by Père Anton, who had been teaching her in the ways of the Church. Her classes would be over shortly and what Alain was proposing was entirely possible. Forgetting about Mark and everyone around them, Tamson threw her arms about the man she already considered husband and kissed him scandalously on the mouth.

"Yes, yes, *yes!*" she answered, staring into his eyes with undiluted joy.

Disregarding the disruption they'd caused, Alain lifted a reproving brow. "I said I was *tempted*. I haven't asked yet," he reminded her impishly.

Her delight only slightly jarred, Tamson thumped him on the chest in mock disdain. "Dance!" she ordered, hurriedly resuming her position beneath the curious gazes cast their way.

"Monsieur Le Marquis, might I have your consent for the honor of dancing this next selection with your wife?"

"But of course, *mon ami*. It is the least I can do for

all your assistance of late." If Alain was upset, he failed to show it. Indeed, he acknowledged Mark's request and graciously placed Tamson's jeweled hand in his.

The cloud of happiness which had engulfed Tamson disappeared as Mark Heathcote claimed her and ushered her to a place in line. The harsher side of reality was back in full force as the musical ensemble struck up a lively tune. Its traveling steps combined with the allemandes right and left and the constant changes to circles required most of their attention and made conversation beyond small talk all but impossible. When it was over, however, Mark effectively brushed off her other offers to dance by declaring her thirsty and swept Tamson off to the punch table on the opposite side of the room from where Alain conversed with his colleagues.

Upon securing a fruity selection laced with choice brandy, rather than the unadulterated version beside it, Tamson found herself gently but resolutely ushered out to the gardens, which were terraced toward the narrow stretch of water separating the island city from the land side. In the distance was the Côte des Neiges road which crossed it, the route the La Tour coach had taken from the city through the moonswept fields on either side.

"At least he takes good care of you now, Tamson," Mark commented appreciatively. "A new gown?"

Tamson hesitated, thrown off guard by the unexpected observation. "Why, yes. How did you know?"

"The way the ladies were cooing and ogling, it was evident they hadn't seen it before. It appears the rumors of your husband's family's destitution aren't quite true."

"You haven't seen them attending the bevy of parties that have filled these last months, have you?" Tamson challenged, somehow put off by the cynical note in her companion's voice. "Alain has been carrying them financially. I purchased Isabelle's gown out of monies I made myself."

"Indeed? You've found yourself a vocation aside from nursing?"

"Painting," she answered smugly. "And I help with the cleaning and running of the house."

"Have you taken to eating salads and frogs as well? It wouldn't surprise me. After all, you've fallen in love with your enemy."

Tamson looked away to spare Mark the anger that flashed in her eyes. He couldn't help being hurt any more than she could help defending her new family. "Did you risk bringing me out here to demonstrate your powers of observation or just to show how boorish you can be?"

"No . . . to both charges," Mark added, his tone tinged with frustration. "I'm paid to be observant and I didn't mean to be boorish. It's just that . . .Tamson, I'll be leaving soon. When I do, it will be abruptly."

He placed a hand on her shoulder, his fingers tentatively testing the softness of her shoulder where the gathered pale gold brocade fell away provocatively. It was like the darker velvet trim which adorned it, so very soft and feminine.

"I'm asking you once again. When I go, come with me back to your home, where you belong."

Tamson stared at the quicksilver ribbon of water beyond the garden. "My place is with my husband, Mark. I'm very sorry, but I can't change what has happened, what separated us, any more than I could leave him now. Please try to understand."

The tender touch of his fingers suddenly chilled, harsh and biting as a northern wind. "Understand?" Mark turned her toward him, his expression a mingle of incredulity and anger. "The woman I love wants to wallow in the throes of defeat with an enemy who allies himself with savages that slaughter her own innocent people?"

"We're not so innocent, Mark," Tamson retaliated stubbornly. "We exiled peaceloving people, separating families, mothers from children, men from wives! We confiscated their property and are handing it out to our own, without the slightest twinge of conscience! Innocent?" she repeated, her voice rising with a slight tremor. "How innocent are the ones who ordered blankets infected with smallpox to be abandoned to the Indians, knowing they would be taken back where women and children would be wrapped in them?"

"Dear God, you destroyed the blanket, didn't you?"

"Alain did," Tamson informed him succinctly. Although there had been a report of a smallpox outbreak in one of the Iroquois villages, nothing of consequence had evolved in the city. The sisters at the Hotel Dieu, however, were treating each case of fever with extra caution. "You knew, didn't you? You knew before your enemy found you out."

"This is war, Tamson."

"Not against women and children!"

"All right, *both* sides are guilty!" Mark conceded, exasperation invading his speech. "But war is that way. Innocents suffer right along with the guilty."

"Oh, I'd wager not! The guilty are sitting somewhere in a comfortable office handing out these senseless orders. They're the ones they ought to put on the front lines, not the poor devils who have no choice but to follow orders like the deaf, dumb, and blind."

"Madame, mon Dieu, take pity on this poor man! He, like myself, is among the deaf, dumb, and blind! It is not he who is responsible for the hostilities."

"Alain!" Tamson gasped, startled by the nearness of her husband's voice. She turned to see him standing on the steps of the mansion. How long had he been there? A quick glance at Mark told her her companion was thinking much the same thing.

Alain came down off the small portico and strolled toward them, her light cloak thrown over his arm, indicating their impending departure. "And to think I came out here to rescue my wife from a persistent admirer, only to find *him* in need of rescue. When Madame La Marquee wishes to make a point, her voice tends to rise with her fervor."

"Your wife does not approve of this war."

"Who does?" Alain quipped good-naturedly. "It's a worthless nuisance for most of us, is it not? Only the corrupt profit. That is the way of war." He draped the cloak over Tamson's shoulders and fastened it with marked authority.

"We're leaving?" Tamson ventured, her heart still frozen within her chest at Alain's unexpected appearance.

"Oui, we must, I am afraid. Henri has sent word that Marielle is ill. Isabelle and Joseph are seeing to the carriage now."

The fear which had haunted the La Tour household since the destruction of the possibly infected blanket hardened within Tamson's chest like a block of ice as she met Alain's somber gaze. Of them all, Marielle was the one who had slept on the blanket and the most likely to suffer for it. Yet, the child had been playing that afternoon and happily helping her mother and Tamson dress. The only sign of distress was because she was not able to go with them.

If anything happened to Marielle, she'd never forgive herself for breaking her word and venturing into the market . . . and she certainly would never forgive Mark!

By the time they arrived at the La Tour house, the physician had already completed his examination. The child suffered with a high fever. What it was a prelude to was a matter of question at this point. The cook had become concerned when the child appeared pale and would not eat her supper. Upon checking the little girl, she was running a fever and, in lieu of the reported outbreak of smallpox among one of the Iroquois villages, Henri immediately sent for them as well as the physician.

"It could be just one of those childhood things," Alain consoled Tamson later as they lay in each other's arms. Beside the bed on the chair were the layers of clothing and accessories he had helped Tamson out of, but not in the original spirit of passion spawned at the party. They were both worried about their niece.

Isabelle insisted on staying the night in Marielle's room, leaving Tamson to get a good night's sleep so she could relieve her in the morning. It was hoped during that interim that the fever would break.

"I cannot count the nights my mother spent up with my sisters—three, mind you," Alain specified, "only to have them up and running about the next day as though nothing had happened. Children are like that."

Tamson wasn't certain just whom her husband was

trying to convince as he continued to stare at the ceiling. He loved the little girl in the other room as much as his sisters. Her heart swelled. He had enough love for them all and her besides. Leaning up on one elbow, she bussed him on the tip of his nose.

"What was that for?"

She smiled lazily. "For being you."

He returned the gesture. "And that was for being you, madame, although sometimes when you are yourself, I worry."

Tamson cocked her head at him indignantly. "And just what does that mean?"

"It means when I find you discussing politics with my colleagues, my knees get, how do you say, full of water?"

"They turn to water," Tamson giggled. "But why?"

"Because I don't want anything to happen to you, *ma petitesse.*" He brushed her hair back behind her ear gently, his gaze boring deeply into her own, pouring out loving concern for her. "I worry that in your enthusiasm for your ideals, that you might let something slip which could jeopardize you . . . *us!*" he added, in such a way as to melt her heart.

Nor did Tamson want anything to come between them, not now that the troubled waters separating them had been bridged by their love. She reveled in the way Alain stroked her body—touching, kneading, teasing until he had maneuvered her beneath him, his passion-hard flesh as eager as her yielding desire to meld as one. She basked in his warm gaze, watching the hunger glower there as it did in her own.

As he dropped down to nuzzle her breasts, savoring each in turn as if it was a mere morsel of that which he

craved, she purposely forced all thought of Mark Heathcote from her mind. She wanted no hint of the quandary
in which Mark had placed her. Out of love and loyalty,
she would not leave Alain. Out of loyalty and obligation
to the man she had inadvertently jilted, she would not
tell her husband about Mark. If that made her a traitor,
she couldn't decide. All she knew was what her heart
compelled her to do. Love left her no choice.

Twenty

Marielle suffered from the measles. As Alain had predicted, the fever was one of those childhood things. Yet, when a few days later he found himself confined to bed with the same fever and rash, he was no longer smug. It seemed that, while all his sisters had suffered the disease at an early age, Alain had escaped it and considered himself immune.

When the "childhood thing" he'd alluded to put him in bed for a full week, his frustration, and consequently everyone else's, knew no bounds. That Tamson could hardly stifle her amusement at the sight of him, peppered with a rash as he lay against his pillows, did not improve his humor.

Because of his confinement, however, Mark Heathcote was forced to visit Château La Tour daily and keep Alain appraised of the activity in the office. Tamson made any number of excuses to leave the room, fearful of betraying their previous acquaintance, although Alain was so involved in his work that she doubted he'd notice.

If Alain knew he was speaking with an English spy, much less that she was aware of it and had not told him, Tamson was certain he'd never forgive her. He'd come to trust Mark, enough to involve him in a subterfuge of his own, sending confiscated goods from La Friponne to the starving Acadian refugee camp. Both men agreed that there was no one better to steal from than the thief himself.

The three weeks Mark was away helped to assuage Tamson's guilt for her reluctant deceit, although Alain went straight from his bed to the office to take over. Well, almost. Once the fever and aches subsided and the rash was all he suffered, he abandoned his irate manner at being confined to take advantage of the time to a most devilish end. The time she spent in his room had actually become an embarrassment, despite the fact that they were man and wife.

It would become even more so, if what she suspected was correct. Not that Tamson would mind Isabelle's teasing at all, were the fact that she was well overdue for her monthly inconvenience. The very idea brightened her face even more as she left Château La Tour and started toward the Parish Church on her way to the hospital.

Late-arriving patrons and carts bound for the market were coming in from the fields beyond the city by the Côte des Neiges road. Sooner than follow their route, however, and risk getting involved with that traffic, she turned down a side street by the nunnery's gardens and cut through them to the hospital itself.

If a baby was indeed on the way, it was just as well that she was all but finished with her studies in catechism, for, busy or nay, a wedding would have to come and soon. Somehow she didn't think Alain would object, much as he hated such formal occasions. Naturally, they would keep it small, she thought, ever mindful of the austerity enforced by the war. Whatever it was to be, all that mattered was that they would be truly man and wife.

Upon emerging from the nunnery's serene enclosure, now bright with summer's flowering beauty, Tamson's personal excitement was superseded by yet another in the waiting hospital corridors. The confusion was beyond that normally created by the return of French soldiers from a march. Beds were being filled as the men were brought in, as usual, but it was the chatter that seemed unusually ceaseless and pitched to a fervor. Something was definitely amiss.

By the time the day at Hotel Dieu had come to an end, Tamson had heard enough about Montcalm calling back the offensive on Chouaguen to believe the rumors this time. A note from Alain confirmed the urgency of another march permeating the air. He would be home very late, if at all, he'd written. Soldiers were passing all about her, each bent on carrying out his own duties, so that there was no one available to see her home.

Although Tamson wasn't thrilled with the idea of walking the streets unescorted, the sun was still bright in the west because of the long summer days. Besides, the Market Place was usually abandoned by now, the vendors having returned to their homes further inland or across the St. Peter's.

Keeping to the main streets, thick with soldiers moving about with a purpose, Tamson perused the shop windows, those that had not already been shuttered, when she heard someone call out her name from across the street. Turning in surprise, she saw Alain's younger cousin making his way toward her. No doubt he had just left the tavern on the corner, where a sign depicting

King Louis in uniform astride a white horse swung over the door.

"Bonjour, madame! It has been many weeks since I have been treated to your company and that of my family. I take it all is well?"

"Alain and Marielle have suffered the measles, but aside from that, all is the same."

Armand cocked his head at her in a dubious fashion as he slipped his arm through hers. "How is it that you stood my cousin in your boudoir during that time? That is to say, you have not exactly been enamored with him."

What was it that made this man so spiteful where Alain was concerned! Tamson reined in her question behind a tolerant smile. "It was my pleasure, monsieur, not that that is any of your business. We had spent so little time together since arriving in Montreal, what with his work demands."

Armand stopped short, halting Tamson as well. "Come now, *Mademoiselle Stewart,* you needn't continue your charade for me."

"Armand, will you stop slandering my husband and myself! Just because you have made yourself miserable with your gambling and drink, is no reason to inflict your sorry attitude on others!"

Tamson withdrew her arm irritably. "You are not an unattractive man and can be perfectly charming when you are sober! The problem is, you are rarely sober."

Instead of taking offense or showing the least remorse, her companion offered a patronizing smile. "That, mademoiselle, is what I intend people to think, but I can assure you, despite the liquor I have purposely spilled on my coat, I am very much in possession of my senses when I am on duty."

Armand had always made her feel ill at ease and at that moment Tamson felt even more so than usual. At any rate, she was not going to argue with him in this strange humor of his.

"If you are on duty, monsieur, then do go about it and leave me be. I'll not listen to your petty insults to Alain."

She would have stepped around him, but he blocked her path and, to her astonishment, grabbed her wrist with a steel grip.

"What *are* you doing, monsieur? Alain will not understand this at all!"

"Doing my duty, mademoiselle. You can come peacefully to the Citadel like a lady or I can take you in, bound like a common thief. Either way, you are under arrest."

He was mad! Tamson thought. "For *what?*"

"Espionage, what else?"

"But . . ."

"You are the daughter of an Albany merchant, not a Scottish trapper, and your mother is English, not French. You were educated in England and kidnaped by my cousin in his zeal to find his Acadian family, whose loyalties are also under serious investigation. He has presented you to everyone as his wife when we both know, mademoiselle, that no such marriage took place."

How she remained standing with the tide of weakness that washed over her was beyond Tamson's understanding. Of course Armand could not know that their marriage was invalid, solely because of her non-Catholic faith.

"I don't believe you. Alain said we were married."

Armand chuckled to himself. "A clever one, my cousin . . . *in some ways*. I am not certain even I would have the audacity to carry off such a deception."

Incensed that he should cast such doubt on Alain, Tamson slapped him soundly on the cheek with her free hand, the sting of her palm leaving its imprint on the officer's clean-shaven face. "You should be ashamed to suggest such a thing!"

"Mademoiselle, you will not do that again. The next time, I shall retaliate, I promise!" he swore in such a manner as to leave no doubt as to the validity of his threat. "I also promise that if you tell us the name of your English accomplice, that I will recommend you for a prisoner exchange rather than the hangman's noose. And do not deny this. We have intercepted his courier with a message to your father, telling us all about your liaison."

Moving once again under the force of her companion's escort, Tamson stumbled for footing. He was wrong about Alain, but not about Mark. Her worst nightmare was unfolding and she could not gather her wits enough to stop it. She glanced about her frantically, searching for anything, any means of escape. Who would have believed the drunken Armand was a member of French intelligence?

"Please!" she managed, struggling sufficiently to slow Armand's deliberate stride. "Don't take me down the main streets. Think of your family, if not me," she implored fervently. "Besides, when you discover I am innocent, neither of us will look foolish."

A gaze much like that of her husband's studied her frightened expression. "Very well, mademoiselle," he conceded graciously. "However, I would have you think very carefully about telling me the name of your English admirer. I do not think Alain would be as objective as I were we to call him in to question you."

Tamson felt ill with fear, but held her head erect as she walked at her captor's side through a back alley. The light was quite dim, yet, even so, Armand seemed to possess the instincts of the rat that he was. Whatever was she going to do, she thought, scanning the dim shadows for anything she might use to escape.

In the corner of her eye, she caught a glimpse of movement. Before either she or Armand could react, a man lunged from his crouched position behind a rain barrel and brought the butt of a pistol down across the back of her escort's head.

Tamson's belated scream was abruptly smothered by the hand of Armand's assailant. Nonetheless, it rang loudly from within, almost deafening her to the man's plaintive command.

"Quiet! It's only me . . . Mark!"

Relief usurped the panic that stiffened her body, its tears welling in her gaze as he loosened his grip and turned her toward him. Upon seeing them, however, he gathered her back to him.

"It's all right, Tamson."

"Oh, Mark, he . . . he thinks I'm a spy!"

"I suspected as much when I saw him confront you on the street. You looked like death had apprehended you." Mark smoothed her hair gently away from her face. "Did he say how he knew?"

Tamson thought a moment, her mind a tumbling daze. "They intercepted one of your couriers with a message to Father."

Mark uttered an oath, the exact words politely distorted for his companion's sake.

"What am I to do?"

"What I've been telling you all along. Come with me." A moan from Armand drew his attention. "After we dispose of this gentleman." He drew a knife from his boot. "You'd best turn your back, love."

Seized with alarm, Tamson grabbed his arm. "No, you can't!"

"Tamson, he knows about us!"

"I won't let you kill him! He's Alain's cousin!"

"I don't care if he's my own! It's his life or ours!"

"Can't we just tie him up and hide him until you escape?"

Mark started to argue when his intended victim moaned again. With a swift blow from the hilt of his knife, he quickly rendered the man back into a deeper state of unconsciousness.

"Would you have us both hang for his sake?"

Tamson stood her ground, her chin set stubbornly. "I won't let you kill him."

Instead of vocalizing his irritation, Mark unleashed it by ripping his victim's belt from his trousers and proceeded to bind Armand La Tour's hands behind his back. A handkerchief served to guarantee his silence and the man's scarf proved useful to decommission his feet.

His disposal, however, was another matter. Damnation, he couldn't believe he was letting the bloke live! He searched the alley urgently. "Stand back," he warned, the means coming into view, "and keep watch!"

Twenty-one

The fading sun having dropped behind the building across the street, it was impossible to continue processing the lists of supplies requisitioned for Montcalm's impending march to Chouaguen, at least without lighting lamps. Irritated that the task might have been done had Marc Lepage returned from his afternoon summons to the Château de Vaudreuil, Alain shoved the manifests in the top drawer of his desk and slammed it shut, venting some of his tension in the process. What he would not give to spend a few days among the *couriers de bois* in Prairie, celebrating the last season's success and preparing for the next!

Jacques Dupré had stopped by that morning, but the choking responsibilities of Alain's office barely afforded enough time to complete their business, much less go across the street to the tavern to share a drink with his friend and partner. The governor's office was satisfied with its share of the pelts and Alain was more than pleased with his cut of the under-the-table investments Gaspar and Jacques had made for him behind enemy lines, where the gain was much higher. The news from Albany, however, was less satisfying.

Alain scowled, wondering not for the first time since Jacques' departure if he should tell Tamson of her father's misfortune. Damn the man—dealing furs with the *couriers de bois* was one thing. It was accepted and practiced by those higher up in colonial influence than Stewart. Alain himself was involved in such an alliance.

Trafficking plundered goods from the savages, however, was another. At least, that was what the man had been accused of. Somehow, Alain found it hard to believe. Squire Stewart was a shrewd businessman, not a fool, and certainly not a traitor! There was a code of ethics, even among the black-market traders.

The young man heaved a sigh and tossed his jacket over his arm. Regardless, the chance of Stewart's helping find Marie La Tour and her daughters was almost nonexistent now. With the aspersions cast against him, Belcher and Lawrence, the masterminds of the Acadian exile, would not likely continue any association with him.

Alain swore beneath his breath as he reached for the door latch. There had even been speculation that the squire would lose his land and holdings, not to mention his life. While Alain wanted Tamson as his wife, he didn't want her this way, robbed as she had been of her past which she'd held dear. No, he decided, he would not tell Tamson. He'd . . .

Alain's introspection claimed his attention so completely that when the door burst open, he narrowly missed being driven against the wall by the unexpected intruder. Carrying with him a peculiar stench beyond that of his customary liquor, Lieutenant Armand La Tour staggered into the office and caught himself on the desk. Disheveled and breathless, he spun about and caught his obviously aching head in his hands.

"*Dieu*, but I am undone!"

"Drunk appears to be the more appropriate word," Alain observed dispassionately. His cousin had an uncanny habit of appearing when things were going badly, proving the proverb that they could always be worse. "Have you been sleeping in an alley or . . ." He broke off as Armand removed a bloodied hand from the back of his head and wiped it on his sludge-stained leg. That was what the smell was, the greenish brown slime found in stagnant water. *"Mon Dieu,* but what have you done to yourself this time?"

"I have done nothing, monsieur. The damage was done by your wife's lover."

"You must have hit your head too hard, *mon ami."*

Armand winced as he pressed the bloodied scarf he'd pulled from his belt to the back of his head. "I arrested Tamson for espionage, Alain."

"You *what?"*

Alain's incredulity was sufficient to hide the icy panic which thrust itself mercilessly through his chest at the mention of Tamson and espionage in the same breath. Armand's penchant for stirring up trouble had gone too far this time. He grabbed the front of his cousin's coat roughly and shook him, as if to remove the incriminating link from his liquor-sodden brain.

"You idiot! Where is she?"

"Off with her English lover, I presume," his uninvited guest managed through the choking constraints of his collar. "He hit me from behind and . . . and that is all I know, except that I awakened stuffed in a barrel. But for some children playing in the alley, I would still be there."

"Where's Tamson?" Alain demanded once more.

"I will tell you what I can if you will but allow me sufficient air."

Reluctantly, Alain complied, although the temptation to strangle his troublesome younger cousin was great. He fought back the runaway emotions rioting within and backed away with measured deliberation on the off chance that Armand *was* in possession of his wits and Tamson was indeed in danger, rather than dining with his family at that very moment.

"Then be quick about it, monsieur. If my wife has been abducted, I would rather set about finding her than listening to your absurd accusations."

Once assured that Alain did not intend to throttle him, Armand restored his jacket to order with obvious indignation. The glare he shot back at his barely restrained assailant, however, was not that of an intimidated man. It was almost smug, as though he were enjoying some superior grasp of the situation as yet unrevealed.

"Among my other vices, *cousin,*" Armand enunciated without the least hint of affection, "I work for the French intelligence."

The very shock of Armand's revelation was sufficient enough to fuel Alain's existing alarm over Tamson's safety to full-fledged fear. He had gravely underestimated his frivolous cousin, he realized, as the man went on to explain his reason for arresting the Marquee de la Galisonne. With each unfolding detail, Alain leaned more and more against the back of his desk chair, as if, ounce by ounce, he was being drained of strength. He knew instantly who the spy was.

He'd had a few suspicions concerning Tamson and his new assistant. Armand merely confirmed them. Tamson *had* met Marc Lepage before. They had been romantically involved. Except, Alain had actually hoped Tamson would admit to having met Marc during her year's study in Paris, that he was no more than an old admirer. The world had been known to be so small as to allow for such reacquaintances.

Oddly, the fact that Marc Lepage was English and a spy was the hardest part to accept. Even though Alain had been giving his suspect assistant enough leeway to incriminate himself, both romantically and politically, he'd liked the young Frenchman who had restored his faith in his fellow countrymen. He'd hoped that the surveillance he maintained of Lepage's activities would amount to naught but an excuse for some unfounded jealousy. While love had not dulled his instincts to make him the total fool, he had, he realized, become careless.

Even as Alain digested the impact of Armand's information, the final missing piece to the puzzle fell into place. The missive to Squire Stewart, which was intercepted by the French, had been written by an outraged lover. If Alain recalled correctly from her furious threats early on in their acquaintance, Tamson's fiancé had been called *Mark* and was a Carolina planter's son—a fact that would easily account for his excellent command of the French language.

Who else could Marc Lepage be, but Tamson Stewart's fiancé? It fit too well to be coincidence, he thought morosely as Armand finished his story with an account of being discovered in an old back alley rain barrel by a group of boys playing hide and seek.

"It is hard to tell when I would have been found, had one of the little fiends not chosen my barrel to conceal himself."

"So what is it that you propose, cousin?" Alain asked warily.

"No one else knows except my superior, if you are concerned about your . . . *mistress*. I do not think the girl is guilty of anything except harboring the identity of a spy. If we can but find them, she might be spared for a prisoner exchange."

Instinct told Alain that more was amiss than capturing a spy, despite Armand's admission of his actual profession. For one thing, his cousin was deliberately trying to provoke him. Determined to keep cool, Alain let the slanderous reference to Tamson pass for the moment.

"You haven't alerted the guards to look for a spy trying to escape the city?" he queried. An officer of the intelligence surely would not overlook so important a detail.

Armand smiled slightly, caught in his lie. "I have told them that a spy has been suspected of kidnaping the Marquee de la Galisonne as a hostage to escape the city and must be stopped at any cost."

Such as Tamson's life? The idea churned in Alain's stomach. "How astute of you."

"If you help me, cousin, it will certainly look better for you. I'd rather be a cuckolded husband than a traitor."

Once again, Alain overlooked his cousin's poorly veiled glee. He was frantically trying to think where Marc and Tamson might be hiding out, for surely they would wait until dark to make good their escape. The marquee was too well known to sneak out of the city in broad daylight . . . *unless she went willingly.*

He steeled himself against the cold blade of that suspicion. "I know of a place to start looking."

"Good!" Remarkably recovered, Armand slid off the corner of the desk and started for the door after Alain. "You will not regret your cooperation, *mon ami.*"

Alain turned abruptly in the entrance, momentarily stilling the rampant emotions tearing from within lest they be betrayed in his voice. "She is no spy," he stated flatly.

"Oh, I agree, monsieur. The lovely marquee is but a means to catch one, nothing more."

A means to catch one. To Armand, perhaps, Alain mused disconsolately. To him, Tamson Stewart meant everything. He inhaled deeply with renewed resolve. He'd fight his cousin and all of New France if he had to to save her. Her danger had been brought on by him, not the Englishman. Had he been Tamson's betrothed, he would be doing exactly what Marc Lepage, or whatever his name was, was doing—taking her back. Again the gnawing question haunted his mind: had she gone willingly?

It was dark enough now that the lanterns were being lit along the streets. Soldiers, both on and off duty, were still everywhere, but afforded Alain and the disheveled Armand little more than a disdainful glance. They would be marching before the week's end and there was too much revelry available in the interim to bother with a drunken officer and his civilian companion.

"You are going *away* from the waterfront!" Armand observed, dubious and confused when Alain turned up St. Jean Baptiste. "Do you not think they would try to escape by sea?"

"I am going to the only place I know that they have met!" Alain snapped impatiently.

Dieu, but he hoped they would not try to escape by land. A Carolina planter, for all his military training, did not stand a chance of making it safely back to the colonies cross country, especially with a woman in tow. Not even Alain had dared such a feat with all the Indian and military action separating Montreal from Albany.

"Monsieur! Monsieur Le Marquis!"

"Get out of here, you shriveled little rat! We've no time for the likes of you!"

Alain turned in time to see Armand kick the old man known as Oncle Souris, sending him sprawling into the mud of the street.

"Wait!" Pushing past his cousin, Alain stooped over to help the elderly soul to his feet and brushed at the stains on his tattered clothing. "I apologize for my cousin, Oncle Souris. We were in a hurry to go to the old warehouse on the north side of town. Do you know it?"

Oncle Souris cut a suspicious glance at Armand La Tour and rubbed the bearded chin that almost touched his long, narrow nose. Although he appeared bewildered, his small eyes were bright and alert, confirming that he had understood Alain's subtle message.

"Oui, your old oncle, he knows it. The things I could tell you about that place," he cackled, slapping the patched knee of his trousers.

"Alain!"

"A moment!" Alain answered his irate cousin with equal impatience. "Have you seen *rats* there, Oncle?"

Souris grunted. "Humph! That's where they began to take over my tunnel . . . big ones, *pretty* ones . . ."

That was all Alain needed to know. They had gone to the place where Oncle Souris had frantically reported to Alain that the marquee had been taken not long after Marc Lepage arrived in Montreal. As he started to pull away from Souris's claw-like grip, however, it tightened.

"But they are not there now."

"What the devil is the old fool running on about?" Armand demanded.

Alain swallowed his exasperation. "Do you know where the rats are, Oncle?"

Souris cast a wary look at Armand once more. "I know a lot of things," he evaded with decided pique. "More than an *old fool* is given credit for, I might add."

"I fear for her safety, Oncle."

The hardness in the old man's gaze wavered as he turned back to the husband of the kind mistress he'd kept dutiful watch over. "I took you there once, monsieur. You meant to save your kind wife that time as well."

The trading post on the Market Place! That was more like it, Alain thought, clapping the old man gratefully on the back. "I owe you much, *mon ami,* but this will have to do for now." Reaching into his pocket, he fished out a coin and folded in Souris's gnarled hand.

"Your charity becomes you, Alain, but do you think this is the time?" Armand asked, breaking into a sprint to catch up with his cousin, who was making haste through the dark shadows of a hospital on their right.

"That was not charity, monsieur. I rewarded Souris for telling me where your spy is," Alain called over his shoulder. "There is little that goes on in this city that Oncle Souris does not see."

Although the old man had him wondering for a moment if he'd not lost his mind for trusting him, Alain mused. Still, even half mad, Souris had come through. He was devoted to his pretty marquee and was always lurking about, so Tamson had once confided to Alain after pointing out the old man peeking around the corner from one of the alleys as they'd walked one evening from the Hotel Dieu.

When Alain had rewarded him with a coin for alerting him to Marc's initial rendezvous with the marquee, Souris became diligent in keeping a watchful eye on both parties. Tamson had been coerced into accompanying the man that time. She'd been clearly upset, according to Souris. But was it the same now?

But for a single candle braving the darkness in the well-provisioned storehouse next to the trading post, there was no other light. A canvas had been pulled down over the shuttered windows and an old blanket hung over the door, lest even that filter through the cracks of the ill-fitting frames to call attention to the building's occupancy. The shadows of stacked barrels, crates, and bags were cast upon the ceiling, taking all manner of hideous shapes and seeming to move with the slightest draft.

Although the warmth of the summer day still lingered, Tamson was cold. The very thought of dropping through that hole in the floor and crawling through the damp, dark tunnel beneath filled her with dread. Yet that was nothing compared to the despair that filled her heart and soul and kept her on the edge of tears.

Mark had made her situation clear, despite her attempts to rationalize the merit of remaining behind with her husband. If Armand La Tour knew that she had harbored an English spy's identity, then his superiors also knew. She was an accomplice by association.

Since Alain had no idea of her crime, he was likely to suffer being labeled a fool rather than a traitor. His work for the Governor General would rest in his favor. At least, that was what Mark had told her.

Tamson was no more certain of that than she was of anything else at this point. All she knew was that her heart felt as if it were being stretched in two and she was helpless to stop it. Alain would not understand. He'd never forgive her her inadvertent treachery. Then there was the possibility of the baby . . .

"There, love. I promise, everything's going to be all right. It's the waiting that's the hardest."

No, it was the leaving! That's what she wanted to cry out to the man who had brought all this about. Instead, she allowed Mark his misunderstanding of her quiet tears and accepted the warm and comforting arm placed about her shoulders. Her desperation craved solace, whether it was born of the right sentiment or not.

Besides, she could not truly hold Mark accountable. Like Alain when he'd kidnaped her, her companion had done what he felt he had to do. They were all victims of the war.

Inevitably, however, he would have to understand that things could never go back to the way they were. Her girlish infatuation had been replaced by a woman's love that no amount of gallantry and understanding on his part could change.

And Mark had been quite chivalrous, Tamson admitted with a degree of gratitude as she ventured a look at his somber countenance. Despite the natural anger and frustration that flashed in his gaze only when she exasperated him to his limit, he had been as gentle with her as time and circumstance would allow. Were their positions reversed, she doubted her more volatile husband would be as understanding . . . at least, at first.

Now that she knew the real man behind his quick temper, his less reserved manner was one of the things that excited her about Alain. Her heart constricted once again. She would not ever truly live without him again, especially if she was with child. She closed her eyes to hold back her utter despair as Mark tenderly hugged her to him.

"I still love you, Tamson," Mark averred wholeheartedly, as if to banish her misery.

His watchful vigil abandoned momentarily, he placed his loaded pistol within reach on the crate which served as her chair and dropped to her side. Troubled over leaving Armand La Tour alive in the alley, he'd investigated every sound in the building since they'd taken refuge there, as if he expected the man to reappear. "What has happened between you and Alain doesn't matter. You were vulnerable and frightened by the savages and he, such as it was, was the only civilized alternative with whom you might seek comfort."

"How very generous of you, Monsieur *Lepage.*"

"Alain!" Tamson tore away from Mark at the sound of her husband's voice. Searching the tall shadows cast by stacked crates, she saw him step beyond into the light, his cousin Armand La Tour at his heel.

"I would not reach for that pistol, monsieur!" Armand warned, leveling his own weapon at Mark.

Her thoughts only for Alain, Tamson rushed toward

him, briefly blocking Mark from Armand's sights. She
didn't see Mark seize the opportunity she unwittingly
presented. All she witnessed was the sudden panic on
Alain's face as he lunged at her with a loud, "Non!"

His tackle carried both of them to the ground above
the simultaneous roar of gunfire. They had no more
than landed when Tamson felt herself being dragged
into cover. Still dazed, she fell back as Alain urgently
disentangled himself from her and drew the lethal hunting knife he wore tucked in the calf of his boot. Beyond
him lay Armand La Tour, his discharged pistol still
smoking while the stench of the burned powder permeated the damp musty air. A single dark hole oozed scarlet in the midst of his forehead.

"Alain . . ."

Tamson's plea died as her companion raised a silencing finger without glancing her way. His attention was
fixed on the other side of the room where Mark had
been. She held her breath as he peered above the stores
protecting them, uncertain as to what she prayed he'd
find. She didn't want Mark dead, too, yet alive, he was
a threat to Alain. A second look at the curved blade of
the knife in her husband's capable hand, however, forced
her to reassess her estimation of the Englishman's advantage.

"You are unarmed, monsieur. I would suggest that
you hand Tamson over to me now."

"And you are running out of time, Lepage. Do you
think your shots went undetected?" Alain queried with
a deadly calm. In the silence that followed, distant
shouts answered the question for them both.

"*Dieu*, Alain!" Mark swore, giving in to his exasperation. "If you think half as much of your wife as

you have led me to believe, you will let me take her away from here! It's all you've thought of, sparing her from this coming winter's hell."

"We were friends then, monsieur."

Tamson looked at Alain in surprise, not only that he'd grown comfortable enough to discuss his private life with his assistant, but that he'd not yet given up the idea of her leaving. She'd thought she'd convinced him that she would not go with Henri and Isabelle, or anywhere, for that matter.

"And surely she has been incriminated by your cousin! Would you risk her hanging for treason as well?"

Alarmed by Alain's silence, Tamson touched his arm. "I won't leave you," she whispered.

A far-from-reassuring gaze fell upon her hand, prompting her to withdraw it. Icy fingers of dread inched along her spine as she searched his fiercely thoughtful expression for an indication of his feelings. When he did speak, his tone as much as his words mercilessly shattered her short-lived relief.

"Why then, madame, did I find you in your lover's embrace?"

There was no anger in her husband's glacial appraisal. The accusation lacked the characteristic ferocity of his temperament, yet she reeled from the assault as though he had driven his blade into her chest.

A telltale click of Mark's pistol hammer abruptly drew Alain's attention back to his adversary. "To fire that again will narrow down the search for you, monsieur. Consider that I have not yet killed you and put away your weapon."

Tamson realized the merit of Alain's remark. While

Mark was reloading his gun, Alain had had ample time to use his knife. "He's right, Mark! He has a knife and, as a voyageur, is quite good with it," she verified, eager to avoid any lethal confrontation between the two.

Again the emotionless eyes of her companion spared her a moment's appraisal, but a strange, dragging sound intruded. Even as Tamson heard it, she knew its implication. Mark had been wounded by the unfortunate Armand's last shot, most likely in the leg or foot. Would Alain be next? Neither of them deserved to die, she lamented, the idea churning like a sickness in her stomach.

"*Alors, monsieur.* It is obvious that neither you nor I wish this to go further. What you suggest does have some merit. Since it is also apparent that you are wounded, I think that you will not be able to do as you say without help."

"*You* would assist me?" Mark countered skeptically.

The strain in Mark's voice revealed the truth of Alain's observation, but Tamson was too stricken by the direction of her husband's thoughts to notice. Obstinately, she rose to her knees, oblivious to exposing herself to possible pistol fire.

"I won't leave you, Alain! I was upset because I thought I was being forced to and Mark was trying to comfort me. I'm your wife. I love you."

Unmoved by Tamson's impassioned confession, Alain shook his head. "Non, Tamson, you are not my wife. You have never been my wife."

"What?"

"So what do you say, Lepage? Shall we work together or waste more time."

"I'll see your knife."

Alain held up the knife so that his adversary might confirm its existence. "And you'll ease the hammer to rest on your pistol."

Tamson sprang back from her initial shock and grabbed Alain's arm as he cautiously started to rise. "Non, I don't believe you!"

"Believe what you wish," Alain replied indifferently. "Shall we put away our weapons, monsieur?"

"I said, I don't believe you!" Tamson insisted, pulling Alain about so that he had to face her. "We're married!"

For a brief moment, Alain glanced over her shoulder at the wary man tucking his pistol into his belt and then back at her. "I merely told you so to keep you from getting hysterical and unmanageable, like you are becoming at the moment."

Once again, Tamson fell back in disbelief. It wasn't possible! He couldn't have fooled her so completely, not after all they'd shared, the relationship they had . . . or did have. She inadvertently glimpsed the still Armand La Tour on the floor a few feet away. Was he telling the truth? she wondered, staggered beyond her ability to reason this out.

"I have but one request, monsieur, in exchange for my assistance."

Mark averted his sympathetic gaze from Tamson. "Yes?"

Alain pointed to a leather satchel resting by the open floorboards. "That you leave that behind. Whatever you carry back to your superiors will have to be in your head." It didn't sit well with the young Englishman, but neither did anything else Alain had done so far. "You have killed my cousin and betrayed my trust, Marc Lepage. Yet I am willing to assist you if you trade those documents for the girl. Although I owe allegiance to no one but myself, I have my limits as to what I will tolerate."

"The French will lose, we both know that. They cannot hold out as they have been forever."

"But I will not intentionally contribute to the loss."

"You bastard!"

Distracted by Heathcote's argument, Alain reeled from the angry blow of Tamson's palm against his face. He touched his inflamed cheek tentatively, his voice willfully impassive. "I do believe that is an accurate description, *ma chérie*. So go to your Mark, who is both high-born and legitimate. If you are lucky, I will get you both out of here in one piece. What do you say, monsieur? Will you leave the bag, or will we delay your departure even further?"

The shouts which had echoed faintly following the exchange of gunfire had grown louder, indicating the searchers were getting nearer. Mark shifted his weight to relieve his bloodied leg and nearly lost his balance. As he grabbed for support, Tamson rushed to catch him, fleeing the French devil who had broken her heart with his callous candor.

"Leave the bloody documents! Just get me away from him before I shoot him myself!" She glared back at Alain. "To think I went to all those classes with Father André, that I believed you and loved you for your sense of honor, that I . . ."

A noise at the front of the building caused her to break off. Alain hurried forward and grabbed Mark's other arm. "Come, monsieur. Your decision has been made." He kicked the satchel across the floor beyond his adversary's reach upon reaching the open boards, lest the temptation to go against his word be too great.

Despite her obvious reluctance to drop down into the black hole beneath, Tamson did so out of some inate sense of survival which had taken over amidst her shock. There was no time for emotion now and thought was impossible without it. She steadied Mark as Alain lowered him, becoming part of a team with one purpose . . . escape. If there would ever be such a thing for her, she thought, fighting the anguish which pushed through the anesthesia of her stunned state of mind.

After taking the candle down into the abyss, Alain carefully eased the floorboards back into place to conceal their means of escape and turned toward the direction of the river. Refusing his offer to relieve her of helping her companion, Tamson stubbornly plodded through the mud, her feet making plucking sounds in the eerie silence. Her resilience when provoked still amazed Alain, even though he had counted heavily upon it to get her to leave with her fiancé. The torture would be to bear her wounded looks and outbursts until she was on her way to a safer and better place than that to which he had taken her.

"I told you there were big rats in my tunnels . . . English rats." came a loud voice.

Tamson's ear-piercing scream filled the passage, spurring Alain to clamp his hand over her mouth despite his own start at the voice he recognized as that of Oncle Souris. He should have expected the old man to lurk somewhere within the dilapidated network of passages. Timidly, their hidden companion emerged into the sphere of light cast by the candle.

"I am sorry, madame, I meant you no harm."

"The English rat is going to save the marquee from being charged with treason, Oncle Souris. We must help them get away."

"Madame?"

Tamson nodded in affirmation upon her self-appointed guardian's questioning look. "I will be safer with this man, Oncle. *He* loves me," she added, her accusing, injured look running Alain through.

"Come, we're wasting time," Alain snapped impatiently. "Where is your boat, monsieur?"

"He's hidden it in some bushes growing near the west ditch." Upon seeing Alain's astonished look, Oncle Souris cackled. "I watch good for the marquis' coin, that I do, non?"

"That you do, *mon ami.*"

"But we will miss our bonne marquee, non?"

"Perhaps," Alain managed tautly. "But first, we must see her on her way," he added, taking the arm Mark had used to support himself against the tunnel wall to speed them along.

The moonlight bathed the wharf area outside the walls of the city, diminishing the effects of the candle as soon as they were in sight of the tunnel opening. Grateful that it was not too long a distance between the exit and the ditch beyond the corner stockade, Alain moved the brush concealment away and stepped outside, where the fresher scent of rush and river water replaced the still musty stench of the tunnel. Due to a protrusion in the wall itself between them and the Market Gate, they would not draw attention from the patrol stationed there.

With luck, Alain thought, taking care to stay close to the wall as he looked overhead, the guards in the stockade would be distracted by the ongoing search within the city rather than keeping watch on the few overturned canoes belonging to traders.

"Keep low, madame," he whispered as the others emerged. "I will help your friend. And say nothing, nothing at all."

Tamson could hardly say a word if she'd wanted to. While she could personally shoot Alain at the moment, she did not want him hurt. As for Mark, she didn't love him, but felt the same way about his welfare. Her own danger never once occurred to her, such was her concern for the two men who accompanied her, nor did the reason the two enemies worked now as allies. When her foot caught on a root, however, and she sprawled forward onto the cool wet sand, neither Alain's warning to keep quiet nor her frozen heart could stifle the small shriek knocked from her by the fall.

"Arrêt! Who goes there?" came a shout.

"Quick, take this one!" Alain instructed sharply, flipping the light bark canoe closest to them on its bottom. "There is no time to reach your boat now!"

He helped Mark into the vessel and turned to reach for Tamson when a musket shot rang out and a ball sliced into the water just beyond them.

"Watch your feet so you do not step through the bottom!" he cautioned, lifting her easily over the side and placing her between the two plank seats while Mark scrambled to find the paddles.

"I'm sorry!"

"Just lie there until Mark says it is safe."

Another shot bit into the sand a few yards away as Alain scrambled to his feet to shove the boat off. With his shoulder jammed against the bark hide and pitch, he heaved with the force of his desperation to keep Tamson from harm, digging deeply into the sand with his feet as he did so. The *troupes de la terre* were not known for their expert aim as their Canadian counterparts of the marine were, but the musket balls were coming too close for comfort.

Just as he reached the knee-deep water into which he pushed his precious cargo, shouts erupted from the Market Gate, where a squadron of soldiers broke through. Suddenly, with a voice twice his size, Oncle Souris started running toward them, shouting at the top of his voice.

"Stop, stop! The spy has killed Lieutenant La Tour and taken the Marquis and Marquee de la Galisonne hostage! You must not shoot!"

"Get in!"

Alain turned away from Souris's diversion to see Marc Lepage pointing his pistol at him. "What?" he demanded blankly.

"I said, get in, you idiot! You're with us now, whether you're the King's most loyal subject or not!" Mark reached down and drew Tamson up. "Tell them I'll shoot you and your husband if they do not hold their fire."

"Au secours! Don't shoot! He will kill us!" she shouted, her terror not at all a charade.

To Alain's amazement, old Souris's plan was working, especially now that it was reinforced by Tamson's plea. Upon seeing the men lower their guns in confusion, he sprang into the canoe and took the seat opposite Lepage. Mark tossed him one of the paddles.

"Row, you French bastard! I think I'm going to be sick." The man was incredibly pale, his face made more so by the blanching moonlight which made them easy targets.

Alain bit back an oath of frustration at the ceaseless games fate was playing with them. It was enough to give Tamson over to a man he'd once considered a friend and help them escape, but to be forced to go with them was beyond even his capability to have foreseen. "Where?"

"To the *Bonne Femme,* that two-masted schooner there in the distance. She's readying to sail even as we speak."

Digging powerfully into the water with the paddle, Alain remarked grimly, "For *all* our sakes, monsieur, I hope so."

Twenty-two

The *Bonne Femme* was indeed ready to sail. The riggings were crawling with crew members when Alain brought the canoe up against its side. She was a trim vessel, the light sort that could outrun and outmaneuver the heavier warships. A privateer's dream, Alain thought, just as the canoe was his chosen choice of escape. He glanced up expectantly for a line to be dropped to them. Once Tamson and Lepage were aboard, he would make his way to landfall and on down to Prairie, where he could blend with his fellow voyageurs.

"This is Captain Mark Heathcote! Throw down the damned ladder!" Mark demanded, his pain robbing him of patience.

A smiling face appeared over the rail belonging, Alain assumed, to the captain. "But that, I am afraid, *mon ami,* is impossible, now that you have awakened the whole town to your grand departure." He looked down at Tamson appreciatively. "And, not that I would object to offering passage to such a lovely lady, but you said nothing about bringing along companions."

"You'll be paid well when we reach Oswego—you know that."

So that was what the Englishman had been waiting for, Alain realized—confirmation of the impending offense at Chouaguen, or Oswego, as the enemy called the English stronghold. It explained his reticence to leave for Quebec when it appeared the major campaign was going to be from Carillon rather than Frontenac. He had to be ready to travel the moment Montcalm's plans were made, which were hailed by the requisitions going through the commissary office.

Instead of remaining where he might report other enemy offenses, the young English captain had evidently grown restless to leave Montreal because of Tamson Stewart. Still, Alain had to give him credit. To make his escape on one of the supply ships bound for Frontenac was the height of audacity. From there, he could proceed to Oswego on his own, ahead of the French forces. It might have worked had the man not let his heart rule his head.

"Ah, but the problem with that is," the ship's captain was explaining, "that I must get past the French ships at Présentacion and Frontenac, which no doubt will be looking for me, since so many saw your escape by boat. You can rest assured that everything floating between here and Frontenac will be suspect." The man shook his head, as if genuinely apologetic, or at least regretful in the sense that he was losing the chance to make a considerable profit. *"Non, mon ami,* I do not wish to have you and your friends found among the supplies we carry for the Captain General's army when we are stopped at the head of the river. It is too risky, even for me."

"You lying bastard!" Mark shook his paddle at the man in his helpless fury. "We've a lady with us!"

The captain leaned over, waving a reproving finger

at the Englishman. "And such language in front of her! What manners are you English taught?"

Not unfamiliar with his companion's frustration, Alain leaned forward on his paddle as the master of the ship dismissed them with a cheerful, *"Au revoir, mes amis,"* and turned to the business of getting his ship underway with the tide. Fate, it seemed, had not yet had her fill of ripping him inside out.

"We cannot take the ship by ourselves, monsieur," he pointed out flatly to the fuming officer opposite him.

"Well, this damned boat is going to sink if we don't do something!" Mark lifted his wounded leg out of the water that had seeped into the bottom.

"My dress is soaked," Tamson concurred anxiously. "What is to become of us now?"

Her dark-honeyed gaze could consume Alain like wildfire, could touch him like no other. But wide with fear and glazed with tears, it was his undoing.

"I will take you home, ma . . . madame," Alain altered quickly, avoiding the endearing *ma petitesse* which came to his mind.

Much as it pained him, he had to make her want to go back to Albany. Her English captain would take care of her, even if Squire Stewart was in no position to do so. As for himself, he would simply disappear into the north country. To plan further than that was to invite additional interference by the whims of Lady Fate, for fate surely had to be female, fickle as it was.

"Overland?" Mark asked skeptically.

Alain liked the idea no more than his companion. "Have you another suggestion?"

The officer shook his head in resignation.

"But the canoe!" Tamson reminded them. Having

had to sit in the bottom across the hard cedar framing, she felt she was more aware of the incoming water than either of her companions.

"Remember the sponges Jacques and Gaspar used, madame?"

"But we have none, monsieur. They must have fallen out . . ."

She broke off as Alain produced the sponges which had been lashed neatly under his seat. "I believe you know what must be done."

Lips thinning, Tamson took them from him.

"And I would recommend that you remove . . . carefully . . . all but one of your petticoats. Soaked with water, they alone are enough to sink us."

"Good God, Beaujeu, would you have her undress in front of us?"

"Although I will see nothing I have not seen before and you, monsieur, have the option of looking away, the alternative of trying to swim to shore with her *and* her petticoats in tow is not in the least the better of the two options."

"Really!" Tamson swore in indignation.

She snatched up the skirt of her dress, fairly glowering at Alain, with no idea the relief her renewed spirit instilled in him. That was more to his liking, he thought, taking up his paddle again. He glanced over her head at Mark—*Heathcote,* he corrected mentally—to see the officer looking decently in another direction. An idealist, he mused in halfhearted disdain, for in spite of all that had happened, there was still something about the young man that Alain admired. But for Tamson, and Tamson alone, they might have been good friends.

After Tamson tossed her dripping petticoats over the

side, Alain followed suit with his jacket. Despite the unexpected turn of events, he felt a surge of relief, as if floating away with the garment was the smothering role he'd been forced to assume as the Marquis de la Galisonne. Now he could stretch his unconfined shoulders to his heart's content.

The carefree life which had been calling to him was just two miles on the other side of the river. There he would find people he could depend on. He could almost see Jacques' face when he walked into the campsite, where his compatriots were no doubt singing and dancing as if the night were as endless as the supply of liquor they had purchased.

A smile toyed with lips that, until that moment, had been fixed in a grimly pressed line. One glance, however, at the girl frantically sponging out the bottom of their craft was enough to erase it as quickly as it had appeared. His own celebration would have to wait, he thought, unaccustomed to the heavy feeling which bore upon him at the realization that his future life, no matter how appealing, would not include her.

It couldn't, he told himself even as he began to entertain the thought of taking Tamson with him. She was born to better things and deserved more than living the life of a squaw, which was what traveling with him and his companions would amount to. She would come to truly hate him, rather than react from the stings of her wounded pride as she was doing now.

No, seeing Tamson safely to English-held territory was the greatest gift he could give her now that he was no longer a marquis, he concluded reluctantly. Then, perhaps in time, she would forgive him. Besides, who was to say that after this war was over they might not reunite? Even now, he had enough put aside to give her the life she deserved. What he lacked was a country in which to share it with her.

"Where are we going?" Mark Heathcote's question ended Alain's silent speculation abruptly.

"To Prairie de la Magdeline. There we can get supplies for the journey to Champlain."

"Or we could continue upriver. The same reward awaiting the captain of the *Bonne Femme* could be yours were you to act as our guide."

Alain chuckled to himself. "You do not lack for boldness—that I can say for you, Monsieur Heath . . ."

"Captain . . ."

"*Captain* Heathcote," Alain amended graciously. "But if I refused to let you carry the documents no doubt stolen from the Chateau de Vaudreuil itself, not to mention my office, what makes you think that I would deliver you with your much-awaited news to your English superiors at Chouaguen? Non, monsieur, I intend to take advantage of the heavy military concentration devoted currently to that passage and take the opposite as well as the most direct route to the lady's home."

"I have a gun."

"So you do . . . and you also have a bullet in your leg. In time, Captain, I do not think your pistol will be of much use to you. Forget your mission and be grateful for the lady's presence."

Alain did not need to elaborate. He was certain the captain knew that without Tamson, he'd be left to fare for himself, wounded in enemy territory. As Alain had told him earlier, for Tamson's sake, he would spare the

Englishman's life and help them escape. But he would not be party to treason.

After a prolonged silence, Alain motioned to the bloodied wound, now wrapped with a strip of one of Tamson's sacrificed petticoats. "When we put in at Prairie, I will see if I can get the ball out—that is, if you trust me."

Bitterness crept into Mark's reply. "Do I have a choice?"

Alain did not answer. It wasn't necessary. The point had been made. He was in charge now, *whether he wanted that responsibility or not.* Was it only a year ago that he'd given up his carefree existence as a *courier de bois* for the sake of a pretty colonial girl, whose picture had once beguiled him? *Dieu,* but how this war had changed things!

Aside from campfires outside the village of Prairie de la Magdeline, there was no other sign of activity. The town itself was a dark silhouette of sharp-pitched rooftops and a single steeple against the moonlit sky. The traders, however, both French and Indian, kept the night alive with their cheerful singing and shouts of amusement that drifted down the shore to where Alain had beached the canoe.

It wasn't a cold night, but Tamson shivered uncontrollably in Mark Heathcote's jacket and leaned within the circle of the officer's arm as they huddled on the bed of grass their rescuer had made for them. Alain was not so certain that her wet clothing was solely responsible for her tremors. He knew by the way she kept looking nervously toward the campfires that she recalled vividly the torturous night she'd spent at the hands of savages in that same spot.

More than anything, he wanted to take her into his arms and soothe away her fears, but there was much to do before morning and he couldn't encourage her to stick to her resolve to remain with him. She belonged in New York with her own people, away from the inevitable deprivation of Montreal's coming winter.

Leaving the couple with the canoe propped up over them for cover lest the few clouds gathering in the west made good their promise of impending showers, he made his way toward the flat of ground beyond the village. With luck, he would find his partners and get the clothes and supplies they needed to appear inconspicuous when daylight brought the search parties, which would inevitably come from the island city across the river. Their journey beyond that was in the hands of the same fate which had brought them this far . . . and in the noble hearts of one Gaspar Le Boeuf and Jacques Dupré.

How she ever fell asleep in Mark's arms was a wonder to Tamson. Despite the gay notes of the fiddle in the distance, all she could hear were the shrill shouts and laughter of the drinking, gambling Indians camped among the French traders beyond the village walls. Yet, when Alain shook her gently and coaxed her away from her sleeping companion, she rose with a start.

For a moment, she'd actually forgotten where she was and started to throw herself into her husband's embrace to seek warmth and comfort. However, when she inadvertently jostled Mark Heathcote's leg, causing him to jerk into wakefulness with a gasp of pain, reality slapped her as coldly as the hide bundle Alain put in her hands.

"Put these on, madame . . ."

Tamson's heart leapt at his choice of words, but instantly, he shot it down. *"Pardonez-moi,* I meant to say *mademoiselle."*

It had been a mistake, just as trusting him with her heart had been, she realized morosely. She untied the thong about the bundle and shook out what appeared to be a fringed shirt like the one he wore, made of soft buckskin. With that were a pair of woolen trousers, leather leggins, and a bright blue tasseled stocking hat—all of which was designed to disguise the fact that she was a female.

There was no need to show her disdain, for she doubted Alain would pay her heed. The man she'd known had died back in Montreal and the rough and heartless voyageur who had kidnaped her had taken his place. Besides, she recognized the sound reason for the disguise. Their situation was desperate and there was no choice but to obey Alain Beaujeu completely. Whatever his purpose, he would save them. She believed that much in him and his abilities.

She focused on the man helping Alain tend to Mark's wound. She knew that she knew him, yet his name eluded her. What was the man's name, she puzzled, digging back into memories she'd tried to forget. Gaspar! That was it.

She would have spoken except that he, too, was absorbed in watching Alain probe the dark, seeping wound beneath Mark's torn, bloodstained trousers. Mark had turned a deathly white, perspiration glistening in the light of the lantern Gaspar held over his leg. Teeth clenched as tightly as his eyes, he turned his face to the side as if to ignore the painful search of his living flesh for the ball from Armand La Tour's pistol.

Torn between going to comfort Mark and obeying Alain's terse command, she reasoned the latter course the most practical. There was little she could actually do to lessen Mark's pain and this was no time to hamper their escape by incurring Alain's wrath. And—she wasn't sure she could stand up to him in her own wounded frame of mind.

Regardless of how unwitting it had been, she had done enough to antagonize Alain, she thought, treading on the very mental ground she'd resolved to avoid; not that he would ever believe her story. Disconsolate, she stepped to the other side of the canoe for privacy to change. Damn the man—it was he who had committed the worst treachery and yet, it was she who suffered relentlessly from guilt. To think, all those months his lies had been cruelly calculated, not born of circumstance beyond his control as hers had been.

She forced her attention to dressing as quickly as possible while her male companions were occupied. The hide clothes were warm and dry, even though they reeked of the creature which had once occupied them—animal or human, she wasn't sure. The shirt hung down past her knees and, but for the gay sash tied snugly about her waist, she would have lost her trousers in less than two strides. While the stocking cap and soft-soled moccasin boots were easy to put on, the remaining strips of leather and thongs were a mystery.

As she pondered the problem, a terrible cry, pitifully smothered, emerged from the other side of the canoe. Tamson rushed around in time to see the officer's head loll backward and to the side, lifeless and still. Ice formed in the pit of her stomach.

"Dear God, is he dead?"

"He has but fainted, mademoiselle," Alain answered, terse and patronizing. Apparently not about to offer assurance, he continued his ministrations without regard for the unconscious state of his patient.

"He will awaken again, mademoiselle," Gaspar filled in for her, the crooked scar on his cheek stretching as he gave her a bolstering toothless grin. "It is the Almighty's way of relieving his pain, nothing more."

With little alternative, Tamson sat down on a blanket and waited for them to bandage the now free-bleeding wound, which they had washed with some sort of liquor—a cheap brandy, she thought. From their soft exchange of observations, the young man would recover well enough if serious infection did not set in.

Mark did come around as Gaspar and Alain lifted him to his feet to carry him back to the voyageur camp in the darkness. They made him a bed on the ground and one for Tamson beside it. When Alain started to leave again, it was all she could do to quell her panic. The memory of the last time he'd left her in Prairie haunted her as she watched him disappear once again into the darkness with Gaspar, but this time he wasn't going far. He was only going to destroy the canoe and the evidence of their landing.

It had to be done. It wasn't going to be like before, she told herself sternly as she settled down under the blanket, because this time she was staying put. She'd be safe among Alain's friends. Even if he hated her, he wished her no harm. That was enough for now.

Once again, however, her heart squeezed with anguish and she knew that it really wasn't. Nothing short of Alain Beaujeu as the loving husband he had been would ever heal her wounds. Yet that, it appeared, not only never was, but was never to be.

Twenty-three

Tamson Stewart was hardly the spoiled little debutante he'd kidnaped, Alain mused from his squatting position near the fire. The young woman had shown as much bravery and stamina as any man during the perilous journey which had brought them into English-held territory where no telling campfire had been possible for days now, with both ally and enemy roaming the forests.

Yesterday they'd met a war party of savages making their way north with livestock stolen from some unsuspecting homestead. As he'd covered an ashen Tamson with his body, hiding in the underbrush while the Indians passed them by with their plunder, he hadn't been able to resist brushing the top of her hair with his lips, but she'd been too frightened to notice.

It was just as well, he thought, glancing over to where the girl leaned against a tree, her eyes closed. He didn't wish to encourage any hopes about their future together. It was better that she thought him a deceitful bastard. It would make leaving her easier . . . for her.

Alain picked up a pebble and tossed it, striking the tree beside her, but Tamson never stirred. A scowl creased his forehead as he exchanged a concerned look with Jacques. It had been the same since they'd put

ashore on the south side of Lake George. She'd slept
the moment they stopped, too exhausted to eat. Not that
the dried biscuits were that tempting, Alain mused laconically. She hadn't even complained about that. In
fact, he wasn't certain that she'd eaten her share that
morning.

After pushing himself easily to his feet, Alain crossed
the distance between them and gently felt the excess
material blousing about her sashed waist. The search
awakened her with a start.

"It is all right, mademoiselle," Alain assured her,
"except that you did not eat this morning." He patted
the bulge of the hard biscuit which she'd tucked in her
shirt. "It is no wonder you are so tired. You must eat."

The amber brown eyes which had driven stakes
through his heart with every glance during the first part
of their journey were now dulled with fatigue as she
stared up at him. "I was too frightened to eat." She
rested her head against the tree again and closed her
eyes. "Now I'd rather sleep until it's time to go."

"You do not feel well?"

"As if you'd care," she mumbled sleepily.

Alain straightened, aware that Jacques and Gaspar
were as intent upon their conversation as he. "We'll
stop early today."

"I think we might even have a fire," Gaspar spoke
up.

Alain nodded. "Oui, I have been smelling it, too."

Every once in a while, there was a slight wafting of
woodsmoke in the air. Since it came undoubtedly from
the same direction as the war party, it was not likely the
Indians would double back. The smoldering remains of
the homestead would serve to disguise their own fire.

Perhaps then, they might tempt the girl to eat and see that she got a good night's sleep.

Much as he hated to bother Tamson, Alain roused her from her nap and suffered another accusing look before he got the group underway again. *Dieu,* but he would be glad when she was safely with her own people and he in the wilderness with his friends, although even they treated him as if her misery were all his fault. They had not said as much, but Gaspar and Jacques had a gift of expression.

Surely they could see that she was not up to accompanying them into the wilds of the north, much less suited for the life of a squaw, which was what she would have to live in order to survive. Tamson was meant to wear silks and satins, not buckskins. Her domain should be a home, not a lodge made of sticks and hides. With their life in Montreal behind them, there was no choice but to return her to her father.

No choice, he told himself, not for the first time since leaving New France. No matter how much he wanted to take her into his arms and reaffirm all that had passed between them, he couldn't allow it. Even his ability to keep Tamson in the style to which she was accustomed, something for which he would sacrifice his wanderlust readily, could not insure a future together. Not only did his investments await him, but a hangman's noose as well for kidnaping the girl. There was simply no choice!

It was late noon when they bridged a wooded rise overlooking the clearing and the smoking remains left in the wake of the savages. From the distance, there was no sign of bodies, but since the savages had not carried hostages with them, Alain knew there had to be. Leaving Tamson with Mark Heathcote amidst the cover of the trees at the forest's edge, he and his fellow traders went down to investigate.

Tamson was almost too numb with fatigue to register the icy dread settling in her empty stomach at what the men might find. Yet, nothing could erase her recollection of the heinous capabilities of the redskinned savages. Compassion welled in her heart for the victims and she prayed that they had died before suffering long from their captors' fiendish torture.

That Alain had insisted she not accompany them was one of the few blessings she'd experienced since leaving Montreal. Not that she blamed Alain for their relentless pace. Their lives depended on it. Sheltered as her life had once been, she realized that. All three Frenchmen took a great risk to come this far south, not only for her sake, but for Mark's. They might have easily abandoned the wounded officer rather than taking turns carrying him when he could no longer keep up on his own. That was why she'd done her best to endure the journey without complaint.

Ironically, the pace had been a blessing in disguise. Her weariness had dulled the merciless pain of Alain's rejection. As the days had passed, the edge of her despair had worn off and her eyes no longer glazed over each time she looked at him. It was almost as if she'd become detached from everything except keeping up and tending Mark. Now, even that was becoming difficult, she thought, taking up Gaspar's canteen to dampen the cloth on Mark's forehead again.

All she wanted to do was sleep. She didn't care whether or not she ate. She didn't want to think. That was too painful. Nor did she wish to comb her hair or make some attempt at bathing to alter her shameful state of dishevelment. She just didn't care anymore. Given the chance, she felt she could drift away forever to a world where the heartache of Alain's betrayal couldn't touch her.

The first snap of dry twig nearby did not penetrate Tamson's dulled consciousness. She'd grown used to that sound, just as she'd grown accustomed to the rustle of the leaves overhead in the summer breeze. However, when she heard what sounded like a strangled sob no more than a few yards away, Tamson came to her feet with a bloodcurdling scream.

Without a weapon, she grabbed the closest thing she could lay hands on—a dry limb which had broken off one of the trees—and stood frozen, staring into the thicket of wild berries growing at the edge of the woods. It had to be an animal, she thought wildly, for if it were a savage, he would be upon her by now.

She glanced down the hill and was relieved to see Alain abandoning the search of the smoldering ruins, racing toward her with rifle in hand. Suddenly the berry patch began to tremble and Tamson shrieked in panic, "Alain, hurry!"

"Au secours!" a small, pitiful voice implored with equal terror. "Please! Please help me! Do not let them shoot!"

Startled, Tamson looked again at the leafy cover until she was able to make out a white bonnet, beneath which were wide frightened eyes as blue as a summer sky. It was a young girl! From the homestead, no doubt, she thought, suddenly overwhelmed with compassion for what the child had probably been through. The poor thing had no doubt been hiding there since this morning, wondering where her parents were. Worse yet, she might have seen what had happened to them.

Dropping her bark-covered weapon, Tamson stepped forward and held out her hand.

"Tamson, non!" Alain shouted, lumbering toward her breathlessly, his ordinarily cool blue gaze frantic as he waved her away from the brush. Behind him, Jacques and Gaspar had started back up the hill as well.

"It's all right!" she assured him. "There's a child in the bushes! A little girl, I think."

Alain eased the hammer on his rifle as he drifted to a loping stop and followed Tamson's pointed finger with a narrowed gaze to the blackberry thicket, which still trembled as its occupant retreated deeper into its center.

"It's all right, little one! We won't hurt you!"

The child froze again, uncertain, wide blue eyes staring out at them both.

"Dieu!" Alain swore in relief. He leaned over, hands to his knees, and tried to catch his breath. Too distracted by the child, Tamson failed to notice the way his hands shook as he straightened or the way his face had paled beneath his bronzed skin.

"She was speaking French at first," Tamson told him, taking his gun so he might approach the thicket.

Alain looked back at the child and waved at his approaching companions. Upon regaining his wind, he knelt down and, in a gentle tone, called out to the girl in his native language. "Come, *ma pétitesse*. I will not harm you. We saw the savages. They are gone."

Struck by the sudden tenderness in his voice, Tamson wondered that any creature could resist Alain Beaujeu. Neither of them, however, was prepared for the enthusiastic outburst that resulted. The bushes erupted with a loud squeal of excitement and the girl, who was not so little after all, tore out of the thorny hideaway, heedless of the thorns which lodged in her clothes. Crying hysterically in French, she charged into Alain's open arms, nearly bowling him over in the process.

"It *is* you! It *is* you! *Merci à Dieu!* I give all my praise to God! Our prayers are at last answered! Maman, she promised they would be, but I had given up. May God forgive me for my doubt!"

Alain was clearly taken aback by the outburst which finally wound down to incoherent sobs. Gently, he pried the young woman away from him, still incredulous, and stared at the pretty scratched face of his charge, distorted with a mixture of disbelief and joy. She was a beautiful girl, not quite grown, Tamson thought, equally taken aback by her outburst. Perhaps fifteen or so . . .

Her speculation abruptly ended when Alain ventured, his voice uncertain. "Liselle?" Suddenly, he had the same overjoyed reaction as the girl in his embrace. *"Mon dieu!* Hush!" he cooed brokenly. "Hush, *ma bonne petite."* He pulled her against him fiercely and rocked her, whispering over and over, *"Merci à Dieu, merci à Dieu, merci à Dieu . . ."*

Liselle! Tamson reflected, eyes misting at the emotional reunion of brother and sister. Liselle was the middle one, whom Alain had fondly described as precocious and awkward at the ripe age of sixteen. The poor thing!

Tamson glanced suddenly at the smoking ruins where Jacques and Gaspar had returned and her heart stilled. Oh, dear God, no!

"Maman said that you or Papa would come, b . . .

but it has been so long!" Liselle managed, adding to the dread building in Tamson's mind.

"Maman?" Alain repeated, suddenly struck by the same fierce alarm. "Maman was here?"

Tamson met his tortured gaze over the girl's shoulder and, despite his cruel betrayal, her heart went out to him. The cabin was so badly burned, no one could have survived the fire. Not now, she prayed. He didn't deserve any more torment. He'd suffered enough for two men.

"Non," his sister denied, missing his anxiety completely. "She is in Annapolis with Laurette."

"Annapolis!" Alain exclaimed, echoing Tamson's surprise.

"In Maryland," Liselle went on. "We were separated when New York would not take us all."

Tamson wasn't sure whether to be relieved or nay. She would never get over the shame of the deeds committed by her fellow countrymen on innocent people.

"And Annette?"

"Annette, she is married and this is . . . *was*," Liselle corrected shakily, "her husband's farm."

Tamson was unable to contain her dismay any longer, for this news was no better. "Oh, Alain!"

The outburst brought Liselle's gaze to her for the first time. It looked as though a feminine version of Alain was peering out from beneath the rim of her bonnet, so alike was her Beaujeu blue gaze. "Oh non, it is not like that! Annette and Tom were not at home. They are clearing their new home site by the creek. With the baby coming and me underfoot, Tom's small cabin was becoming crowded."

"*Dieu!*" Drained of emotion by relief, Alain fixed

his attention on the sky overhead until he could regain his voice.

"They left you here alone?"

Dark lashes fanned against tear-scalded cheeks and Tamson caught a glimpse of the mischievous creature Alain had described to her. "I was *supposed* to join them when my chores were finished, but I decided to pick enough berries for a pie to surprise them. I was here when the Indians came and hid there in the bushes until they were gone, just like you and Papa told me to do. I was not coming out until Tom and Annette came home." Liselle glanced mournfully at the smoking embers of her sister's home. "But now they have nothing but ashes!"

Alain held her tightly as she gave way to another torrent of despair, kneading her long dark braids in his fingers as if still finding it difficult to believe that she was real. "It will be all right, *ma petite*. That you are safe is all that is important."

Reduced to ragged breaths, Liselle pulled away and gave Tamson and Mark a cursory look before focusing her attention on the two Frenchmen making their way back up the hill. "Is Papa with you?" she asked hopefully.

Tamson cringed inwardly, feeling the pain of Alain's gaze. He gently lifted his sister's chin and stared down at her with such compassion that Tamson almost envied her. He'd alluded to his devotion to his family and now she saw it—in his eyes, in his manner, in his voice.

"*Non, ma bonne Liselle.* Much has happened since I last swung you about in circles until you were too dizzy to stand. But that is something we will discuss later, after we find Annette."

* * *

There were mostly ashes, but with everyone sifting through the rubble, they were able to salvage a few things. Those, however, all fit in the single hamper Annette Beaujeu Malone had packed for the day spent helping her husband clear the place for their future home. Although her Beaujeu-blue eyes were glazed as she tried to salvage what was left, the dark-haired beauty in the loose-fitting dress had tried to make the best of their loss, for her husband's sake, if for no other reason.

"We have all that is most important to us and more, non?" she asked Tom Malone, echoing her brother's earlier sentiment. She made a brave attempt at a smile. "We and Liselle are safe and now Alain is here. This is the best bad luck I have ever had!"

Tom Malone hadn't said much to Alain, much less the others. He'd greeted them politely upon being introduced, but for the most part, he'd spent his time raking through the debris with a vengeance, as if stirring the embers might make the dwelling rise again. His gaunt face was smudged from his efforts as he looked down at his wife. For the first time, Tamson saw the man's stoic front falter, not with despair but with complete adoration.

"I've never seen the likes of ye, lass. You can make the best out o' the nearest nothin'." Then, as if he realized that he had drawn everyone's attention, he actually blushed at his tender folly and withdrew the hand he'd gently placed against Annette's swollen abdomen. "If all them French up there are like her, we'll never see the end o' this blasted war. No offense intended, o' course."

"Your winning of this war, monsieur, will lie, not in the . . . how do you say, *pluck* of the French, but, in the fact that there is a lack of unity, which, I fear, will be New France's undoing," Alain replied amiably. "That is why so many like myself and my friends have left to return to a country that knows no king."

"Now there's a fine thought!" Tom agreed heartily.

Annette looked from her brother to her husband in astonishment. "Listen to the both of you. You speak treason!"

"No king an ocean away really cares about his subjects in the colonies," Alain protested stubbornly. "*Dieu,* not even our own Canadians came to the rescue of innocent women and children being shipped off like cattle, separated from the men and each other."

"A bloody damned outrage, to my thinkin'!" Thomas agreed. "I never saw such a sight as them that came off that ship. Herded like animals, they were, scared and hungry. Except for Annie, that is." Again he cast an affectionate look at his wife. "She was standing like a rock in a runnin' stream, waitin' for her sisters and mama. Not bein' much in height, o' course, she was havin' a time of it, so I pulls her off to the side and lifts her up on a barrel."

"At first I thought he was trying to abduct me," Annette injected, chuckling gently.

"Aye, and the fierce look she gave me was enough to kill a lesser man. Instead, it melted me heart right in me chest."

"He grinned at me like a simple mule and pointed

at the others coming off the ship, saying *Look, lass, look. Pretty lass, look!"*

"I went down to the docks to see about some tools and come back with two French colleens with the damnedest blue eyes I've ever seen."

Annette went on to tell how she and her sister had been separated from Marie Beaujeu and Laurette before leaving the ship. Later, her search among the refugees proved fruitless. Whether her mother and sister had been among those indentured by the ship's officers in the first group that disembarked or were carried on to another destination down the coast, she'd had no idea.

"What would you have done if Mama and Laurette had been with me?" Annette teased suddenly.

"Come home with four women, I guess. Ye'd have come along a lot quicker, to be sure!" Tom snorted, a good indication of the trouble his wife had given him in the beginning of their relationship. "I tried for three weeks to talk her into leavin' that hellish camp . . . even tried to find your mother meself."

"I told him I didn't believe in love at first sight. That I would have to know him better," the older sister injected, her twinkling gaze belying her smug tone.

"So I missed gettin' in me crops and stayed in New York till this last spring with me mother. After a month, Annette and Liselle moved in as well to help her, her bein' a seamstress and them both bein' mighty handy with a needle. Me'n Annie shod the horse Christmas and by God's grace, this comin' Christmas we'll have us a healthy babe."

Tamson wondered if Tom's wide show of teeth was anything like the mulish grin his wife had described. As the two went on with the story of their romance, she couldn't help but sigh in envy. She and Alain had once had that special glow, no matter where they were. It was a bond born of their love for each other. She regarded him quietly, wondering if he too was reminded, but, to her disappointment, he was intent on clinging to every word about the fate of his family.

Tom's mother was the seamstress for the wife of the *Mercury* editor, who saw to it that ads were placed in all the major cities down the coast in hopes of locating Marie and Laurette Beaujeu. Then, just before Tom was ready to leave in the early spring with his new wife and sister, word came that Marie Beaujeu and Laurette were in Annapolis, where Marie had used her Paris education to acquire a position teaching French and music.

"They hope to earn enough money to cover their lodgings and make the trip to New York before the baby comes," Annette said wistfully. "I suppose that is where it will be born now."

Tom sobered at his wife's remark. " 'Tis just as well, lass. I'm regrettin' ever bringin' ye back up here, least-wise, while the war's still ragin'. I could'a took up a job at the shipyard. Now I will. There's no need to build something for the heathens to burn, even if there was time to cut and dry the timber to raise it between now and winter." His expression, despite his attempt to hide it, was so forlorn it tugged at Tamson's heart.

"Hah!" Annette exclaimed, hugging his arm to her before addressing her brother. "He is like you. He chokes in the city!"

"There's too many people tellin' a man what to do! At least here, I only had you and the mite over there!" Tom nodded toward Liselle, who had relieved Tamson of bathing the feverish Englishman so that she might enjoy the wild turkey Gaspar roasted over the spit, fire posing little problem since the charred remains of the house and chimney still smoked.

"I'm not a mite—I'm a young woman now," Liselle protested good-naturedly. It was evident the in-laws enjoyed their teasing rapport. "I'm nearly seventeen and . . . and look, Alain! I have a bosom now!" The slender girl puffed out her chest as much as it would go, for she was not as round and well-proportioned as her older sister.

"Liselle!"

"But he is my brother!" the more precocious of the two siblings countered with an utterly guileless expression.

"Is *that* what that is?" Alain exclaimed, falling in with the risqué devilment. "I thought two of the blackberries she'd been picking had dropped down her neck."

Even Tamson laughed. What a delight it must have been to share the same house with such a loving family, she thought enviously. While Aunt Penelope was a dear, she lacked a sense of humor and such a thing was ne'er heard of at the school for young girls, except among the schoolgirls themselves after the matron had retired.

"I think she's beautiful."

Liselle gasped, staring down at her patient, who, until now had been in a state of semi-conciousness. Mark Heathcote held her startled gaze and reached up to touch the long dark braids which hung from beneath her cap, but his weakness from his wound was such that his hand fell back to his side limply and he closed his eyes once more. The movement held the astonished Liselle in uncharacteristic speechlessness for a long while.

Suddenly she looked up at Alain. "Is this one married?"

"Liselle!" Annette's cheeks pinkened in embarrassment for her bolder sister.

Undaunted, Liselle lifted a stubborn chin and added in a condescending tone, "I only meant that he must be married and thought that I was his wife."

It was a smooth recovery, but it fooled no one, including her brother. With a knowing grin, Alain pushed himself to his feet and turned to help Tamson up from the log which served as her chair. *"Non, ma bonne Liselle,"* he tossed over his shoulder, "he is not married and I happen to know he has excellent taste in women."

Shocked at first by the sudden switch of Alain's attention, Tamson warmed under the blue embers kindling in his gaze. Naturally, he'd made the comment to accomplish the utter destruction of the younger girl's composure—and quite effectively, for Liselle blushed a fierce red. When Alain Beaujeu chose to charm, he was devastating.

"I will help you make up your bed, mademoiselle," Alain said to Tamson, "and then Tom and I will go relieve Gaspar and Jacques from the watch. They will be leaving us in the morning."

"They?"

Somewhere among the embers of her hope, a spark ignited at his choice of words. Did she dare think he was changing his mind? After all, even if he was having a change of heart, he did not deserve to be taken back with open and eager arms.

"I will see you and your captain to safety and catch up with them later," Alain added in a matter-of-fact manner, dashing her expectations. "Tomorrow, you may even sleep in a real bed at the inn next to the ferry."

Tamson answered with a strained smile, trying to hide her feelings. A few feet away, Tom tucked Annette in, taking special care to insure his unborn infant's warmth before kissing her lightly on the cheek. When she forced herself to look away from the sweet intimacy the two shared, her envious gaze locked with Alain's.

For a moment she thought he might give way to that flicker of emotional indecision. Instead he smoothed out the blankets for her and rose, wiping his hands on his trousers.

"Bon soir, mademoiselle. Take heart. You are almost home."

Twenty-four

Almost home. Tamson tossed on the leafy bed, finally turning so she could stare into the fire, which was now reduced to embers. Somewhere there in the trees beyond, Alain kept a protective watch over his loved ones with the same dedication as his brother-in-law. Much as she wanted to think that she counted among them, she no longer had reason to. If he truly loved her, how could he leave her, simply drop her off like a piece of baggage and be on his way?

Emotion clouded her eyes and she blinked it away willfully, wishing her fatigue would work its anesthetic wonder once again on her heart. Emotion would not do, she chided herself sternly, the memory of Alain's admonishment the night they'd escaped Montreal ringing in her ears. *I merely told you so to keep you from getting hysterical and unmanageable like you are becoming at the moment.*

Nor could she simply lie here in insufferable silence, a more rebellious part of her nature insisted. She'd always been one to reach for what she wanted—and usually got it. She'd overcome the alleged barrier of religion to marry Alain Beaujeu. Was she going to let him put her aside now without a fight?

If she'd traipsed over high and low country from

Montreal to New York, enduring Alain's cold disregard, then she could certainly stand up to him now and weather the result. He couldn't possibly hurt her any more than he had already. He either loved her or he didn't, and whichever way it was, she wanted the truth.

With more spirit than she'd been able to summon of late, Tamson threw off her blanket, inadvertently fanning smoke from the fire toward the place where Jacques and Gaspar lay sleeping. Climbing to her feet, she studied the dark forest pitted against a clear starlit sky and then started in the direction Alain had taken, her blanket wrapped cloak-like about her shoulders to ward off the night chill. This was likely the last chance she'd have to speak with him alone, perhaps forever.

She'd heard Alain say he was going to take the watch down by the creek, which ran through the forest toward the land where the Malones hoped to build their future home someday. As she ventured into the trees and out of the bright moonlight, however, it was Tom Malone who she found first.

Although he gave her no more than a cursory glance, Tamson grew warm about the neck and face imagining what he was thinking when he congenially pointed further downstream to the place where Alain sat hidden in watch. "If I was you, lass, I'd hum a merry tune, lest he think a drunk savage was comin' up on 'im and make a terrible mistake."

Keeping Tom's advice in mind, Tamson did just that. It was no more than the tune to one of Marielle's favorite nursery rhymes, but, walking alone in the vast forest would not permit her to manage anything requiring more concentration. Animals, snakes, and insects of all varieties surely lurked in the dark surrounding her.

Undaunted, at least in appearance, she boldly
tramped on, determined not to give Alain the opportunity to call her a *silly goose* again. She was a woman,
a woman in love who deserved the full truth.

"*Dieu,* what manner of squeaking mouse is wandering about the woods instead of sleeping cozily in her
bedroll?"

Alain's wry comment came seemingly out of nowhere, killing the last note of the melody in Tamson's
voice and choking off her sharp gasp. Motionless, she
waited until he revealed his hiding place. Instead of
getting up from his comfortable position propped
against a tree, he motioned for her to enter into his
secluded retreat.

"How can you watch anything in here?" she queried.

"I can see out between the branches, but I listen more
than I watch. Savages use animal calls to communicate.
One familiar with the ways of the forest night creatures
can tell which are real and which are not . . . most of
the time," he admitted with a unassuming grin. Then
he was wary again. "And to what do I owe the honor
of this visit, mademoiselle? Do Gaspar and Jacques
snore so much that you cannot sleep or is it that you
fear the savages."

"Neither, actually. I've just been thinking."

"About home?"

"About us," she answered, grateful that her voice did
not crack with the rush of emotion sweeping through
her. "There *is* an us, Alain, even if it is not recognized
by the law or the church. I do not see how you can deny
it after all we . . . well, all we've shared." Of their own
accord, her cheeks began to burn at the thought of the

tempestuous nights and giddy afternoons, the lazy mornings . . .

"We were a charade, Tamson, no more."

Tamson raised her gaze to Alain's face, but he was not looking at her. Instead he stared out at the nearby creek, a sparkling ribbon cutting whisperlike through the earth-brown forest floor. The slivers of moonlight shining through the needled canopy highlighted his rugged features, tempting Tamson to trace them with her finger. He was evading the answer just as he'd evaded any contact between them since they'd left Montreal.

It was something she could not let him do. She wouldn't be ignored. He'd tell her the truth she deserved. Impulsively, she yanked on the leather thong which held his long dark hair in check at his neck.

Her unexpected act startled him. *"Sacré bleu,* what are you about?"

"Trying to get your attention," she answered in complete candor. "I've been wanting that all evening, Alain Beaujeu . . . or actually, the whole bloody trip!"

Lips thinned, her companion exhaled through his nostrils, as if blowing off his annoyance at her intrusion of his privacy.

"And damn you, you owe me the courtesy of listening to me!" She grabbed his face between her hands and forced it toward her. "And looking at me." Tamson rose up on her knees, her resolve suddenly undermined by the realization of just what she did look like. Her belligerent expression faltered. "I know I don't look like much in these awful skins and my hair hasn't seen a comb in days, but I *am* a woman, Alain . . . a woman very much in love with you."

"Tamson . . ."

"And as that," she went on, silencing him with her raised voice, "I deserve the truth from you." She swallowed dryly, all too aware that it might not be what she wanted to hear, yet she pressed on. "That's all I ask."

To her surprise, a grin flashed across his face. "Don't look like much?" he echoed, effecting a lightheartedness. "Mademoiselle, I am only glad that the animals which once occupied those skins cannot see how much better you make them look. That alone would kill them."

It took Tamson a moment to realize what he was doing. It was his more charming version of evasion, but it was evasion nonetheless. Anger reinforced her flagging spirit.

"I'm serious, Alain Beaujeu!" she declared, taking him by his fringed shoulders and giving him a rough shake. "Damn your soul, you look me in the eye and tell me that I never mattered to you, that it was all a cruel trick to get me to act the obedient captive, and I'll go home without another word." She shook him again when a renegade sob came out of nowhere to interrupt her defiance. Not now, she prayed, forcing back her anguish as she grabbed his face between her hands and insisted through clenched teeth, "Just don't lie to me anymore!"

Before her eyes, Alain's expression grew stonelike. He made no effort to pull away, nor did he show any further sign of intolerance or exasperation. *"Très bien, mademoiselle.* No lies."

Tamson sniffed back her emotion, wiping her stinging eyes with her sleeve. Nervously, she brushed back the short, copper-gold curls which had escaped her braid in an effort to regain her composure. She leaned back, crossing her arms over her breast as though she feared it might need protection.

That alone was nearly enough to make Alain abandon all his resolve. He sifted through the words that came to his mind, words about how what had passed between them should never have been and there was no future in continuing such a relationship, but they were not the ones that came out, driven by his restraint-wearied heart.

"I love you, Tamson. I wish I did not, but that is like wishing that we had never made love or lived as husband and wife. It cannot be undone. It simply is."

"Oh, Alain!"

Alain caught Tamson as she threw herself into his arms and sealed his lips with a kiss—a long, fervent, grateful expression of joy. Her tears wet his lips as he held her, giving her rein, for to abandon his own will to the sweet, ardent temptation would be both their undoing. *Dieu,* but how was he going to convince her that love alone would not solve all their problems?

"I knew it!" she whispered breathlessly. "Even when I was hurting so much, I just couldn't believe you could change so heartlessly. There's always a noble reason when you try to deceive me."

"Tamson . . ."

"We have more chance of happiness together than we've ever had, what with your family and mine coming together here. Can't you see?" she rushed on shakily. "After all, what is there to go back to in Acadia? Your lands have been given away! You have nothing there and all manner of opportunity here."

"To be hanged, you mean." Alain hated to crush her again, to see another wounded look haunt her gaze.

"You've done enough for Mark and me to . . ."

He put his finger to her lips. *"Dieu,* Tamson, can you not see the folly of it? Politics are the least of my worries. Your father, he will not be so easily assuaged. It is you, *ma petitesse,* who does not take this seriously."

"I'll handle Father," Tamson shot back eagerly. "He wouldn't hang the father of his grandchild!"

Were it not for the tree at his back, Alain would have reeled back at her hastily blurted argument. Mentally, he still did. Perhaps he had misunderstood. His jaw clenched as he ventured cautiously, "You have reason to think that you are?"

"Not since before Monsieur Ailleboust's party," Tamson answered, reading the calculation that ran rampant through his mind concerning her monthly indisposal.

Such was Alain's shock that he failed to note the telltale quiver in her voice. "But you have been upset. I have heard such things cause these inconsistencies. It is uncertain, non?"

But then there was her fatigue, he reasoned, not to mention her lack of appetite. Still, it could all be a mistake. Ailleboust's party. That was what, six weeks ago? That was not so much beyond, he thought, having heard his mother and father speculate on just the same subject . . . except that his parents had discussed such a prospect with anticipation. This was . . .

Before Alain could decide just what his reaction to Tamson's declaration was, his cheek burst hot with the sting of her angry palm. Startled, he put his hand to the inflamed area as the girl struggled to her feet and glared down at him.

"You're absolutely right, monsieur! It *is* uncertain!

But I can tell you what I am certain of!" she, hands flying to her hips in absolute fury. "I'm tired of begging for crumbs of affection. To hell with you, Alain Beaujeu! If I am carrying your child, I'll be just as glad that you're gone, because you, monsieur, do not know the meaning of the word *love*. You think it grows in your breeches, not here!" she swore, striking her chest. "I . . . oh, to hell with ye, ye swaggerin' blackguard!"

The tree shook as Tamson fought her way through the low-growing branches out into the clearing. She heard Alain call her name, but she could take no more of his ambivalent manner. She meant it. To hell with him!

"Tamson!"

"If ye so much as come a step closer, I'll scream the bloody forest down about your ears!" she shrieked back, her high-pitched whisper sharp and brittle with intent. She'd not only made a total fool of herself, throwing herself into his arms in utter forgiveness as she'd vowed not to do, but she'd let her suspicion about the baby slip out in the process.

Alain paused and leaned on his rifle as he watched the petite figure in the oversized buckskins pace off, making more thunder with her angry moccasined feet than a spooked buffalo. He swore in silent vehemence, when what he really wanted was to run after her and drag her back to show her his real feelings. He also knew Tamson well enough to let that Scottish temper cool before trying to get near her.

Sacré bleu, a child was exactly what he'd tried so hard, yet apparently ineffectively, to avoid. *Not because he did not want one,* he argued with himself, but because it would make their separation so much harder on both of them. Shoulders sagging in defeat, Alain climbed back into the brush and fell against his tree. As he did so, he discovered the blanket Tamson had left behind and breathed a short sigh of relief.

She would be back, he told himself. Then they could talk this out reasonably. Again he tried to calculate the time that had passed since he'd been bedridden with the measles, for that was surely when it had happened. Six weeks, maybe seven, he guessed generously.

Despite his consternation and guilt, a smile spread on his lips, revealing even white teeth. Tamson had a ready answer for everything. Her father would have to accept him as the father of her child. *Dieu,* but dare he even dream that this might somehow change things? The saints knew he wanted to spend the rest of his life loving Tamson Stewart.

Yet, for the first time since it all began, it appeared as if his luck was changing. They'd escaped Montreal, effectively ending the lives of the Marquis de la Galisonne and his wife so that, without retribution, Joseph and Isabelle could start over in France at the estate Alain did not need or want. They'd survived the dangerous journey through savage and military patrolled lands, bringing the Englishman and Tamson into their own territory, only to, incredibly, find his sisters and discover his mother's whereabouts.

But he was not quite the romantic that the woman he loved was. While Mark Heathcote had insisted he would speak on Alain's behalf with the government to enable him to become a colonial, he would have no sway with Tamson's rightfully outraged father. The last thing Alain wanted was for Tamson to be torn between him and her only family. Families should not be torn apart, physically or emotionally. There had been enough of that in these hellish times.

The only chance he and Tamson had for happiness was the baby—*his baby.* A feeling of wonder swept over him in spite of his hopeless frustration. *Mon Dieu,* a baby! A son, perhaps. Or a daughter, he amended, not the least bit particular. Could he abandon his child as well as its mother without so much as a fight? Alain buried his face in his folded arms at the onslaught of yet another perspective to his quandary.

Having reached the quiet campsite, Tamson sat on one of the logs pulled about the fire for benches, trying to hold back the agony flaying her heart. It wasn't at all the way she had planned. She'd asked for the truth, but she got more than she wanted.

She hadn't intended to mention the baby. It just slipped out in her rush of enthusiasm over Alain's admission of love . . . or what he *called* love. Never would she have dreamed Alain would have been so adverse to the idea that she was carrying his child! The look on his face! One would have thought she'd told him she was going to shoot him point blank between the eyes!

Or perhaps she *should* have guessed, she thought, recalling Alain's initial avoidance of her bed. No doubt it was more fear of getting her in a family way than any religious conviction that had been at the root of his resistance. A child would make it more difficult to get rid of her later, which was what he'd intended all along. Tamson closed her eyes and rubbed her arms, chilled more by her despair than the damp night air. She'd even left her blanket!

"Mademoiselle may I have the favor of your attention, *s'il vous plaît.*"

Tamson started out of her melancholy to see the source of her misery kneeling in front of her. His rifle rested across his knee and his thick raven hair, still untethered, hung past his collar in disarray. One lock fell forward on his somber face as he leaned toward her, giving him a perfectly rakish look. But for his blue eyes, he'd have looked the savage. No, not quite, an inner voice argued. He was uncertain. It showed in the awkwardness of his manner.

"I would ask your forgiveness for my reticent behavior back there, Tamson."

With uncharacteristic apprehension, Alain glanced over his shoulder at the sleeping figures surrounding them before, only mildly reassured, he returned his gaze to her. Nonetheless, it was only after he'd wiped damp palms on his knees and fortified himself with a deep breath that he proceeded.

"Perhaps we might go somewhere more private."

Tamson shook her head. "Whatever you have to say, sir, I will hear it here and now." She almost regretted the words the moment they were out, for annoyance reared in the pale blue of his gaze. Even as she watched, however, he forced it into submission and nodded.

"Très bien."

Again he glanced about, his Adam's apple bobbing as he swallowed dryly, lips poised as though groping for words.

"I admit that I have not known for certain what I was doing since I fell in love with you . . . or perhaps I should say, with your picture." He was actually sheepish, she thought, taken aback by this very different side of Alain Beaujeu. Why, he was even perspiring. She could see the damp film glistening on his forehead as his gaze darted to the fire and back to her. "It is silly, non? But then, you make me crazy, *ma petitesse.*"

His hand shook as he gently wiped the wet tracks left by her tears with the back of his hand. "So crazy that I am going to ask something of you, which I have no right to do."

"Wh . . . what?" Tamson refused to anticipate the question. She didn't think she could stand yet another disappointment, even if he was kneeling before her in a pose that suggested all her anguish was in vain.

"Tamson Stewart, I wish that you would give me your hand in marriage at the church in the village tomorrow, or tonight if you wish." Her breath caught in wary exultation, as though she still did not trust her ears. "And then our union will be so legal in the eyes of God and man that you will not be able to get rid of me, even if you wish."

"And . . . and what if this is a false alarm? What if I'm not really with child?"

With a bone-melting look that would not release her, Alain took her hand and raised it to his lips, tenderly planting a kiss against her first knuckle. "Then we shall try again." The second knuckle got its turn. "And again," he said, moving on to the third. "And again." Proceeding onto the last, he whispered, his impassioned gaze still locked with her own, "And again . . . until we have a house full of laughing little girls with bright curls and big brown eyes that will steal the heart of any man . . . like her maman, non?"

Whether Tamson chuckled or sobbed, she couldn't say. It was a half hysterical noise of elation and disbelief. "And boys?"

"Enough to make us wish for more girls," Alain answered, his rakish self surfacing with the promise of her acceptance.

"With dark hair? And blue eyes that will cause a girl's heart to trip each time they find her?"

"They will be their father's sons, will they not?" At Tamson's chiding look, Alain put his hand to his chest. *"Mon Dieu,* am I wrong? It is not my eyes that have won your heart, mademoiselle? My charm then, *non?"*

"Non." She went into his extended arms and placed her head against his shoulder as he hugged her.

"My dark, handsome looks?"

"Non."

He lifted her face to search her gaze. "Then what, pray tell, was it, *ma pétite,* that has blessed me with such a determined and devoted bride-to-be?" He hesitated a moment, suddenly confronted with the fact that she'd not actually said yes to his proposal. "I *have* been blessed, *non?"*

This time Tamson could not help but laugh. "Yes, you have been blessed. I'm not letting you get away this time!"

"Then what is it to which I owe such a blessing?" His voice dropped to a playful rumble. *"My lovemaking?"*

Once again Tamson shook her head. Finally, she placed her hands against his chest and stared at him through a joyous mist. "Your heart, Alain Beaujeu. Your brave, noble, loving heart."

The devilment Alain had mustered to cover his uncertainty died in the face of Tamson's sweet assault. "There are times, *ma chérie,* when this heart has failed in all three of those qualities."

"It had its reasons and all of them unselfish. There

is little, Alain Beaujeu, that you do solely for yourself. You always take others into consideration, even those who were once cruel to you—like Joseph and his wife."

Their gazes locked and their surroundings faded with the heart-to-heart exchange. Nothing stood between them now; the truth had made it all insignificant compared to the bond forged by their unselfish love for one another.

As Tamson melted against him, drawn by his wordless bidding, Alain touched his forehead to hers and whispered huskily, "Alas, mademoiselle, I fear now I am going to have to prove you wrong, for I am doing this," he murmured, his arm closing about her waist as if never to let her go again, "solely for my own sake."

His was a tender plunder, gentle and probing. Where *surrender* may have been the only acceptable term for his searing possession, Tamson went beyond that, caressing, adding fuel to the wildfire that reached its all-consuming flashpoint. Her body came alive, eager for the stirring caress of his hands, starved for the bountiful feast he provided.

"There! You owe me sixty sous, *mon ami!*"

"I was hoping I would, you old jackal!"

While Tamson did not hear Jacques Dupré collecting his wager from his companion Gaspar, Alain did. Confused when her lover's worshipful lips broke into a toothy grin and he backed away, she looked up at him blankly, still caught in the heat that had enveloped them. Vaguely, she felt the hands that had been most deliciously exploring the round curves of her buttocks move hastily to the less scandalous region of her waist. It was only as Alain looked over his shoulder and spoke, however, that she realized they had an audience.

"The least you two might have done was *pretend* to sleep! When did you place your bets . . . last week in Prairie?"

The two men exchanged amused glances, suppressing their laughter for the sake of the two females sleeping on the other side of the campfire.

"It was a year ago, I believe. When we first met the mademoiselle," Gaspar admitted.

"You were wearing Cupid's arrow right between your eyes, *mon ami.* You just couldn't see it," Jacques chimed in, striking himself on the forehead in eloquent demonstration. "I am only sorry that we will not be present for the wedding. I hate to miss the chance to kiss the bride."

"Well, we can't have that!" Too elated to let even the thought of her two traveling companions' departure dampen her joy, Tamson rose with Alain's help and walked over to where the two voyageurs were rolling up their blankets. Approaching Jacques first, she stood on tiptoe and bussed him on the cheek. Suddenly, she was caught in a bear-like hug and kissed full on the mouth.

"If I am going to kiss a woman," he explained, upon releasing her, "I am going to make it worth my while! That kiss may have to last me through a whole winter, non?"

Tamson cast a disconcerted look Alain's way in time to catch his reassuring wink. Nonetheless, she was more restrained when she reached up to Gaspar. Unlike his gregarious partner, however, the more wiry of the two returned her chaste peck in the same fashion with a warm, energetic hug.

"Viva l'amour!" he teased. His smile was so wide,

his hawklike nose nearly touched his chin. "If we must lose our partner to matrimony, it is better that it is to such a kind and gentle woman as yourself, mademoiselle."

"But this is not the last you will see of us, be assured!" Jacques warned them amiably. "We will be back to bounce our nieces and nephews on our knees and teach them how to hunt and trap, since our Alain will be too fireburned to remember!"

"You're going *now?*" Tamson asked, upon watching the men take up the sacks into which they'd stuffed their bedrolls. For some reason, she thought they were going to take up the watch her husband-to-be had abandoned.

"It is a clear night, mademoiselle, too pretty to waste on sleep."

"Or spend it listening to two lovebirds coo," Jacques remarked dryly before seizing Alain's arm and shaking it firmly. *"Bon voyage, mon ami.* We will remember you in the wilderness as usual."

Alain hugged Jacques fiercely and backed away. "I owe you both much."

"And we will collect," Gaspar promised, reaching out to shake Alain's hand as he added, *"wherever* you finally settle down. The voyageur, he knows no country, non?"

"And no allegiance except to his friends," Alain finished in agreement.

"Au revoir, monsieurs," Tamson whispered as the two Frenchmen turned away from the camp. "God speed."

Beside her, Alain echoed softly, *"Va avec Dieu."*

Twenty-five

The small church at Bull Ferry had no bell, nor was there an organ to celebrate the occasion. It was a single room with open rafters, crude benches, and a hard-packed dirt floor. All that set it aside from the other structures of the village were the furnishings—stone statues of the saints and the small altar with its hand-stitched scarf and accouterments of gold and silver.

After a long dissertation in Latin, the words of the ceremony itself were short and to the point. Yet none ever sounded so beautiful to Tamson as her husband swore before God to love, keep, and protect her until death separated them. Ironically, it was she who was perspiring, now that she'd finally gotten Alain Beaujeu to the altar. Her voice shook with emotion, but somehow, with the reassuring squeeze of Alain's hand, Tamson made her vows at the prompt of the priest. Soon they were bound at the wrists by his embroidered satin sash, listening to the pious Latin prayer for happiness and love under God all the days of their lives.

When the scarf was removed, Alain had stood all the propriety his restless nature would allow. He gathered his bride into his arms and kissed her most irreverently until she was nearly in a swoon from want of air. Surrounded by his two excited sisters and new brother-in-law, he and Tamson thanked the priest with a contribution and left the small building as husband and wife.

With more gold coin from the heretofore untouched purse he'd had Jacques acquire on his behalf before leaving Prairie, Alain arranged for food and lodgings for the wedding party at the small inn by the ferry. Although it was impossible to share his wedding night alone with his bride, for the inn had only two upstairs rooms, one for men and one for women, he made the most of her company and that of his family over the post-nuptial meal. Their long tavern table next to the open window afforded them the benefit of the afternoon breeze and allowed him to see his buckskinned bride as he hoped he would always see her—radiant and happy.

Even Tom and Annette managed to shake off the clouds of their recent ill fortune to join in the celebration, although the word of the Indian raid had certainly circulated the village and filled its citizens with alarm. The fact that he was French and a stranger had certainly earned him his share of speculative looks, although his English bride and the English officer in his company helped to placate them.

Yet, not even their suspicion could dampen Alain's mood. He wouldn't let it . . . not on the day he'd married the girl of his dreams. And he had walked into this knowing the wariness would come. For Tamson and his child, he was even willing to face her father's rage and try to make peace. The rest of their future depended on how convincing Mark Heathcote could be of Alain's political neutrality.

"Maman will be so happy to see that she now has not only a new son, but a new and very pretty daughter!" Liselle cheered, raising a cup of ale to toast the bride and groom. "I think it is so romantic! Perhaps some day I will be carried off by a handsome stranger and we will marry and . . ."

"I think Mama will be even more thrilled to have *two* grandbabies on the way!" Annette interrupted.

"I *think!*" Tamson reiterated, lest things get too carried away.

Alain had not been able to keep the news to himself. It had been his only release, since they had not been able to finish what his fiery engagement kiss had started. Instead, he went to Tom Malone at sunup, then awakened Tamson with a kiss and rolled his sisters out of their beds by unceremoniously snatching their blankets out from under them to share his news.

"Lass, I knew ye was with babe the first time I laid eyes on ye. An expectin' mother has a special look like no other. I just wasn't clear as to which o' the men ye was partial to, no offense intended."

"None taken, Tom."

"Speaking of the *other man*," Liselle piped up brightly, "I think I'll go over to the doctor's and see how Captain Heathcote is doing. If he wakes up and finds a total stranger tending him, he might take a turn for the worse."

"I've heard it happen many a time," Tom remarked dryly, exchanging a knowing look with his wife. " 'Twouldn't do to have 'im set back none."

Instead of answering, Liselle poked an impish tongue out at her brother-in-law and ducked through the open door of the tavern.

"I do believe the mite's taken a likin' to that militia man," Tom observed, fondly watching her through the window.

The moment they'd arrived at Bull Ferry, Alain and Tom had carried Mark Heathcote to the home of an elderly doctor whom the villagers refused to let retire. They'd spirited the man from his gardening to see to the festering wound on Mark's leg before Alain went on to make the arrangements for the wedding. Just before the ceremony, however, the prospective groom checked back with his ex-rival to find the patient sleeping peacefully, his wound freshly lanced and drained of the strength-robbing infection.

"Wait until she sees Mark in uniform. He does cut a fine figure," Tamson blurted out without thinking. A dismayed "Oh!" escaped her lips as she turned anxiously to Alain in time to see that damnable brow of his arched at her. His dancing gaze, however, gave him away and she struck him playfully on the chest. "Arch that eyebrow all you wish, monsieur, 'tis *you* that I married."

"So it is, *Madame Beaujeu.*"

Alain lifted her hand to his lips and caressed it with a wanton look that ran her through. Color spread from her neck to her hairline, reflecting the heat pouring through her at his unspoken suggestion. Yet, she would not curse fate that that night she would again be denied her husband's bed. Regardless of how fierce their mutual longing was, she was his and for now, that was all that mattered.

Nonetheless, there was no harm in basking in the glow of Alain's gaze. And if her thoughts wandered scandalously to the carnal edge, why not? After all, this was her wedding day.

"Well, I'll be buggered, look what's here now that we don't need 'em," Tom announced.

Reluctantly, Alain withdrew his attention from the passionate promise in his wife's eyes and looked up at the door where six members of the colonial militia stood, squinting to adjust their vision to the change in the light. They were oddly dressed in mismatched uniforms, but that was not so odd for those not part of His Majesty's Royal Forces. As they moved inside, the priest from the church followed and, after a moment, pointed to the table where the wedding party was seated.

"There they are. That's the ones whose place was burned by the savages and the other's Mrs. Malone's brother and his new bride."

"Typical," Tom commented dryly. "It's always safer after the redskins are gone."

The captain of the group, a rather stocky but nonetheless sturdy fellow, approached their table and took off his hat in deference to the ladies. With a loud cough, which he cast to the side, he cleared his throat and held out his hand.

"Mr. Malone, I be Captain Irons of the New York militia. We heard you'd had a Injun raid on your homestead. Can ya tell me what tribe?"

"I'm not sure. Abenaki or Wyandot . . ." Tom glanced at Alain for help.

"Abenaki."

The captain looked over at the voyageur. "So ya saw 'em?"

"Oui, I saw them as they were leaving with the livestock. There were only twelve or so . . . a small scouting party, I believe."

"And where were they headed, *monsure?*" the man added derisively in a poor attempt at the French address.

"Toward Lake George . . . possibly Fort William Henry."

"And o' course, ya didn't try to stop 'em."

Hair rose instinctively at the nape of his neck at the censure in the captain's manner, but Alain replied succinctly. "Monsieur, I had a wounded and feverish colonial officer and my wife to consider. The three of us would make a poor showing against a dozen savages whose bloodlust had not yet been satiated. Non, I let them pass and hid my friends in the trees."

"I unnerstand from that little Acadian girl that ya brung Captain Mark Heathcote and this young lady all the way from Montreal through enemy territory. That's quite a feat."

They'd taken Liselle? Alain's gaze darted to the door, but there was no sign of his sister. "It was as much by God's grace as skill."

The captain lifted his hand and two of the armed militiamen came forward, rifles poised. "Well, I guess the Almighty's grace is run out where you're concerned, *Monsure Alain Beaujeu.* Guess He's as fed up as us with the way you damned Frogeaters set Injuns against innocent folks. To my notion, would'a served ya right to find your sisters hairless and bug-eyed dead."

There were too many to take without risking harm to Annette and Tamson, Alain reasoned, even if Tom Malone were to assist him. Bewildered as to what had put these men so quickly on to him, Alain glanced at Tom Malone uncertainly. Had his brother-in-law tipped these men off? No, he could see the man was just as taken back as he. Then who? Alain wondered. Mark Heathcote? Is that how Tamson's former fiancé repaid him for saving his life?

"Just what are you getting at, sir? My husband is a neutral!"

Distracted from his quandary by his wife's outburst, Alain saw the way Tamson tilted her head in that defiant challenge that had first won his heart. However, it could also be annoying, especially to one not affected with love.

"Don't try it, Beaujeu! Just take it out slowly and put it on the table, if you please."

Although Alain had already had second thoughts about taking the captain with his knife and bolting through the window, he'd inadvertently moved his hand toward the hilt of the blade, lest the captain take exception to Tamson's objection. At the hammer click of the rifles, he did exactly as he was told.

Not the least daunted, however, Tamson did not back down. "I demand to know why you are harassing us like this! My God, we've just come through enemy territory and this is hardly the reception I expected from my own people!"

"Because, *Miss Tamson Stewart,*" the captain answered, reaching into his jacket as if searching for something. "This Frogeater is wanted for kidnaping, stealing livestock, and leading an Indian raid on your father's property."

Tamson's heart lodged against her throat as the man found the elusive paper in his jacket and unfolded it before her. There it was in black and white—a 10,000 pound reward for the capture of Alain Beaujeu offered by Squire James Stewart. "Well, I'm certain Father will drop all the charges after I speak to him," she managed not so convincingly.

"You gentlemen aren't militia then, are ye?" Tom

surmised contemptuously. "Ye're bloody bounty hunters!"

Captain Irons held up his hand, halting Tom as he
started up from the table. "Now we've no quarrel with
you, Malone, 'ceptin' we'll be takin' your wife an' her
sister to Albany to Squire Stewart. You're welcome to
tag along, but we'll be takin' your weapons."

"The bloody hell ye will!"

"Non, Tom!"

Heedless of his wife's restraining hand, Tom shot up
like an enraged bull to charge the man at the end of the
table, unaware of the accomplice who had slipped up
behind, rifle butt poised to stop him. Annette's warning
became a cry of alarm exploding with the crash of it
against the back of his head. She tried to catch him as
his legs crumbled beneath him, throwing him forward
across the table.

"He don't take much to invitations, does he, Cap'n?"
Tom's assailant chuckled, checking the butt of his rifle
for blood.

"You'll not get a penny from my father, you blunder-
ing bully!" Tamson shouted, stepping forward before
Alain could stop her.

"Oh, but we will, Miss Stewart, and likely get us a
bonus to boot, considering we stopped this marriage
before it . . . *took effect,* so to speak," he added meaningfully. "Now, 'twould be a shame to see a pretty girl
like you dressed in widow's black, so ya'd best behave
yerself." He looked beyond Tamson's shoulder to the
somber Frenchman standing behind her. "Gents, take
our prisoner into custody. The ladies can remain under
guard here at the inn tonight."

"Wait!" Tamson seized the sleeve of Irons' jacket and jerked it urgently. "I'll go with my husband."

"I don't think you'll appreciate the rest of the company he'll be sharin', miss. A blockhouse ain't a place for a lady."

"Do as he says, Tamson," Alain advised her grimly. "We can work this out when we get to Albany."

"Cocksure of yerself, ain't ye, Frogeater?"

"Why is it you wish to take me as well?" Annette demanded, drawing Irons' attention from her brother to where she held Tom's head in her lap, trying to stop the bleeding with her kerchief.

"Me 'n' the boys just come to fetch ya, you puttin' that ad in the paper so helpful like, but lo and behold, when we come, here's the squire's daughter and her kidnaper as well." The captain looked at his men and laughed as though sharing a common jest. "We'll sit right comfy after this 'un, eh, mates?"

"Alain?" Panicked, Tamson pushed her way to Alain as his hands were roughly tied behind his back.

"Stay with Annette and Tom. These men would not dare harm any of you. Not even your father would condone that and they know it."

"But I don't think the squire'd care what shape you was in when ya got to Albany, Frogeater, since he's got a hangman's noose just waitin' ta greet ya."

Tamson's knees nearly gave out at the threat, but she held her ground. Sick with fear for Alain, she forced it back and rallied. "If you harm one hair on his head, so help me, I'll put a noose around *your* neck, ye potbellied excuse for a man!"

Irons caught the hand that lashed out at his face and forced it down to Tamson's side. "How I treat our prisoner depends on just how well you and the other ladies behave, missy. Now, am I makin' meself clear or do I have to give you a demonstration?"

The man's signal was barely perceptible, but Tamson caught it and tried to pull away in protest. "No!"

The man next to Alain smashed the butt of his gun into his stomach before he saw it coming, nearly driving him to his knees. With sheer determination he struggled to remain upright, to convince Tamson he was all right, when he saw the brass glint of a second's musket flash before his pain-blurred vision.

In less time that it took to blink, his forehead burst with white agony, propelling Alain into the log wall behind him. Blood poured from the gash over his unseeing eye as he inched down the wall and suddenly in place of the blinding light, there was none at all.

Twenty-six

The homesteads hacked out in a forest-ridden landscape became more and more numerous and woodland trails gave way to well-trodden roads the morning of the second day. These signs of civilization lifted Tamson's wearied and battered spirit. Shortly after Irons had passed out some cold firecake, a hard-doughlike concoction, to stave off starvation, they met an army supply train bound for Fort William Henry outside of Albany and adrenaline began to pump through her veins. Home and help was close now, close enough to override her exhaustion from a poor night's rest and renew her restlessness to end the bounty hunters' reign of terror.

While Captain Irons and two of his men rode over to speak to the officer in charge, Tamson tried to listen for the sound of running water. There was a little falls where she and Mark had picnicked somewhere in this area, if she recalled correctly. She stared at the rise where the river should be, yet she didn't trust herself to be certain. If she made a run for it in the wrong direction, there could be hell to pay for the others. Unless she could convince the bounty hunters that she couldn't wait to see her father.

She glanced toward Irons speculatively. Squire Stewart could end this nightmare—she knew it. He'd do so for her sake, if for no other. He could keep Alain from going to the prison in the stone fort above Albany. If only she were sure of the way . . .

"The river is over the rise there, mademoiselle! Do you not recognize it?"

Tamson met Alain's knowing look. Despite her anxiety over the swollen bruises which had closed one of his eyes, she smiled. That was how it should be between man and wife, knowing each other's thoughts before they're even expressed. That was how close they'd become, how strong their love was. No, nothing was going to take him away from her . . . not now.

"Then home must be over there." She pointed south.

Instead of answering, Alain nodded and then stiffened at the sound of the approaching horse belonging to the guard who'd wandered over to watch the parade of wagons and soldiers.

"That's enough outta you, Frogeater!"

Alain, too, had stood the bounds of restraint too long. For the first time since leaving Bull Ferry the morning before, he stood up to his tormentors. It was bad enough that they'd used every excuse to badger him, but the sheer terror on Tamson's face as she'd watched helplessly had been more unbearable than the physical torment. Bracing himself, he leaned into the man's horse, causing it to stagger sideways before he gave way to its brute force.

He struck the ground and rolled to his feet, moving out of the tangle of the rope before it could be used against him. Breaking into a run, he proceeded to wrap it about the feet of the horse to which it was attached. Enough of a distraction might give Tamson the lead she needed to break away for help, not for himself, but for his sisters. He didn't want them subjected to more humiliation than they'd endured already.

As a gentleman, Squire Stewart might be persuaded to look after them, although Alain did not share his wife's anticipation that her father would speak in his behalf. To what degree Stewart had lost influence as a result of his alleged involvement in trading plundered goods with the enemy was a question that would soon be answered. His hope remained with the officer they'd left behind at the ferry and the gentleman Alain had asked Tom Malone to fetch with all haste to.

Watching as the remaining two militiamen sought to put the suddenly rebellious prisoner in his place, Tamson was torn between rushing to Alain's aid and seizing the opportunity the distraction afforded. In a split-second decision, she chose the latter. They would punish Alain now, whether she stayed or fled.

She kicked the roan with her heels and dug in as the animal, unaccustomed to such aggressiveness, leapt forward to climb the stretch of rock-studded grassland. Although it felt as if a portion of her heart remained with the man fighting overwhelming odds, another seemed to well with the exhilaration of escape. The fast gallop not only freed her of the smothering midday heat but of the equally unbearable and suffocating bondage she'd endured in body and spirit.

A rolling wheat field waited beyond the crest of the hill. As if sensing the sudden uncoiling of frustration and anxiety in its rider, Tamson's steed thundered down and across it, oblivious to the gentle slap of the stems on its underbelly or the temptation to snatch a mouthful from its bounty. Tamson would have whispered grateful and encouraging words to the roan were her heart not lodged against her throat.

It wasn't until she reached the other side that she dared to glance back to see the result of the confusion she'd left behind. Alain had evidently succeeded in keeping three of the guards at bay, for far in the distance, a lone rider followed her in heavy pursuit, his horse's neck stretched on the same plane as its back and tail. Recognizing Captain Irons' faded blue shirt billowing about his stocky frame, Tamson spurred her roan on once again.

God deliver her to familiar ground, she prayed in fervent silence, before she was overtaken by the man's more powerful horse. Even as her thoughts formed, however, the lather which had built up on her mare's red and white mottled coat slapped her face, underscoring the futility of her situation. She couldn't possibly reach Annanbrae before Irons caught them.

The sight of a small rushing creek dividing the cultivated field from a spacious pastureland and a familiar orchard beyond, however, revived her flagging hope. Ahead, in a small grove of chestnut trees, was the little house that Squire Stewart had first built for his wife and new daughter upon arrival in New York. He'd rented it to Adam Stilwell, the town schoolmaster. If her father could not come to her aid, surely his tenant would.

Tamson looked over her shoulder again, confirming what her ears already told her. Irons was rapidly gaining ground some hundred or so yards behind. Yelling at the top of her voice, she kicked the panting, snorting roan once more and headed straight for the cottage.

"Adam Stilwell! Help! Help me!"

The door was open on the porch as Tamson yanked

tight on the reins in the cottage yard. Before the horse was able to stop completely, she rolled off its back, falling to her knees with the momentum. Behind her she could hear the slowing hoofbeats of Irons' horse. She knelt there only long enough to wipe away in instinctive distaste the spatter of the roan's lather which had flecked her face.

"Help! Mr. Stilwell, help me!" she shrieked, scrambling half on her knees and half on foot to the planked floor of the porch.

Suddenly, one of the laces of her moccasins caught in a crack where two of the boards joined, seizing her up short, and she sprawled outright, scraping her palms over the timeworn wood. But for her buckskin sleeves, her elbows and knees would surely have suffered worse. The breath driven out of her by her fall, she tried to pull herself upright when she spied a pair of brown boots, worn but meticulously polished, in front of her face.

Somehow she found her voice. "For the love of God, help me, sir, I . . ."

Her remaining plea gave way in relief at the answering click of a hammer over her head, before she heard her protector demand of the approaching Irons, "What is the meaning of this, sir?"

"Only doin' what ye're payin' me to do an' more! We not only got two of them French gals ye sent us for, but we got him what took yer little girl and Miss Tamson 'erself!"

"Tamson?"

The man's voice was all too familiar to Tamson, but it was out of place. It belonged at Annanbrae, not the tenant house. She knew it nonetheless. It gave her the strength to push herself unsteadily to her knees, her raised gaze meeting one and the same amber hue as her own. "F . . . Father?"

It *was* him, an inner voice assured her, except that he looked . . . *different,* she decided after a moment, lacking a more suitable word. He was haggard, rather than his usual robust self. Where lines of laughter had added character to his handsome face, more severe ones told of heavy burdens previously unknown. Where cherry cheeks reddened by his daily rides across the estate had once glowed round and ripe, his skin sagged loose and pasty-hued over prominent cheekbones, as if the life had been drawn away.

Still, it was he, James Stewart—her hope. It was the man who had had the answers to all her quandaries since she was a wee thing bouncing on his knee. Clumsily, Tamson crawled to her feet and into James Stewart's open arms. "Oh, Father!"

"For the love o' God, lassie, did the bastard make a heathen of ye?" Stewart gasped, managing to prop his rifle against the rough-hewn outside wall. "Bless ye, I hardly knew ye!" He pulled the braided length of hair inside her shirt out, as if to be certain she was not the malnourished lad she appeared and was truly his daughter.

He'd lost weight, Tamson realized amidst her dizzying joy. She backed away and shook her head, smiling through the glaze blurring her vision. "No *he* made me his wife, Father." Suddenly, remembering Irons' presence, she swung an accusing finger in the bounty hunter's direction, smile fading. "And that man snatched us from our wedding celebration, took Alain's sisters against their will, and marched us over high and low road like bloody prisoners! I demand you have him and his men arrested at once!"

"She's been a bit of a handful, sir. I reckon that Frog-eater's got her sweet-talked to a fair-thee-well."

"Oh, my God, it *is* her!" a shrill female voice sounded from behind them.

Tamson's answering retort was crushed from her by the woman who rushed out of the house and seized her in an enthusiastic embrace. "P . . . Prudence!" she managed in a squeak of acknowledgment.

The housekeeper thrust her away for just a second, touching her face with joyful reverence, before drawing her to her again. "God bless you, sir!" she called out to Irons over her charge's shoulder, her voice breaking with an uncharacteristic sob. "I thought we'd never see her again!"

"That man took me prisoner! He still has my husband!" Tamson decried in frustration from within the smothering embrace.

Prudence stiffened. "Husband! Faith, don't tell me that young Heathcote found you!"

"No, ma'm. Heathcote's back at Bull Ferry with a festerin' leg," Irons spoke up. "Same place I fetched this'n up from her weddin' supper . . . *just in time,* if ya get my meanin'."

Upon realizing the drift of popular opinion shifting toward Irons, Tamson pulled away from the stricken housekeeper to face her father. "No, it wasn't . . . and I am perfectly sane," she averred, reading correctly the dubious cast of the gaze that fell upon her. "It's this bloody war that's crazy! It's made enemies of good people . . ."

"What are ye tryin' to tell me, lassie?" Squire Stewart quietly interrupted.

His impassive tone unsettled Tamson as she shifted beneath a gaze that almost begged her to deny her declaration. She'd been prepared for ranting and raving, not this uncharacteristic complacency. She'd always been able to disarm her father's hot temper.

"That . . . that I'm carrying your grandchild, Alain Beaujeu's baby. That we're married and that I love him. That he was bringing me home when these men abducted us. That you've got to do something to save him!"

"Poor child's gone half mad!"

"I am not mad, Prudence!" Tamson snapped, the sharpness of her voice, combined with her savage appearance, driving the housekeeper back with a gasp.

"The man's a murderer!" Prudence declared.

It was Tamson who faltered this time, icy panic skittering up her spine. Had death resulted from the raid which carried her away? "Carleton?" she asked anxiously.

"Carleton's fine. Dinna fret," her father assured her.

"Then *whom* did Alain murder?" she challenged, tossing up exasperated hands.

"He *could* have murdered my Carleton," Prudence declared. "You may not recall the fierceness on his face, but I see it every night in my dreams, him dragging you off with those savages."

"I've forgiven him. I pray you will, too, Prudence."

"When hell freezes!"

With no quarter there, Tamson swung back to her father. "He did it because he loved his family. He now loves me and would fight just as hard for me and his child."

Instead of answering her, Squire Stewart picked up his rifle from the wall where he'd propped it. "Prudence, take the lassie inside and make her look like a white woman!"

"No, I'm going back for Alain!" Tamson yanked free of the housekeeper's grip and leapt off the porch to catch up with her father. "I wish to lodge a complaint against this man and his men to his superiors. Then we'll take Alain and his sisters to Annanbrae and try to make up for the unforgivable indignities they've suffered at the hands of these . . ."

James Stewart put his hand over the restraining one Tamson placed on his arm and looked at her with such sadness that her anger and fear for Alain and his family wavered momentarily under the sway of yet another alarm—an instinctive one. "Nay, child, we'll do nay such thing. Things have changed this last hellish year. 'Tis we who are the tenants now."

Tamson glanced at the house again, disbelief claiming her face. She'd been so worried about Alain and her father's state of health that she'd not had time to inquire as to why James Stewart, not to mention Prudence, was here at the schoolmaster's. Annanbrae lost? The concept was more than she could comprehend. "What happened?"

Prudence put a sympathetic arm over Tamson's shoulder. "Come into the house, child, and I'll tell you all about it. Let your father see to his business."

Again Tamson rebelled. While her father wasn't raving, he had shown no sign of taking into account a single word she'd said in Alain's behalf. "No, I have to go with him!"

"Would ye have me hung for shelterin' the enemy, lassie? Strike me blue, I've lost everything as it is on the false accusation that I cavorted with the French and their savages for profit from their plunder! I canna afford to defend Beaujeu, even if I were inclined to, *which I am not!* Ye'll never know the hell he put me through." He afforded her buckskins a scathing look. "By the look of ye, ye'll be excused for your sentiments where the bastard's concerned. God knows what ye've suffered yourself."

"I've been through nothing compared to what you're doing to me now!" Tamson swore fervently. "Father, *please!* Mark will swear Alain saved our lives . . . that he's no threat to us or England."

" 'Tis nay pretty favor you're askin' for this time, lassie. I'll see him safe to the fort and bring the girls back here, but that's all I'll do. If he's innocent as ye say, he'll keep."

"What about the reward?"

"Aye," Stewart acknowledged to the bounty hunter. His shoulders fell as though yet another burden had just been laid upon them. "Ye'll get your reward, such as I have. 'Twas offered before all this," the man said, motioning toward the cottage.

"Father, this man treated us like the enemy!"

"For the love of God, Tamson, this is war! They were doing their duty to fetch you here!"

War! If she heard that used once more as an excuse for injustice she would scream! "If that forgives them, then it forgives Alain for what he did! Father, please, take me with you. Help me save him."

Without warning, James Stewart's reserved manner snapped. He thrust his finger at the panting, lathered mare. The thunderous rise of his voice was more in keeping with his old self, though it offered Tamson no comfort.

"What will ye ride, lassie, a dead horse?" he challenged. "I've *one* steed left to my name, such as it is, and *I'll* be takin' that! Now there's the end of it, Tamson girl!"

"Promise you'll see he's not hurt!" Tamson retaliated. She didn't want to push her father beyond his obvious limits—she just wanted desperately to force him to help her save Alain from imprisonment.

"Ye sure ye're with his child?"

Tamson nodded, praying with all her heart that she wasn't lying. She wanted Alain's baby. She wanted both father and grandfather to be happy over it. She wanted peace, at least among those she loved.

Like the one raging within her, a terrible battle waged in James Stewart's gaze as he turned away and forced his clipped reply. "Then I'll do what I can do and nae more."

Twenty-seven

"I wish you would not do this!"

As oblivious to Annette's plea as she was to her father's and Alain's orders, Tamson climbed onto the wagon which was borrowed from the main house. "Wild horses couldn't keep me away."

"But the doctor . . ."

"Is overreacting! I feel fine, I have felt fine, and I will be fine."

That wasn't exactly true. This morning was the worst yet and, damn her luck, it had been impossible to hide. While she wasn't certain the cause was as much her worry over Alain's fate as it was the baby, she'd spent an hour futilely retching. Her sister-in-law assured her it would be a short-lived inconvenience, but Tamson had her doubts in the midst of her misery.

She knew they were all concerned. In the weeks that had passed since arriving in Albany, she'd lost enough weight that even Alain had noticed through the small hatch in the opening of his cell door, despite the point she'd made of visiting in the afternoon when she was at her best. They'd kept him at the fort, for fear of citizens storming the local gaol and taking justice into their own hands, for the devastating news of the French victory at Oswego had hewn English outrage to a finer edge than ever.

"Alain will not like it. You know that." Annette was not one to belabor a point, but when she spoke, her words were well chosen and to the point. "He will be angry."

"That will be his problem," Tamson responded, knowing that while her sister-in-law's prediction was true, Alain wouldn't demonstrate his displeasure.

He hadn't so much as given the slightest weight to her first plea of responsibility for his being in this predicament, when he had every right to. He had warned her that this would happen, but she'd refused to believe it.

Instead, he'd only expressed his love and concern for her. Was she eating enough? Was her family too hard on her for marrying him? Why wouldn't she listen to the physician and rest, at least until she recovered from the hard and dangerous journey?

The ride into Albany passed quickly. Liselle and Squire Stewart maintained an involved conversation on horses, each giving their estimation of any they saw along the way. At least her father had warmed to Alain's sisters, but then, who wouldn't? Liselle's interest in horses had been the a great help in melting James Stewart's war-hardened heart.

As they drove by the locust-lined approach to Annanbrae's manor, Tamson studied the two-story Georgian mansion which had not changed while the rest of her life had. It was as magnificent and imposing as ever, reigning from atop the knoll her father had chosen. Outbuildings appeared as specks of white through the green foliage adorning its orchards and lawns. A strange carriage waited in front of the wide paneled door under the portico where two men stood, deeply involved in conversation.

From the road, she could not make out who they were. One was most likely the solicitor who had arrived earlier in the week to announce that its new owner was coming from New York for a stay before the winter set in. Perhaps the other was the man himself, she speculated, since Carleton and Prudence, who had been summoned as witnesses, were most likely already at the courthouse where the civil trial was to take place.

The military hearing, which had taken place three days ago, had declared Alain to be what he claimed, a Canadian neutral. Considering her choice of Alain over him, Tamson would be forever indebted to Captain Mark Heathcote for honoring his word to absolve Alain of any political affiliation.

Mark had accepted the news of her marriage graciously and shown nothing but the greatest concern for her welfare during his daily visits to the tenant house since his arrival in Albany. Now, however, the civil charges, which Tamson naively thought her family could simply drop at her request, were more threatening to her husband than those of espionage.

"Look, there's Mark!" Liselle shouted excitedly, spotting the officer conversing at the door of the large green shuttered building with the sheriff and another man. As they drew closer Tamson recognized William McShane, the young lawyer to whom Beatrice De Lancy was now engaged and who had recently been appointed by the governor to represent the Crown.

"Captain Heathcote," Annette reminded her sister with quiet consternation.

Demure did not exist in the gregarious Liselle's vocabulary any more than *coquette* did. Her feelings for Captain Mark Heathcote were written all over her face. Infatuation or nay, Tamson feared for Liselle's heart, for Mark, nine years her senior, treated the young girl more like a precocious child than a prospective love interest.

Leaving the officials of the court, Mark started toward them, answering Liselle's wild wave with a more reserved one. His leg still pained him as evidenced by the way he favored it. Although he'd arrived from Bull Ferry with a cane, he'd done away with it as a nuisance the moment he reported for duty at the fort.

"Mrs. Beaujeu, I do believe motherhood becomes you," he drawled gallantly, offering his hand to assist Tamson down from the wagon.

"Has that bullet affected your eyesight as well as your leg?" Tamson quipped.

She was all too aware that, but for her sash and petticoats, she looked like a waif in ill-fitted hand-me-downs. Mark's hands lingered at her waist as he searched her anxious gaze, making Tamson feel ill at ease for Liselle. Instead of voicing concern, however, he chose a lighter course.

"I've fallen off a bit, too, but for entirely different reasons," he added mischievously.

"What was Mr. McShane saying?" Tamson asked, shifting from the small talk to more important matters.

In his quest to ferret out those sympathetic to the French, William McShane had failed to win a conviction against her father. During the grand jury hearings, the attorney seemed determined to make up for the loss with Alain.

"Lord Loudoun is sitting in on the trial with the magistrate," Heathcote answered candidly.

"Loudoun?" her father exclaimed in astonishment. "What the devil is His Lordship's interest in Beaujeu?"

Mark shrugged. "Giving the mayor a rest, I suppose," he ventured wryly.

Almost as popular a scandal as Tamson's marriage to Alain Beaujeu was the ongoing battle between the new commander-in-chief of the English military and Albany's mayor concerning the billeting of His Majesty's soldiers.

"Who knows, maybe Alain will be the next mayor of the city."

Still concerned over her husband's trial, Tamson managed a chuckle at Mark's facetious comment. Since his July arrival in the colonies, the new commander-in-chief was now demanding its citizens freely house its inundation of fresh troops from England.

The number of complaints lodged against the official on both accounts had been shocking to anyone except a native of the city. Albany's population only took issue with the trade of *plundered* goods, but the fur trade was quite another matter. Until Loudoun, having vowed to remain neutral and unaffected by the war, the city had literally done so by virtue of its ongoing commerce with the enemy.

"The mayor has been lying low since His Lordship threatened to order all the troops on the continent to Albany if the man and the town's citizens did not comply with his directive to house his officers," Mark informed them.

As an outsider, he was as bemused as he was amused by the curious conflict. The other colonies condemned

Albany for its ambivalent loyalties. "I don't know how these people expect the King to protect them and not quarter his soldiers."

"But they didn't need protectin'," the squire pointed out, adding, "though they will now that the free tradin's stopped."

"Ah-hem!"

Distracted by Liselle's rather obvious ploy to gain his attention, Mark immediately abandoned the latest political gossip to lift her off the back of the wagon. "Forgive me, *ma petite ange de miséricorde* . . . my little angel of mercy." Once he set her down, he proceeded to gallantly kiss her hand.

The sound of approaching horses diverted Tamson's attention, however, as the carriage which she recognized as the one which had been in front of Annanbrae swept past them to come to a stop directly before the courthouse. Two men emerged from it, both of fair complexion and richly attired. To her astonishment, a third followed, dressed in a plain homespun suit, poorly fitted to broad shoulders thickened by hard work.

Tom Malone joined them as they walked into the courtroom. He had fetched the gentleman from New York whom Alain had sent him for, although for the life of her, Tamson could not imagine how a Dutch merchant could be of any help.

Prudence and Carleton Ware had saved them a seat on the left of the magistrate's bench. The two servants, like her father, had given truthful incriminating statements to the clerk of court despite their change of heart toward the defendant.

Upon hearing Tamson's self-edited version of how she and Alain had fallen in love and the sacrifices he'd made for her, they had, at least, appeared to be on her side if not her husband's.

The courtroom was hot and close, more smothering than standing in the full sun outside. The mingled scent of perfume, tobacco, and sweat stirred by the fans of the women moved Tamson to accept Prudence's thoughtful offer of the seat nearest the open window. Although she wanted to be directly behind the railed area where the prisoner and his jailers were to stand, she would hardly help Alain's cause if she were to become sick.

As she settled down, she looked across the room and inadvertently locked gazes with Beatrice De Lancy. The minister's daughter, who had once been her friend, glanced away rather than acknowledge the slight inclination of Tamson's head and turned to whisper something to the Whittington sisters next to her. Neither of her acquaintances had bothered to speak since giving their testimonies to the clerk of court about the raid on the day they'd visited Tamson.

A shuffle at the side door drew Tamson's attention to where the sheriff and prosecutor entered the room, followed by Alain Beaujeu. Thankfully, the bruises and cuts inflicted upon him by Captain Irons' men had healed, save one wealed scar over his eye, and he was able to walk upright with dignity rather than bent in pain from the fractured ribs the military doctor had wrapped tightly.

No longer in the filthy buckskins in which he'd traveled from Montreal to Albany, her husband hardly looked as though he'd been imprisoned for weeks, but was quite handsome. The clean clothes Tamson had brought him, combined with a bath and fresh shave, made him appear more like the Marquis de la Galisonne than the voyageur whose expertise in survival techniques had saved both her life and Mark's, too.

Tamson could not help but wonder as she glanced about the room if the fluttering of the ladies' fans hadn't increased as her own pulse had. Not the least jealous, she would accept any favor her husband won within these walls. A smile toyed with her lips at the thought and she turned back, only to be captured by the sharp, probing gaze she had just admired. Alain was not pleased to see her.

I'm fine, she mouthed, smiling in answer to the silent reprimand. *I love you.*

Alain glanced inadvertently at Squire Stewart and back to her.

And he does, too, Tamson conveyed quietly, earning a skeptical arch of her husband's dark brow.

Although her father's merchant lawyer friend, Mr. Jeffries, had offered to present his defense before the magistrate, Alain insisted on representing himself. With Tamson and her father all but penniless, his sisters had offered to sell their horse to pay for his defense, but he'd refused to let them do so. He knew Tom Malone needed the animal to make a living for Annette and the child she carried.

Besides, he'd argued, there was nothing to defend. He had indeed committed all those charges made against him, except for the latter—assault with intent to kill. If he'd intended to kill Carleton Ware, the man would have been dead. He'd convinced everyone that a defense attorney was a waste of money.

"All rise for His Lordship Sir Wilfred Beekman, Magistrate of His Majesty's court and His Lordship, the

Earl of Campbell Lord Loudoun, Commander-in-Chief of His Majesty's forces in these colonies."

Tamson stood as two bewigged gentlemen entered the courtroom. The first was swathed in a scarlet robe which made him look as though he had neither hands nor feet. He approached the raised bench and stood at his seat waiting for his colleague and guest, who had been integral in the decision made in the military hearing the previous week. When Lord Loudoun stepped up upon the platform, his military regalia glittering in the sun's rays, the magistrate took his seat and the assembly, aside from the sheriff, Alain, and his jailers, followed suit.

Amidst the squeaking of benches and shuffling of feet, Sir Wilfred spread the documents on the desk, studying them through the spectacles resting on the end of his bulbous nose. Lord Loudoun, taking the opportunity to survey the crowd with his narrowed dark eyes, nodded ever so slightly to someone in front of Tamson, drawing her gaze to where the two men from New York sat next to the witnesses' bench. That Alain and Lord Loudoun had common acquaintances struck her dumb with amazement and once again she wondered who this merchant Van Rensselaer was.

"This court is now in session!" the magistrate announced, slamming his gavel on the bench more for decorum than need. Every man and woman sat ready to hear each word concerning the scandalous marriage of Tamson Stewart to her enemy and kidnaper.

"Alain Beaujeu, you stand charged by the Crown for the following catalogue of crimes against the citizens of His Majesty's colony of New York." The man's booming voice startled Tamson, for the judge was small in size compared to the giant Scot sharing his bench. "Kidnaping, horse theft, and attempted murder. How plead you, sir?"

"Guilty to the first two, your lordship. Not guilty on the last."

Tamson inhaled sharply, along with the rest of the onlookers. God in heaven, what was he doing? Mr. Jeffries had advised him to plead not guilty to all three charges. Prudence and Carleton were prepared to testify that, while they'd seen the man who had abducted the squire's daughter, they couldn't say for certain that it was Alain Beaujeu! Her father was going to say that he was seeking Alain's family as a favor to a former business associate and she had already prepared a story of meeting Alain in Montreal, where he had rescued her from her captor. It had all been planned!

"But there were mitigating circumstances which I would ask your lordship to consider before passing sentence, circumstances which can be verified by witnesses."

Sir Wilfred glanced over at William McShane and was not disappointed to see the disapproval written on the attorney's face. Due to the inability of the clerk of court and sheriff to summon a sufficient number of qualified jurors, the magistrate was elected to make judgment, thus denying McShane his day in court.

"All witnesses come to the fore and be sworn!"

Tamson rose and accompanied the Beaujeu sisters, Mark Heathcote, her father, and the Wares to the seating set aside for them. As she passed the New York associates who had answered Alain's summons, she afforded them a curious glance, wondering why they did not join the group.

The Clerk of the Court approached each of them in turn with a Bible, repeating, "Do you swear by Almighty God that your witness will be true?" After all had replied in the affirmative, they were permitted to sit upon the bench reserved for the active participants.

"I would have this brief, Monsieur Beaujeu. But for His Lordship's request, I would not be inclined to hear you at all beyond your admission of guilt. Is that understood?"

Alain inclined his head. "Completely, Your Lordship." The chains about his ankles dragged on the floor as he turned toward the witnesses. "In order to save time, I will state what I would have His Lordship hear and you may simply request these good peoples to verify it."

"So be it."

"The two lovely dark-haired ladies on the bench are my sisters," Alain began, "and they, like my mother and youngest sister, are very dear to me. When they were taken from their homes and exiled on English ships to unknown destinations, I did what any man would do. I became angry.

"In that anger," he went on, "I contrived a plan to find them using a former business associate who was now my enemy because of a war I did not wish to become involved in. Because he knew people who could find my family, I kidnaped his daughter."

The admission set off a wildfire of comments, requiring the magistrate to call for order with his gavel so that Alain could continue. When he did, Tamson gripped the rail in front of her as if clinging to the hope he was tossing away with his admission, not only of kidnaping her, but of promising the Indians who helped him the squire's horses for their effort.

"There is no one to testify in my behalf to the fact that I asked my Indian friends that no blood be spilled, except for the fact that none was, which is highly unusual in a savage raid, is it not?"

"Were you not shot, Mr. Ware?" the magistrate inquired sharply.

Carleton Ware cast an apologetic look at Tamson. "I was, sir."

"But that was by *my* hand," Alain objected, "not by the savages. It was in self-defense, for Mr. Ware had fired first."

A shout of indignation rose from somewhere in the back of the room, but the judge's gavel stayed the others that rallied to it.

"I am a voyageur, monsieur, and my prowess with weapons is to be considered. Had I intended to kill Monsieur Ware, he would not be here to testify one way or the other. I would be willing to demonstrate my marksmanship, if the court questions it, but . . ."

"Not necessary," the magistrate growled, cutting Alain off. "So you state you committed the first two offenses because your family was removed in an act of war and you claim self-defense in the latter?"

Although Sir Wilfred was clearly impatient to be done with the matter, Alain was not flustered. "Oui, but there is more that you should know, monsieur."

Sir Wilfred shot a sideways glance at Lord Loudoun. Upon seeing his nod, the magistrate sighed, giving Tamson cause, for the first time, to think that perhaps the guest magistrate had not been invited. "Get on with it then, sir."

"I found my father dying in an abandoned fortress in Quebec, to which some of my people had escaped. It was there that I realized the futility of my anger and that I had met one injustice with another. I was in the act of returning Squire Stewart's daughter to her home when I was captured."

"Nearly a year later," the magistrate pointed out.

"Winter was upon us, so for her sake, I remained in Montreal . . ."

"And in the spring?"

Alain smiled and turned to Tamson. "By then, monsieur, it was *I* who was the captive. She would not leave and I could not bring myself to force her. Love makes a man do rash and sometimes unjustifiable things."

The flutter of fans throughout the room increased at the warm look he bestowed upon her. Would that the women there could decide his fate at that moment, she thought, venturing to look at her friends across from her. Even they, who had been frightened witless during the raid, were not immune to his charm. Indeed they studied him with renewed interest spawned from the romantic side of their nature.

"Is that true, Mrs. Beaujeu . . . that you would not leave when you had the chance?"

"It is, sir. Alain tried to make me go, but I wanted to remain at his side as his wife for the rest of my life. It was I, sir, not he who . . ."

"Thank you, madame." Alain turned from her to Mark Heathcote before she could finish. "But for Captain Heathcote's arrival, we both might still be there."

Tamson bit her lip in frustration. Even if it blemished her reputation, the people needed to hear how Alain had spent the winter as her husband *in name only,* when he might have ruined her; how he'd treated her like a marquee, depriving her of nothing; how he'd given up the free wilderness life he'd preferred and endured the job in the commissary for her sake and comfort.

As it was, Mark Heathcote made the latter clear. As he had in the military hearing, he told of how Alain hated his job and was caught in the midst of a political tug of war within New France's regime in his commissary job, shuffling smuggled goods and luxuries about for the noblesse and officials while his own displaced people starved. Yet, the young Acadian endured it for Tamson's sake.

Then Alain's part in Mark's escape, despite the fact that the captain intended to take Tamson away from Montreal by force, was brought to light.

"He might have saved Tamson and left me wounded and helpless to escape, but he did not. There's no doubt in my mind that the prisoner is one of the most honorable men I know and that he did what he did in an act of desperation because he loved his family. He then did what he could to set it right, which led him to a capture he might have avoided, had he been a lesser man."

Tamson took heart at the impressed quirk of the magistrate's thick, grey-white brow. She watched the man shuffle through his papers and then pull one out to study it. Lord Loudoun leaned over to see which testimony it was and then sat back, arms folded in what appeared to be satisfaction.

Could the charges be dismissed because of Alain's help to an agent of the English army? She only knew they could not be dropped by those offended by them, for the Crown was the prosecuting party in this particular case, under William McShane's initiative.

"Have you anything else to say, Mr. Beaujeu?" Sir Wilfred asked at last.

Alain shook his head. "Nothing except to thank Your Lordship for permitting me to speak and to express my gratitude to those who have supported me in this matter, even if their motives have been for the protection of my beloved wife and unborn child." He bowed toward them. "I could not in clear conscience permit anyone to perjure themselves for my sake."

Tamson's hand flew to her throat where a lump of emotion was wedged stubbornly. The very quality which had won her love and respect was now going to take him away.

"Then stand ready for judgment, sir."

Taking up a small black square of cloth, Sir Wilfred ritually perched it upon his head and slammed the gavel down, thunderous in the sudden hush that fell over the room. Unaware that she'd risen in her unbearable apprehension, Tamson held her breath as the magistrate began to speak.

"Alain Beaujeu, the Supreme Court of Judicature of George the Second, by the Grace of God of Great Britain, Ireland, and the colony of New York, King Defender of the Faith, hereby has heard your plea and finds you guilty of kidnaping and horse theft, the punishment for which according to law is *death by hanging.*"

Twenty-eight

"The Crown finds you not guilty of assault with intent to kill," Sir Wilfred went on, but Tamson was oblivious to all but the words *death by hanging*.

But for her father's quick response, she might have collapsed upon the floor. Her cry of protest emerged as no more than a moan as the beamed ceiling of the room whirled over her head. As it was, he caught her in his arms and eased her down upon the bench between himself and Prudence Ware. It was her fault, all hers! she bemoaned, dizzied from shock. She'd insisted he stay. She'd insisted on marriage . . . and for what? To become a widow?

"Tamson!"

Alain's frantic voice drew her out of her swoon more than the ministrations of Prudence Ware, who dabbed at her damp forehead with a freshly laundered handkerchief while Alain's sisters fanned her with theirs. Tamson blinked and made out her husband's face as he leaned over the railing of the prisoner's box, battling against the jailers who restrained him. From out of nowhere, her physician appeared in his stead, evidently having watched the affair from the gallery, and shoved a small vial under her nose.

"You can't die!" she sobbed brokenly, trying to avoid

the jolting odor and see past her attendant to Alain. "I don't want to live without you!"

Suddenly the ammonia was gone and in its place was a milky concoction, which the doctor put to her lips. "Drink this, girl," he coaxed sternly. "I warned you not to come."

Tamson obeyed, just to get the vile-tasting sedative out of her face, and then tried to get up, but her father and the physician would not let her. "I must go to him!"

"Be calm, lassie, or ye'll be thrown from the court!" her father cautioned, desperate with concern and sympathy.

In the background the magistrate called the room to order with his gavel and shouted over the dying din, "Is the lady well enough or will you remove her, sir?"

Her father's warning, driven home by the magistrate's question, worked far faster than the sedative. She had to contain herself, Tamson thought furtively. "I'm fine!" she insisted. Far from it, she wrapped her arms across her chest in an attempt to master the involuntary shivering that assaulted her in the overwhelming heat.

"She is well now, Your Lordship," the physician answered, none too certain.

Trying desperately to keep from crying, Tamson brought her stricken gaze to Alain and nodded in a pitiful attempt to reassure him. Although he'd moved back to the center of the railed area and ceased to struggle against his guards, his fists were clenched, white as his face.

She'd never seen him so frightened, his blue eyes wild as if he were about to explode with anxiety. Suddenly it occurred to her that it was not for himself, for he paid no heed to the magistrate, but for her.

"We'll proceed with the sentencing, if you are so disposed, Mr. Beaujeu," Sir Wilfred reminded the distracted prisoner.

Tearing his gaze from Tamson, Alain squared his shoulders as though he too needed fortifying. "My wife, monsieur, she is with child. She does not mean . . ."

"Yes, yes, yes! I am well acquainted with such things, *being a father of seven.*" The resulting levity of the judge's wry aside was curtailed with the suspense that permeated the room. "Alain Beaujeu, in consideration of Captain Heathcote's testimony to your exemplary aid to an agent of the King and of the fact that Squire Stewart and his manservant Carleton Ware have sworn that they wish no retribution considered on their behalf, this court chooses to waive the death sentence. In its stead, you are sentenced to an indenture of seven years, the said indenture to be auctioned off following this trial."

The gavel struck the desk again, silencing myriad responses from the gallery, both for and against the decision.

"What?" Tamson whispered to no one in particular, not trusting her ears.

"He's not going to die!" Annette assured her, grabbing Tamson in her enthusiasm and drawing her into a joyous hug.

"And we owe it all to Mark!" Liselle chimed in, nothing short of adoration in her eyes.

"Not quite," Heathcote admitted wryly. "Now I see that I never stood a chance against that silver-tongued devil. Half the women in this room are in love with him. Did you hear the approval?"

"They certainly changed their tune," Prudence Ware

agreed. "I always say there's more to most things than meets the eye and that young man's no exception."

Moved aside in the rush along with the stiff-lipped Carleton, James Stewart spoke up softly. "I'm glad for ye, lassie. I wouldn'a ha' ye lose a true love for a' the world."

As he had her mother, Tamson thought, reading the rest of her father's sentiments in his gaze. She glanced to where Alain stood and back to the squire again, torn between throwing herself into one's arms with joy and thanking the latter for his change of heart. Her decision was made when her father motioned toward Alain with an inclination of his head, but the gesture eased her conscience as she broke through the cluster of well-wishers to reach the man she loved.

"You should not have come, *ma chérie,*" Alain chided, trying to return her embrace despite his chains. "When you fainted, I thought I would not live to be hanged!"

Tamson put her finger to his lips. "Don't even speak of such a thing!" Her chin trembled, betraying the threat to her control. "I came . . ." She touched his face with her other hand, her eyes over-bright. "I came so close to losing you!"

No longer feeling the slightest bit inhibited by the austere surroundings of the courtroom, she replaced her silencing finger with her lips, conveying the relief raging through her. Salty tears spilled down her cheeks, unashamed, as Alain returned her kiss with a fervency of his own, his chained hands grasping the excess material at her waist as if he'd never set her free again.

Soul to soul, they communicated all the things left unsaid in the last strained weeks. Oblivious to the slam of the gavel on the magistrate's bench, it wasn't until the gallery quieted and the judge's chiding words became distinct enough to register that they parted. Even then, it was with unabashed reluctance.

"Mrs. Beaujeu, it would please the court for you to resume your seat so that we might proceed and be done before the noon hour."

Alain smiled down at her, his gaze fierce with passion as he stepped back from the rail. Tamson returned to the witnesses' bench per the judge's instruction and took a seat next to James Stewart.

Now her father *could* do something. Surely somehow they could come up with the money for the indenture—selling more furs, perhaps.

"Father . . ."

"Dinna ask, lassie. If I'd had a pence to spare, do ye think I'd have given up my horse? The store is our livelihood now. I already owe on that."

Tamson's face went blank with uncertainty. "But what will we do?"

"Pray whoever buys his service will permit ye and the bairn to go with him."

Faced with yet another crisis, Tamson searched the room furtively. Sir Wilfred opened the bid. What would happen if no one made an offer? she fretted, the prolonged silence answering the judge's request growing loud in her ears. She was about to ask her father when one of the strangers from Annanbrae spoke up.

"One hundred pounds sterling."

A collective gasp echoed in the room. The observers strained to see who had made such a substantial offer, for, while Alain was an able man in his prime, few in the wartime economy could afford such a sum.

"Mr. Rensselaer has bid 100 pounds sterling. Are there any other bids?" Again silence ensued. "Going once . . . going twice . . . sold to Mr. John Rensselaer of Annanbrae! Clear the court, sir!" Sir Wilfred ordered the sheriff. "We've papers to sign."

It happened so quickly that Tamson was still staring at the stranger when he asked that Alain's chains be removed. The moment he was free, Alain was at her side, this time embracing her fully. Her head pressed against his chest, Tamson could hear his beating heart, steady and assuring as the quiet strength of the arms enveloping her. If time had come to a stop at that moment, she would not have cared, for she was exactly where she wanted to be for eternity.

However, it did not. Too soon, Alain gently pulled away to extend his hand to the stranger from New York who had purchased his indenture. "Mr. Rensselaer, I thank you for coming."

"How could I refuse, sir?"

The tall, blond-haired gentleman clasped Alain's extended hand warmly. It was hardly the gesture of a total stranger, Tamson noted, a flicker of suspicion stirring in her mind. However, when Lord Loudoun joined the group, it flared full force and she knew some sort of conspiracy had been afoot.

"Young man, you are a lucky devil if there ever was one! I take it I can still count on your cooperation?"

"I gave my word, Your Lordship."

"For what?" Tamson looked at her husband expectantly.

"Part of my pardon from the military required that I swear allegiance to the King of England."

Perhaps to the men standing about him, it was a small

gesture, but Tamson was aware of its significance. He had prided himself on owing allegiance to no man and would not take such a vow lightly. Once again, she was overcome with awe at the extent of his love and sacrifice for her.

"Beaujeu, I would suggest that you and your wife take our coach to Annanbrae. I've had a room prepared for you," John Rensselaer informed him, a decided hint of smugness in his gaze, as if that too were part of a pre-existing plan. "After I sign your contract of indenture, Lord Campbell and I are going to the Crown Tavern whilst you familiarize yourself with the place. You'll be there for a good while, I'll wager."

Had Rensselaer known the outcome of the trial before it took place? Tamson puzzled silently. And surely Lord Loudoun had not attended the trial to remind Alain of his oath of allegiance! Suddenly it dawned on her what the New York entrepreneur had said.

"At Annanbrae? Did he say we'll be at Annanbrae for a good while?" She pressed Alain's arm in utter confusion.

"Mr. Rensselaer has been in need of an overseer for his company's investment," her husband explained, grinning at the way her whiskey-dashed eyes grew wider at the news. He pulled her closer to him, lest her knees give out from the shock. "We'll be running the place for the next seven years by the look of things."

"Annanbrae?" she marveled again, glancing over to where her father stood, listening in silence. It was so hard to believe!

Following her gaze, Alain excused himself from his companions and approached James Stewart, his hand extended tentatively. The squire looked at it and then met the young man's gaze, impassive. Tamson crossed her fingers and held her breath, wishing he'd do something, anything, to break the sudden stillness. It was Alain, however, who took the initiative.

"Although I do not deserve your forgiveness, sir, I hope you will not mind offering a small farm boy advice on running an estate."

James Stewart snorted in derision, still ignoring the outstretched hand. "Ye sly devil, I should ha' known ye'd find a way out o' this, ye always bein' the fox. 'Tis the means that has me puzzled."

"I learned from a master, monsieur, not to put all the chicken's eggs in the same basket, non?"

"Meanin' ye been tradin' with someone other than meself all these years?" Stewart declared, his eyes narrowed with interest. "Then tell me this, laddie, who was it got the pick of the furs?"

"The highest bidder," Alain answered glibly. "I do recall that to be your own advice, was it not?"

To Tamson's astonishment, not to mention relief, her father roared in amusement, his stern demeanor abandoned abruptly as he shook Alain's hand. "Damn me, ye French swearin' bastard, ye got my daughter, fathered my grandchild, and it's you now, runnin' Annanbrae. 'Tis a hellish turn o' things, to my notion. Strike me blue, I'll not offer ye one piece of advice!"

"Father!" Tamson gasped at the equally sudden reversal of humor, for Stewart's quick smile had faded, thinned into an ungiving line.

"I'll let ye squirm a bit, like ye made me do this last year, and maybe, just when you're about to lose your wits, I'll save your undeservin' skin!"

He glanced at Tamson's anxious countenance and

once again a hint of humor surfaced, twinkling in betrayal of his true feelings. She could have struck him for his mischief at a time like this, were she not so grateful to see it.

"Now get this girl into that coach and off her feet! I'll tolerate a lot from ye, laddie, but not a whit of nothin' where Tamson is concerned."

"But where do *we* go?" Liselle intervened, confusion afflicting her bright expression. She looked from Alain to the squire and back to her brother.

"To Annanbrae with us, *ma petite.* We have the room, non?"

"Of course," Tamson replied, basking in her husband's attention.

"But I already got us a room at the tavern, paid for," Tom Malone protested. "Me 'n' the girls'll join ye tomorrow, if the invitation still stands."

"Good!" Mark Heathcote chimed in. "I was hoping I might invite the three of you to join me for supper this evening . . . a celebration of sorts."

"Très bon!" Liselle grabbed the officer's arm in her sudden excitement and delight. "But that is just wonderful! And I already have on my best dress!"

It wasn't by accident that their plans were falling into place so that Tamson and Alain could be alone. Mark, Tom, Rensselaer . . . even Lord Loudoun was brimming with smug satisfaction.

Tamson didn't understand the how or why of it. All she knew was that her prayers had been miraculously answered.

After stopping long enough to shake hands with some of the citizens who had witnessed the trial and been won over by the testimony, Alain escorted Tamson to the waiting coach. As he climbed in after her, Tamson heard her name called through the window and looked out to see the Whittington sisters.

"We just wanted to say we're glad things turned out so well for you, Tamson," Abigail said.

"And that we're sorry we had to testify, but Beatrice's fiancé was insistent," Amanda chimed in. "I know he means well, but sometimes Willie McShane lets his appointment by the Crown go to his head."

Abigail ushered her sister back from the coach as the driver snapped the reins over the horses. "We just wish you both the best!" she shouted.

"Thank you . . . both of you!" Tamson leaned through the open window and waved gratefully. "And tell Beatrice I understand her support of Willie. Love has a loyalty all its own!"

As the coach turned up Beaver Street and the buildings blocked her view of her friends, Tamson moved away from the window into Alain's waiting embrace. As he pulled her onto his lap, he nuzzled her neck and planted a kiss against the pulse quickening there.

"My sentiments exactly, *Mrs. Beaujeu.*"

Tamson grabbed his head and shoved it against the heavy upholstered seat back to avoid his passionate assault until her questions were answered. "Did you know you were not going to hang yesterday when I visited you?"

"I *hoped* that would be the case. My associates from New York and the results of the military hearing won Lord Loudoun's support. The magistrate's favor depended on the hearing this morning."

"Why didn't you say something?"

Alain tightened his grasp about Tamson's waist as

she started to pull away. "Because I was not certain. What good would it do to give you false hope?"

"False hope is better than no hope!" Tamson bit her trembling lower lip. "I have been . . . I . . ."

"Hush, *ma petitesse*. It is all over now. We are together and that is all that matters," Alain whispered against the top of her head as he cradled her in his arms.

Tamson sighed shakily. "I'm sorry. It's just that . . . I just keep crying and crying and I can't stand a crybaby, but . . ."

Catching her chin with his finger, Alain lifted her face to his. "I understand that such a thing is to be expected in mothers-to-be! And as of this moment, I promise that you can cry all you wish and I will do my best to kiss each and every tear away!"

Her sniffle gave way to a giggle as Alain proceeded to make good his words, kissing each crystalline droplet streaking her reddened cheeks.

"You're rather cocky for a bond servant, monsieur, don't you think?"

Alain chuckled as he drew away. His lopsided grin made him look boyish and roguish at the same time. He'd wanted to keep his secret until he was alone with Tamson in the master bedroom of Annanbrae, but he found he could hold it no longer.

"Not exactly," he demurred.

"I agree with Father. You are brazenly bold."

"Non, I admit to that. It is my being the bond servant that I deny, madame."

Tamson wriggled away from him. "What are you saying? I saw you auctioned off . . . and none was too anxious to have you either, I might add!"

Instead of rising to her good-natured taunt, Alain

touched the tip of her nose and traced a distracting line down to the ruffled dip of her bodice. "I was purchased by the business in which Mr. Rensselaer is a stock-holder."

"So?" Tamson squirmed involuntarily at the warm trail left by his wandering hand across the fullness of her breasts.

"Mon Dieu, but I think you are becoming more buxom, non?"

She slapped his hand away. "So?"

"So," he picked up, cheeks drawn to contain his humor. "I am the other stockholder." He threw up his hand. *"Voila!* In a manner of speaking, I purchased myself."

Tamson's mouth fell open in shock.

"It was agreed at the military hearing by Lord Loudoun that I was permitted to keep my holdings if I swore allegiance to the Crown of England and agreed to billet the King's soldiers for as long a time as needed."

He ran his hand beneath her skirt, fingers climbing playfully up her stockings and over her garters, but Tamson was too dumbfounded to protest, even if she were of a mind to. "So when I pay back the company for its investment in an overseer, I shall own Annanbrae. What do you think of *that,* Mrs. Beaujeu?" he queried in smug delight.

"I don't know whether to smack you or kiss you!"

"I prefer the latter."

"You're too big for your breeches, Alain Beaujeu!"

A look of sheer devilment settled on Alain's face as, without warning, he lifted her out of his lap and set her on the seat opposite him.

"What the devil are you doing?"

"I am about to remedy the situation of which you speak, madame," Alain answered deviously, working at the fastens of his trousers restraining yet something else he could no longer hold back.

Tamson's shock melted at the sight of his arousal, now freed of the binding garment lying about his ankles.

"Here?"

"Just a sampling of our wedding night, non? Besides," he said, pulling down the shades of the coach. "We are in the market traffic, or hadn't you noticed, *ma chérie?*"

She hadn't. That was how captivated she was by her husband's unbridled desire, how much her longing made her oblivious to anything else. After coming so close to losing him, nothing else mattered. Only Alain, only their love, only his touch . . . not just at this moment, but forever.

WATCH FOR THESE ZEBRA REGENCIES

LADY STEPHANIE   (0-8217-5341-X, $4.50)
by Jeanne Savery
Lady Stephanie Morris has only one true love: the family estate she has
managed ever since her mother died. But then Lord Anthony Rider
arrives on her estate, claiming he has plans for both the land and the
woman. Stephanie soon realizes she's fallen in love with a man whose
sensual caresses will plunge her into a world of peril and intrigue . . .
a man as dangerous as he is irresistible.

BRIGHTON BEAUTY   (0-8217-5340-1, $4.50)
by Marilyn Clay
Chelsea Grant, pretty and poor, naively takes school friend Alayna
Marchmont's place and spends a month in the country. The devastating
man had sailed from Honduras to claim his promised bride, Miss
Marchmont. An affair of the heart may lead to disaster . . . unless a
resourceful Brighton beauty finds a way to stop a masquerade and keep
a lord's love.

LORD DIABLO'S DEMISE   (0-8217-5338-X, $4.50)
by Meg-Lynn Roberts
The sinfully handsome Lord Harry Glendower was a gambler and the
black sheep of his family. About to be forced into a marriage of convenience, the devilish fellow engineered his own demise, never having
dreamed that faking his death would lead him to the heavenly refuge
of spirited heiress Gwyn Morgan, the daughter of a physician.

A PERILOUS ATTRACTION   (0-8217-5339-8, $4.50)
by Dawn Aldridge Poore
Alissa Morgan is stunned when a frantic passenger thrusts her baby into
Alissa's arms and flees, having heard rumors that a notorious highwayman posed a threat to their coach. Handsome stranger Hugh Sebastian
secretly possesses the treasured necklace the highwayman seeks and
volunteers to pose as Alissa's husband to save her reputation. With a
lost baby and missing necklace in their care, the couple embarks on a
journey into peril—and passion.

*Available wherever paperbacks are sold, or order direct from the
Publisher. Send cover price plus 50¢ per copy for mailing and
handling to Penguin USA, P.O. Box 999, c/o Dept. 17109, Ber-
genfield, NJ 07621. Residents of New York and Tennessee must
include sales tax. DO NOT SEND CASH.*